Daughters of Lyra

Felicity Heaton

CONTENTS

HEART OF AN EMPEROR

Princess Sophia, one of the beautiful and strong daughters of Lyra, has had it with the never-ending row of suitors that her father, King Sebastian Lyra I, has lined up for her. When the latest suitor turns out to be the emperor of Varka, a species known for their lack of emotions, nocturnal lifestyle and bloodlust, Sophia wants little to do with him.

But when she greets the emperor and his two attendants, Sophia realises that a Varkan makes her heart beat like no other man before him and might just win her after all. Only, it isn't the emperor who was caught her eye.

Regis, Count of Sagres, is transfixed from the moment he meets Sophia. She pushes him to the brink of surrendering control to his bloodlust with every beautiful glance and smile she throws his way. But would she ever marry a male who doesn't know the meaning of love? Fear of the bloodlust makes Varkans retain an iron grip on their emotions, but Regis is willing to surrender control and risk everything to win Sophia. And Sophia will do whatever it takes to make him see that Varkans can love and that she wants no other man in the universe, including triggering his bloodlust and putting the whole palace in danger!

Will Regis's feelings for Sophia be enough to stop him from hurting her and killing the entire palace? Will Sophia be able to love a man that the universe sees as a monster? And will she still love him when she realises the Varkans' deception?

CHAPTER 1

Sophia stood in the expansive white square in front of the palace and watched the biggest and blackest fighter ship she had ever seen descend into the royal port of Lyra Prime. It wasn't just the colour of the sleek curvaceous craft that made it black to her. It was what it contained. Another black cloud to mar her perfect blue Lyran sky. With a sigh, she tossed her long dark hair over her shoulder and ran her fingers down the twin braids that started at her temples and flowed down the front of her pale blue empire-line dress. Her eyes tracked the ship and she toyed with the braids as she always did when nervous or angry. How was she going to get out of this one? She glanced at the palace and then back at the ship as it landed, sending a plume of white dust up into the air as the thrusters fired.

Her father had gone too far this time.

It had been bad enough when he had brought a Minervan suitor to the palace. At the time, she had thought it had been a joke and the man had been a friend of her mother's. No. A suitor. As though she couldn't find her own husband. After she had dismissed the Minervan, things had only taken a turn for the worse. So far, her father had brought a new suitor every month. Dazkaran, Sekarian, Terran, Sirian, and several other species that she didn't care to remember had sent suitors to court her. She had turned them all away. Her father might be the king of Lyra now that her grandparents had gone to Iskara, but he had definitely gone too far this time.

In the heat-hazed distance, three black-clad figures shimmered, striding towards her.

Varkans.

Sophia swallowed her trembling heart and straightened her back. They didn't frighten her. She had been reading up on them. At least, she had read what she could find, which wasn't much. There hadn't even been a picture of the royal family in the computer or the books. They were one of the most technologically advanced species in the universe, creating things that everyone had heard of, yet they had somehow remained the most mysterious. It was that mystery that frightened her, not their apparent bloodlust.

Her father and mother stopped beside her. Her mother was still as beautiful as ever. As always, she wore her long black hair in an elaborate bun, drawn away from her pale face. Her eyes were as dark as her father's, but seemed blacker with the makeup surrounding them. Her parents did look so very regal when they stood together like this, King Sebastian and Queen Terea of Lyra.

The confident click of heels on the white stone of the square ceased. Sophia took her place beside her mother and turned to face the Varkans.

It seemed she would still have to wait to know what they looked like.

Stood before her were three tall, slim males, all dressed in black high-collar knee-length jackets, black trousers and polished knee-high boots. Silver embroidery decorated two of the men's jackets, three columns of bright buttons down their fronts that shone like full moons. The third man, stood between the other two, had gold embroidery on his jacket and a deep red and gold sash that cut across from his left shoulder to right hip. The emperor she presumed. She wished that she knew what he looked like.

It was impossible to tell when they were all wearing black visors that covered the top of their heads, the two curved sides coming to meet in a point in front of their noses. All she could see were their mouths, jaws and necks. All of them were pale. The man on the left had lips like her father's, curved and hinting at beauty. The emperor's lips were a thin compressed line that made her wonder what he was thinking. She couldn't sense his feelings as she had been able to with her other suitors. The man on the right.

Sophia paused.

His lips were perfect. Curved, full, and intensely kissable. She dragged her eyes away from him and back to the emperor.

Her father stepped forwards.

"Emperor Varka, may your species flourish and may eternity be within your reach," her father said and Sophia noticed the emperor's lips tilt slightly into a smirk, as though her father's words amused him. Eternity. Apparently, it was something that Varkans already held within their grasp. They flourished rather well too. Perhaps her father should have chosen a better Lyran greeting. "May I introduce my daughter, Princess Sophia of Lyra."

Sophia stepped forwards past her father to greet the emperor and instantly the other two men were in front of him, both holding one arm out to block her path, their other hand on a weapon at their waists. They looked like swords. She frowned.

"You must understand, little one, it is not wise to approach our species so flagrantly," the emperor said, voice deep and edged with an eerie echo. She glanced at the small black triangular device attached to the left side of his throat. Did the translator make his voice echo, or did all Varkans sound this way?

"I apologise. I had only wished to greet you." She bowed her head, already wishing that the Varkans were gone. If she couldn't go near him, how was he supposed to court her? Out of the corner of her eye, she glanced at the male with the perfect lips. Maybe she didn't want them gone just yet, not until she knew his face. "I am Princess Sophia of Lyra. May I enquire as to your guests' names?"

She could feel her father's eyes on her, and her mother's. None of the suitors had brought company with them before. It wasn't such an unusual question to ask.

The men moved back into their positions and then the one on her left stepped forwards.

"Attendant Second to Emperor Varka, Count of Aeris." He bowed very stiffly and then stepped back. Her right eyebrow rose. She didn't catch a name in there unless she was supposed to call him Count of Aeris.

The man on her right stepped forwards, an aura of confidence surrounding him. She watched his perfect mouth as he spoke, mesmerised by the movement of his lips and the deep echoing timbre of his voice.

4

"Attendant First to Emperor Varka, Count of Sagres." He bowed with grace and when he was rising, the sun hit his visor and she swore she caught a flash of his face.

Her heart pounded.

If she had, then he was handsome enough to rival any Lyran, even her father.

She curtseyed and then fixed her attention on the emperor so she didn't appear rude. It was difficult to keep her eyes off the Count of Sagres but she managed to make it through the rest of the greeting ceremony without looking at him. When they were walking to the palace, she reached out a little to try to read him. The area he occupied was there and she could feel it, but she felt nothing from him. It was as though he wasn't there.

"Sophia, dear," her father whispered as they led the way into the palace, accompanied by four Lyran guards. "You seem tense. Do relax. If you are worried about the rooms for the attendants, then you need not. They are already being arranged."

Sophia wasn't worried about rooms at all but she didn't correct her father. It was probably better that he presumed she was fretting over tiny details rather than battling her desire to look at the Count of Sagres again. She felt drawn to him, under a spell that commanded she look at him. Keeping her face forwards, she walked under the grand archway that led into the darker interior of the palace and smiled as the cooler air hit her. There was a collective murmur from the Varkans and a shuffling noise. Had they removed their visors? Suddenly, not looking at the Count of Sagres seemed impossible.

One of her attendants, Caria, hurried over to her and Sophia stopped to see what she wanted. Tiptoeing, the dark haired girl whispered in her ear, curtseyed and then stood to one side. Sophia glanced at her parents before slowly turning to face the Varkans, her heart thumping in her throat. Her gaze fell on the Count of Aeris first, her nerves and the anticipation of seeing whether the Count of Sagres was as handsome as she thought making her take the long route. The Count of Aeris was handsome, his beauty exactly as his lips had promised. The emperor was also handsome, but there was a cruelty about his features, a darkness that she didn't like. She knew that in terms of wealth and power he was a good match, and that marrying him would advance relations between Varka and Lyra and strengthen the peace, but for some reason he made her wary. Her gaze shifted, finally falling to rest on the Count of Sagres.

He was stunning.

His moon white skin was a stark contrast to the chin length tendrils of his black hair. It hung in ribbons, parted down the centre and caressing his cheeks and the defined straight line of his jaw. The sensual curve of his lips drew her gaze and she imagined how they would feel against hers—soft but strong, caressing hers in a kiss that she knew would be commanding, passionate and consuming. She dragged her eyes away, up over the fine aristocratic line of his nose to his eyes. They met hers and the deep red colour of his irises shocked her for a moment. Blood. They were the colour of blood. All of their eyes were dark crimson.

Regaining her composure, Sophia stepped forwards and curtseyed to the emperor.

"Your room is ready, your highness. Rooms have also been prepared for your attendants. One of my attendants will show you to them," she said and intimated for Caria to come forward. The young girl did and curtseyed so low that Sophia wondered if she would be able to get back up.

With a smile, Caria turned and started walking up the hall. The Count of Aeris led the way, followed by the emperor. He looked at her, his red eyes briefly meeting hers before he turned away. She had felt as though he had been assessing her with that glance. It made her nervous. In a few hours, she would have to sit and talk with him. Normally her research into the species helped the conversation but she still knew little about the Varkans. Perhaps she could ask him, at the risk of looking ignorant. The Count of Sagres passed her and her eyes followed him, studying his noble profile. Why couldn't he have been the emperor? She would gladly spend hours shut in the drawing room talking to him.

When the Count of Sagres had disappeared around a corner, she noticed that her parents had also gone. Behind her, excited chatter burst into life, shattering the silence in the hall.

Sophia sighed and turned to face her other two attendants, Alexa and Zalina.

"What is it now?" she said, relieved that she would have a few hours peace before yet another courtship began.

"Nothing, miss." Alexa curtseyed, holding the skirt of her corseted deep blue dress and lowering her head. The equally dark blue veil covering her hair fell forwards to mask her face. She pushed it back and rose.

"Nothing?" Why didn't she believe that? She looked at Zalina, knowing the younger girl had no skill at lying.

"Nothing—the Varkans are handsome." Zalina covered her mouth, her tanned cheeks darkening and ringlets of her brown hair falling down across her face when she shook her head.

Sophia laughed and looked along the corridor in the direction that the Count of Sagres had gone.

"They certainly are."

Sophia smoothed her black hair back into the bun that her mother had helped fix it in and then toyed with the two long braids she had insisted on keeping. She hadn't been able to find the peace she had wanted before the meeting. Her attendants had insisted on getting her ready early, plastering her face with pale make up that she abhorred and painting her lips ruby red. The colour of blood. Blood. She frowned as she remembered the Count of Sagres's eyes. Against his dark lashes and pale skin, they had been startling. Perhaps his species truly had a bloodlust as the books said.

She straightened her dress out, pulling the top half about so it covered her ample breasts a little more and making sure that the high waistband sat underneath them. Her attendants had tried to make her wear black, but she had changed out of the dress the moment they were gone and had put her empire-line sky blue one back on. She was a princess of Lyra. She was going to wear the colour of Lyra.

Minutes passed and she fidgeted on the long deep blue couch, wondering if the emperor was planning to make an appearance. She glanced around the expansive cream room and then at the rich dark wooden door. Perhaps it was still the fashion to be late on Varka. On Lyra, it was rude.

The door opened and she shot to her feet. Her eyes widened when she saw it was the Count of Sagres. He stood on the threshold of the room, his hand still on the door handle. Her heart leapt and pounded. There was no denying the attraction she felt to him. Her mind had been constantly on him from the moment they had met and now that he was before her again, she wanted nothing more than to look at him, to drink her fill of his handsome face and those stunning red eyes. She blinked, looking into his eyes, wondering what he was thinking as he stared at her. He looked at her a moment longer and then stepped to one side. Emperor Varka passed him and paused.

"You may leave. I will report in before retiring," he said and the Count of Sagres nodded before closing the door, leaving them alone.

Her shoulders slumped. For one happy moment, she had thought the Count of Sagres would be staying.

She forced a smile for the emperor when he took her hand and kissed the back of it. Sitting back down, she held her hand out, intimating the couch opposite hers and fearing that he would choose to sit next to her instead like some of her suitors had.

Thankfully, he took the desired seat. She smiled again, unsure what to say to break the dreadful silence. By Iskara's wings, her father was going to pay for this torture. Hadn't he learnt anything when his parents had arranged his wedding? Perhaps she could run away as he had. She grinned inside. The shock and worry would probably kill him.

Perhaps she could run off with the Count of Sagres.

Her eyes widened again, that thought shocking her. Did she want to run away with the count? The idea flustered her enough that her cheeks burned.

"Is something the matter?" Emperor Varka said with a slight echo to his words. Sophia stared at him, shaking her head. "You look ill."

"No, I am fine, thank you." She straightened up and smiled again. "A little too much sun today perhaps."

"It is dreadful," he said, voice droning enough that she clearly got the message that he didn't like her sunny planet.

"It's beautiful," she countered, ready for an argument if he overstepped the mark. Emperor or not, she wouldn't let anyone insult her home world.

"You must understand, little one, that Varkans are not accustomed to such strong sunlight. I merely meant that it was painful for me, not that it is not beautiful, in short spells."

Short spells? She could spend the entire day lazing in the gardens under that strong sunlight. It did explain the visors though. She had read that none of the planets in the Varka system rotated like hers. On one side of each was permanent daylight. On the other side was permanent darkness. She was beginning to get the impression that Varkans were from that side.

She could ask the emperor, but for some reason she didn't want to. Her gaze drifted to the door and her thoughts to how handsome the Count of Sagres had looked. Shocked too. He had hidden it well, but something about either the room or her had surprised him. It was probably the awful make up she was wearing. It dawned on her that she didn't want to talk to the emperor.

She wanted to speak to the Count of Sagres.

"You are as beautiful as your planet," Emperor Varka murmured, his voice so low that it sent a shudder down her spine. She dragged her eyes away from the door and smiled at him, taking his flattery even when it revolted her. As a princess, she had grown accustomed to disgusting men fawning over her and seeking her attention. "Although I hear that you have had many suitors in the past, I can assure you that none of them can offer you what Varka can."

A frown threatened to crease her brow. She held her smile. Did he honestly think that he could haggle for her hand in marriage? She wasn't interested in how many planets her future husband had, or how rich and powerful he was. The only man she would marry was the one who loved her, and whom she loved.

Relaxing a little, she settled in for a conversation that she knew was going to feel like an eternity rather than a few hours.

There was only one thing keeping her remotely interested in the emperor as he told her of his wealth and the might of the Varkan Empire.

He knew the Count of Sagres.

Her gaze drifted to the door.

She wanted to know him too.

CHAPTER 2

Regis, Count of Sagres, walked out onto the balcony of his room. The palace gardens stretched below him, white paths glowing ethereally in the evening light. A light breeze blew across them, washing his face with the lingering warmth of day and carrying the scent of roses. Far to his left he could see the port where they had docked. If he leaned forward, he could see the square where the royal family had greeted them.

Where Princess Sophia had greeted him.

Her lack of knowledge about his species had been evident the second she had thought to approach a Varkan emperor without warning. Still, it was understandable. His kind never had been ones to tell the universe about themselves. They were feared enough already.

Regis leaned against the white stone wall of the balcony and stared at the distant city. Tall pale spire-like buildings rose at the centre of it. The financial district was the closest group. Beyond that, even taller buildings pierced the sky. The Lyran parliament. His fingers flexed and he clenched his fists. They ran the military. How many of his kin had he lost to Lyra? His hand fell to the sword hanging at his waist. The feel of its hilt beneath his fingers was comforting. The war was over now. A tentative peace bridged the gap between his species and the Lyrans. They were here to strengthen that peace through marriage.

A sigh escaped him when a full moon broke the horizon, blood red but slowly turning to white as it rose. He watched its progress and then smiled when another moon appeared a distance away from the first, this one crescent. He studied them both and realised that the first moon partially eclipsed the second. It was beautiful. It added a strange sense of magic to the falling night.

He missed the moon of Varka Prime. It glowed purple, a pale lilac that reminded him of the flowers his mother and sister had preferred. It had been long decades since their passing.

In all that time, he had never left Varka Prime. His duty had been to the people and the struggle for peace for his species, while his friend Van, Count of Aeris, had left to join the military. Regis wished that he could have that freedom too, but knew that it wasn't possible. He had a duty to do.

The darkening sky lured his attention to how quiet it was on this planet at night. He looked down at the garden where it sprawled thirty metres below him and then leapt over the wall, landing silently in a crouching position on the balcony above the garden. He straightened and walked to the top of the steps that led down into the maze of paths and flowers. It was a beautiful night for a walk. It had been some time since he had felt so relaxed and at peace with the universe.

Regis followed the steps down into the garden and let his feet find their own route amongst the winding paths. The flowers were beautiful, especially so when the moonlight touched them. He gave a brief thought to the fact that the emperor hadn't reported back and that he might miss him, and then shrugged it off. He wanted to walk the garden. If he needed him, the emperor would easily be able to sense him here.

Perhaps he was still speaking to the princess. Regis frowned at that thought. It had been several hours since he had left them alone together. Maybe the offer his species had laid on her table was palatable. A firm peace between their species, the technology of Varka at their disposal, and a marriage that would connect them with other species of similar prosperity. Not to mention the fact that Varka were offering Lyra the second planet in their system for a military base station. Varka Two was a deal breaker. The Lyrans had desired a presence in the Varka system for nearing a century and had fought hard to win one.

Unfortunately for them, his species had fought harder.

The Lyran Imperial Army were no match for them.

Regis stopped and looked back at the palace. It was bright in the moonlight, the white stone glittering. Most of the windows glowed warm and amber from the lights inside. A few of the balcony rooms were in darkness. Without thinking, he reached out with his senses and focused on each room. The unlit ones weren't all empty. Their occupants were sleeping. The lit ones contained one or two signatures. A light sweet perfume of Lyran lilies came from one, carried down to him on the cool night breeze.

The princess.

Her room was distant from his, close to the rear of the palace, near to where he was now in the garden. He knew it was her. Her scent was unique in the castle and had stayed with him all day. He stared up at her window, a part of him willing her to come out onto her balcony. He had read Terran literature about a star-crossed match and their tender balcony scene. He had read a lot about love in an effort to understand it.

Looking back at the moons and the myriad of twinkling stars, Regis took a deep breath of night air that filled his heart with warmth and did something he hadn't done since his beloved mother and sister had died.

He sang.

Sophia sat cross-legged on her expansive bed, hungrily devouring the information in the computer pad about Varka that the emperor had given to her. Much of what she had read so far had contradicted that in the Lyran archives. Apparently, Varka Two rotated like her planet, with equal day and night across the sphere. It was the planet they were offering Lyra in exchange for her. The planet where her uncle had fought twice and almost died both times. Her family told her not to concern herself with such things, but she couldn't help it. She knew there was peace between Lyra and Varka now, but she couldn't forget their bloody history.

She paused and her breath hitched in her throat when she moved to the next page of information on the pad.

Varka Prime was stunning. The sight of it sent chills chasing over her arms and down her spine. The picture was of a city with beautiful pale cream towers decorated with jade and gold, or blue and silver. Intricate patterns of those colours surrounded the windows and doors, and adorned the bridges in the foreground. A wide river snaked through the city. Her eyes followed it into the picture and stopped when she saw a building in the centre of the city, high above everything else on a hill. A waterfall spilled from arches where the building met the hill and the water cascaded down into the city. Flying buttresses supported its tall spiked towers. She had never seen anything so beautiful. It even surpassed her Uncle Balt and Aunt Kayla's home on Lyra Five. It was breathtaking.

Sophia eagerly read the passage of text below it and frowned when she realised that the building was the emperor's palace.

Her frown increased when a lilting male voice drifted through her window, singing in a language she didn't recognise. She tapped the translator in her ear and wondered if it was working. The song was beautiful, so soft and melodious that she needed to hear it clearer. She slipped from her bed, leaving the computer pad there, and crossed her room to the balcony.

The sky was stunning tonight, the moons shining so bright that they lit the world in silver. She looked down at the garden and her frown melted away when she saw who was singing. It couldn't be. The Count of Sagres?

Her gaze followed him as he walked slowly through the garden, seemingly oblivious to everything, even her.

His song was like that of the Sonaran, a mythical sea creature that lived on Lyra Seven, her system's outermost planet. Apparently, its song lured you to a sweet death. His song lured her.

Conscious of her bare feet and nightdress but not caring about either, Sophia snuck through the palace and out into the garden. She needed to hear it closer. She had never heard such a sombre but beautiful song.

Her footsteps were silent on the pale stone path that wound through the garden. She approached the count from behind, slow and cautious, remembering how the Varkans had reacted earlier today when she had moved too quickly. His hand drifted out to brush the pale blue rose heads as he passed and he raised his face to the moons. It felt as though he was singing to them.

He was stunning even in the low light, his uniform cut to show his figure. The jaw length strands of his black hair shifted in the breeze, the moonlight making them shine. She wanted to look into his eyes again, to see his handsome face.

The small white pebbles of the path near the fountain scrunched when she stepped on them and she lifted her foot, cringing at the noise. Too late. The singing had stopped and she could feel him looking at her.

"Please, don't stop." Sophia smiled her apology into his eyes. "Continue. Do continue."

He shook his head, the jaw length dark ribbons of his hair moving with the motion. In this light, he looked even paler and his eyes were pools of midnight.

"I apologise for disturbing you, your highness." His voice was as deep and smooth as she remembered it from his introduction, its echo no longer startling her. The sound of it sent her insides trembling in a strange way.

"You weren't, really you weren't." Sophia stepped forwards, her brow furrowing as she tried to convince him to continue. If anyone had disturbed someone, she had disturbed him. She shouldn't have come down. She should have known that he would stop if he realised someone was listening. A frown crossed her face when she realised that the translator wasn't broken. She could understand what he was saying. Had he been singing in a language that the device didn't recognise? "It was beautiful, although I couldn't understand it. Was it a song for the moon?"

He smiled, sending her heart pounding. "A song for a goddess, sung in the old language as it should be."

Her cheeks flushed.

"I am sorry." He stepped up to her, holding his hand out. "I have not properly introduced myself. Regis, Count of Sagres."

She placed her hand into his and his thumb closed over her fingers. His gaze held hers. Regis. A count. She hadn't found anything about the societal structure of the Varkans so far. Was a count high up in court? Her cheeks blazed again when she realised that he wasn't letting go of her hand.

"I've been reading about Varka," she said to break the silence and his fingers left hers.

He held his hand out to one side and she started walking with him, nerves fluttering in her stomach. She hadn't asked the emperor anything about his species. They had only talked about the glory of Varka and the things that she would gain from marrying him.

"Is it true that one of the planets in your system rotates?"

He nodded and placed his hands behind his back, locking them in the curve above his backside. "It is. It is uninhabited for that reason."

She frowned. "Why?"

"Because we cannot bear the light for too long, and the Wraiths cannot bear the darkness. We occupy only the planets that keep one face to the sun."

"What side are the Varkans from?" She glanced at him, her gaze tracing his noble profile and committing it to memory. He was a count and he travelled with the emperor, which meant that he had to be important. But would he be important enough for her father? In her heart, she knew that her father intended her to marry someone of a higher rank—a prince, a king or an emperor. She hoped with that same heart that she could change his mind and make him see that she had to marry for love, had to marry a man who she had feelings for, or she would never be happy.

"The side of darkness, as I am certain you suspected." Regis drew her out of her thoughts and brought her attention back to him.

She nodded this time. He seemed at home in the dark and all of them had made it clear they were uncomfortable with the bright Lyran sun.

"Is it always dark? I saw a city in a picture. It had looked like evening there."

"The dark side we live on is freezing. We have built a series of interconnected shielded cities where a dim day is artificially created and the temperature is controlled." He looked up at the moon.

Varkan technology sounded as amazing as her uncles and father had told her it was.

"Is it always so dark though? It looked like night was falling."

"It is set to a preferable brightness, otherwise it hurts our eyes."

"It looks too dark to me." She looked up at the moon he seemed so fascinated by. Or was it moons? Did Varka Prime have only one, or none at all? She hadn't read anything about it.

Her eyes fell back to him. She had never met a man as handsome as he was. There was such beauty in his features, such elegance, but there was strength too. His whole air spoke of it, of power and authority. It stirred her blood and made a warm feeling settle in the depths of her chest. She would give anything to have him command her, to have his demanding lips on hers and his hands gripping her with all of his strength.

"When you marry the emperor you will live on the dark side. You will need to become accust—"

"Marry the emperor?" Sophia interjected, stunned to a standstill by what he had said.

He turned and looked at her, a single dark eyebrow raised in intrigue at her outburst. She didn't care if it wasn't very princess-like to speak in such a fashion.

"That's a little presumptuous," she continued with a glare. "I'm never leaving Lyra and I'm certainly not going to marry your emperor."

His dark eyes narrowed as he frowned. "Why not?"

There was an edge of malice to his tone that she didn't like. Suddenly she could sense his feelings and they were all anger. Had she offended him with her rejection of his emperor?

"I don't love him!"

His frown didn't shift. "What does love have to do with breeding?"

Her eyes widened and she stared at him, unsure what to say and wondering if he really had just said that.

"Breeding?" Mortified, she trembled on the brink of unleashing her own anger but clenched her fists instead, desperate not to do anything that would disturb relations between Varka and Lyra. This man was a count and the first attendant to the emperor. He could have power enough over the emperor and his species to sway them into war with Lyra. She bit her tongue but it was no use. She couldn't stand there and let him say such things about her. What sort of picture had he made of her in his mind? What kind of person would marry purely for the sake of breeding? "I... I won't marry someone that I don't love."

It was his turn to look shocked but there was something else in his eyes that didn't quite match his expression.

She reached out to his feelings, trying to discern them. The anger had gone. No, perhaps a little remained. Something else was crushing it though, consuming him. Some sort of upset. She couldn't quite tell what it was.

"What is love that you place such great importance on it?" Regis snarled and stepped up to her, towering over her in a menacing way that made her heart pound painfully against her ribs. His lips compressed into a thin line of fury.

What was love?

The question threw her long enough that before she could find an answer, he was gone, striding away and leaving a trail of anger in his wake that surrounded her and made her heart heavy.

What was love that she placed such great importance on it?

13

What sort of question was that?

Now that she was alone, she realised how cold it was and how numb her toes had become. She went back to her room, mulling over his reaction to what she had said as well as his question, and thinking about the fact that she had sensed his emotions when she hadn't be able to before.

Closing her door, she threw herself onto the bed and picked up the computer pad. The answer had to be in there somewhere. There had to be a reason for his outburst and the fact that she could suddenly feel him.

She would find it, even if she had to read all night.

CHAPTER 3

Sophia peeked around the corner and watched with relief as her father disappeared into the distance, surrounded by guards and taking the dreaded emperor with him. She had told her attendants to inform the party that she wasn't feeling well and it seemed her father had decided to take the tour of the city without her. A fatigued smile touched her lips but quickly faded when she remembered what she had learnt by reading all night. She just couldn't believe it.

She had to find the count and find out for sure.

Her plan could have easily backfired. She had realised that as she had watched her father leave with the emperor. The emperor might have asked his attendants to go with him and then she would have had to find another opportunity to speak with the count alone.

She leaned against the wall behind her and wondered where he could be. The emperor would be gone for a few hours. The palace was so large that it could take her that long just to find the count. She had once spent a whole day trying to find her cousin, Amerii, in this place. They had kept missing each other by seconds. She hoped that didn't happen with the count.

Regis.

He had said that his name was Regis. And he had taken her hand. And his touch had been far warmer than she had expected.

With a sigh, she started her search, making sure to hide whenever someone passed, ready to pounce if it was him or disappear if it was her mother or a guard. She had sworn her attendants to secrecy and told them to stay in her room. She couldn't risk them revealing that she wasn't sick.

An hour into her search and she was beginning to wonder if the count was in the palace at all. Her feet hurt from walking in the delicate shoes her attendants had chosen for her and more than once she had almost tripped over the long skirt of her deep blue corseted dress. She could barely breathe in it now. Perhaps she should have convinced her attendants to choose something a little more suitable for an expedition. Trousers and flat boots sounded good.

Those two things made her think of Amerii again. It had been a while since she had seen her younger cousin and she wondered where she was in the galaxy. She was probably making a name for herself in the army, just as her father, Uncle Acer, had done.

Blindly turning a corner, Sophia started when she saw someone was there and didn't relax even when she realised it was Regis. He stopped walking and stared at her. He still made her heart pound whenever she saw him, his beauty otherworldly and entrancing. He straightened his back, standing tall, his long black jacket emphasising his figure, and then his gaze shifted to one side. Sensing he was about to leave down the nearest corridor, she hurried to him.

"I never realised." The words came out as one. She took a deep breath to steady her nerves. "I'm sorry if I offended you last night. I never realised that Varkans didn't know love."

It had taken her almost an hour to absorb that information and make sense of it. The thought that a species in the universe didn't know love seemed unbelievable. It was something that she had presumed happened to everyone.

"I want to know," he said with a solemn edge to his voice, his gaze not leaving hers. "I have studied it but do not understand it. I want to feel what it is that other species in this galaxy place such importance on... but I never will."

The idea of that made her sad and she took his hand on impulse, squeezing it. He looked down at their joined hands, his eyebrows raised and eyes wide.

"Varkans must be able to love. You must feel attached to something. You must be capable of feeling it." Her own words sounded stupid to her ears. Her heart told her that he would know if he could feel love. Someone on the Varkan planets would have felt it by now if the species could.

"What symbolises love?" He moved closer to her, his fingers closing around hers. He raised her hand. "Does this?"

Sophia's eyes widened. "No. Maybe for some people. This is... sympathy perhaps."

"What symbolises love to you?"

She stared at the floor, at their feet only inches apart. She could see herself in the reflection on his black boots. What was love to her? Her thoughts strayed to her parents.

"A kiss," she said with confidence and a smile as she remembered how her parents would kiss when they thought no one was watching. To her, a kiss was love. It held love or it had no meaning.

Before she could even squeak, Regis had grabbed her, dragged her into a dark room and was kissing her. Her eyes were wide as his mouth glided over hers, sending thrill after thrill chasing across her skin and buzzing along her nerve endings. She closed her eyes and hesitated for only a moment before clutching his upper arms and returning the kiss. His tongue brushed her teeth and she parted her lips to let it pass, her own coming to meet it. He backed her into the wall, his body against hers, the pressure of it making every inch of her burn with desire. No one had ever kissed her like this. It was intense, mind-blowing, and even though she knew that she should stop him, she couldn't bring herself to push him away.

She wanted to cling to him, to hold him and beg him to never let her go. She could kiss him forever.

Her tongue brushed his canines and she flinched at their sharpness.

His fingers closed around her upper arms, pressing in and gripping them so tight that it hurt. She wriggled against him but he deepened the kiss and pushed her against the wall so hard that she struggled to breathe.

A metallic taste filled her mouth.

Blood.

She couldn't breathe.

Her heart exploded with panic, thundering at the thought that she was running out of air and Regis wasn't letting her go. She released his arms and pushed her hands against his chest, trying to shove him off her. His grip tightened again and she whimpered in pain. His mouth didn't leave hers. She shoved him and closed her eyes so tight that a tear ran down her cheek. With one final push, he stumbled backwards.

Sophia choked on the air as she breathed deep, her heart still pounding with fear.

Before she could say anything, Regis pulled her back into his arms, holding her so gently that it confused her. He said something that she didn't understand, a language similar to the one he had sung in, and stroked her cheek. Closing her eyes, she leaned her cheek against his chest, too tired to fight him again. Her head felt light but heavy at the same time. It spun occasionally, making her legs feel weak. She had never been so frightened.

"I am sorry, your highness," he whispered into her hair, his fingers still caressing her jaw and hair. "I was not in control of myself."

Sophia coughed and drew another lungful of air as she thought about what he had said. He wasn't talking about the kiss. It was what had happened afterwards. It was her blood.

"Understand that I would never consciously hurt you."

She frowned.

Stepping out of his embrace, she reached out behind her and touched the control panel beside the door. The lights slowly came on.

Regis flinched away but not before she saw how red his eyes were. Crimson. Not the dark red they had been before. She continued to frown, wondering what had happened to him to make him almost hurt her.

He turned away. "Do not look at me like that... do not look at me at all!"

Suddenly, he was gone. The window was open and the warm midday breeze was drifting in, tousling the long thin curtains and washing over her.

She hadn't even seen him move.

Her hand rose. Her fingers pressed against her lips. He had kissed her and it had been nice, more than nice, until she had cut her tongue on his teeth and everything had changed. He had changed. Her blood had altered him. Could this be the bloodlust that the books and computer spoke of? She'd thought it was just a figure of speech, something to sum up their violent nature in battle. Did it mean something else? She didn't understand.

Sophia went to the window and looked out at the bright square below, but couldn't see Regis anywhere. There was so many questions that she wanted to ask him. He had to be back in the palace somewhere. The Lyran sun was too strong for him without his visor. She was about to go to find him again when she thought the better of it.

He had told her not to look at him.

She had felt his shame and horror. A moment before she had broken free of his arms, she had felt his remorse. And before that, when he had been kissing her, she had tasted his hunger.

If she went to him now, while he was still feeling such muddled emotions, he would turn her away. She needed to give him some time alone. She needed to find someone else to answer the question burning within her.

Looking back out of the window again, she smiled when she saw her father walking the square alone.

He would answer her.

She took the quickest route down through the palace, unable to leap from windows like Regis. She had read Lyran Imperial Army reports that stated Varkans had strange abilities—a strength like no other species, bones that wouldn't break when they leapt from great heights, and an urge for violence that made them natural soldiers. She wouldn't have believed it if she hadn't witnessed it herself.

Coming out in the square, she looked around for her father and spotted him walking towards the garden.

"Father!" She ran after him, lifting the skirt of her deep blue dress so she didn't trip. He turned and gave her a smile.

"I see you are feeling better." He placed his arm around her shoulders. The sleeve of his loose pale blue shirt tickled her neck. She looked up into his near-black eyes and smiled at the concern in them. Her father had always made her feel better. "Although you are a little flushed."

Sophia touched her burning cheeks. It was Regis's kiss that made them blaze, not her phoney illness.

"Father, can we walk a while?"

He nodded and they headed in the direction of the garden. Sophia struggled for a while, trying to find the courage to ask her question. It was difficult enough to ask her father this. It would have been impossible to ask Regis.

"What are Varkans?" Her voice trembled.

Her father sat down on one of the benches in a shady corner of the garden, ran his fingers through the strands of his black hair and then patted the spot beside him. He crossed his legs and adjusted his dark blue trousers. Normally her father didn't dress so informally but it was hot out today. A smile touched her heart when she remembered how they normally passed hot sunny days swimming in the crystal clear palace lake. Sophia sat sideways, facing him. His pensive expression unsettled her.

"You seem troubled by them." He cupped her cheek and his brow furrowed with concern. His dark eyes searched hers. "Is it the emperor?"

She shook her head, nerves churning her stomach.

"The Count of Sagres?"

Her eyes widened.

Her father laughed. "Your mother was right. The moment they arrived she knew that it would not be the emperor who captured your heart."

Sophia placed her hand against her chest and looked at it. "My heart? How can someone who cannot love capture my heart?"

She sighed when her father placed his arm back around her shoulders and pulled her close. It was comforting to feel the weight of it against her and his firm grip on her shoulder. It had been a long time since she had been a child, and since she had turned mating age, but it still made her believe that he wouldn't let anything bad happen to her.

"You must have noticed that it is difficult to sense their emotions."

She nodded.

"Varkans control their emotions to control their bloodlust. The species do not feed in the same manner that we do. Intense feelings bring out their bloodlust."

Her hands fell into her lap. Bloodlust. Was her father suggesting what she had feared, insinuating that Varkans drank blood for sustenance and that it affected them? When she had been close to Regis, she had been able to sense his feelings, but after she had cut her tongue and he had tasted her blood, his feelings had been so intense that she had felt them.

Everything he had felt, she had felt too.

She had never experienced another's emotions before, not like that. It had been overwhelming.

She opened her mouth to speak but her father raised his hand, silencing her.

"I do not think it is I who you should be posing these questions to. I will detain the emperor again so you may ask the right man for the job." He smiled at her when she gave him an unimpressed look and then rose and walked away.

The right man for the job. Her eyes scanned along the palace and stopped on the room she knew was Regis's. Perhaps her father was right. Regis was the one she should be asking, even though she was afraid to. He was Varkan after all. If anyone could make her understand the species, it was him.

CHAPTER 4

Regis stalked around his room, grabbing everything that he had unpacked only hours ago and tossing it back into the large cases on the floor. He was a fool for thinking that he could do this. His father would have been sorely disappointed with him if he had still been alive.

He paused by the window. The curtains and the tall windows were open. The world outside was still painfully bright, stinging his eyes enough that he thought about putting his visor back on. He didn't. He walked to the edge of the room, standing on the threshold of the balcony, and stared out at the city. He had never seen such a blue sky before. Sophia wore nothing but blue. Even if she did agree to marry Emperor Varka, it would be impossible to convince her to leave this place. She loved it as much as any Varkan loved their home world.

As much as he loved Varka Prime.

Although her skin was pale and her eyes and hair were dark like a Varkan, she was a completely different creature. She craved the sunlight while a Varkan needed the darkness.

With a growl, Regis unbuttoned his black jacket and tossed it onto the expansive bed beside his sword. Bare-chested, he walked into the bathroom and stared at himself in the mirror above the marble basin. Dark red eyes glared back at him. He knew what she had seen when she had looked at him in that room. It was the exact reason his species were so secretive. Other species didn't understand their ways and their needs. When they discovered the truth about them, their view changed. His kind became something else entirely in their eyes.

Monsters.

When she had looked at him, she had seen a monster.

He hung his head forwards, grasping the edges of the basin for support, and closed his eyes.

He wasn't a monster.

Or perhaps he was.

He had almost killed her after all. Something with feelings, with a heart that could love as well as merely hate, wouldn't have done such a thing to someone so beautiful.

A knock at the door made him tense. His fingers tightened against the basin edges, threatening to smash the stone. He pushed away from it and went back into his room, throwing the rest of his clothes into the waiting trunks.

Another knock.

"I wish for no company, Van. Leave," Regis said, hoping the younger Varkan would do as he had asked. He had known Van since they were younglings together on Varka Prime and under normal circumstances would welcome his company, but not today. These weren't normal circumstances. He would leave a note for Van, the Count of Aeris, and then make his way to the ship. His friend would understand.

They knocked again.

Perhaps he wouldn't.

Regis's temper frayed when another knock sounded and he stormed to the door.

"Van!—" He yanked the door open and stared at the blank space were Van's face should have been. His gaze dropped almost a foot to a crimson-cheeked Sophia.

She smiled nervously and glanced along the hall in both directions.

"Will you let me in?" Her anxiety showed in her voice and her beautiful dark eyes.

Regis stepped back to allow her to pass. She took a step and then stopped, her eyes widening slightly when they fell on his bare chest. Her cheeks darkened and she hurried past him and into the room. Closing the door, he watched her standing in the middle of his room, looking over his luggage. She turned to face him, her mouth open and shock in her eyes.

"You're leaving?"

He nodded. "I must."

"Why?" She looked away, back at the trunks.

"I cannot remain here." He went to his trunks and closed the lids. "Not now."

"Not now?" She took a step towards him, her dark eyes wide and entrancing. Each shy glance she had ever given him flashed across his memory, making his blood burn.

His gaze shifted to her neck and his hunger rose. The world became brighter as his eyes altered and he waited to see how she would react to the sight of them so vivid with bloodlust.

She touched her throat, delicate fingers caressing skin that he longed to devour and taste.

"You want my blood... and you're leaving because of that?"

There was an incredulous note to her voice that amused him on some sick level. She didn't know what she was dealing with. Whatever she had learnt about his species and their bloodlust couldn't prepare her for the reality. The darkness and violence, the need, were things that were impossible to put into words that any but a Varkan could understand.

"I must." He turned away from her and pressed the dark pad on the front of the cases, locking them and registering his imprint with them so none but him could open them.

She huffed and grappled with the lid of one of the trunks, trying to prise it open, clearly wanting to unpack his things as though that alone would make him stay. Her efforts were futile but it didn't stop her. There was a sense of sheer desperation about her actions and her feelings. He could sense them as clearly as he knew she could sense his when he was close to losing control. One of her parents had more than one species blood in their veins. Perhaps her mother. It seemed likely that a daughter would receive her mother's gifts.

"Why?" Sophia surrendered her attempt to open his luggage. Her jaw was set tight, her lips beautifully compressed into a thin line that said she wasn't going to give up so easily. What was she fighting for so vehemently? Was this the true face of love?

Did she love him?

A voice at the back of his mind laughed and mocked him for thinking such ridiculous things. A princess wouldn't lower herself to marry someone she knew wasn't of royal blood. Their trip here would prove him right in that. No matter what she said, it was wealth, power and connections that she wanted from marriage.

Not love.

"Why?" She moved closer to him, seemingly unaffected by his half-dressed state now. He was under no illusion about her innocence. She had never been alone with a man like this before. Anger coloured her cheeks as much as the sight of his bare chest had. "Because you want to bite me?"

If only it were so simple.

"You do not understand." Regis walked over to the bed to retrieve his jacket.

Before he could put it on, she had crossed the room and had come to stand only a few feet away. The sound of her heart pounding filled his senses and he could feel the warmth radiating from her. She pushed a strand of her long black hair from her face and glared at him.

"Father says that Varkans control their bloodlust." She grabbed his sword off the bed and unsheathed it a little.

"What are you doing?" He grabbed her wrist but not before she had managed to run her finger along the blade.

His eyes widened.

He stared at the drop of blood as it blossomed on her finger. She held it up, her palm facing the ceiling so the drop remained perfectly balanced. His lips parted and his teeth sharpened. His heart thumped hard against his chest, faster than he had ever felt it beat before.

His breathing turned heavy as he stared transfixed at the tiny bead of blood. Fire consumed him and a desire for violence was born in its midst. He trembled as he held her wrist, his fingers tightly closed around it, aware that he was probably hurting her but unable to care at that moment. He was lost. His mind raced forwards to imagine every possible outcome of this moment. A wave of bloodlust stronger than he had ever experienced hit him and he could see himself killing all in the palace just to get to her, to have her all to himself.

He could see himself killing his friends.

Her family.

Everyone.

It was torture to see all that in one single drop of blood and know that if he tasted her, drank from her, the feelings he had now would increase in strength one hundred fold.

He would lose his mind.

"You can love, Regis... you're just too afraid of how those feelings control you," she said and his gaze snapped to hers. "Well they control everyone. We're slaves to them too."

His breaths shortened as the hunger rose.

"Is it just blood making you lose control?" she whispered, sinful and tempting as the blood itself. "Or is it *my* blood? Is it *me*?"

He frowned at her. Was it her or her blood? He had been battling for control over himself from their first meeting in the square. He hadn't smelt her blood back then. He had only smelt her perfume of Lyran lilies.

"I'm not afraid, Regis." She removed his hand from her wrist. Entranced, he stood there, watching with a sense of inevitability as she raised her hand and the precious drop of blood towards him, knowing he wasn't strong enough to stop her. "Not of love or these feelings. Not of you or your hunger."

She wiped her finger across his lower lip, smearing it with the rich taste of her blood.

"Tell me that you didn't want me before you had a taste." Her voice was a sultry whisper that made him realise that she didn't know how dangerous what she had done was. He couldn't control himself any longer. "Tell me that you didn't feel something that night we spoke in the garden."

He shuddered and licked his lip. Bringing his hand up, he touched his mouth and then brought it away. His fingers shook, paler now than they had been. He couldn't control himself and he wished for her sake that he could.

He frowned and tears filled his eyes, hot and rebuking.

Was this love?

This desire to protect her, even from himself, even when he knew that he wasn't strong enough?

"Tell me that you didn't want to kiss me and I will believe that you cannot love. I will leave."

He stared at her.

"I wanted you the moment I saw you." He grabbed her around the waist and crushed her lips with a kiss so consuming it felt impossible to sate. His tongue thrust into her mouth and hers came to meet it, tangling and gliding against his in a way that stirred the fire in his blood. He growled, picked her up, and continued to kiss her as he lay her down on the bed, only half-aware of what he was doing.

She moaned on contact with the soft bed and he ground his teeth, closing his mouth and struggling for control. Her hand came up to caress his cheek, bringing the scent of her blood with it. It was too much, too intense. It shattered what little control he had retained and sent him over the edge.

He poured all his hunger and need into his kiss, claiming her mouth for his own just as he longed to claim her blood and her body. The feel of her delicate warm fingers stroking his cheek drove him on, luring him into enacting all the sinful thoughts running through his mind. He closed his eyes and fervently kissed her, his body hardening as her tongue caught his teeth and a flood of sweetness filled his senses. Her hands lowered to his arms as he devoured her mouth, seeking out every molecule of blood, desperate to taste each one. Her fingers flexed around his muscles and then held them tight as her body went rigid and a moan escaped her. He groaned at the feel of her body brushing his, stirring his desire until a red haze fogged his mind.

He needed her.

She didn't protest or put up a fight as he dragged the skirt of her dress up to reveal her legs. He broke off the kiss and stared down at their long shapely forms, the sound of her heartbeat and her rapid breathing filling his ears. With a growl, he grabbed her and pushed her up the bed, so he was level with her hips. He pushed her dark blue skirt away and ran his hands over her thighs. She shook beneath him, trembling in a way that his body matched as he stared wide-eyed and open mouthed at her bare legs.

He wanted her.

She would be his.

Every Varkan would know it.

With a snarl, he sunk his fangs deep into her thigh and sucked hard, pulling a mouthful of her blood and then swallowing down the sweet nectar. She shrieked and her hands grasped his shoulders, shaking with the pleasure he could sense in her. He drank deeper, lost in the haze and his need. One thought pounded his skull as he clung to her legs and held onto her.

She was his.

A loud banging disturbed his solitude, his moment, and he raised his head. Seven signatures on the other side of the door. All meat. All dead. He roared at them, a warning for them to leave before they met their deaths. They banged again and ordered him to open the door.

Sophia muttered something, her eyes closed and face flushed with desire. The scent of it filled the room, suffused his senses along with that of her blood. He growled at the thought of their moment being disturbed, at the thought of those men daring to intrude and interrupt her pleasure.

Kneeling on the bed, he narrowed his eyes on the door.

He roared.

"In the name of Iskara and the King of Lyra, open up!" several men demanded at once.

Addled by the blood, Regis grinned. He would open up. He grabbed his sword and unsheathed it. He would open up and then he would open them up.

He ignored Sophia's feeble protest as he left the bed and stalked towards the door, intent on protecting what was his.

CHAPTER 5

The weird dizziness and warmth evaporated in a heartbeat when Sophia realised that Regis had opened the door. Tall burly armoured guards poured in and she screamed as she raced to cover her legs and sit up. Regis roared and she reached out to him. Kneeling on his bed, she could only watch as he fought the guards, his eyes blazing red and his mouth bloodied. Her blood. She flinched when he blocked one of the guards' blades with his bare arm and it sliced into it. She had done this to him. She had made him lose control.

She reached out again, desperate to speak but unable to find her voice. He ran one guard through, gutting the man, and roared as he attacked the next. What had she done? She hadn't meant for it to turn into this, for it to go this far.

Her heart ached when the guards finally disarmed Regis and piled onto him, pinning him down. She couldn't watch as they carried him away, didn't want to hear his shouts of protest. Even though he was speaking the old Varkan language and she couldn't understand the words, she knew that he was angry. She could feel his outrage and his hunger.

Sophia didn't understand why he felt those feelings though. Was it because of her? Was he angry at the disturbance? She had been, at least at first. She sat in silence in the empty room and lifted her skirt. Her fingers traced the neat set of red marks on her flesh. They didn't hurt. The whole area felt numb. In fact, she felt numb. Her initial anger at the guards' arrival and Regis stopping biting her had faded to guilt and misery.

She had driven Regis into biting her and now the guards had probably taken him to the palace cells. Her father would probably have him killed.

It was all her fault. She touched the mark on her thigh again. It had felt so good though. She had tried to keep quiet but it had been impossible. The wave of pleasure and sense of connection to Regis had been overwhelming, sending her out of her mind.

The door opened and she covered her leg, smoothing her dress down over it. She frowned when she saw it was her mother and turned away to stare at the window. Night was falling. How long had she been sitting here thinking about what she had done?

Her mother sat beside her and placed her hand over hers. It was comforting, warm, and made tears fill her eyes as she felt she no longer had to be strong. Her mother would understand. Her mother would never be angry with her, not about anything, and certainly not about something concerning love.

Sophia sighed. She had been such a fool and where had it got her? She had convinced Regis to lose control and she still hadn't been able to discern whether he felt love. His feelings had been so strong and, while there had been a connection to him, and she had felt tenderness and devotion within his emotions, she hadn't felt anything that she could distinguish as love. Now, Regis would pay the price for her mistake. He would be punished, not her. It should be her.

"What will happen to him?" she whispered, staring at her mother's hand where it covered her own. She could feel her mother's sympathy and understanding.

"They are holding him in the cells for now."

Sophia forced a smile when her mother brushed her hair behind her ear. She didn't want to think about her appearance. It was probably obvious what had been happening in this room before the guards had burst in.

No, they hadn't burst in.

Regis had gone to fight them.

She had felt his need to protect her.

"Will they kill him?" Her voice trembled and she looked up into her mother's dark eyes. Sometimes, it was as though she was seeing herself in the future. They were so alike. Perhaps that was why her father doted on her so much and tolerated her sometimes wild ways. "I have to speak to father and tell him not to kill him."

Her mother's grip on her hand tightened, stopping her from leaving the bed. She looked back at her.

Her mother laughed. "Do not be so overdramatic. They are only holding him because he is trying to kill anyone who goes near to him, even his kin. Your father asked me to take you down there. The Varkans believe that he will calm down if he sees that you are not harmed."

Sophia frowned. "Will they take him away?"

Her mother's eyes widened.

"You've fallen for him!" she said with a strangely serious expression, one that unsettled Sophia.

She blushed. "It's pointless. He says he can't love."

"I know love when I see it and can feel it," her mother said on a laugh.

"Feel it?" Sophia clutched her mother's hand. "What do you mean, feel it? I can't feel it. I tried... this is all because I tried to see if I could feel that he loved me."

"Love is not one feeling that you can sense, child." Her mother sighed and smoothed her hair, pushing each rogue strand back into place. "It is the culmination of many feelings. It is something you have to see with your eyes. That boy... no... man, very definitely a man, loves you or he would not be shouting your name from the cells."

"He is?" Sophia couldn't believe what her mother was saying.

Her mother nodded. With a grin, Sophia stood and raced from the room, running for the cells. She held her skirt high so she didn't trip as she bounded down the steps that led into the dungeon beneath the palace. It took a moment for her eyes to adjust to the dimness and then she rushed on. Her heartbeat quickened when she heard Regis. He was shouting something but she couldn't understand it. The old language again. Other voices joined his as she followed it, trying to find him.

She skidded to a halt when she turned a corner and saw a row of men stood in front of one of the cells. She raced over and pushed her way through the guards, coming out beside her father and the emperor. The Count of Aeris was pinned with his back against the bars, Regis's arm across his throat. Regis snarled, his eyes still bright red even in the darkness, and went to bite the count.

"Stop!" she screamed.

Regis froze and looked up at her.

"Beauty has timing at least," the Count of Aeris drawled and she gasped when she saw the blood on his cheek and throat. "Although you might have come quicker to tame your beast."

Regis snarled and released the count. She went to help the count but stopped when Regis roared. It froze her blood and she tensed.

"It is not wise to anger him." The Count of Aeris got to his feet and rubbed his neck. "Soothe him. Bring him back to us."

She stared at him and then at Regis. "I don't know how."

Emperor Varka stepped forwards and Regis growled again. "Speak with him. He has been calling you."

"But he'll speak in that old language won't he? I don't understand—"

Regis reached out to her and she realised that she didn't need to understand anything he said, she could feel it all in him, every emotion behind whatever words would leave his lips. They would tell her what he wanted to say.

She stepped up to the solid steel bars. Varkan steel. All the bars of the cells at this end of the palace were Varkan steel. It was supposedly indestructible, even to the species who mined it. They had placed him here because they knew he wouldn't be able to break out. He growled and reached for her again, black claws scratching impatiently at the air.

Taking a deep breath, Sophia placed her hand into his and frowned when he drew her slowly to him, his grip so light that it stunned her. He closed his eyes and she walked forwards, following her hand. Silence filled the dungeon and she trembled as he leaned his cheek against her hand. It was strange to have such power over one so strong. Her presence alone had calmed his thirst for violence. Opening her hand, she furrowed her brow and touched his cheek. He was bleeding. Long thin lines cut across his face and his neck. The wound on his arm where he had blocked the guard's blade was deep, blood coating his forearm. His chest was marred with cuts and scratches, smeared with blood. His blood.

"Who hit you?" She looked over his face again, and he opened his eyes and looked at her. He said nothing in response, merely leaned into her open palm and held it against his cheek.

"I have not enjoyed your deception and you have a lot to answer for," her father said behind her. She presumed he was talking to Regis.

Turning to look at her father, she pleaded him with her eyes. "Release him, father. It was all my doing. Punish me instead. I made him bite me. I'm sorry. Please don't hurt him anymore. I am a woman, and I can accept responsibility for my actions."

Tears streaked her cheeks and as the first sob broke free of her lips, Regis growled and pulled her against the bars. She closed her eyes as she felt his arms around her and a strip of his chest against her cheek, edged by cold steel where the bars pressed in.

"No one will be punished," her father said and she smiled. "But there will be some explaining to do once the Count of Sagres is calm."

She blinked away her tears as her father turned to the Count of Aeris and Emperor Varka.

"Take the Count of Sagres to his room."

A guard near the cell door opened the lock and the door slid open, forcing Regis to release her. The moment the door was out of the way, he grabbed her and wrapped his arms around her, holding her so close that she couldn't help smiling. He still wanted to protect her.

The Count of Aeris tried to get her free but Regis clawed at him, making it quite clear that he wasn't going to leave her. She looked at her father to see him standing with his arms folded across his chest and a grim look on his face.

"Can I go with them?" she asked.

An amused smile touched her father's lips and she frowned.

"You are much like your mother in matters of love. When I saw you enter this universe thirty Lyran years past, I had a thought that you would be like me, but I see now that you have grown into a woman as headstrong and wilful as your mother, willing to sacrifice yourself for one you love," he said and she blushed and dropped her gaze to the floor. She had never thought of herself like her mother in personality as well as looks.

"Perhaps there is a little of you in me too, father, for I was willing to run away to avoid an arranged marriage."

He frowned. "My sweetest daughter, you did not believe that I would give you to a man whom you did not wish to marry?"

"I thought perhaps you might, if they offered the right things in exchange."

"Never!" He stepped forwards to touch her face but Regis growled and held her tighter. Her father smiled and shook his head. "I would have kept you for my own forever but I knew that you were lonely and desired to meet someone to call your equal, your love. Having found such a good match in my Terea, I thought you might wish to look beyond the sphere of Lyran society for your love. I only invited these suitors so you might be able to find someone you loved without having to leave... foolish as it sounds... here."

Sophia smiled. She didn't think her father was foolish for trying to bring the universe to her. She only wished that perhaps he had done it in a more tactful manner such as a ball or something where she wasn't meeting one species at a time. It had been the thought of a queue of them waiting for their time with her that had made her uncomfortable. It had made her believe that he wanted to give her to the highest bidder. She hadn't thought about the fact that he had kept her here and had continued to refuse her desire to travel while still granting her the freedom to do as she pleased.

"Forgive me?" He looked as though he wanted to put his arms around her.

Her smile widened. "Of course. Although, I never wanted to leave here. I still don't."

"You mean you'll refuse to leave?" The Count of Aeris stepped forwards, a frown marring his beautiful features. "Even if the emperor... no... even if Regis will marry you, you will not leave Lyra Prime?"

"Regis knows that I will not leave this planet. Lyra Prime is my home. What does it matter if I remain here even if Regis marries me?"

"It will matter a lot when Varka—"

"Van, that's enough," Emperor Varka said and she blushed with shame when she looked at him. "We will take the Count of Sagres to his room."

"I'm sorry about all this." Sophia tried to move but Regis was holding her too tight. "I think I might have to go too."

Her father nodded.

Taking Regis's hand to show him that she wasn't going to leave him, she started walking. He released her and followed, holding her hand so tight that she could feel her bones creaking. He was strong. He was incredibly strong. Yet she had brought him to his knees. She followed the emperor and count up through the palace, back to Regis's room.

"Emperor Varka," she said and the man didn't respond. She walked a little quicker to be closer to him. "Emperor Varka?"

The man turned to look at her with wide eyes and then smiled. "What is it, little one?"

They stopped outside Regis's door and she glanced at it and then looked back at the emperor.

"I'm sorry. I don't love you. It wouldn't have worked."

He continued to smile. It held a hint of darkness that unnerved her. Something about it, about him, spoke of intimate knowledge of violence and death. He looked like the royal assassins did sometimes when she chanced upon them in the city.

"Give the Count of Sagres more blood and he will calm down. We must call home to apprise them of the situation but will not be far away. If he loses control, we will sense it and come to you. Come, Van."

With that, he was walking along the corridor. She had expected more of a protest or perhaps disappointment. He didn't seem at all bothered that Varka's ties with Lyra weren't going to be strengthened through marriage. Perhaps he was only thinking of the money he could save and the fact that Lyra wouldn't be getting Varka Two.

She opened the dark wooden door and walked in, leading Regis to his bed. He sat down on it and she was relieved when she released his hand and he didn't make a fuss. She could sense him watching her, studying her every move. His feelings were still as strong as they had been when they were last in this room together, ebbing and flowing through him, through her. Looking him over, she sighed at the cuts that marked his pale skin, cutting over the contours of his muscles. No one had admitted hurting him. Had they all been guilty to some extent? Even his friend and the emperor? Even her father? She supposed they weren't to blame if they had hurt him in order to protect themselves. After all, he had been attempting to kill the Count of Aeris when she had arrived at the cell.

"Are you alright?" She touched his cheek. His blood red eyes never left her face. "I'll clean you up."

She went to the bathroom, unsure of what to do. She had never had to clean wounds before. She ran water into the stone basin until it felt cold and then wet a cloth with it. She returned to Regis and sat beside him on the bed. He turned to face her when she did and for a moment, his eyes flickered to her throat. Ignoring the spark of desire it lit in her, she cleaned his cuts, carefully washing away the blood, and bound the wound on his arm. She couldn't help noticing how fantastic his body was, or the white scars that marked his skin. He wasn't a stranger to wounds and pain.

Her gaze wandered his body until it reached his hands. They rested on his knees, relaxed but holding them. She could sense the tension in him, the desire to touch her. It seemed he was in control of himself, at least for now. She frowned when she noticed a black finger thick band that ran up both of his arms on the outside. She looked a little closer at it, fascinated by the intricate markings that created the line, markings that varied from slashes to swirls to what looked like symbols. Her eyes followed the black line upwards over his biceps to his shoulder and from there up his neck. They were beautiful.

Without thinking, she ran her fingers down the line nearest her, tracing it and revelling in the warmth of his skin. The marks were familiar but nothing came to her—nowhere she had seen them before or what they might mean.

Dropping the cloth, she took hold of his hands, one in each of hers, and then ran her fingertips along the marks, following both at the same time towards his neck. When she reached it, she caressed the line of his jaw and then brushed his lower lip with her thumb.

Regis growled, grabbed her upper arms, and pushed her onto her back on the bed.

Give him blood.

That was what they had told her.

Sophia shut her eyes when his mouth closed over hers, his kiss stealing her breath and setting her body on fire.

Give him blood she would.

CHAPTER 6

Sophia stared at the ceiling when Regis's mouth left hers and he kissed a trail along her jaw and then down to her throat. She swallowed and lay sprawled out on the bed, ready for anything. Ready for everything. A moan left her lips when he kissed her throat and then wrapped his lips around it, sucking the skin. She longed for him to use his teeth.

She ached for him to bite her.

She would give anything to feel it again.

Involuntarily, her body arched against his, her thigh rubbing between his legs. He growled and sucked her throat harder, but still didn't bite her. She would surrender everything to feel it. Her birthright, her family, her blood. There wasn't anything she wouldn't sacrifice in exchange for him.

It didn't matter that he wasn't the emperor or that her species would gain nothing from the match. She didn't care.

She only wanted him.

She loved him.

Her eyes shot wide when he nicked her neck with his teeth and she shuddered along with him when he growled and sunk against her, his body half covering hers. Her hands swept up his arms and she clawed his back, lost in the glimmer of pleasure and the promise of exquisite ecstasy. His hand roamed down the other side of her neck and covered her right breast. She bit her lip and moaned her approval, hoping to encourage him.

They had told her to give him her blood.

She wanted to give him more than that.

So much more.

Regis growled again and shifted, moving to kneel between her legs. Sophia gasped when he ground against her and she felt his hard length. Her heart raced. She had decided to give herself to him but it still hadn't quite prepared her for the reality of it or the fact that he didn't seem quite with her.

She had thought perhaps that he would come around a little once he'd had a taste of her blood. Right now, he didn't seem at all conscious of the fact it was her.

Or was he?

"Regis?" Sophia whispered as he devoured her throat with kisses so intense that she yearned for his touch. They drove her wild with need and when he pushed his hand beneath her skirt and placed it over the bite mark on her thigh, it sent her out of her mind. She raised her body into the touch, into him, and threw her head back. Her breasts pressed against her corset, straining for contact with him. Her heart ached and thundered, begging him to relieve her.

He muttered something in her ear, his breath hot and sultry, his words carrying a promise of seduction even though she couldn't understand them. She longed to know what he was saying, what words he husked against her skin between kisses.

He felt hungry, full of desire and passion as strong as her own. There was an aura of desperation around him, of hope and fear.

Her hips bucked into his touch when he pressed his hand against her mound, fingers teasing her through the material of her underwear. She willed him to remove the snug material, to invade her body with his own and take everything that she was offering him.

"Regis." As she uttered his name in sheer need, he ran his fingers over the front of her underwear and she blinked as she felt cool air against her. His fingers quickly followed it and she realised he must have used his claws to rent the material in two. She gasped at the thought of him touching her with his claws out and then relaxed when she looked at his other hand and saw his fingernails were normal.

Her eyes met his and she opened her mouth to speak but her words came out in a garbled moan when he slipped his fingers into her folds and drew wetness up to her pert nub and circled it. The feel of his touch was intense, mind-blowing.

Regis growled, a pleased smile on his face.

She had to stop him. She needed to know that he was actually in there, that it was him speaking to her and he was conscious of what they were doing. Her hands pressed against his chest but he didn't stop. His fingers slid lower and she melted into the bed when he inserted one into her slick channel.

"Regis?" She bit her lip and stared into his eyes.

They brightened, turning crimson.

"Shh, Sophia, before you turn me insane. I am already half there." He flashed her a smile that was all sharp fangs before burying his face in her neck and kissing it.

At least he was still with her, even if he was on the verge of losing control again.

He needed blood or, well, she didn't know what he would do or how violent he could become. The others had told her to give him blood to calm him down. Taking hold of his other hand, she brought it up to her neck and then remembered that his claws were retracted and she really didn't want them out again when he was touching her down there. She had to cut herself though. She had to convince him to bite her and take her blood before he lost control. She could feel that he was slowly regaining a sense of awareness about her and his surroundings. She didn't want him to lose that again. She wanted to make love with him, not have him lost in a haze of bloodlust as he had sex with her.

His finger moved inside her and all reasonable thought left her. She gasped with each plunge of it into her core, each smooth slide that sent sparks of hunger gathering in her abdomen. She writhed against his hand, moaning into his ear and desperately trying to retain a sense of cohesion within her thoughts so she could figure out a way to make him bite her.

He thrust against his hand where it covered her mound and the solution dawned on her.

He wanted to bite her.

She didn't need to make him.

She only had to let him know that she wanted it too.

There was something else that she wanted first. She wanted this torture to end and him inside her. Her hands skimmed down his back to his buttocks and she slid them around to the front of his trousers. He lightly bit her neck as she undid the front ties of his trousers and her heart thumped hard against her chest when she swallowed her nerves and slid her hand inside. The feel of his hard shaft in her hand was electrifying. She licked her lips as her mind raced to imagine it inside her, stretching her body and making it his. She ached for that moment.

He ground his length against her hand and she instinctively wrapped her fingers around it, gripping it. A groan left him when he thrust again, his length pushing through the tight circle of her fingers. His tongue traced a line along her throat that left her tingling. Insensitive. Was this why the patch around his bite mark on her leg felt numb? Could he anaesthetise the area that he was going to bite? It explained how she hadn't felt any pain earlier when he had bitten her thigh. She had felt only pleasure.

His finger slid free of her body and he removed her hand from his length. She swallowed her pounding heart as he moved between her legs and the head of his shaft pressed into her. Closing her eyes, she waited with bated breath. It was torn from her throat in a deep sigh as he pushed into her, filling her body with his own. She licked her lips again and clung to him, wrapping her arms around his shoulders and pushing her fingers into his hair. He thrust into her, slow and deep, taking her out of her mind as her body hummed and tingled with each plunge of his length. He moaned against her throat and then growled. Before she could even think about reacting, his fangs penetrated her neck and he pulled on her blood. Her entire body arched into his as a wave of heat crashed through her followed by a shockwave of pleasure. This time, she bit back the scream as she climaxed.

Regis growled and continued to thrust into her, drawing on her blood at the same time. She held his head to her, not wanting him to stop drinking. He didn't. He drank deeper, biting hard enough that she felt it this time. It hurt, but the intense feelings of arousal and desire that it brought with it made the pain seem a small price to pay. His hand went to her breasts and he growled into her throat as he sliced the front of her corset open. She gasped at the cool air as it washed over her body and then at the feel of his bare chest against hers. She wished they were fully naked, but didn't want him to leave her. She wanted him to stay inside her. Wanted to feel him.

He thrust deeper inside her and she raised her pelvis up, drawing a moan from him. His drinking slowed but remained deep enough that her head spun with each mouthful he took from her. Her thighs trembled against his as warmth coiled tight in the depth of her stomach again. His pelvis slammed against her clit with each frantic plunge of his length into her and before she knew what was happening, heat exploded through her again. Her body convulsed around his, milking his shaft and this time sending him crashing over the edge with her. He jerked up hard inside her and shuddered as he spilled himself. Her harsh breathing was joined by his own as his fangs left her throat and he licked the wound, pressing kisses against it occasionally.

Her eyes widened when he rolled onto his back, taking her with him so she was lying on top of him, and then closed when he wrapped his arms around her. She

33

drifted off to sleep as Regis whispered words to her that sounded a lot like the song he had been singing to the moons.

Sophia sighed as she woke and then smiled when she saw Regis lying beside her, half dressed and looking as wanton as she probably did. She reached out to push the long strands of his black hair away from his face so she could see it better and then paused as it hit her.

She would have to marry him now. In her haste to have him, she hadn't thought about the consequences. She hadn't thought about protecting herself. He murmured something in his sleep and smiled. He had a beautiful smile. If they had a child, perhaps it would also have his smile. In a way, she hoped it would have his eyes too. Now that she was used to them, his eyes were stunning.

She brushed his hair away from his neck and ears, and smiled too as she mused what life would be like with him. Her smile faltered when she realised that she might not have a life with him. Her father hadn't consented to the match and Regis might not want to live on Lyra Prime. What if her haste had left her pregnant and Regis didn't want to stay with her? What if he didn't love her enough or still refused to believe that he could love?

He could. Her mother was right. Everything Regis had done had proven that he loved her. She had felt all the feelings in him, everything that she had been feeling herself. He couldn't deny that he loved her. Would it be enough to make him stay on a planet that didn't suit him though?

Or was her love for him enough to make her leave Lyra Prime for a world and a species that she knew hardly anything about?

A place where the brightest the day got was evening light?

Her fingers traced the black band of marks that started just behind his ear and followed them down his throat and over his shoulder. They were so familiar.

It dawned on her where she had seen them before.

They had been in one of the books from the palace library.

Pulling her clothes closed around her as best she could, she rushed from the room intent on reaching hers unseen.

There was something important about the marks.

Something very important.

She had to know what.

CHAPTER 7

Regis smiled up at the hot Lyran sun through his visor. It warmed him to the bone but it wasn't the reason that he was smiling. He lowered his gaze to the garden and his smile widened as he saw Sophia. She was beautiful in her flowing sky blue empire-line gown, her wavy black hair tumbling around her smooth graceful shoulders. He laughed with her as she danced around, her smile broad and infectious. The laughter of the two small children joined theirs and he stopped to watch them again, fascinated by the sight of her and the younglings.

Younglings.

Their red eyes told him that they were Varkan. Or at least in part they were Varkan. They had their mother's beauty.

His younglings.

Their younglings.

He had never seen such a beautiful sight as her playing with them, never in his long years. A sigh escaped him and he allowed himself the moment of whimsy as he watched them. In this moment, he was no longer a commander of his people but a man with a family.

It was a beautiful dream.

No. It would be a beautiful reality.

Sophia turned and looked at him, waving as she laughed, the light breeze tousling her hair and dress.

She was a beautiful reality.

He flinched and gritted his teeth as something hit him. The dream slipped through his fingers as the pain came again and he was torn from sleep. He frowned as he opened his eyes and then smiled when he saw Sophia kneeling beside him on the bed.

"You utter sekta no uso cruskin nyaaeso!"

She hit him again with something rectangular and very hard. His head ached and he blocked her next strike with his arm, unwilling to be beaten up any more. His translator hadn't understood the last part of what she had said but judging by the thunderous black look in her eyes and the fact that she was beating him to a pulp, he deduced it wasn't words of love.

"You lied to me."

He understood that.

Sitting up, he placed his hands out behind him to prop himself in place and looked at her. The marks on her neck were deep and sore. He had been a little harder on her than he had hoped he would but the bloodlust had been too intense and he hadn't been able to stop himself from losing control.

"Lied about what?" he said, his head still reeling. One moment, he was dreaming about their future family and the next he was being hit with, he glanced at what she was holding, a book.

35

"You." She opened the book. She turned it to face him and he stared at the markings on the page. Perhaps some things about his species were better documented than he had expected. He hadn't let slip about these markings so it must have been his father or one of his other predecessors. With a sigh, she dropped the book and her shoulders slumped. "Why didn't you tell me?"

He picked the book up and looked at the drawing of the markings and then at his arms.

"Because I had to know." He closed the book, placing it down on the bed. He looked at her, at her sore eyes, and realised that she had been crying. Why? Was it because of what she had discovered or something else? His gaze lowered to her stomach and then darted back to her face.

"You had to know what?" New tears rose into her eyes and he longed to reach out and wipe them away.

Was this also love? This past day had been incredible. He had learnt so much, gained so much, and now he felt as though he was standing on the edge of the cliffs of Varka Three, one step away from falling to his lonely death. If he said the wrong thing now, if he couldn't convince her that he hadn't lied to her, then he would lose everything.

Without her, life wasn't worth living. Eternity would be a bleak darkness without this ray of light before him.

His own shoulders slumped as he realised that the Terran tale was true. He understood it now. Love was consuming, beyond mortal control. The star-crossed lovers had killed themselves—one because they believed the other dead, and the other because they woke to see their love had died. Neither had wanted to live without the other. Both had chosen death over life alone.

A decision he would gladly make should Sophia turn her back on him because of his deception.

"It was not easy. Please believe me, Sophia." Regis took her hand. When she didn't snatch it back, he took it as a good sign. This was all frightening and new. Never before had he been so scared that someone would leave him. Never had he relied so heavily on one person for his future happiness. "I desired to tell you at every turn, with every furtive glance you threw my way, but I had to resist and see what you would do. When you rejected the emperor because you could not love him, and when you sought my company, I knew that you were growing attached to me but I still could not dare hope or reveal the truth."

He sighed and squeezed her hand.

"Sophia, I admit that while we were en route to Lyra Prime, I decided to switch with Sirus and see what would happen. You have had many suitors and rejected them all. I wanted to spend time with you to discover whether you were only waiting for the right amount of money, planets or power to come along or whether it was something else that you were looking for."

"You lied."

He closed his eyes and raised her hand, pressing it against his cheek. He opened his eyes again and looked at her. The frown she wore was beginning to fade.

"Know that I did not mean to deceive you. I only wished to observe proceedings, hoped that perhaps I was wrong and there was something else you sought. When you admitted that you wanted to love your future husband, I wanted to rejoice and cry at the same time. You had chosen the one thing I could not give and I had begun to long for your company and the sight of your beautiful face."

A blush touched her cheeks and he stroked her right one with the backs of his fingers.

"But you can love." Sophia took hold of his hand. "I have seen it... felt it."

"You have made me realise it." He squeezed her hand and sighed. "Although I fear you will no longer love me."

"It's foolish, but when I met you, I longed for you to be the emperor so I could spend time with you. I hated the emperor."

"Do you still hate the emperor?" he said with a hopeful look.

Her frown melted away and she sighed. A smile curved her beautiful lips.

"I'm an idiot, but I think I love him."

Regis smiled, warmed by her confession and the fact that everything was out in the open now.

Almost everything.

"Would you marry the emperor?"

"I don't think the emperor should talk about himself in the third person." She frowned again. "Your name is Regis though, yes?"

He nodded.

"And the Count of Sagres bit?"

"Count of Sagres is the name traditionally given to me as Emperor Varka. It was a risk to use it, but it is not well documented."

Sophia stared at him. Regis was a count, and also the emperor. The man she had thought was the emperor wasn't the emperor at all. She couldn't believe this. It was almost as strange and fantastical as the thought that he couldn't love. She had wanted Regis to be the emperor, and it had turned out that he was. Was this the deception her father had spoken of?

"My father knows, doesn't he?"

"Does he?" Regis frowned.

"Down at the cells he mentioned a deception and that someone had to explain something. It must be this."

"The cells." Regis looked pensive, as though he was having difficulty remembering being there. "It is not clear. Perhaps he does. Everything between leaving you here and seeing you there is a blur."

"The bloodlust?" Sophia said and he nodded again. She stroked the back of his hand and then the start of the marks running up his arm. "You really are the emperor, aren't you? You're not going to suddenly announce that the Count of Aeris is the emperor?"

He laughed, although it sounded strained to her. "No. Van would make a terrible emperor. He is a better tactician than politician. He is the commander of our finest fleet."

"And the other one?"

"Sirus?" He lowered his gaze to watch her hand. "He is my first attendant and bodyguard. Although I do not need one."

She could believe that. Having seen Regis fight, she couldn't imagine anyone besting him if he was in control of himself. Her fingers followed the marks up to his elbow.

"Were you going to tell me?" she said with a frown, hoping his answer would be yes. She hoped that he had been intending to tell her sooner rather than later. She hoped that he would have told her before she had found out from her father.

"Were you going to tell me?" he countered and her frown intensified.

"Tell you what?" she said, unable to think of any secret she had withheld from him.

He lowered his hand to her stomach. Her eyes widened and her mouth fell open.

"Varkans are very sensitive to female times of needing and pregnancies. A Varkan pregnancy develops quickly. A Varkan's ability to see the future of their family develops faster than that." He smiled and she was stunned to see the tenderness in it and the affection that filled his eyes as he stroked her stomach. "There will be two."

"How do you know?" She placed her hand over his, shocked by how sure he had sounded.

"I have seen them. A boy and a girl. Playing under the Lyran sun with their mother."

When he smiled at her, she wondered how he could have ever said that Varkans couldn't love. There was so much affection and love in his expression and in his voice.

She hesitated and then smiled. "Do they have red eyes?"

He nodded.

"I think I might be the first Varkan to ever say this." He looked nervous for a moment and cleared his throat. "I love you."

Sophia grinned and forgot that she had been angry with him. It was impossible to be angry with him when he looked at her like this, so full of devotion and love. She was about to throw her arms around him when she stopped herself.

"You saw us here?" She wanted to make sure that she had heard him right.

He nodded. "In the gardens."

"But you're the emperor of Varka. You can't live here and I've already made up my mind to leave with you. How could you see us here?"

"Perhaps because I had already decided to stay here. The dreams can change. I am willing to change with them. We could make both palaces our homes."

"Spend some time here and some on Varka Prime?" It sounded too good to be true. She knew it was a long journey between the planets but perhaps the Varkans could invent a type of space travel that would be even faster than sub-space. She could happily spend half a year on Varka Prime if she knew she could bask in the sun of Lyra Prime for the other half. If they were having twins as he said, then she wanted her family involved with them. She didn't have a clue how to look after children and everyone would be more than willing to help.

"Whatever you wish for, you will receive, my love."

Sophia threw her arms around him then and dragged him down to the bed. His mouth claimed hers and she sighed inside over his tender kisses and the fact that his hand remained against her stomach.

"Regis?" she whispered when he kissed down her neck.

"Yes, Sophia?"

"Will you lose control again... if you taste my blood?"

"No, not now."

"Not now?"

"Not now that you wear this." He kissed the mark on her throat. It was something she hadn't read anything about and now she wished she had so she could understand what was happening.

"Why not?"

He drew back and looked at her. "Because it tells everyone that you are mine."

"I'm yours?" She wanted to hear him say it again.

"Forever mine and mine alone. No one will dare touch you." He caressed the marks on her throat and warmth spread out from their centre, suffusing her entire body. She closed her eyes for a moment to relish the feel of his fingers against her and then looked at him. "To bite someone's neck is the equivalent to... well... marriage."

"Marriage?" Her eyebrows shot up and she went to touch her neck but touched his hand instead. A jolt ran through her and she bit her lip at the sudden hunger that followed. She wanted to feel him against her, their bodies as one again. She cursed him for being able to make her feel like that from just a touch, for making her forget what she had been talking about. "Marriage?"

"There will be an official ceremony of course, both here and on Varka Prime. The people will wish to meet their empress. If you will have me?"

And she had been worried that he was going to leave her. She blinked, too stunned to form a response. He had already marked her as his but he still wanted to marry her.

"Are you going to talk to my father?" she said and he nodded again. "I think I should go with you and perhaps we should bring Van and the other one too. We might need all the protection we can get."

"Why?" He frowned at her.

"My mother will be there."

"And?"

It didn't seem to be sinking in.

"Well, you see, I already have ties to your species."

"You do?" His frown didn't shift.

"My mother isn't wholly Minervan. She's part Varkan. My father can feel things but it's strongest when my mother is with him."

His eyes shot wide. He paled to a shade of white Sophia didn't like.

"She will be able to sense the pregnancy," Regis said in a distant tone, his eyes bright but unfocused. Clearly, he enjoyed the idea of having to face her parents as much as she did.

"Your bags are packed and I have nothing I'd need to take with me." She sat up. "We could run away."

He sat up too and frowned at the luggage.

"No."

"No?" The thought that he might actually stand up to her parents made her squirm inside. She didn't want to start a war between Lyra and Varka and if Regis went to face her father alone, that might happen. Both of them seemed unduly stubborn. "Then let me go alone. My father won't deny me."

He looked uncomfortable. There was a buzz over the intercom beside the door. She tensed and looked at Regis.

"Open the door, Sophia," her father said over the intercom.

Regis stood and put his jacket on. She could only watch as he buttoned it and then did his trousers up and fastened his sword around his waist. He gave her a smile, swept the long strands of his black hair out of his face, and then strode to the door. She curled up on the bed and hugged her knees to her chest. At least they were both dressed. Perhaps her father wouldn't put two and two together. If he did, she prayed to Iskara that he made five.

Regis opened the door. Her father walked in and Sophia smiled until her mother stepped out from behind him. They both looked at her, their shock written on their faces. Sophia opened her mouth to explain but Regis stepped between them.

"I, Regis, Count of Sagres, Emperor Varka, kneel before you." He unsheathed his sword and knelt in front of her father. She leaned forwards, anxious to see what he was going to do. He balanced the sword across both of his palms and lowered his head. "Your highness, Lyra I, King of Lyra, I offer you my sword."

"Your life?" her father said and Sophia started forwards but stopped when Regis looked at her.

The sword symbolised his life? No.

"My life, in exchange for your daughter's." He looked up at her father. He raised the sword up, offering it just as he had said. She shook her head, afraid that any exchange he spoke of would be taken literally by her father. She could see the anger in his eyes and knew that both he and her mother had sensed what had happened to her. Her father would have felt it from her mother. "I willingly give my life for hers."

"Regis," Sophia whispered and reached out to him. Tears blurred her vision. She bit her lip and sobbed when her father took the sword and held it tight in one hand. "Father?"

She cringed and flinched away when he brought the sword down and there was a harsh thud.

Silence reigned.

"I do not understand," Regis said and Sophia opened one eye and then the other. Relief filled her swift and sweet when she saw that he was unharmed and that her father had buried the sword point down into the wooden floor.

"My daughter loves you," her father said on a sigh. "Enough that she has given herself to you. I cannot cause harm to one my daughter loves, not when it would in turn cause harm to her."

"Sophia." Regis stood. He held his hand out to her and she went to him, slipping her hand into his and holding it tightly. Her stomach fluttered with nerves as she stood before her mother and father with him. He turned to her father. "You will give your daughter to me, to protect from this day forward?"

Her father nodded. Her mother smiled wide and looped her arm through her father's.

"I give my daughter to you on one condition."

"Anything," Regis said.

"That you promise to love her until the end of your days, whenever those may be, and beyond them."

"I will always love her." Regis turned away from her father and looked at her. She blushed when he took both of her hands and held them, his thumbs caressing her fingers. "I will always love you, Sophia. I am no longer afraid of these feelings or how little control I have over them. For you, I embrace them and the fear they bring, just as you embraced it for me."

Sophia bit her lip and smiled when he pulled her into his arms. She rested her head against his chest and listened to his heart beating strong. Her heart. She had captured it just as he had captured hers.

She cursed her parents when she saw them still standing by the door and tried to shoo them away. Her father gave her a look that said he wasn't going anywhere.

"One more condition," he said and Regis looked at him. "Sophia is Lyran and will live many long years just as the rest of our species, but not as yours. Give her a wedding present when you are married in two night's time."

Sophia frowned. "Two nights?"

"Hush," her mother said with a knowing smile. Sophia couldn't believe it. If they intended for her to marry Regis in only two nights then they must have been setting everything up from shortly after she had spoken to her father in the garden.

"I will give her any present that she desires," Regis said and she smiled at him.

"Give her this one. Give her the aeturnalia solis."

Regis' expression changed to one so serious that she was dying to know what her father had said. She hadn't understood it. It had sounded like the old language that Regis had spoken.

"I will," he said and her parents left.

Sophia looked at Regis, eager to know what it was that she would be getting as a present. It sounded interesting but the look on Regis's face made her worry. She hoped it wasn't anything to do with him dying again. The thought of him leaving her was terrifying. She didn't want him to ever leave her side, and definitely not on her wedding night.

In two night's time.

Night.

She was getting married at night? Evening at least. She wanted to see Regis's face during the ceremony.

"Regis?" she said as he wrapped his arms around her and the door closed. "What's aeturnalia solis?"

He brushed the waves of black hair from her face and smiled at her.

"Something I would have given you without his asking, but only with your permission."

"Permission?" She frowned.

41

"It goes with this." He stroked the mark on her throat. "Think of it as love everlasting."

"Love everlasting?" She remembered what she had read about Varkans. "Or life everlasting?"

He smiled and cupped her cheek. "Both, for you."

"Love everlasting," she whispered as she stared into his eyes.

Eternity with Regis. It sounded wonderful.

Taking his hand, she placed it over her stomach, holding it there, and kissed him. She wasn't going to leave this room until the ceremony in two night's time. After that, she wasn't going to leave Regis's side forever. She smiled when Regis nicked her lip with his teeth and kissed her harder, stealing her breath away but in control this time, just as she knew he always would be from now on. Now that she was his.

Always.

And soon he would be hers.

Forever.

The End

HEART OF A MERCENARY

Princess Miali, one of the beautiful and strong daughters of Lyra, is an ambassador for Lyra. Her true identity is kept secret to protect but it's her beauty that puts her in danger when slavers attack her ship while she's in cryo-sleep. When she wakes, she finds herself heading for the markets, her only company the ship's handsome young Minervan doctor. Kosen makes Miali's body react like no man before him, sending her hair floating with her positive emotions and making her wonder if she might just be falling for her captor.

Kosen has been part of Nostra's crew since his two sisters were sold into slavery. His only desire is to gain enough money to buy them back, and Miali's sale will get him just that. But the more time he spends with her, the more he realises that the path he chose was a mistake and the life he's led is a shameful one. When he discovers Miali's secret, he agrees to help her escape, and not just because she promises him the money he needs. Miali fascinates him with her beauty and the way her body reacts to him, and he can't help believing that they might have a chance with each other, and he might have a chance at a better life.

Can Kosen help Miali escape the slaver vessel and the terrible future that awaits her at the markets? Will he be able to save his sisters and change the course of his life? And will Miali be able to convince Kosen to stay with her?

CHAPTER 1

Miali walked along the corridor between the bridge and her room, her thoughts miles away and running through her schedule and recent events. They were safely en route to Dliaer. She glanced out of the oval windows running alongside the corridor and stopped when she saw Sekaria Prime slowly disappearing into the distance. Its bright blue orb was dazzling under the light of the twin suns.

It was beautiful.

The backdrop of the Andromeda galaxy only made it more stunning. A smile touched her lips and she gave herself a moment away from her duties as an ambassador to take it all in. All of her life she had dreamed of seeing space as her father and mother had. Now she was finally able to travel amongst the stars whose names she had memorised, following ancient shipping routes that predated her grandparents.

Sometimes she missed her parents and their home on the Nebula-Lyra II, the ship her father, Remi, captained. Her mother, Emmanuelle, had told Miali that her father had always been homesick when in space. Perhaps she had picked up this trait from him. Her long silver hair floated upwards. Miali frowned and smoothed it back down again.

That was definitely something she had inherited from her mother. It was a Dazkaran trait that she wished she didn't have. It made it impossible to keep some things secret.

If she liked a male, her hair would betray her feelings, rising and swaying with them. If she was happy, it floated in the air as though she was underwater. They had tormented her in school about it, so much so that, much to her annoyance, her father had pulled her from lessons and had her privately tutored instead. He had only been protecting her, but she had wanted to spend time with the children of the other officers on the ship. She had wanted to be normal.

The communicator bracelet around her wrist bleeped. Miali looked down at it. It was time to turn in. Soon, the ship would drop into sub-space and it always made her feel sick if she was awake when it happened. The other ambassadors on the ship understood her need to be in cryo-sleep when they travelled in sub-space but didn't know the reason for it. The ship's doctor had explained to her that her sensitivity to her feelings amplified her fear and the reverberations of the ship. Those combined to make her nauseas and gave her panic attacks.

It was a nice change to have someone treat her as an adult and a normal person for once. The doctor hadn't picked on her because of her part-Dazkaran roots, or fussed over her because of her royal blood. In fact, no one here did.

That was probably because no one here knew that she was born of Lyran royalty.

Her father had agreed that it was best to keep that fact about her hidden. He had spoken to parliament and the military, and had arranged a new identity for her under the same name. Her uncle, Sebastian, the king of Lyra, had issued her the position of Lyran ambassador.

They had pulled so many strings to make her safe and give her this chance of living her dream of a normal life. She thanked them so often that they were probably sick of hearing it now. Whenever she wrote to them about a planet that they had agreed a new treaty with or a new species they had made contact with, she always thanked them for giving her this wonderful opportunity.

The universe was a fascinating place full of so many kind and generous species. It was more incredible than she ever could have dreamed.

Making her way to the cryo-sleep chamber, Miali read the files stored on the small computer pad that she held. The other ambassadors on the ship had all filed their reports on the meeting on Sekaria Prime and their thoughts on the topics they would broach at the meeting on Dliaer. She hadn't had the time to write hers yet. She had spent the remainder of her time on the planet seeing the central city.

All of the other ambassadors on the ship were male and often teased her because of her desire to see the cities they visited. She didn't mind if they thought it was a female thing to do. She loved to see them. Once, she had even managed to convince a few of the men to join her. After that, the others had teased her less, turning their taunts towards those men instead.

Miali giggled to herself about the constant torment those men had been given since their tour of the city. It had been on Minerva Four. Months had passed since then.

The ship's doctor greeted her at the door to the cryo-sleep chamber. She smiled at the grey-haired man and finished reading the reports on her computer pad as she stepped into the sleek curved white metal and glass pod that the doctor had prepared.

"I'll take it from here, Doc." A familiar male voice made Miali look up and she blushed with her smile when she saw it was Eryc, the Terran ambassador. They had met as children on Lyra Five, her Uncle Balt and Aunt Kayla's planet. Her aunt was the last surviving member of Terran royalty and had gathered all of her scattered people there when she had married Balt. Eryc thought that she knew the royal family because she was a friend of Renie, Balt and Kayla's eldest daughter.

"You're thinking about Lyra Five again aren't you?" Eryc said with a wide smile, his chocolate brown eyes warm with it.

"Maybe." She handed him the computer pad. "It's been a while since I've seen Renie. I bet her brother Rezic has her off in the wild depths of space somewhere looking for ancient tat."

Eryc laughed. "You know Renie and Rezic. They're inseparable. I'll never understand why they want to haul arse around the universe looking at dead things."

"And they'll never understand why we travel from planet to planet forging new peace treaties and maintaining relations with other species." Miali reached for the strap above her right shoulder at the same time as Eryc. Their hands touched, hers covering his. She froze, her heart beating a little harder, and then took her hand away. Eryc looked at her for a moment before pulling the strap down and clicking it into place with the array of other straps over her stomach.

Miali willed her hair to stay put. She wasn't stupid. She had seen the way that Eryc had been looking at her recently. In Iskara's name, half of the men on the ship had been looking at her that way. Considering that they spent most of their time in space and that she was the only female onboard, she could understand the flirting and the looks they gave her. She was beginning to give a few of them looks in return but that was where it stopped for her. She had never been the kind of woman who could have flings. Her feelings were too strong and she knew that she would want more than just a short romance. She wanted love.

She hoped that the heated looks that Eryc gave her weren't just because it had been months since they had spent longer than a day on any one planet.

After all, the way that things were going, she was starting to get the impression that she might like him and, given enough time, that like might become something else.

Something more than friendship.

He clicked the last of the straps into place and tugged them, checking that they were secure. With a flash of a smile, he stepped back. The doctor checked her vitals on the monitor beside the pod and then touched the panel below them. As the door closed, the doctor walked away but Eryc remained. He had done this the past few times that they had sent her to sleep. It was comforting to see him there when she was sent under and then to wake to see him still there, as though he had been waiting for her the whole time that she had been asleep.

"See you when you wake up, sleeping beauty." Eryc held his hand up and smiled again.

Miali nodded and then everything went black.

Miali's head ached when she came around and she frowned when she found herself faced not with the cryo-sleep room and Eryc, but with a tall, very broad and ugly bald man in black. The man grinned to reveal twin rows of pointed teeth. Her mind felt as though someone had scrambled it and although she knew that those teeth meant something, she couldn't piece it together. He grabbed her around the throat, squeezing so tight that she couldn't breathe. She tried to push him away as panic lanced through her but her arms wouldn't work.

Dazedly, she looked over at her right arm. She blinked when she saw a thick black metal band encircling her wrist, holding her arm out horizontally. A metal bar extended out from the band and joined it to a wall a foot behind her.

Miali swallowed to clear the dry sticky lump from her throat and quickly looked at her other wrist. A similar cuff wrapped around it, the bar holding it rigid. A glance at her feet revealed they were blurred. When her eyes finally managed to focus, she saw that they were shackled to the wall too, spread shoulder width apart. Her gaze tracked up her legs.

Her heart jumped in her chest when she saw that her deep blue and black skin-tight flight suit was no longer done up to her neck.

Someone had opened it far enough that her cleavage was on display. It must have been the man. She wriggled in a desperate attempt to get free, afraid of what the man might do to her and not caring that the metal cuffs bit into her wrists where her flight suit ended. The man laughed at her, deep and menacing, and tightened his grip on her throat.

"This one has spirit." He chuckled and shoved her head back towards the wall.

Something clicked. His hand left her throat. Cold steel pressed against it. She struggled but couldn't move her upper body. He had put a collar on her and fixed it to the wall like her arms and legs.

"What do you want?" Her small voice trembled and her gaze darted around the dim room. The only light was a tiny pinhole beam on the ceiling. It pointed straight at her, dampening her vision. She could only see the man in front of her. The rest of the room was in shadow. She could hear others but couldn't see them. The thought that others were watching her, could see her so vulnerable and exposed, made her skin crawl. "Where am I? Where is everyone else?"

The man laughed again. "All in good time. For now, shut your pretty trap. Slaves got to learn to be quiet."

Slave?

A wave of nausea hit her.

It wasn't just the thought that she was now a slave that evoked that feeling. There was something else. She focused on her surroundings and her stomach lurched.

In Iskara's name, they were travelling in sub-space and she was awake. Wave after wave of sickness swept through her, crashed over her, until she was fighting a constant battle to stop herself from vomiting.

Slave?

Miali gasped at air. It was cool and refreshing but didn't stop the nausea from growing worse as her panic increased. Some people had her. They must have attacked the ship while she had been asleep.

"Who are you?" she said, voice shaking along with her body.

The man grinned and backhanded her. Pain shot out in all directions from her jaw and cheek. Flashing white dots punctured her vision. She closed her eyes against them and the sight of this terrifying reality.

"Quiet!" He grabbed her roughly by the jaw and dragged her head back around. She squinted through the pain to look at him. Those sharp teeth. It dawned on her. Minervan. "Think of me as your master, for now. Can't say you'll be needing this where you're going."

He took the translator from her ear, her voice alteration device from her throat, and the communications band from her wrist. With a chilling laugh, he walked away, disappearing into the gloom. The sight of his teeth wouldn't leave her. A Minervan? Why did a Minervan want her? Slave? Master?

Her head pounded from fear and pain.

Slave runners?

A door opened and she saw a corridor and then the silhouettes of several people. One was easily recognisable as the man who had spoken to her. He was tall and broad, but not in a muscular sense. Clearly, he was living well from trading the people that he captured, selling them into slavery. Two people just as tall followed him. Both male judging by their shape. One was as large as the man she had met and the other was far slimmer. The last silhouette was clearly a female.

A female working in the slave trade?

Perhaps she was a slave herself.

When the door closed, the light above Miali dimmed and then went out. She tried to look up, but couldn't move her head enough. The collar around her throat dug in, stopping any attempts to escape. The metal was sharp at the edges and her wrists were already sore. Questions filled her aching mind.

Her hope that the others were alive faded when she remembered that this was a slave ship. From what she had read about and seen of slavery, male slaves were rare. Females brought the best price at market. She had heard of the incredible prices that some of them had fetched, and how prized they were by their masters.

Her aunt, Kayla, had suffered years of slavery with a Sekarian trader, thankfully only working in his warehouse. If Uncle Balt hadn't saved Kayla, someone might have discovered that she was Terran royalty. They would have sold Kayla to the highest bidder. Her owner would have prized her as a whore.

Was she facing such a fate now?

What if these men knew that she was Lyran royalty? No. They couldn't. Her family had been careful to give her a false background and to alter the records of the princess with another's picture so no one would recognise her as the daughter of Prince Lyra IV.

White spots appeared across her vision again. It was a struggle to hold onto consciousness as the combination of nausea and fear threatened to take the universe away again. She blinked rapidly, clinging to the darkness and trying to calm herself. A stronger wave of sickness crashed over her and swept her away into the inky black.

Miali groaned when she came around, her throat aching from having her head hung forwards against the collar while she had been unconscious. She screwed her face up and then slowly opened her eyes. The dark greeted her, as menacing and chilling as before. Staring into it, cold fear crept down her spine. What would happen to her now? Where were the rest of the crew? Where was Eryc? Were they really all dead?

Her stomach had settled. They must have come out of sub-space. In fact, she couldn't feel the ship moving at all. Perhaps they had docked.

A bright burst of light blinded her and she flinched away from the open door. When it closed again, the pinhole light above her came on. She squinted as her eyes adjusted to it.

A man stepped under the light, his black spiked hair and equally black eyes betraying his species as much as his sharp teeth did when he spoke.

"Not a word."

Another Minervan.

This one was young and handsome.

And he spoke Lyran.

CHAPTER 2

Kosen approached the female slowly. He ran his gaze over her from her heavy boots up her slender legs to her ample cleavage and from there to her beautiful face. She was a siren that could make any male's blood boil. It was exactly as their contact had promised them. She would fetch a good price at the auction on Minerva Nine in four days time.

Her silver hair shimmered under the spotlight, glowing in a way.

She was more beautiful in the flesh than he had imagined she would be. He had never seen such a figure matched with a goddess's face and silver hair. There was none like her at the markets.

"Food." Kosen showed her the small black protein pack in his hand.

Her nose wrinkled up and she turned her head away. He frowned and then realised that her tight flight suit was dirty. Whatever she had had in her stomach was now down her front.

With a sigh, he walked over to the side of the room and placed the protein pack down on one of the containers. He picked up a cloth and went back to the female. He hadn't expected that he would be cleaning as well as feeding her but they had to keep her presentable. The smell of sick on her might lower her value. He needed her to fetch the best price.

"He frightened you that much?" Kosen muttered and wiped the vomit off her clothes. She struggled when he cleaned her chest. It didn't stop him. Years of working in the slave trade had taught him that she wasn't really a woman. She was an object that would soon pass from his hands to another's. If he saw her that way, he wouldn't care what happened to her.

It was best this way.

Yet, he was speaking Lyran to her. He was talking a language that disgusted most of his species, even though a member of the Minervan royal family was now the queen of the Lyran people.

To him, Lyran was a musical language.

"Cruskin nyaaeso!" The female lurched forwards. Her rebellious actions only served to press her breasts against his hands.

They both froze.

She immediately shrank back and spat in his face, as though he had touched her on purpose. It was her fault for arching into him.

A tirade of foul language spilled from her lips. Lyran was beautiful sometimes at least. When she spoke it, she said every word with so much venom that it sounded Minervan.

"I said to be quiet," he warned and finished cleaning her. "I've never had a prisoner be sick down themselves before. Try not to do it again. I don't think Nostra deserves such a violent reaction."

"Nostra?" she whispered, as though saying it quietly meant that she wasn't breaking the rules.

"The man you met earlier." Kosen couldn't believe that he was talking to her. Something about her made him respond. He had seen captives frightened before but never to this extent.

"Not him," she said and he looked at her. Her dark eyes were only a shade closer to brown than his were. They were wide and round, rimmed with long thick black lashes. "Not sick for him."

She swallowed with a look of discomfort. When he saw the red marks on her throat, he frowned. Nostra had put the collar on too tight. Kosen reached around her to loosen it. Damaged goods sold for less.

The moment his body touched hers, she moved back as far as possible. He rolled his eyes and waited for her to spit at him again. As though he would intentionally press himself against her. He wasn't Sasue.

"Keep still." Kosen moved the collar onto the next latch, giving her more room. "There."

She was frowning when he stepped away.

"Why were you sick?" He studied her. She was paler than when he had first seen her. She needed to eat, but he knew without trying that she would refuse the protein pack if he offered it to her again.

"Sub-space."

That one word made him frown along with her. When they had boarded her vessel, she had been in cryo-sleep. Their contact had mentioned that they would find her there. Had she been in cryo-sleep because they had been travelling in sub-space?

"We're stationary now." He stopped himself before he mentioned their location. The less she knew, the better.

"I know," she whispered and closed her eyes, swallowing hard as though she was trying to stop herself from vomiting again. "Others with me."

"Don't think about them."

Kosen went to the crate and placed the cloth down. His gaze slid to the protein pack. It was worth a try. He was here to get her to eat after all. He picked it up and walked back to her.

"Will you eat?"

She shook her head. This wasn't good. If he failed to convince her to eat, Nostra would kill him. They had elected him with this female because he was the youngest and nearest to her age in relative terms, and the safest option. If she didn't eat, she would lose weight. As it was, she was already borderline. Bags of bones didn't sell well. In fact, they made less money than damaged goods.

"They're dead." Her voice was a broken whisper and her dark eyes shone with tears.

This wasn't what he needed. Crying females were impossible to deal with and difficult to keep emotional distance from.

Normally, he left the room.

He couldn't leave her though.

With a long sigh, Kosen went over to the crate and picked up a clean cloth. He went back to her and tried to wipe her tears away but she lowered her head and turned it away from him. He tried again and she turned her face the other way. He growled in frustration and ground his teeth, his jaw tensing so hard that his teeth creaked.

He offered the protein pack. She shook her head and kept it hung forwards. Nostra had ordered him to remain with her until she had eaten. At this rate, he wasn't going to be getting off the ship before they left dock in a day's time.

He dragged a crate across the room and sat down on it. There were supplies that he needed to get before they broke port, but he was willing to wait for her to become hungry. It couldn't take that long. As far as he knew, Lyrans ate quite frequently. With her stomach empty, she would soon be asking for the food. He picked his nails to pass the time and then toyed with the protein pack, shifting the black liquid contents from one end of the rubbery casing to the other. It amused him for a few minutes at best. Next, he tapped out a rhythm on the crate beneath him, trying to recall a tune from his youth.

Slowly, she raised her head again and looked at him. Kosen could feel her eyes on him, studying. He let her drink her fill of him and take him all in. He wasn't much to look at. Probably just another bastard Minervan to her. Regardless of the fact that her queen was Minervan, she would still hate his kind. Lyrans had always hated them. Minervans had always hated Lyrans in return. Nothing would change that.

"Did you kill them?" she whispered.

His gaze shifted to her.

He wasn't going to lie to her. Perhaps if she knew the truth, she would be more cooperative. The quicker that she lost hope of being rescued the better. They needed her to behave herself. Normally, they had weeks to break a captive's spirits. This time they had barely days.

"Not all. Some," he said and her focus fell to the floor.

A string of perfect Minervan swearwords issued from her lips. His left eyebrow rose. She knew his language. He reminded himself that she had been an ambassador. It shouldn't be so surprising that she would be educated and would know some of the primary languages of the galaxy.

Kosen frowned when her hair suddenly flattened.

She hadn't moved but it had. Was there something about her that their contact hadn't mentioned? Kosen went over to her and brushed his fingers through the long silver locks of her hair, studying them and ignoring how she flinched away. There was definitely something different about her. He had never seen a Lyran with silver hair before. The contact had only told them that she was beautiful and Lyran. When they had seen a picture, her silver hair hadn't been evident. They had only seen her beauty and had immediately agreed a cut of her sale price with their contact, knowing that this time they would make a fortune.

A Lyran with silver hair though.

Something about that didn't seem right.

Kosen looked closer. She hadn't altered its colour. She was naturally silver haired. It would definitely add to her price. He combed his fingers through it and when he touched her cheek, her hair moved again, the tips of it shifting as though a breeze had caught them.

When he went to touch her hair, she spat in his face and lunged forwards, attempting to bite him. He leapt backwards to avoid her teeth and glared at her as he wiped the spit from his face. She was a passionate one. Nostra would probably have to gag her at the auction. With a mouth like hers, she was likely to lower her price by swearing or attempting to bite anyone who tried to inspect her.

"Don't touch me," she growled and glared back at him. "Murderer. Minervan."

The way that she had said those two words together made them sound as though they were the same to her.

They were definitely going to need to think things through before they reached the auction. She might be worth a fortune, but she could easily lower her price. Kosen sat back down on the crate and studied her closely. She glared at him, her eyes never leaving his face even as his roamed her body. Nostra was right to take a risk on her, but the fight had damaged their ship and now they all had blood on their hands. Before now, he hadn't needed to kill anyone. It had brought back memories of that night and the nightmare returned each time that he tried to sleep. He relived every moment in vivid detail, a strange combination of that night, killing the other passengers on her vessel and of her.

"If you eat, I can leave." He offered the pack to her again and she looked as though she was considering it.

"If you leave, will another come?"

She was wary too. Intelligent. She was clearly thinking ahead and concerned that another with a more sinister objective than his one of feeding her might come along should he leave.

"No one damages the merchandise," he said, flat and emotionless. "It's something we've all agreed to and the punishment is severe enough to make us all think twice."

"Severe?" She frowned.

He made a chopping motion with his fingers.

Her eyes widened.

The threat of having their sexual organs cut off should they lower a slave's value by any means seemed enough to stop most from trying to get physical with one. Most. Not all.

"Now eat." Kosen held the pack out to her.

She looked at her hands and smiled politely. "I am afraid I cannot."

He ripped the pack open with his teeth, stepped up close to her, and pressed the opening against her lips.

"Eat."

She opened her mouth. A strange jolt rocked Kosen when her tongue peeked out to touch the protein pack. It disappeared back into her mouth, coated in sticky black liquid, and she pulled a face of pure disgust. Seeing that she was going to refuse him again, he waited for her to open her mouth and then pushed the pack into it. One squeeze and she was gulping it down in a desperate attempt to stop herself from drowning. He wasn't normally so rough with the captives but he wanted to get away from her before he experienced anything remotely close to what he had felt on seeing her soft pink tongue sensually stroke the pack.

When she choked, he pulled the pack from her mouth. She glared up at him through her hair, her eyes black and full of hatred. Good. Perhaps she would learn to be more cooperative and then he wouldn't have to be around her as much.

Kosen checked the protein pack to make sure that she had eaten it all and then pushed the crate back against the wall of the small dark room. When he reached the door, he stopped and looked back at her. She was watching him, her eyes wide in the dim light. Her silver hair had fallen down her front, cascading over the tight flight suit and spilling across her cleavage. Her lips parted as though she wanted to say something. Whatever it was, it would probably ruin this momentary illusion of beauty before him.

This fleeting feeling of attraction.

Closing his eyes, he turned and walked out of the door. He pressed the panel to close it and then his fingers danced across the pad, punching in a combination of symbols that would seal the door to any but him. He could easily justify what he was doing. She needed rest and as the ship's tactician and doctor, he had a right to lock her away. If Sasue were to visit her, he didn't know what would happen. Sasue had a thing for innocence. It lured him like a Polaris moth was drawn to fire and ended just as badly, at least for the innocent.

He couldn't risk anyone harming her.

No.

He wouldn't let anyone harm her.

CHAPTER 3

The young man was back. He sat in the corner, just in the shadows. Miali could make out his silhouetted figure and the computer pad he held lit his face. What was he was doing? A mocking voice at the back of her mind said that he was probably writing down her vital statistics and figuring out how much she was worth.

Was she worth the death of all those people on her ship? Surely, it would have benefited these people to sell those men too? It didn't make any sense.

Unless their ship wasn't large enough to keep all of them captive. Her cell was small, the walls on either side only a few feet from the tips of her outstretched hands. It seemed a little longer than it was wide, but not by much.

"Are you feeling better today?" The was looking at her.

Her eyes met his. The light of the computer screen made his skin pale blue. His black eyes held hers. Every moment from their last meeting flashed across her eyes—every brush of his body against hers. Her hair shifted. She cursed it when the man's gaze moved to it and then cursed herself for thinking about the strange way that she had felt when he had been close.

He stood and walked over to her, reaching around behind him. His movements drew her attention to his tight black flight suit and the belt that circled his narrow waist. The suit left nothing to the imagination. He was all lithe muscle, hard and compact. He pulled a device out and ran it over her.

"Where are you from?" He methodically scanned her body and then her hair. It was behaving itself. She thanked Iskara and then cursed again when he brushed his fingers through her hair and it reacted. It hadn't reacted to a male's touch in years. Why did it have to react to him, now, when she needed to remain incognito?

She didn't like him. This man had murdered people that she knew. He might have killed Eryc.

"Lyra." It wasn't a lie but it wasn't the answer that he was looking for either. He ran the device over her again and then frowned at the display.

"Not wholly Lyra." He touched the screen in several different places. A smile tilted his lips and she stared at them. A warm feeling settled in her chest as she studied the subtle curve of his lips and the hint of dusky pink about them that darkened where they met. Her hair shifted again, floating upwards. His look turned to one of fascination and his voice lowered to a whisper that felt too intimate. "Where are you from?"

Miali swallowed her words, unwilling to tell him in case it made him realise who she was. It didn't seem as though they knew who they were dealing with. Whether or not that was a good thing, she didn't know. It was bad for them. They would make less money. However, if they did know, that would also be bad for them. If they were planning to auction her at a market, they would need to announce that she was Lyran royalty in order to get the best price. Any Lyran, Terran, Varkan or Minervan army personnel in the area would come to her aid.

She looked up at the dark ceiling and the pinhole of light. Would her family have realised by now that she was missing? Her ship should have made it to Dliaer. Her family would have been expecting contact from her. Normally, she spoke to them every few days. It must have been almost nine since her last contact.

Would the army come for her?

Would her brothers come?

Her father?

He would kill all of these Minervans in a heartbeat to protect her, just as her two brothers would.

She wanted them all dead. She wanted them to suffer as her companions had.

Staring at the man, Miali hoped that he could see in her eyes every ounce of anger she was feeling. She hoped that he knew it was all for him. When she was free of these shackles, she was going to kill them all. This wasn't the way she had imagined the universe. She had known that the slave trade was alive and booming, but she had never thought that someone would capture her and turn her into a slave. She had never imagined how horrifying it was, and somehow she knew that this was only the beginning. Soon she would face the markets and then what?

"I shall not ask you again." He tried to touch her.

She moved her head to one side, desperate to avoid him.

"Good. Then I will not have to answer you." Miali spat the words at him and leaned back as far as the collar would allow.

His fingertips grazed her cheek and sent heat sweeping through her. She cursed the way her body reacted to his touch, as though it wanted to feel it, longed for it. This man had killed her companions. The hands that he touched her with had blood on them.

He muttered something about her hair and scanned it again with the device.

"Not Lyran," he whispered and tilted his head to one side as though fascinated.

"What does it matter to you?" she hissed and glared at him. "Will I fetch a prettier price if I'm a mixed species? Or are you worried that I'll be worth less?"

He frowned at her, his eyes dark and holding a hint of anger. What right did he have to be angry? He had killed her companions, imprisoned her, and intended to sell her to the one with the best offer. If anyone had a right to be angry, it was her.

His device beeped. He looked down at it and smiled again.

"Dazkaran." He glanced at her out of the corner of his eye. "Interesting."

On the screen of his device was what looked like a DNA strand and information written in symbols that she recognised as Minervan. It was a medical device.

"Are you a doctor?" she said and he raised his head, his eyes meeting hers.

"The closest there is to one on this ship. You're part Dazkaran." He took hold of a strand of her hair and let it slip through his fingers. "That's why your body reacts so strongly to your emotions."

His look turned thoughtful.

"Sub-space affects you because of this."

She was beginning to wonder if he was more interested in her as a science project than a slave that could potentially make him rich.

She nodded. "It makes me sick. Something which you and sub-space have in common."

He smiled at her, as though her words had no effect other than amusing him.

"I thought so," he said and she concentrated on the ship. It was moving but far slower than before. It wasn't in sub-space. She gave him an incredulous look. He had said that he was the closest thing to a doctor on this vessel. Had he ordered the captain, that horrible mountain of man, to travel through normal space?

Why?

"You should eat." He walked across the room and came back with another disgusting protein pack. The taste of the black goo had made her want to retch and the texture of it had made it impossible to swallow. She shook her head and kept her mouth firmly shut. He wasn't going to fool her into eating it this time. He sighed and pulled the crate out again, placing it in front of her.

When he sat down, he toyed with the pack just as he had done before. He seemed more patient than the other man and a lot younger. He almost seemed too young to be a doctor on any vessel, even one this small. Minervans aged at a similar rate to Lyrans. He had to be close to her age.

"If I don't eat, what happens?"

"To you, or to your value?"

"My value," she said, that word hard to swallow. Her father had always said that she was priceless. How much would he pay for her? He would probably give everything he had for her safe return.

"It goes down," he said and for some reason that answer pleased her. What he said next made her reconsider her plan to starve herself. "If you don't eat, the man you met, Nostra, will punish me and will send another man to feed you. Sasue is the one of us most likely to resort to violence to get you to eat. If that doesn't work, he'll probably do things to you that could result in you losing your mind. It would make you quieter at the auction but would probably lower your value a little."

"But you said..."

His look soured. "Sasue has been running slaves long enough to know how to get his pleasure without tainting the goods." He stared at the floor, as though he couldn't bring himself to look at her. "He's sick. I don't want that to happen to..."

Miali frowned. To who? To her? This man was confusing her more and more by the second. Perhaps if she ate then he would leave her alone again. But then, if he did that, the other man he had spoken of might come to see her. What was stopping him from coming to this room?

"If I eat, will you leave?"

He nodded.

"If you leave..." She bit her tongue to stop herself from saying it. Shackled to the wall, she was vulnerable, and that frightened her. If the man called Sasue came, she wouldn't be able to stop him from doing things to her.

"I will lock the door." It was as though he had read her mind. "Only the captain can overrule my decision about keeping you locked away."

A moment of uncomfortable silence stretched between them as she looked into his dark eyes. He lowered his head again and stared at the protein pack.

"You seem different to him." She found herself relaxing a little. She watched his slender pale fingers as he played with the packet of black goo. Either it fascinated him as much as her hair did or he was avoiding looking at her.

She wished that she could sense people's feelings like her cousin Sophia could. That ability would be handy right now.

"This wasn't my profession of choice," he whispered and squeezed the pack. All of the liquid oozed up to one end. "I didn't want this blood on my hands."

Unsure how to respond to such a confession by a man who was her enemy, Miali stared at him and remained silent. He turned the pack over and sighed when it fell from his hands, hitting the metal floor with a thud. He stared at his upturned palms, a frown creasing his brow.

His fingers curled into tight fists and he leaned forwards, resting his elbows on his knees.

When he looked up at her, she could clearly read the pain in his eyes. It made her believe every word that he had just said. He hadn't wanted blood on his hands. He gave a frustrated growl, scooped up the protein pack and threw it against the wall as he stood.

She opened her mouth when he stalked into the darkness, afraid that he might leave and forget to lock the door. His company was preferable to being alone. When she was alone, she kept thinking about that other man that he had mentioned. When she was alone, she felt vulnerable, trapped and unable to defend herself. She would rather he stayed so he could protect her. He seemed a reasonable man and she had a strange impression that he might care about what happened to her.

Relief blossomed inside her, as warm as the Lyran sun, when he reappeared out of the darkness and walked up to her. Stopping close to her, he dragged a hand over his spiked black hair.

He turned away and hung his head.

"Why am I here?" he muttered under his breath.

Miali frowned at his back, wishing that she could see his face.

Those words had held a hint of frustration and self-loathing. She wanted to know if he truly felt those feelings or whether this was some kind of act.

She laughed internally at herself. What benefit would there be to him acting this way? There was no benefit to him being here at all that she could see. If he wanted her to eat, then he could easily force her. He seemed to want to be here with her and that thought made no sense at all.

"Why am I here?" she echoed his question and he looked over his shoulder at her.

"Because you are valuable." He turned to face her, so close that she could feel his breath wash over her skin when he talked. "Beautiful, young, intelligent. You're everything those sick terk'naks at the markets desire."

Terk'naks. She knew that word. Her older brothers had taught her to swear in several languages. There wasn't an equivalent to this word in Lyran but she understood the meaning enough to know that he didn't approve of the type of person who bought a slave.

"If you loathe them so much, why are you here sending people like me to a life of torture at their hands?"

He frowned and his dark eyes flashed with something akin to anger but it seemed stronger. A moment of hesitation and then his fingers brushed her cheek. His palm was warm against her skin, sending tingles dancing through her each time they touched.

"You are much like them." He swallowed and his eyebrows furrowed. "I'm sorry. It's you or them."

Before she could ask what he meant by that, he had walked out of the door. Her cheek felt cold from the absence of his hand against it and her head ached as she tried to make sense of everything he had said.

Some of it was perfectly clear, but that last part she didn't understand at all. Who was she like? Why was it her or them?

How could a man who so clearly hated the people who bought slaves, work in the slave trade?

Miali stared at the door and then looked up when the light began to dim, shrouding her in darkness. Her heart rate increased as the black closed in on her, sending waves of cold chills over her body.

Why was this happening to her?

Was anybody going to come and save her?

CHAPTER 4

Kosen punched the code into the door and listened to the locks click into place. He leaned one arm horizontally against the wall beside the door and pressed his forehead against his forearm. His eyes closed. What was he doing? His duty was to feed her and ensure her health remained good. Feeding a captive and checking their health normally took him no more than a few minutes. He didn't normally care if they wanted to eat or not. He made them eat.

What was so different about her?

Why was he sitting in her cell for hours watching her, studying her? Why did he go to sleep in his quarters each night thinking of her?

She was beautiful.

She reacted to him.

But she was a slave.

She was meat to be sold at market, not a living thing. When he had started in this line of work, he had promised himself that he would only ever see the captives as that. He had spent years ridding himself of any glimmer of feeling concerning the women that passed through his hands. Why now? Why her? Why was she making him feel this way?

"She getting to you, Doc?" Sasue's deep voice sent a shiver of disgust down Kosen's spine.

Kosen pushed away from the wall and stared blankly at Sasue, taking in the twisted grin on his ugly face and his patchy matted long black hair, sections of it bald from the scars on his scalp. Sasue's bulky frame blocked the corridor. He pressed his hand against the door and stroked it as though he was touching the female on the other side.

"She got spirit. I can help you with her, if you get what I mean." Sasue grinned to reveal long sharp teeth. "Let me in, Doc."

Sasue's enormous hand flattened against the door.

"No." Kosen went to walk away but Sasue grabbed his arm. Kosen looked down at Sasue's hand where it was wrapped around his slender forearm, his fingers thick enough that he could probably snap the bone if he wished. Kosen sighed and prised Sasue's hand off him, unafraid of the brutal Minervan. "I mean no, Sasue. No one touches the captive. She's too valuable."

He walked away.

Sasue started banging on the door, shouting lewd things at the female on the other side. Kosen's temperature rose to boiling point as he listened to the vile diatribe. It was a struggle to stop himself from going back and forcing Sasue to leave. When Sasue went into intimate detail about the things he was going to do to the female once he had broken the door down, she shrieked.

Kosen's restraint snapped.

He ran back up the corridor, his hand going to the knife attached to the rear of his belt. Sasue turned to look at him with a wide grin, as though he was coming back to open the door. Kosen sprung at Sasue, grabbing the collar of the large male's flight suit, and brought his feet up. He pressed them into Sasue's chest and slammed him into the metal grate floor of the corridor. His knife was against Sasue's throat before he could react.

Sasue's grin faded.

"Leave," Kosen snarled, breathing deep to catch his breath.

Sasue glared at him. Kosen pressed the knife into his throat until it nicked his pale flesh and a bead of black blood lined the blade.

"Leave," Kosen repeated and stood, stepping off Sasue.

Sasue picked himself up, rubbed his throat and then licked the blood off his palm. For a moment, Kosen thought that he would retaliate but then he turned and walked away. Kosen exhaled sharply.

What was happening to him?

He had never stopped Sasue from uttering such disgusting vulgar words through the door at captives before. He had never cared until now.

Kosen went back to the door and checked that he was alone before punching in the code. The door opened and the light slowly came on, illuminating the female. She was beautiful. More beautiful than his sisters had been. Some sick pervert would pay dearly for one as pretty as she was.

The door closed behind him and he locked it from the inside.

She was breathing fast, her eyes wide with panic. She probably thought that he was Sasue. He stepped out of the shadows, showing her that it was only him. Her eyes widened further and she wriggled as she shook her head. Following her gaze, he realised that she was staring at the knife in his hand. Slowly, so he didn't frighten her, he slid it back into his belt.

"I won't hurt you." He sat down on the crate. Nostra would punish him for attacking Sasue. Their captain didn't tolerate fighting amongst the crew.

"That shouting." Her face was now so pale that her hair looked dark. The silver strands were flat against her head. It had to be a sign of her fear. When she was happy, when her feelings were positive, her hair floated. It was fascinating.

"Sasue," he muttered. "I won't let him near you."

Silence.

"Did you come back to make me eat?"

Kosen frowned at her. He had forgotten that she hadn't eaten yet. Feeding her was the last thing on his mind right now.

Right now, he just wanted to get his head straight. He needed to know what was different about her and why he was acting this way after all these years.

"No." He leaned back, staring up at the ceiling, at the dot of light shining down on her. "I have a question though."

Did he really want to ask her this? If he asked and she answered then there was no going back. He would have overstepped the mark and broken the rules he had laid down for himself when he had joined this venture. He had to know though. He needed a name to go with her beautiful face.

"What do they call you?"

At first, she frowned and looked as though she wouldn't answer. After long seconds of silence, her frown disappeared and she sighed.

"Miali."

It brought a smile to his lips. "Named after a princess, huh?"

And then he looked closer at her, at the way she bit her lip and turned her head away, at how beautiful she was and how silver her hair shone.

And it dawned on him.

"My mother named me Kosen. Do you know what that means in Minervan?"

She shook her head, still looking away from him.

"Seer of truth." He frowned and stood. "And I do. I saw the truth back at the Varkan steel mines that worked men's fingers to the bone and tore families apart. I saw the truth the day my father made a small fortune by selling my two younger sisters into slavery. I saw the truth the day he left... and I can see the truth now."

She looked at him, her eyes enormous and full of fear.

"Not named for a princess." Kosen stepped up to her and caught her cheek in his palm, forcing her eyes to remain locked with his. "You are the princess."

He laughed at how cruel fate was being with him and her. She would make the crew of this ship a fortune, enough for each to live richly for the rest of their days. Only no one here knew that she was a princess. The contact hadn't told them, which meant he couldn't know either. She had been offered to them as nothing more than a beautiful Lyran—a specimen of perfection.

What they had received was a death sentence.

"Shh," she whispered and glanced past him to the door before her eyes met his again. They pleaded him. "Don't tell them. They don't know, do they? No one knows. To the world, I'm just an ambassador. If they were to find out—"

He pressed his finger against her lips, silencing her. It was soft and warm under his touch. "I won't tell them."

The betrayal in those four words didn't bother him in the slightest. Since setting eyes on her, he had been more loyal to her than to Nostra and the crew of this ship. The moment he had found her in the cryo-sleep pod, he had been thinking about her constantly. He even dreamed of her, although she was muddled into his nightmares.

A smile curved her lips and set his heart racing. It had been too long since a female had affected him so much with such a small gesture. The slightest tilt of her lips or hint of tender emotion in her eyes and he was ready to pledge his allegiance to her and her alone.

He couldn't. He stepped back, distancing himself. She was beautiful but she was a means to an end. He needed the money that she would bring him. He had to save his sisters. He couldn't save her.

"If they find out." She frowned, as though she couldn't bring herself to say anything more. She knew as well as he did how Nostra would react if he discovered her lineage. They would drop into sub-space again and would sell her tomorrow on the black market rather than at the auctions in a few days time. Nostra wouldn't risk her family coming after her or any Lyran army officer discovering her whereabouts.

They would be lucky if they could get someone to buy her at all, but if they did, they would never need to sell another slave again.

He would buy back his sisters.

He would be free of this life.

But at what price?

Could he live with himself knowing that he had sold her into slavery? Miali. A name as beautiful as her face.

His heart thumped harder, betraying his desire to touch her as his hand trembled at his side. She stared deep into his eyes, their dark depths still pleading him to help her, speaking to his soul. It waged war against his mind, leaving him torn between helping her and condemning her.

"You mentioned that your sisters are slaves."

He silently cursed her for bringing that up at this moment, when he stood balanced on a knife's edge.

"To free himself of a life of slavery, my father sold them. That night still haunts me. I couldn't do anything to stop him. I tried. I was no match for him in a fight. I fell unconscious to the sounds of my sisters screaming and when I woke, they were gone."

Kosen sat back down, not daring to risk continuing to stand so close to her when he desired to touch her in order to gain some comfort and was barely strong enough to stop himself. Whenever he fought, the memories of that night haunted his sleep again for weeks afterwards. Now, when he closed his eyes, he saw the fight on her ship mingled in with his fight against his father. It tormented him. He hadn't been able to save his sisters. He wouldn't be able to save her.

"Your sisters are slaves, and you work to send others to a similar horrific fate. What kind of a sick man are you?"

Her words rocked him to his soul, making him nauseas as it struck him that she was right. He was sick. In order to get money to save his sisters, he had resorted to condemning others to the life of a slave. He was no better than his father. His father had sold them to save his family. Now he sold strangers for a similar reason.

He was going to sell Miali and he knew that whatever horrors his sisters had lived through, they would be pale compared to those that awaited her. As a princess, as a Lyran, she would be prized by her owner. He would take great satisfaction in using her repeatedly, favouring her above any other slaves that he might own.

She was right.

What kind of sick man was he?

He had thought that he had been doing right by trading people that he didn't know for those that he loved. Those people meant nothing to him. His sisters meant everything. He had even managed to fool himself into believing that at first and that he had no other choice. Now he could see that this wasn't the only way of saving his sisters. Minervans prided themselves on their valour and strength.

What valour was there in this?

What strength?

He was weak and shameful. It was little wonder that he hated himself and the things that he had done. They haunted his sleep, pervading his dreams. Every face of those that he had helped sell into a life of hell had stayed with him, lived in him.

The thought of seeing Miali's face amongst them was too much to bear. He couldn't live with the idea that he had traded her life for his sisters. She wasn't a stranger to him. No stranger could make him feel this way. Staring into her dark eyes, he could see how easily life as a slave would break her. The thought of Sasue touching her had frightened her half to death. How would she survive the touch of a master?

"I only wanted to save my sisters," he whispered and hung his head forwards. His eyes unfocused. "I have no right to call myself Minervan."

Burying his face in his hands, he asked Arkus for forgiveness, strength and guidance. He couldn't allow them to send Miali to her death but he couldn't sacrifice his sisters either. He had to find a way to save them all.

"Do you know where your sisters are?" Miali said, her voice smooth and coaxing.

Kosen looked up at her, into her eyes. How could she bring herself to look at him after what he had done to her? He should have saved her just as he had wanted to back on her ship.

The sight of her sleeping, so unaware of her fate, had made him consider moving her to one of the escape capsules and setting her free. He wished that he could set her free now, but he couldn't think of a way. If she escaped, Nostra would know that it had been his doing. Nostra would kill him. His sisters would never be saved.

"I know." He thought about the last time that he had seen them. "I have been to their master's home on Minerva Seven. I have watched them but couldn't find the strength to save them."

A hint of sympathy touched her expression, shining in her eyes. "A Minervan bought Minervan women for slaves?"

He nodded.

"What is the universe coming to?" She sighed and then tugged at her wrists. "Will you help me?"

"I cannot. And you should not think about trying to break those bonds. Only Nostra can open them."

"I see."

She had changed. Her fear was gone. In front of him now was a woman who was in command, one raised to be strong and get things done. Looking at her now, he could see why she was an ambassador for Lyra. Few males would stand in her way.

"How long until we arrive at the markets?"

"If they don't discover from our contact that you're royalty, then we will reach the open auctions in two days."

"And if they do?"

"Tomorrow, and it will be the black market."

Her face paled. "You mentioned a contact."

Kosen stood when the door behind him opened and Nostra walked in. When their contact stepped out from behind Nostra, Kosen turned to look at Miali. Her dark eyes were wide with shock and her skin was the colour of stars.

Tears shone in her eyes. Her mouth opened and a single word left her lips. "No."

CHAPTER 5

Miali stared at the man who was evidently Nostra's contact. The only other survivor of her ship.

"Eryc?" She shook her head in disbelief. It couldn't be true. They were friends. She had known him since they were both children. She had been falling for him. She had cried when she had thought that he was dead.

He couldn't have sold her into slavery.

Anger overcame her initial disbelief and she lunged forwards, growling with effort as she tried to get her wrists free so she could attack the man who had betrayed her. The metal cuffs bit into her wrists but she didn't feel any pain. She only felt intense anger. Hatred.

"Restrain her, Kosen, before she damages herself," Nostra ordered in Minervan and the younger Minervan moved towards her.

Miali fought him as his hands caught her upper arms and then stilled when his chest pressed against hers.

"You'll only hurt yourself," Kosen whispered in Lyran and she looked at him. He was incredibly close, his mouth barely inches from hers. A smile touched those lips, sending a flush of heat through her. Her hair threatened to rise but he smoothed it down, surprising her, and acted as though he was checking her neck. He gathered her hair and twirled it into a knot at the back of her head, restraining it. "Not a word."

She dipped her chin and then looked past him to Nostra and Eryc.

"She isn't eating," Nostra said in Minervan as he crossed the room and picked up the discarded protein pack.

He threw it at Kosen, hitting him in the face.

"You had one order. Make her eat. If she doesn't eat and her price goes down, it comes out of your share!"

Miali leaned away when Nostra approached her. Instinct made her turn towards Kosen and hide her face. Hope bloomed in her chest. If Nostra tried anything, would Kosen protect her?

She had come to realise something.

She wasn't the only one feeling something. Kosen felt something for her too. If she could only be alone with him again, she was sure that she could convince him to help her. It was terrible to use his attraction against him, but if that was what it took to escape a life of slavery, then that was what she was willing to do.

A quiet voice at the back of her mind said that it wouldn't be so bad. If he touched her, she would enjoy it. There was no denying that. Her whole body responded whenever his skin grazed hers or their eyes met and his were holding a hint of desire.

"I will," Kosen said, so close to her face that his warm breath washed her skin. Her body heated with the feel of it. "I returned here to see to it that she ate."

"Then see she does." Nostra bent to pick up the protein pack.

Miali lurched forwards, managing to hit Nostra in the head with her hipbone. He growled and his fist slammed into her stomach, knocking the breath from her and sending a shockwave of pain ripping through her body.

She collapsed forwards as much as she could, her hands jamming into the tight cuffs and the metal collar scraping her jaw. Kosen's hands shifted to under her arms and he lifted her, supporting her body so the restraints no longer bit into her skin. Why was he doing this for her? Nostra would surely notice that Kosen's actions went beyond stopping her from damaging herself.

Nostra tossed the pack onto the crate that Kosen had moved to be in front of her. He paused and looked over his shoulder.

"And Kosen?"

"Yes, Captain?"

"If you touch Sasue again—"

"He was trying to get to her," Kosen interjected and Nostra's eyes darkened. Miali shrank back, afraid that the two men would fight. Pure anger twisted Kosen's handsome face, turning it dark. "If he tries to break this door down again, I will see to it that he won't be fit to leave sickbay let alone touch a female."

Nostra held his gaze and Miali expected him to put Kosen in his place. Surprise claimed her when Nostra grinned, turning him even uglier as his scars pulled against his skin and his sharp teeth were revealed, and then laughed and clapped a hand down heavily on Kosen's shoulder.

"I am seeing a new side to you, Kosen, one which I think I prefer. Make sure she eats. We must be ready for market tomorrow."

Kosen tensed at the same time as her.

"Tomorrow?" His expression betrayed none of the shock that she knew he must have been feeling.

"Eryc has informed me of something he had neglected to mention before."

"Now, Nostra. I was not sure until I intercepted a contact she sent out a few days past." Eryc smiled at Nostra in a winsome way. Miali struggled again, filled with a dark urge to hit him. Kosen had a knife. If she could get out of the restraints and get hold of it, she could kill Eryc. Her father and brothers had trained her well.

Kosen's body pressed against hers. She stilled when she realised that their hips were touching and his thigh was between hers.

Her cheeks flushed when he moved and his thigh brushed the apex of her legs.

She hoped that the knot in her hair was holding because right now it felt as though she was flying.

"Take care of our little princess," Nostra said as the door behind him opened.

Her heart sunk into her stomach.

Eryc shot her a wide smile and winked before he walked out of the door. She watched Nostra leave, the door close, and then looked at Kosen.

They were going to sell her on the black market. Panic rapidly filled every inch of her and she did the only thing that she could think of to convince Kosen.

She kissed him.

Before he could move away to lock the door, she clumsily pressed her mouth against his and kissed him. Inexperience made fear pound in her heart. She was still opening and closing her mouth, gaping like a Gavaelian carp, after he had backed off a step.

Miali slowly opened one eye and then the other, dying inside when she saw that Kosen looked as though she had slapped him. His eyes were wide but their black irises held anger. Not quite the reaction that she had expected.

Perhaps she should have taken her brothers up on their offer to get her a couple of men from Lyra Six, the pleasure planet, for her coming of age present.

Maybe then she wouldn't have felt like such an idiot right now and Kosen would have been putty in her hands.

"I'm sorry." She looked down at her feet but could only see her cleavage. Her heart was pounding so hard that she could see it beating. A blush of shame coloured her cheeks and she felt as though she was red from head to toe.

What kind of romantic fool was she that she thought she could sway him with a kiss?

Especially a kiss as pathetic as that one.

He was probably going to tell her how much more she would be worth now that she had proven herself an innocent and was a princess to boot.

She tensed when his hand came into view. He cupped her cheek, his thumb brushing across it. Her cheek was damp. She had been crying. The galaxy had started to look a little blurred. She blinked and sent the tears running down to her jaw. His thumb continued to lightly caress her face as he raised her head. She looked out of the corner of her eye at the wall, too embarrassed to look at him.

"I'll help you," Kosen said and her gaze shifted to meet his. "Although I'm not offering because you kissed me. Just so we're straight."

"Oh." She bit her lip. Why did he have to add that? For a moment, she had thought that perhaps her kiss hadn't been that bad.

"Although..." He dipped his head and her eyes went wide when his lips grazed hers in a light kiss. Her heart thumped so hard that she was sure he would be able to feel it against his chest.

His hand held her cheek as his other claimed her waist. Her eyes slipped shut when he tilted his head and deepened the kiss, his tongue brushing her lips. She tentatively brought hers to meet it and a jolt ran through her when they touched. A moment later, she melted into him, no longer aware of their surroundings.

She was only aware of this kiss, of the feel of his body against hers and the incredible warmth that was filling every inch of her as their tongues stroked one another, their mouths fused as though they were one.

His lips left hers and she stayed there, her head tilted, eyebrows raised, eyes closed and mouth open.

Her breath left her in a sigh.

That was definitely a better kiss than the one she had given him.

"Kosen." She opened her eyes. He smiled at her, revealing sharp pointed teeth that left her wondering how she hadn't cut herself when they had been kissing. "I'm royalty. Whatever money you need to gain your sisters' freedom, I can give you it, in exchange for my own."

He nodded, as though he had already figured out what she had been about to offer him earlier.

"I can't get you out of here though."

She looked at the restraints and remembered what he had said.

Only Nostra could open the cuffs.

"When?" Miali hoped that he wasn't about to change his mind. He looked worried, as afraid as she felt, but there was a flicker of something in his eyes. Her brothers had that look sometimes, and her father. Normally it was before they did something ridiculously dangerous and heroic.

"Tomorrow."

"At the market?"

He nodded.

He was going to wait until the market to set her free. But surely Nostra, Eryc and the others would be there to guard her. She wouldn't be alone with Kosen. How was he planning to help her escape?

"I think now might be better—"

"Not a word." He silenced her with a brief kiss that sent her head spinning, and then pressed his forehead against hers and whispered against her lips, "Tomorrow. Only one person is authorised to enter the medical examination room with you."

"A doctor?" Her breath bounced back from his lips. Her heart skipped a beat and she was thankful that most of her genes had come from her father. Right now, she couldn't imagine how dizzying the beat of two racing hearts would be.

"That would be me," he whispered and reached around behind her. His wrist brushed her neck as he loosed her hair and then ran his fingers through it. "We'll need to move fast. I'll plan it all tonight. You must eat to keep your strength up and to silence Nostra. I'll lock the door with a new combination and keep an eye on everyone to make sure no one comes down here."

The thought of him leaving her alone again made her want to protest but she knew better than to say anything. He was doing all that he could to keep her safe. He had even fought one of his comrades. If he didn't go back to the others, they would become suspicious of him. She could only wait and pray.

"We will drop to sub-space again."

Those words made her feel sick. He opened a pouch on his belt and took out a yellow pill.

"Swallow this. It will ease your nausea and help you sleep through the journey."

She opened her mouth, willing to take the pill if it meant that she wouldn't be ill when they went into sub-space. Kosen had no reason to lie to her about it or try to poison her. She could see in his expression that he only wanted to help her.

When she had swallowed the pill, he turned away from her.

He picked up the protein pack and bit into the corner. The thought of having to swallow the disgusting liquid made her stomach turn but Kosen was right. She had to keep her strength up.

She closed her eyes when he brought the pack to her lips and grimaced as she swallowed down its contents. The gooey liquid made her want to retch but she held it down. When the pack left her lips, she opened her eyes to find Kosen smiling at her.

He really was handsome. His smile made her heart flutter and sent warm tendrils outwards from it. They stretched through her until her whole body was hot, yearning for his touch and the feel of his lips against hers. Her hair floated upwards and his smile widened when he stroked his fingers through it.

"This is beautiful, honest," he said in a low voice as his gaze followed his fingers through her hair. Her breath left her when his eyes met hers and he whispered, "You're beautiful."

"Kosen, I..." There was so much that she wanted to say but, when she thought about it, it all sounded so ridiculous. She wanted to tell him that she thought he was handsome, that a male had never affected her this much before, and that she wanted him to kiss her again.

"Try to get some sleep," he said and she nodded.

She watched him leave, her heart heavy with regret. Now that he was gone, the words came easily, but it was too late to say them. She held them inside, thinking about them and wondering if they were real and not just a reaction to her situation.

The door locks clicked into place.

The lights dimmed.

With the darkness came the creeping doubts but this time the chill didn't reach her heart. She stared into the darkness, at the point where Kosen had stood not moments before. Tomorrow they would take her to market.

She closed her eyes when she felt the ship shift into sub-space and was relieved when she didn't feel sick. Her head felt strangely heavy and she yawned as a sudden wave of tiredness broke over her. Unable to fight it, she began to drift off, wondering what Kosen was planning and whether it would work.

In the comforting blackness of sleep, her mind surrendered its fight against her feelings and her heart took over. She realised that she hadn't kissed Kosen purely to make him help her. She had kissed him because she was attracted to him, because she saw a good man in him, one that she was falling for. She wanted to help him too. She prayed to Iskara that Kosen's plan worked and they would both be free.

One fear settled in her heart and wouldn't leave.

Would he stay with her?

Or would he leave her once he had his sisters?

CHAPTER 6

The cuffs bit into Miali's wrists, holding them behind her back. Her eyes darted around the dark market. Stalls draped with tattered rich brown and dirty grey coverings packed the large space. The air was thick with the smell of spices, food, and medicines. An acrid stench wafted from one of the small tents that they passed and she glanced in, only to choke and turn away when she saw a big fat blue Sekarian male dissecting a young child and dropping pieces into a flaming pot.

Kosen's grip on her right arm tightened, as though he was silently asking if she was all right. She tensed her arm to try to tell him that she was. She had never imagined how horrifying the universe could be. This was worse than any report she had ever read or anything she had ever seen. And she was about to become a part of this darker side of the galaxy, if Kosen couldn't save her. She kept her head turned towards him for a moment longer and then glanced to her left.

Her other arm was held by a man that had to be Sasue. He was at least a head taller than Kosen, and as broad as Nostra. Patchy black matted hair half hid his ugly scarred face. The long strands were each the width of her finger and shifted as he moved, swaying side to side with his heavy gait.

He grinned down at her, his smile showing every disgusting perverted thought that crossed his mind. His muscles rippled under the tight black flight suit when he gripped her wrist a little tighter. She turned away from him, frightened of the things she had seen in his eyes and the way his thumb stroked her arm as light as a lover's caress. Soon she would be free of him. Soon.

Nostra walked ahead of them, his bulky frame and confident swagger clearing a path through the crowd. The people that passed them were mostly males, all as dirty and dangerous looking as Nostra and Sasue. Kosen didn't seem to fit in this underworld. He was pale, face clean, his black hair spiked up. His flight suit fit snugly over his slim, toned body. A glimmer of intelligence shone in his eyes. He was the opposite of practically every male here.

His dark eyes held a spark of concern when they met hers. She went to smile but stopped herself, aware that someone was watching them.

Behind them walked the female crewmember, a beautiful young Minervan with pale gold streaks in her black hair. The gun that she carried looked far too big for her to handle but something told Miali that she wouldn't have a problem. There had been a dark look in the female's eyes when she had seen her. It spoke of hatred and violence. She was as heartless as the male crew was.

Eryc walked beside the female. He wore a black flight suit similar to the Minervans, as though he was a part of the crew now. His cocksure smile hadn't faded. Miali was itching to wipe the intensely smug look off his face and make him pay for what he had done to her. If she couldn't get revenge on him for his betrayal then she hoped that Nostra killed him when she had escaped. He had to pay.

Gunfire erupted, bright yellow laser streaks flashing through the air, illuminating the market.

Miali dropped to her knees, her heart beating painfully fast and her body trembling. Kosen dropped with her and, when she looked at him, she saw that he was holding a weapon. He had a gun. Perhaps they could escape after all.

His body covered hers, his arm tight around her, shielding her. A loud blast shocked her hearing into deafness on her left side. She wished that she could cover her ears when Sasue fired the massive rifle again. He slowly walked forwards until he was beside Nostra.

Nostra held his hand up and Sasue stopping firing. Miali looked through the gaps in their legs at the market ahead of them. There was a fight. One male with a laser gun was facing off against three others. Several dead bodies lay at his feet in a creeping pool of blood. Another blast lit the air and the remaining male fell to join his comrades. A matter of seconds later, the market was back to normal, as though nothing had happened.

Kosen pulled her up onto her feet and held her wrist again. Sasue dropped back and grabbed her other arm. Again, she was walking forward towards her fate. She glanced down at the dead men as they passed, forcing herself to look at them and see what was happening in the universe. Their skin was charred black from the blasts of the laser guns. Blood coated the floor and their bodies. Lifeless eyes stared into infinity.

"Come," Kosen said close to her ear and Miali realised that she had slowed down while she had been looking at the dead males.

Miali turned away from them and held her head high, blinking away her tears as they entered an open square. There were several cages in the centre. Their walls of solid steel bars held the females they contained captive while giving the males milling around a perfect view of them. The females were nude, all huddled together in the middle of the cages, desperately trying to cover themselves. Males patrolled the area, occasionally prodding the females with long poles to make them come out of their huddle. In the midst of the cages was a raised platform. She knew what happened there. If Kosen couldn't save her, she would soon be in one of these cages, naked for every man to letch over, and then she would find her fate on that stage. Her heart continued to beat hard and fast, adrenaline and fear making her shake. Kosen had to save her. She didn't want to become some sick male's property.

The group stopped and Kosen's hand again tightened around her wrist. She frowned at Nostra as he spoke to someone a short distance away. The slim blue hairless Sekarian male glanced across at her, running his gaze down her body, and nodded as though in approval. A twisted smile touched his dark blue lips and a satisfied look entered his all-black eyes. Nostra grinned along with him. Eryc moved past her and Nostra glared at him as he spoke to the Sekarian. She wished that she could hear what they were saying. They were discussing her fate. She wanted to know what it would be if she couldn't escape.

Her heart picked up speed when all three men turned to look at her. It jumped against her chest when Sasue pushed her forwards and she walked towards the Sekarian. His grin widened when she reached him and he moved around her. She turned her head, trying to see what he was looking at and flinched when he placed his hands on her, patting and touching every part of her.

"Well?" Nostra said in Sekarian, an impatient look on his face.

"I will bill her." The Sekarian moved around in front of her. He preened a hand over his bald head, stroking it as he smiled. She hated the thought that he had placed those hands on her. He stepped forwards and she tried to back away.

Her stomach turned when he cupped her breasts and looked as though he was considering opening her flight suit to inspect them.

"She will need medical." He released her breasts. "We make sure you not lie."

Sekarians were an ugly race with an ugly language that she was starting to wish she didn't understand. Some of the languages that the crowds around her were speaking were unrecognisable without her translator. She stopped herself from looking at Kosen. How many languages could he speak? Could he speak enough to get them off this backwater spaceport and across the galaxy to somewhere safe?

"Who is medical officer?" The Sekarian looked at all of the men.

"I am." Kosen stepped forwards, bringing her with him.

"Come, come." The Sekarian waved his hand and started walking towards the edge of the square.

"Make sure she checks out for the highest price," Nostra ordered.

"I want to go with them." Eryc went to move towards her but Nostra's large hand pressed against his chest, blocking his path.

"Sekarians do not like company. Only the medical officer can go with her. Kosen knows what he's doing." Nostra's look darkened and he pushed Eryc backwards when he tried to get past him. "Kosen will take care of her."

"Yes, Captain." Kosen pulled her roughly towards him. There was a hint of apology in his eyes when the wrist cuffs bit into her arms and she flinched. "Come with me."

Her heartbeat didn't slow as they approached the hut at the edge of the square. If anything, it beat faster. She looked out of the corner of her eye back at Nostra and Eryc, afraid that Eryc might try to follow them. If he did, would they still be able to escape? She wished that she knew what Kosen's plan was. At the moment, she couldn't see how they were going to get away.

When she entered the hut, the Sekarian was waiting by a dirty inspection table. The black covering had seen better days and was stained and ripped in places. The thought that he had inspected all those poor females in here made her sick. She glanced back at the door, filled with an intense sense of sadness that she wouldn't be able to save them. If Kosen managed to free her and she tried to save them, she would only be caught again. Nostra would kill Kosen. As much as she wanted to help the females, she couldn't risk anything happening to Kosen. She needed him.

Kosen lifted her onto the table and she lay down, grimacing when her hands dug into her back and trying to remain calm. His eyes met hers, the hint of concern still shining in them. He touched her arm, the brush of his fingers so light that it told her everything that he couldn't. He was sorry, he cared about her, and he wouldn't let anything happen to her.

The apology wasn't because she had hurt herself. It was because he felt responsible for her being in this position to start with, facing a future as a slave. He was sorry because of the things that had happened to her since they had met. He was sorry about how they had met. He was sorry for everything. She didn't hold his past against him. If she hadn't been royalty and someone had taken her brothers as slaves then she would have done whatever it took to free them too. He loved his sisters. He had subjected himself to a life of torment and misery, living with the terrible things that he had done in order to free them.

"We begin." The Sekarian picked up a gleaming silver tool that she didn't like the look of. If he was going to try to put that where she thought he was, then he was going to have to get past her feet first. She would kick him before he even got close.

It dawned on her that the Sekarian was going to be involved in the examination too. Kosen had said this was their best chance of escape. How were they going to get past the Sekarian?

Her gaze shifted to the laser gun hanging by Kosen's hip. Was he going to shoot the man? Laser pistols were notoriously loud. Nostra and the others would hear. Kosen nodded to the Sekarian and then calmly opened a square pouch on his belt. He withdrew a small injection gun and the Sekarian frowned at it.

"What is this?"

"She's part Dazkaran," Kosen said, no trace of nerves in his voice or his expression. "It will make her more sensitive to positive emotions. We want her to look her best so she fetches a good price. The better the price, the bigger your cut."

The Sekarian looked thoughtful for a moment and then nodded, grinning.

He walked towards her feet. Kosen grabbed him from behind and pressed the injection gun against his neck. There was a hiss of air as it fired. The Sekarian convulsed, his eyes rolled back into his head, and then he slumped forwards. Kosen lowered him to the floor. Miali wriggled into a sitting position and looked down at the male. He was dead.

"What was in that?" she whispered and looked at Kosen.

He tossed the injection gun onto the table of tools and then grabbed another device.

"Mercury. Sekarian's are allergic to it," Kosen said in perfect Lyran.

Miali stared at the dead Sekarian. His blue skin had become mottled with grey and had swollen. She would say that his reaction had been a little more than simply allergic. The mercury had killed him.

"We have to move fast." Kosen rounded the table.

She was about to ask him what he had planned when incredible heat blasted against her back and the smell of tin filled the air.

"Keep still," he whispered and she tried to look over her shoulder. He had some sort of cutting device. The heat of it made her skin feel as though it was going to blister right off her bones.

"Are you sure you know what you're doing?" The blazing blue flame of the device touched the metal cuffs and heated them, singeing her.

"I used to work in a mine. I know what I'm doing." The flame touched the cuffs again. "Just keep still. I'm sorry if this hurts."

She wanted to tell him not to apologise. He was doing this to save her after all. She would rather suffer a few burns on her wrists than a life of torture at the hands of some sick pervert.

The metal cuffs dropped off her wrists but before she could move, Kosen's hands were on her arms, stopping her. She hissed in a breath when something cold and wet touched the sore skin of her wrists. A soothing, pleasant cool feeling followed a moment of pain. She kept still as Kosen wrapped her forearms and hands in something. When he released her, she brought her hands around and rolled her shoulders as she looked at the thin black bandages covering her.

"Thank you." She felt a strange lightness inside her, warmth that made her wonder if her Aunt Kayla had felt something similar when she had escaped from her life as a slave.

"Don't thank me." He rushed across the room. She sat on the edge of the inspection table, wondering what she could do to help. He grabbed two thick black blankets from a stack on top of a cupboard and walked back to her. He unfurled one of the blankets and draped it over her head like a hooded cape. She zipped her flight suit up and pulled the black blanket closed around her. Kosen tucked her hair behind her ears, pushing it out of sight. "I haven't saved you yet."

He put the second blanket over himself, covering his head and body with it.

"Come." He reached out for her hand.

She slipped hers into it, her heart pounding as she hopped down off the inspection table and followed him. How were they going to get out of here without anyone seeing them?

Kosen picked up the device that he had used to remove her wrist cuffs and used it to cut through the bolts holding the metal panels together at the back of the hut. He caught the one he had been working on as it fell towards him and carefully placed it to one side.

Beyond it was darkness. Miali followed Kosen into it, tightly holding his hand as though her life depended on it. She couldn't see where they were going but evidently Kosen could because a few minutes later they had come out of the maze of narrow black alleys into the market. She pulled the black blanket forward to cover her face and stayed close to Kosen. His fingers interlocked with hers and her hair threatened to rise when warmth crept up her arm from their joined hands.

His thumb brushed hers.

"Keep going," he said.

She gasped quietly when she looked up and saw several Minervan military officers heading towards them. Instinct told her that they wouldn't help her if she asked. They looked as dark and menacing as Nostra and his crew. Kosen ducked down a side alley, dragging her with him. This place was a maze. She felt as though any moment now they would end up back in the square where they had started.

"I have a confession."

She didn't like the sound of that. It made her heart beat painfully hard.

"What?" She hoped that it wasn't that he was going to sell her anyway and take all the money for himself.

"I can't pilot."

She had thought that they would take Nostra's ship but perhaps they were going to charter one instead. That didn't seem so bad.

"So?" She struggled to keep up with him as he strode through the market. She flinched every time that someone shoved her out of the way. Why was she was being pushed around and he wasn't? When she came up beside him again, she realised that the answer to her question was simple. He looked as though he was ready to kill anyone who came near him.

His eyes narrowed, his black irises menacing in the low light. His jaw was set and his black eyebrows met in a frown so intense that it was clear that murder was on his mind. He bore his teeth at a passing group of males who were staring in her direction and they avoided her completely.

"We have to take public transport," he said over the noise of the market.

That didn't sound so bad.

"I can only afford cargo class. We might be lucky."

Her face fell. That did sound bad. Cargo class on a freighter out of this place was likely to be an experience that she would never forget. It would round off this nightmare perfectly. But she knew that Kosen would protect her. He had been protecting her since they had first met and something told her that nothing would change that now. Or would it? Was he really going to stay with her after she had bought his sisters back for him? Or was he using her as a means to an end? By rescuing her, not only was he clearing his conscience a little, but he was gaining his sisters freedom. Would he leave her?

She pushed her dark thoughts away and clung to Kosen's hand. Her heart said to never let it go. She didn't want to let him go. He looked at her out of the corner of her eye and she managed a smile. Now wasn't the time for such melancholy thoughts. They hadn't escaped yet.

"I can live with that. Where is the port?" She felt stupid for asking when he pointed straight ahead of them and she saw the end of the market.

The dome that covered the port was clear and she could see the stars. They were all wrong. She couldn't tell where they were. Kosen would know.

"What ship are we getting?"

"One to Minervan space." The tone of his voice said that it wasn't up for discussion. The Minerva system was a long way from Lyra. She would rather they were going in the direction of her home system, but she wasn't exactly in a position to argue with him. After all, he had risked his life to save her and it was his money paying the fare.

Miali huddled close to him as they entered the busy port. He went straight for the desk with Minerva as a destination above it, not slowing down even when he reached it. He pushed past everyone in the line and flashed a charming smile at the Minervan female behind the desk. A flare of jealously exploded inside Miali and she stepped up to stand beside him so the female would see that he wasn't alone. Miali didn't pay attention to the conversation that happened between them. For some reason, she couldn't stop looking at Kosen.

He seemed so different from the man that she had first met but at the same time, he seemed unchanged. He was so confident and in control. He had risked his life to set her free, had killed a man in order to do so, and there wasn't a hint of fear about him.

He was so strong. Her heart skipped a beat and pounded hard when Kosen's gaze slid to meet hers. He handed the female some money and took the boarding papers from her. Without so much as a backward glance at the Minervan female, he walked away, taking Miali with him, his eyes not leaving hers.

"Dock eight. The ship there is heading for Minerva Prime but will stop at Minerva Eleven."

She realised what was happening. He was trying to get to his sisters on Minerva Seven.

"We have to run," he said and she barely had time to grab her blanket to stop it slipping off her before they were running towards the gates that led to the docks.

His pace was too fast but she did her best to keep up. By the time they reached the enormous black vessel, she was out of breath. She followed him onto it, ducking through the closing doors. He slowed to a walk as they passed through the corridors and into the cargo class area. They walked through it, past rooms packed with groups of unsavoury characters, and then finally entered one of the rooms. Females, children and the occasional family occupied this one. It was dirty, packed and smelt worse than the market had but it seemed a lot safer than the previous ones.

"This will have to do. It's better than I thought we'd get," Kosen said.

The ship jerked into the air. The thrusters kicked in and the entire ship shook with the force of them as they headed upwards. Kosen held on to her, his arm wrapping around her shoulders and steadying her. Being in his arms felt wonderful, soothing and warming. He walked her across the room and she saw the small compartment they were heading towards. The ship rocked and Kosen's grip on her tightened. He smiled at her when she looked up at him and then stepped into the dimly lit compartment.

Miali collapsed onto a hard seat by what would be a window when the ship had made it out of the atmosphere and they lowered the blast shields.

She looked at Kosen when he drew a small curtain across their compartment and sat down opposite her. Cargo class didn't seem so bad and they were heading away from that hellish market port and her captors.

Her heart rate began to slow at last, she huddled up in the corner, staring at her knees, and wondering what would happen now. They had escaped the market but that didn't mean that no one had spotted them or the ship that had brought them here wasn't following them. Those men wouldn't let her go so easily. She needed to get word to her father. She was sure that he would be looking for her, just as the men would be.

"Are you alright?" Kosen said and, when she looked up at him, he moved and came to sit beside her.

She closed her eyes and leaned her head against his neck as he placed his arm around her. Now that she was away from the market and those men, it was all sinking in horribly fast. She couldn't speak, didn't know what to say. She curled up against Kosen, hoping that it was over now.

Hoping they were free.

CHAPTER 7

Kosen stretched in the cramped compartment and frowned as he slowly came around from a nightmare-filled sleep. His eyes shot wide, sleep driven from him when he saw that Miali wasn't with him. He rushed to his feet and opened the curtain. Relief flooded him when he saw Miali crouching with some children in a small open area near their compartment, playing a game that he recognised from his youth. She didn't seem to care that the children she was playing with were Minervan.

She didn't seem to care that he was Minervan.

She didn't seem to care about the things that he had done.

He watched her playing, studying the graceful way that she moved. She seemed so out of place in this area of the ship, but at home at the same time. The dull grey expansive room was packed with Minervans and the occasional other species. It was clearly a ship that had passed through the port rather than originated at it. He couldn't imagine that most of the passengers here had come from the port or anywhere near it.

Miali looked up and smiled at him before going back to playing with the children, moving the black pebbles around on the green and blue diamonds on the board. The children laughed at her mistake. Kosen leaned against the doorway of their compartment, smiling as he watched her intentionally lose.

"Miali." Kosen tilted his chin up when he said her name.

She said something to the children and then placed a little girl in her position at the board and came over to him. It was strange to see her like this after he had only known her as a captive. He hadn't imagined that she would be so friendly to Minervans, or that she was so amiable. It made her even more beautiful.

It was little wonder that she was an ambassador. She certainly had a knack for convincing people to do the right thing and get along, and she had an amazing capacity for forgiveness. He didn't deserve such forgiveness. He didn't deserve her.

"I was bored," she said with a small shy smile, as though confessing she had done something bad. "You were sleeping and I saw no harm in it."

"They seem to like you." He nodded towards the children. She looked over at them with a fond smile, watching them play. His gaze remained on her, drinking in her beauty and the warmth that she radiated.

"They were teaching me the finer points of cheating at Loretsil. I don't think I have the art but perhaps I'll beat my brothers next time we play."

"Brothers?" He frowned at the mention of her family. He knew little about them, only her name and that she was royalty.

Royalty.

She didn't act at all as he had imagined one would. She had no pretentions and airs. She seemed happy to be amongst common people in the lowest possible class on a public transport freighter.

"Yes. They're both in the Lyran Imperial Army. It wasn't to my taste so I became an ambassador instead. I didn't want danger and adventure like they craved. I seemed to have found myself mixed up in it after all though." She sat back down and looked out of the round window at the stars.

They were already halfway to Minerva Eleven. They would need to contact her family soon to have them rendezvous with them there so he could get the money to save his sisters. He hated to ask her for it, hadn't saved her because of her promise to give him money, but he needed it. He had to save his sisters. He would offer the man who owned them a price that he couldn't resist. He would set them free.

The ship shook and the lights went out.

"That wasn't a ship docking, was it?" Miali's voice came out of the darkness and she grabbed his arm, clinging to him.

"No, it felt like weapons fire."

Blue flashing lights punctuated the darkness and an alarm sounded, deafening him. He looked down at Miali, seeing her in the split seconds when the light was on. She looked frightened. The tight grip she had on his arm confirmed her fear.

The room filled with the clamour of voices and he grabbed Miali's hand and dragged her in the direction of them. It was hard to cross the room in the darkness. The bursts of blue light did nothing to help him find his way. Eventually he made it to the corridor. Everyone that had been in the room with him and Miali now lined the windows of the corridor. He looked out of the window nearest him and his heart leapt into his throat.

"Nostra." He stared at the small old fighter as it fired upon the freighter again and dodged the return fire.

"Cruskin," Miali muttered beside him and he seconded that thought.

This wasn't good.

Crew rushed past him, armed to the teeth. Children screamed and clung to their mothers. Kosen looked down to see one of the children that Miali had been playing with wrapped around her legs. She bent over, the flashing blue lights making her look as though she was moving strangely, and picked the boy up. Kosen watched as she soothed him, speaking Minervan with an expert tongue. He couldn't understand how she could be so calm. They were under attack and it was only a matter of minutes before Nostra convinced the officers of the freighter to allow them to board. Nostra had connections with the Minervan military. He had probably already obtained permission from them to board any Minervan vessel that he wanted.

The small fighter fired again and Kosen grabbed Miali when she stumbled backwards. The child in her arms shrieked and buried his face in her neck. Miali whispered something to the boy and then smiled at him.

"Are you alright?" Kosen smoothed her flat hair. Her expression and actions might not give away her fear, but her hair did.

She nodded and moved closer to him as the fighter ship closed in.

Kosen drew his gun, ready to fight to protect Miali. He wouldn't let anything happen to her.

There was a bright burst of pale purple light similar to what happened when a ship went into sub-space. When his vision came back, an enormous sleek top-class fighter ship was overshadowing Nostra's small fighter. Kosen didn't recognise it as Minervan. If anything, it looked Lyran.

His gaze shot to Miali.

The blue emergency light flashed again, highlighting her face.

She was grinning.

"Perfect timing as always."

Kosen looked back at the huge fighter vessel.

"You know them?" He had the impression that while he had been sleeping, she had been doing things other than playing with children.

"I might have sent a message or two asking for assistance. You needed money after all and I needed passage back to my home. So, I had my home come here."

Home. He looked at the ship. For some reason, the thought of her returning home made him feel queasy. He had expected to have at least a few more days with her.

Two smaller fighter ships detached from the large vessel that Miali had called home and escorted Nostra's fighter, guiding it to dock with the vessel. He didn't want to imagine what fate awaited Nostra and his crew onboard the Lyran fighter. He was only glad that he had chosen a better path for himself to follow, one that would take him away from a world involving slaves.

The passenger freighter slowed to a stop and the Lyran fighter drew alongside it, eclipsing the view out of the window. It was massive. He had never seen an attack vessel on such a grand scale.

Miali was still grinning when he looked at her. She ruffled the hair of the boy that she was holding and set him down on his feet. Dim lights flickered back into life above them.

"Run along now," she said and the boy disappeared into the crowd. It wasn't dispersing. Everyone was watching the Lyran vessel now.

"Home?" Kosen pointed at the ship.

"The Nebula-Lyra II. My father's ship." She looked around them and then back at him. "Do you know where the docking bay is?"

He dumbly pointed along the corridor. She grabbed his hand and dragged him in that direction.

"My father will want to meet the man who rescued me."

Those words sent a chill to his heart and made him nauseas.

Her father?

Was she forgetting that he was also one of the men who had kidnapped her and had intended to sell her into slavery? He was sure that Nostra would be quick to mention that when he met her father.

Kosen tried to get his hand free of hers but by the time he had managed it, they were in the docking bay. He swallowed his thundering heart and pulled himself together. Nostra probably didn't need to tell her father that he had been involved. It wouldn't take much for her father to piece it together. After all, the only place they could have met was on the ship that had taken her. Perhaps they could pretend that he had been a captive too. That would work until her father had spoken to Nostra. Perhaps it was better not to lie. Her father might kill him for such a thing. Perhaps it was better just to avoid the situation entirely.

"This isn't a good idea," he said.

Miali looked at him and he gave her a nervous smile. Understanding visibly dawned in her eyes.

"Perhaps you're right—" Before she could finish that sentence, one of the airlock doors further along opened.

They both looked there. Her hand fell from his as two tall, broad built males walked through it. Their black hair and black eyes made them look Minervan but Kosen knew that they were Lyran. They wore the black and blue flight suit of the Lyran military.

"Miali!" One of the males grinned and came rushing towards her. The other rolled his eyes and walked.

"Aksel," Miali gasped moments before she was wrapped in the male's arms.

Kosen's blood boiled at seeing the man handle her so familiarly. If he wasn't one of her brothers then Kosen was going to kill him.

It was a strange feeling, as violent as others he'd had since meeting her. For some reason, he needed to protect her, to keep her shut away from other males. It all clicked into place in his mind. He really did like her, more than he had thought. He liked her enough that he had attacked Sasue, a man easily able to kill him, and he was considering attacking both of these Lyran males at the same time.

"Miali," the other man said in an official and somewhat displeased tone.

Her smile fell off her face and the man she had called Aksel put her down.

Miali lowered her head as though in shame. "Taelis."

"Come Taelis, show her a little affection. Be pleased that your rigorous and ridiculous training served her well and she was able to escape." Aksel slapped the other man on the back.

Kosen decided that they had to be her brothers. No man unrelated to the one she had called Taelis would dare slap him.

Taelis gave Aksel a thunderous look and then patted Miali's cheek. "Mother was having Snrikiks over this. She's had father flying around half the galaxy looking for you. I am glad that you were able to escape."

Miali cringed. "I didn't do it alone, or use anything that you taught me."

Kosen stepped back and the two males' eyes immediately locked onto him. Perhaps moving had been a bad idea.

"Miali." Taelis stepped up to her. "You appear to have a young man with you."

She grinned but it looked more like a grimace to Kosen. Kosen smiled and then backed off another step when the two men frowned.

"A young Minervan man." Aksel's eyes narrowed with his sly smile. "Don't tell me that he helped you... that you and he—"

"Brother!" Miali shouted and slapped him hard enough that the sound echoed through the docking bay. When her hand fell away from Aksel's face, there was a bright red mark on it.

"What in Iskara's name is happening here?" Another male voice joined them and this one held such a note of authority that Kosen's palms sweated.

When the two males in front of him parted to reveal the owner of the voice and they saluted, Kosen made a small whimpering noise in his throat.

He knew the about sons of Lyra.

Only one had a cybernetic arm that could easily crush a man's throat.

Why did that one have to be her father?

"Father!" Miali bounded over to him and threw herself into his arms. "You were cutting it close."

The captain's handsome face shifted into a wide smile as he held her and then set her back down on her feet.

A cold trickle of sweat eased down Kosen's spine and he considered running for it but didn't think he would get very far with Miali's two brothers only feet from him.

"We have the men who kidnapped you." Her father looked her over. "Did they hurt you?"

"No... Erm, father?"

Kosen prayed that she wasn't about to point the man in his direction. If only he could fade into the darkness and disappear. He had never had to face something as terrible as this. The moment this man realised who he was and what he had done to his daughter, he was going to crush him like a bug.

"Miali has a lover." Aksel grinned.

The heat drained from Kosen in a flash, leaving him cold and numb.

"What?" he said at exactly the same time as Miali, Taelis and her father.

Aksel's face blanched too as all eyes came to rest on him and his father stormed towards him.

"A lover?" her father said, face dark.

"Wait wait wait," Miali chanted, her cheeks bright red.

Kosen held his hands up when her father diverted his course away from Aksel and straight towards him. Miali ran in front of him, trying to block his way.

"Wait, father, it's not like that." Miali pushed against her father's chest and then looked over her shoulder at himself.

Kosen waved his hands in an attempt to tell her not to speak. If her father asked her anything that would make her think about the things that had happened between her and himself, then no matter what answer she gave him, her body would tell the truth.

"He's not your lover?" Her father stopped and scrutinised him.

Kosen frowned at him and had a change of heart as he wondered why it would be such a bad thing if he were Miali's lover. He was a good man who could easily make something of himself. He had been honest with Miali throughout their time together and she liked him. So there was that little fact that he had played a part in her kidnapping, but he had surely cancelled that out by helping her?

He was about to ask whether her father objected on the grounds that he was Minervan when the man stepped up to him, sandwiching Miali between them. When she backed into him, Kosen placed his hands on her upper arms, holding her.

She was shaking.

"Father, I can explain. Kosen helped me escape those men. He was the doctor on their ship." She held her hand up when her father's look turned deadly and he opened his mouth to speak. "Was, father. Was. He helped me escape. Now I want to help him. I need money."

"Money? Lovers? What in Iskara's name is going on?"

Kosen had the distinct impression that this wasn't going well, especially when her two brothers came up behind their father, flanking him and drawing their weapons.

"He kidnapped you. He's one of them. Step aside, Miali," Taelis said, taking aim with his laser gun.

Kosen swallowed hard and stared down the barrel of it.

Miali stretched her arms out across him and shook her head.

"No," she said, her voice shaking as much as he could feel her body was. "Kosen saved me. I promised that I'd help his sisters. He needs money to buy them back from their master. Please, father?"

"Answer something for me, Miali." Her father's look softened and a tiny flicker of hope ignited in Kosen's heart. Perhaps he wasn't going to die today after all.

"Anything."

"Is he your lover?"

Kosen couldn't help looking at her as she struggled for an answer. Her silver hair shifted and she frantically pushed it back down. It seemed to be the only answer that her family needed.

"A Minervan?" Taelis grumbled and shook his head.

Miali whined and then said, "What does it matter if I've fallen for a Minervan? Aunt Terea is Minervan and she's the queen of Lyra!"

All three men pulled faces that clearly expressed that they couldn't deny that. Kosen joined them. It was true. Her family had no right to complain about her choosing a Minervan when they were under the rule of a Minervan female.

His eyebrows rose.

Wait.

Choosing a Minervan?

He stared at Miali but her hair obscured her face. He turned her to face him when frustration got the better of him. He had to see her when he asked this.

She dropped her head forwards, looking at her feet. He cupped her cheek and raised her head up until her eyes met his.

"Fallen for a Minervan?"

Her cheeks flushed.

"No one you know." She tried to turn away. He held her. She was a spirited little thing now that she was free and safe, even more than he had expected, but she couldn't deny it.

"Miali," he whispered and she looked up at him through her lashes.

Her eyes widened as he dipped his head. He captured her lips, not caring about the fact that her father was likely to tear them apart and throw him in the cells, if he didn't kill him outright.

She made a small noise of protest and then melted into him, her hands pressing against his chest as he wrapped his arms around her. A quiet moan escaped her lips as he tilted his head and deepened the kiss, and she began to respond. Her tongue parted his lips and brushed his, her hands sliding up until she had looped her arms around his neck. He frowned and exhaled through his nose when her body pressed against his.

Suddenly, there was only her in the universe, just as it had been the first time they had kissed back in her cell.

The galaxy came crashing back when someone tapped him on the shoulder and he lifted his head to see three unimpressed males.

"Come with me," her father said, his expression grim. "I have a few questions I would like to ask you."

Kosen released Miali and followed her father towards the airlock that led to the Lyran fighter. He glanced back at her to see her standing between her two brothers, worry written across her face.

He really hoped that a few questions meant just that and wasn't code for 'I'm going to crush you once we're in private and my daughter can't see us'.

Holding his hand up, he smiled at Miali, trying to tell her that he would be all right. Her hair floated upwards as she returned the smile and she blushed again as she struggled to smooth it down. Beautiful.

She was an angel of Arkus.

And she had fallen for him.

Just as he had fallen for her.

CHAPTER 8

Miali stared out of the window of the small fighter ship. How long would it take to travel back out of Minervan space to where the Nebula-Lyra II waited for them? Taelis and Aksel had accompanied her and Kosen to Minerva Seven. Her two brothers seemed reluctant to leave her alone with Kosen but now they were busy tending to their new guests. Kosen had gained his sisters' freedom at the scant cost of one hundred gold Lynans, which was only a fraction of what her father had given her.

Kosen had taken his two sisters straight to sickbay. She had only seen them in passing on the planet and when they had been brought onto the ship, but they were both beautiful, with skin as pale and hair as dark as Kosen's. They seemed frail though and wary. Kosen had told her that it would take a long time before his sisters overcame their time as slaves, if they ever did.

Would they like to live in the Lyra system? It wasn't just for their sake that she wanted that. She wanted Kosen to stay with her. Now that she had seen him around his sisters, she knew that he would go wherever they went. She had never seen such an attentive and loving brother. If they wanted to remain in the Minerva system, even after what had happened to them, then he would remain there also.

Her family would never allow her to stay in Minervan space. It was too dangerous for her. From now on, she would be lucky if they would let her leave the Lyra system without an armed escort of thirty men and her two brothers, or worse, her father.

She sighed and watched the planets drift into the distance.

There was a bleep from the control panel beside her quarter's door.

"Come in." Her eyes never left the stars outside.

The door swished open and closed again. Soft footsteps sounded on the plush deep blue material lining the floor. Her eyes half closed when she felt him step up behind her and the ends of her hair shifted.

"Your brothers asked me to tell you that we'll be dropping into sub-space soon."

Miali said nothing. She didn't want to go to sleep, not right now when everything was so uncertain.

Kosen stepped out from behind her and she felt his gaze on her, intent and studying her profile as she stared at the stars and tried to get a grip on her feelings.

"I brought you something."

She looked at him when he held his hand out. On his palm was a deep orange pill.

"What is it?" Her gaze lifted to meet his. He still wore a black flight suit, moulded to his body like a second skin. She ached to peel it off him.

Cursing her thoughts in case they affected her hair, she focused on the pill that he was offering.

"It will stop the sickness that you experience in sub-space."

"Will it send me to sleep?"

He shook his head. "Not this one. I've spent some time altering the active ingredients so there isn't a need for a tranquiliser. It should simply relieve your sickness."

He smiled at her and her heart beat a little quicker.

As she took the pill, something dawned on her.

She really was like her father.

She had fallen for a doctor.

She hesitated a moment and then swallowed the pill.

"There." Kosen brushed her cheek with the backs of his fingers. "Now you should be fine. I'll be right here in case you experience any nausea."

He wasn't leaving her?

"What about your sisters?" She frowned. "I thought they needed you?"

"The nurses from your father's ship are seeing to them. They're resting at the moment." He paused and then smiled again. "I wanted to see you."

He did? Her hair threatened to float upwards and she pinned it down.

"Don't." He removed her hands from her hair. "I love how it reacts."

"Because it gives away everything that I'm feeling," she muttered and pushed it down, clawing at it. "It's hardly fair."

"Miali, what's wrong?" He brushed her hands away before clearing the hair from her face. "You seem tense."

She sighed, resigning herself to whatever happened. If she didn't get her fears out in the open, she might burst. "You're going to leave."

He frowned. "Leave?"

Pushing his hands away, she walked across the room and stared out of the window.

"You have your sisters now. We're even. There's no reason for you to stay and they'll probably want to live in the Minerva system, and you'll live with them."

He laughed but it was a mirthless sound, one born of annoyance. "What are you talking about?"

When he went to touch her again, she avoided his hands and walked to the other side of her bed, placing it between them. She couldn't bear the thought of him touching her if he was only going to leave. She didn't want that. She would rather they had a clean break and she parted ways with him now.

"Miali," he whispered and she ached when she looked at him and saw the hurt in his eyes. They searched hers. "Do you want me to leave?"

"No!" She started towards him and then stopped herself. "Of course not. Why would I want you to leave?"

"Why would you think I want to leave?" he countered and she threw her hands up in frustration.

"You have your sisters to look after."

"That doesn't mean I have to leave." His look turned incredulous and he walked towards her.

"They'll want to live in Minerva."

"No, they won't. They don't. I've had an offer that I'd be a fool to turn down."

Her whole body stopped on hearing those words, even her heart. She stared at him, too afraid to hear what the offer might be. He was going to leave her.

"Miali." Kosen rounded the bed, blocking her way.

Miali knelt on the bed, intent on avoiding him, and went to scramble across it but he grabbed her waist and dragged her back to him. She struggled and he flipped her over, took hold of her wrists and pinned her to the bed beneath him.

"Will you listen to me?"

She shook her head. Why couldn't he just leave? She didn't want to hear the explanations. It hurt too much.

Her hair flattened against the bed. Kosen's shoulders slumped.

"That's something that I never wanted to see." He released one of her wrists and stroked her hair, fanning it out across the soft rich blue bedcover. A sad smile touched his lips. "Don't you want me to stay? Are you trying to push me away?"

"No!" she protested again, ill at the thought that she might be. "I'm just so confused. Surely you'll want to stay with your sisters. My father won't let me out of his sight now, or out of the Lyra system if he's not with me. So you see, it's impossible for us to be together. We're doomed."

"Doomed?" He looked amused. "You truly are as young as you look."

"What's that supposed to mean?" She frowned up at him, offended by his remark. She was young but the way that he had said it made it sound as though he thought that she was a fool.

"You were heading for a life in slavery and not once did you think you were doomed. Now you think you are? You won't even listen to what I have to say. If you did, you'd know that we're anything but doomed."

Her eyebrows rose. "We're not doomed?"

Kosen shook his head and smiled at her. His dark eyes shone with it. She stared up at him, lost in his eyes and musing how handsome he was. Her gaze fell to his lips. She licked hers.

"Far from it. I've spoken with your father and, well, mostly your mother," he said.

His words snapped her out of her daydream about kissing him.

Dear Iskara, her heart was pounding so hard that she felt sick. He had spoken with her parents? With her mother?

"When we were back on your father's ship and I was making the pill for you, your mother was impressed with my skills. I'm an idiot for not recognising her as your mother. I was so focused on my work that I didn't notice the resemblance until she approached me and mentioned that she and your father had agreed that it would be best if I was offered a position that kept us close to one another."

Miali's mouth fell open. "Offered a position?"

"Emmanuelle has offered to train me as her assistant with a view to me becoming a doctor of the fleet. I would remain onboard the Nebula-Lyra II. My sisters would have quarters there and be offered rehabilitation and therapy." His smile suddenly held a hint of nerves. "There was one condition."

Miali cursed her father. He was never one to make things easy when it came to her. She had tried having boyfriends and he had soon chased them off. Of course he would still have conditions now. He had probably banned them from touching each other, or worse, said that they couldn't see each other without supervision.

He had only ever been difficult when what she wanted happened to have anything to do with a member of the opposite sex.

"Miali..." Kosen stopped and sighed heavily. The anxiety in his look only made her heart beat faster. It would be typical of her family to dangle exactly what she wanted in a man in front of her and not let her have him. She willed Kosen to say the words and put her out of her misery. He was staying, but it was over. He hesitated a moment more and then said, "I want to stay..."

"But?"

Kosen wet his lips. It was sheer torture to be this close to him, waiting for an invisible axe to fall and cut all the happiness from her life, when all she wanted was for him to kiss her.

"I made a deal with your parents that I'll stay if..."

"Cruskin nyaaeso, Kosen, spit it out. Just say that you can't see me anymore."

He frowned. "Can't see you? It's quite the opposite. I'm going to marry you."

Her eyes popped wide. Something wasn't quite right about that sentence. It didn't fit. It was all wrong.

"My father said that you can only stay if you marry me? Did I hear that right?"

"No."

She had thought it was too much to ask.

"I read up on your Dazkaran side. It's tradition to ask the mother for her daughter's hand. She agreed and spoke with your father, and they agreed we should marry. If you'll have me, of course... and there's no rush. I can wait until you're ready. I mean, we hardly know each other."

Miali stared blankly at him, struggling to absorb the information and the fact that Kosen might have actually convinced her father to let him marry her.

Her eyebrows rose again.

Her hair rose with it when it hit her.

"You want to marry me?"

"Of course," Kosen said, matter of fact, as though she couldn't have ever doubted that he wanted it. He smiled and leaned down, peppering her face with kisses and running his hand over her forehead and into her hair. "Who wouldn't want to marry you? Although I don't think that I deserve you."

"I think your drug has affected my mind."

He laughed and before she could say another word, his lips claimed hers, stealing her breath away. She closed her eyes and relaxed into the bed, becoming gradually aware of the fact that Kosen was on top of her. Her body warmed with the feel of his pressing against it. Her hair drifted upwards, tickling her cheeks.

Tilting her head to one side, she moaned quietly in her throat when Kosen's tongue tangled with hers and then hesitated a moment before venturing into his mouth. His lips parted, teeth opening with them. She slowly explored his mouth, kissing him deeper than she had ever done.

He pressed harder against her and her tongue caught on his teeth. She loosed a muffled 'ouch'.

"I'm sorry," Kosen said with an air of nerves and an awkward smile.

She stared at his teeth. They hadn't cut her but they were as sharp as they looked.

"I just don't understand why you do it." She frowned at his sharpened teeth.

Kosen frowned too and ran his tongue along them. The sight of it caressing his teeth made her tremble and ache inside.

"All Minervan males do it."

"I know," she whispered and reached her free hand up, touching his teeth with her fingertips. "Why?"

He playfully snapped at her fingers and she jerked her hand back.

"It makes us... sexy." He grinned.

She laughed and his face fell. When she realised that he was being serious, she cleared her throat. Perhaps it did make them more attractive to Minervan females but it didn't do anything for her.

"Sexy how?"

His frown wasn't shifting. He sat up and she pined for the feel of his body against hers. She hadn't meant to spoil the moment with her stupid questions. She sat up and moved closer to him where he was sitting at the edge of the bed.

He looked thoughtful. His black eyes slid to meet hers.

One eyebrow rose.

His eyes narrowed on her, holding such heat that her body flushed and her hair threatened to rise again. She twirled it and tied it in knot to stop it.

He leaned towards her and she was captivated as his lips parted, entranced by their beautiful shape and the sight of his sharp teeth. Thoughts of what he could do to her with that mouth made her heart flutter and her blood boil with desire.

She licked her lips.

He edged closer, his movements achingly slow. She looked down at his hands, yearning to feel them on her, and then back into his eyes.

He whispered one word that made any shred of reserve she had disappear.

"Dominance."

Her lips parted and her breath left her in a sigh. He kept moving towards her and she leaned back to counter his move.

"Strength."

Her back hit the bed and she stared up at him as he moved between her legs.

"Danger."

Her heart beat hard against her chest.

Her breathing quickened.

Perhaps he was right, when he put it like that. She lay beneath him, willing him, waiting for him to make a move. Her throat felt too tight to breathe. Her heart felt as though it would explode if he didn't touch her soon.

With a smile that revealed his teeth, his gaze left hers and drifted down to her flight suit. She watched his face at first and then her eyes fell to half-mast when he slowly undid her flight suit. As his hand passed her breasts, she arched upwards, forcing the two sides of her suit apart. He moaned his approval and continued onwards, until he had reached her navel.

She gasped in air when he dipped his hand inside and trailed wet kisses downwards, from her chest over the curve of her breasts, to her stomach. She longed for him to keep going, wanted to tell him not to stop, but was powerless as she lay on the bed, submitting to him.

His hand skimmed up her thigh, over her waist, and finally settled against her breast. She pushed it up into his palm, desperate to convince him to undress her.

"Miali?" he whispered against her stomach and pressed kisses up to her breasts.

She made a garbled noise in her throat in response when his hands grazed her shoulders and he parted her flight suit and began to pull it down her arms. He groaned when her breasts sprang free and she gasped when his lips caught one of her nipples and he suckled it.

Her hips bucked up, rubbing against his body in a dire attempt to ease the hunger growing inside her. She needed him. Her whole body felt as though it was on fire and only he could bring cool relief.

Her hands went to his hair, tangling in the black spikes. She shrieked a moan when his teeth teased her nipple, sending a shockwave of pleasure rippling through her.

"Shh," he whispered and kissed her breast, flicking her nipple with his tongue. "I'm petrified of your brothers as it is."

She would have laughed had he not wrapped his mouth around her nipple and started sucking it again, tugging it into his mouth and making it painfully hard.

"Miali?" He moved across to her other breasts and laved her nipple.

"Yes?" She squeezed the word out and bit her lip to stop herself from moaning again when he tortured her nipple with his teeth.

Lost in a haze of passion and pleasure, she couldn't deny anything he had said about Minervan males. In fact, she was thankful for it. Sharp teeth definitely made everything sensual and erotic, the added hint of danger making her nerve endings flicker with delight.

"You are going to marry me?"

She laughed this time.

"Ask me again when I'm back in my head, not floating somewhere outside my body."

He dipped his head and licked a path from her breast to her mouth. She sighed into his when he kissed her, fervent and passionate, stealing her breath and stirring her desire beyond her control. She went to grab him but he moved out of her reach, sliding down her body and taking her flight suit with him. Her eyes opened and she stared up at the ceiling when he stripped it off her, leaving her bare on the bed.

She went to say something but all words failed her when he eased her legs apart and darted his tongue between her folds. Her head fell to one side, her eyes wide and mouth open as he licked the length of her, from her slick opening to her pert nub. She moaned and stared at the stars, feeling as though she was going to explode as he devoured her, his tongue teasing and lapping at her arousal.

"Kosen," she said, panting it as the feeling of tightness inside her increased, her body so hot that she was aching for release. She writhed against him and he moaned. The sound of it only drove her on and she threaded her fingers into his hair, clutching him to her, begging him not to stop until she had come undone.

The moment his finger eased into her hot depths, she cried out her release at the universe. Her whole body trembled around him, quivering as she came. He thrust his finger into her a few times, drawing out her orgasm, and then pulled it free. She collapsed into the bed and then tensed again when he lowered his mouth and lapped at her opening, drinking her juices. It tickled.

She pushed against his head, forcing him away from her. Wriggling on the bed, she looked up at him as he stood by her feet, watching her. He grinned and the sight of his sharp teeth sent a flush of heat through her.

"In Arkus's name I've never tasted anything as sweet as you."

If he thought that her taste was amazing, he was in for a surprise. Her mother had warned her that her hair might not be the only thing that she had inherited from her.

Sitting up, she gave Kosen a seductive smile and ran her hands up him. She pulled the fastening on his black flight suit and eased it downwards. Her lips parted and her whole body trembled at the sight of hard packed muscles rippling under his pale skin. She had never seen a body like his, compact but powerful, speaking to her hunger on a sexual level.

She eased the flight suit off him, pulling it down over his hips and pushing it down to his boots. He kicked them off and then stepped out of the suit.

"Now I really don't want you brothers to see us."

She smiled and looked at his long hard length where it jutted out from a nest of black curls. Leaning forwards, she took hold of it, wrapping her hand around its girth, and licked the sensitive head. He was shaking. He would be doing a lot more than shaking soon. She closed her mouth around his cock and sucked on it, moving her mouth up and down. The feel of it gliding into her aroused her. When he thrust forwards, she moaned, wanting more.

He groaned. "I really really don't want your brothers seeing this."

He worried too much.

But, just to be sure they were left alone, she reached over to the control panel on the cabinet beside her bed and locked the door.

He would need it.

If what her mother said was true, he wasn't going to go quietly when she got him inside her.

Kosen groaned again and muttered something about stopping. She did and looked up at him. He had his teeth buried deep into his lower lip, his eyebrows knit into a frown. Taking hold of his hips, she guided him to the bed. Dominance. It sounded like fun.

It only took a slight push to make him fall on his back on the bed. Before he could say anything, she was on top of him. Whatever protest he had been about to form left his lips as a groan when she lowered herself and rubbed her slick groin against his hard shaft.

"Wait..." He held his hands up, breathing hard. "We need—"

She pressed her mouth to his to silence him, kissing him and grinding against him. She needed him inside her now. She was tired of being so innocent and she wanted to be his.

"My mother is a nurse," she said, knowing what he was trying to say. "I've been given sterilisation injections since I turned mating age."

His eyebrows rose and he didn't seem to have a response so she ground one out of him, rubbing herself on his length and tearing a moan from his throat. He felt so good beneath her, the sensitive head of his cock teasing her nub.

"Are you sure you're ready for this?"

She smiled down at him and kneeled, taking hold of his length. "Are you sure you're ready?"

He frowned and before he could answer, she sank back onto his cock, letting it slowly fill her. There was a momentary sting of pain and then nothing but pure bliss. Kosen groaned and his hands went to her hips. His fingers pressed in as he gripped her hard and started moving her on his cock.

The feel of it thrusting into her, filling her and striking deep inside her, tore moan after moan from her throat. Her body trembled as she tensed and Kosen closed his eyes, a heavy frown marrying his eyebrows. She pressed her hands against his stomach and moved up and down on his cock, riding him, her thrusts opposite to his. Her entire body burned, tightening with each plunge of his length into her and each slam of her clit against his pelvis.

The tightness in her abdomen grew, feeling as though it was pulling everything into it like a vortex, sucking all the heat from her body until she was crying out for release. Kosen's hands went to her breasts and his thumbs flicked her pert nipples. She stared down at him and when her eyes met his, the whole galaxy exploded.

A blast of fire and lightning slammed through her, a bright white shockwave that left her quivering and trembling against Kosen's chest, weak and hot. The sound of his heart pounding filled her ears, mixing with the tremendous beat of her own. She shook in his arms and then realised that he was shaking too. His rough breathing matched hers. His length throbbed inside her, spilling his seed.

The only sound Kosen made was a strangled sob.

"Wow." Miali sighed against his chest, waiting for the scattered pieces of herself to fall back into place and the room to stop spinning.

"Wha—"

She managed to gain control of her limbs enough to shift herself around so she could see Kosen. He was staring at the ceiling, pale and trembling, his eyes unfocused.

"What was that?" she breathed, still panting to catch her breath. "Besides incredible?"

He nodded and his gaze fell to her. His pupils widened and narrowed, as though trying to focus.

"There's a lot of you," he said with a drunken grin and went to touch her cheek but missed by several inches. "Which one is you?"

Her mother was right. Dazkaran females did climax in ways that sent males of other species out of their minds.

She took hold of his hand and pressed it to his cheek. "Right here."

He smiled and blinked a few times before passing out. She pulled herself up and smiled down at him. Perhaps she should have warned him but then she hadn't known if she had picked up that trait of her mother's species.

Slumping next to him, she closed her eyes, snuggled against his arm and waited for him to come around.

Hours passed but eventually Kosen muttered something about the cold and stirred. She reached over and pulled the blanket across them.

When he opened his eyes, he still looked a little dazed.

Miali pressed a kiss to his lips and then smiled at him as she brushed the flattened messy strands of his hair from his forehead.

"Better?" she whispered, concerned about the amount of time it was taking him to recover. She hadn't expected it to take this long.

He nodded. "Incredible. A Dazkaran trait?"

She nodded in response and continued to smile. "You asked me a question."

He frowned. "I did? I did... lost it there for a moment."

She laughed as he blinked as though he was still trying to clear his head.

"Will you? It doesn't have to be now. Just someday?" His arms went around her, holding her against him.

The feel of his bare body against hers made her ache to have him inside her again but he didn't look up to an encore. At least not yet. There was still a long way to go before they reached the Nebula-Lyra II.

"Will I what?"

"Marry me... a worthless Minervan who doesn't deserve you?"

She frowned this time and stroked his forehead, her eyes never leaving his. He smiled up at her and it held such hope that her heart warmed.

"A heroic Minervan, the only man in the universe for me, the man who saved me." Dipping her head, she held her mouth bare centimetres from his and whispered, "Yes."

He craned his neck towards her and she kissed him, her lips caressing his in the lightest of touches. It warmed her through until she was constantly smiling against his mouth. He pulled her on top of him, turning that warmth to fire as his body pressed into hers.

She would have to work on his sense of self-worth but she had the perfect solution to that problem. She rubbed her hips against his and he groaned and kissed her harder. His teeth caught her tongue and this time the pain didn't shock her. It only added to the thrill of loving him.

For now, she would stay on the Nebula-Lyra II and perform her ambassador duties from there, greeting dignitaries and visiting planets where the vessel stopped.

She would stay where she was safe and with the man that she loved. She'd had enough of the adventure of deep space. It was time for a different, more pleasant adventure.

She squealed as Kosen rolled her over, nestling himself between her thighs, and kissed her harder.

The adventure of falling in love.

The End

HEART OF A PRINCE

Princess Renie, one of the beautiful and strong daughters of Lyra, loves nothing more than exploring space with her twin brother, Rezic, but when they venture too close to the Black Zone, the barrier between Vegan space and the rest of the galaxy, things turn from exploration to a fight for their lives. With Rezic injured in a meteorite shower, Renie has no choice but to accept help from a vessel within the Black Zone, even when it turns out to be Vegan! Separated from her brother and taken hostage, to be held for ransom, Renie isn't sure what she's going to do…

Until she meets a man in the cells, the most unusual and gorgeous male she has ever seen, a man who seems to be willing to do anything to protect her and makes her pulse race.

Tres isn't enjoying his stay in the cells. The commander has broken his thermal suit, leaving him cold and weak, and his last chance of leaving the Black Zone has been thwarted. But the galaxy comes to him instead, and she's more beautiful, warm and full of feeling than he'd ever dreamed. When he discovers her and her brother's plight, he vows to help her if she'll help him, and when she touches him, showing him warmth, he wonders how touch can be so forbidden and realises that he'll do anything for her.

When Renie is injured during their escape and Tres is forced to stay behind so Rezic can leave with her, will she ever see him again? Will she be able to convince her father, General Lyra II, to go back into the Black Zone and rescue the man she's fallen in love with? And will she still love Tres when she realises just who he is?

CHAPTER 1

Renie frowned when the first beep sounded. She cast her dark eyes across the small bridge of the ship to the display panel on the wall to her right. It beeped again. Switching the ship over to automatic controls, she unclipped herself, her eyes still fixed on the display panel, which now showed diagnostics on something that looked like a planet. She crossed the bridge and studied the panel. Her fingers danced across the panel above, accessing the star charts for this region of space so she could pinpoint their location. She wasn't familiar with this area. It was the furthest from home they had ever been.

She brought the black band around her wrist to her mouth and pressed the button.

"Rezic," she said and waited for her twin brother to answer. No reply. He was probably sleeping. It was her turn to pilot after all. When they had hit space that they didn't recognise on the charts, they had agreed to take shifts at the controls and alert the other if something happened. She felt as though she hadn't seen him in weeks. They had meals together but that was about it unless there was something that needed to be fixed or charted. "Rezic?"

Her communications band crackled when she released the button.

"What?" he said in perfect Terran when she had been about to shout at him in Lyran.

She smiled.

Their parents told them off whenever they spoke Terran around Lyrans or other species. They both preferred it to Lyran. Even their younger sister Natalia had picked up the habit. Too many people could speak Lyran and even though their father was a Lyran, they still insisted on speaking Terran most of the time.

Especially when they were on an expedition.

"I need you on the bridge." Renie lowered her hand and looked at the display again and then the star charts.

There weren't any systems in this area. In fact, there didn't seem to be much at all. The star charts ended around seventy thousand leagues from them. They were heading into space unknown to Lyra.

Rezic appeared beside her, running a sleepy hand through his cropped dark hair and tousling it further than his bed already had. His black eyes matched hers perfectly. They both looked like their father, Balt. Rezic closed one last fastening of his loose white shirt, leaving the top three undone, and rubbed his eyes before tucking the tail of his shirt into his brown trousers.

"I was dreaming a good dream, this better be important." His gravelly voice spoke of how deep asleep he had been and he struggled to stifle a yawn.

Renie hated waking her brother but it was important.

"There's a planet," she said and pointed at the display.

"Very observant." Rezic yawned again. "Is that it? Christ, Renie, how many planets have we seen? I thought you'd get over it by now."

Renie smiled at his grumpy air, knowing that deep inside he was as excited as she was. Or at least he would be when he let her finish speaking and woke up a little.

She pointed to the star charts and the area where the system should be.

"There's nothing on the map."

Rezic eyes narrowed on the chart and then the planet. "It's a class six. Is it beyond the map? Maybe no one discovered it yet."

His voice held a hint of excitement now.

"Maybe, but it should be right here and it isn't. That's inside documented space," she said and before she could utter another word, Rezic was punching in the coordinates and sending the ship towards it.

He moved to the controls and Renie held onto the back of the co-pilot's seat when he shifted the small vessel into its top speed, which wasn't much. The ship creaked as though it was going to break apart. It was a heap of junk, but it was theirs and they had bought it with the money from their first big find in the temples of Marsha Three. Since then, they had explored the galaxy, documenting dead cultures and searching for artefacts.

Their two younger brothers and sister said that they were treasure hunters.

Their parents called them archaeologists.

Or at least they called her an archaeologist.

Renie looked at Rezic, his excited smile bringing out her own as he raced to find the planet on the display.

They called him Lyra V.

Renie moved around the co-pilot's chair and slid into it, buckling herself in.

Rezic had no desire to achieve the throne though. He was happiest out here with her, finding ancient things, charting new territory and cruising space. She was happy here too.

She wondered if things would always be this way. It was many years since their birth, but they were mature now. Their mother said that in Terran years they looked a little over thirty, the age their father had looked when they had married. She knew that it was their mother's way of telling them that soon they would begin to think about finding someone to love. What would happen then? What if Rezic found a woman, other than in his 'good dreams', and decided to settle down? The thought chilled her. She wanted to adventure in space with him forever.

Perhaps whomever they married would be adventurers too and they could buy a bigger ship and continue their journey together.

Renie pulled her knees up to her chest and toyed with the white sleeves of her shirt.

"Is something the matter?" Rezic said with a sideward glance at her. She smiled at him to alleviate his worry, knowing that he could sense her feelings sometimes. The connection they shared as twins ran deep.

She went to speak but the proximity alarm sounded. Both of them looked at the front screen of the ship.

Renie couldn't believe her eyes as Rezic slowed the ship to a halt. In front of them was the planet the ship had detected but it looked nothing like she had expected it to. It was a brown, pitted rock. More shocking than that though was the fact that it was only half a rock that looked as though it had been split perfectly down the middle.

She unclipped herself at the same time as Rezic and went to the display.

"It doesn't make sense," she said and looked from the display to the dead planet. "The readings say it has the mass of a class six planet and it's being displayed as a whole, not a half."

She went back to the window and stared at the planet.

"It's definitely dead," Rezic said and set the computer to scan it. The readings came back quickly. "No atmosphere. Signs that it was once inhabited. Whatever happened here, it wasn't nice. There's a lot of carbon on the planet."

"Carbon?"

"A lot of living things died very quickly."

She gasped and stared at the planet.

"Did the sun collapse?"

He shook his head. "No. The planet would have been wiped out and there's no sign of debris or the sun itself."

Her brother was far superior at science, but none of what he said made sense at all, not on any level. Normally she could follow him quite well. She looked up at his profile. He seemed to be having difficulty understanding it too.

"Why is there only half a planet when the ship says there's a whole one? Where did the sun go?" he said with a frown.

Renie looked around them and then stopped when she noticed something. Her eyes moved from the star spotted space to the left of the planet where it curved, to the blank space on the side that had disappeared.

"Rezic," she said and touched his arm. "Where are the stars?"

She looked at the empty black space in front of her. There was nothing. It looked as though darkness had swallowed half the planet and the rest of the galaxy.

"The Black Zone," Rezic said and she sharply turned to face him.

A chill danced down her spine and along her arms.

"The Black Zone?" she repeated, hoping that he had been joking. "The Vegan barrier?"

He nodded and went to the star charts, pulling up the overview that connected all the separate maps together. He zoomed into the area they were in and pointed out the perfect line across the charts.

Renie's heart thundered against her chest and her palms sweated. It couldn't be. She stepped up to the charts and stared wide-eyed at them.

"The Vegans erected the barrier after the war with Lyra to protect their territory." Her brother swept his hand across the empty area of the chart. "Originally the Vega system wasn't on the other side. It stood sentinel on this side of the barrier. Just after we were born, they expanded the barrier to cover Vega, withdrawing completely. The star charts were erased. All we know now is that Vega is on the other side somewhere. No ship can cross the barrier without permission."

Renie touched the screen. There were systems on the other side, planets that a Lyran had never seen, or at least hadn't seen in hundreds of years. Her stomach fluttered with excitement and nerves.

"If we could cross the barrier—"

The proximity alarm drowned out the rest of her words and she whipped around to face the front screen of the ship. Masses of meteorites were heading for them, coming out of the Black Zone. She ran for the controls for the shield.

"Renie, get down!" Rezic shouted and then slammed into her as the ship rocked. He tackled her to the ground, his body covering hers, shielding her from the meteorites as they battered the ship.

There was a terrifying sound of buckling metal and then darkness. Rezic's body pressed down hard on hers, suffocating her along with the blackness. She struggled to breathe. Panic consumed her and made her breath come in short sharp bursts. The alarm continued to sound and her head felt light as the air rushed out of the bridge. She clawed her way out from beneath her brother and fumbled with the control panel. Finding the shield, she pushed the dial for it to maximum and then hit the emergency beacon.

The air was too thin. Her eyes unfocused as she struggled to maintain consciousness. The lights came back on at a low level, the computer reporting that there were multiple hull breaches and life support was down. The shield would seal the remaining air in, but it wouldn't last for long. Normally the shield gave out after an hour or so.

She fumbled across the panel until she found the emergency life support. She hit the button and a whoosh of air filled the bridge. She gasped, taking the fresh air down deep into her lungs.

She turned where she knelt on the floor and her eyes widened when she saw Rezic. Blood coated the side of his head, dark against his pale skin. Her heart slammed against her chest.

"Rezic?" Renie said, reaching out and touching his face. He was breathing, but barely. She frowned at the wound on the side of his head. He needed a medic. For the first time in her life, she wished she had paid attention to Aunt Emmanuelle when she had given her and her brother basic medical training. Rezic had been distracting her the whole time, mimicking Emmanuelle behind her back. She cursed him and stroked his face. "Wake up, brother, please."

The computer informed her that Rezic's life signs were fading and he needed medical assistance.

"I know!" she screamed and dashed her tears away as she got to her feet. She ran to the door of the bridge but it wouldn't open. Smashing the panel over the manual control, she grabbed the lever and yanked it. Still nothing. "Open the door!"

Her fists hurt as she banged them against the solid metal, willing the door to open so she could get to the medical supplies in the engine bay.

The computer warned her again that Rezic was dying. Renie curled into a ball and sobbed into her knees. She couldn't get the door open. Why couldn't the computer open the door? Why did she have to sit here and watch her brother die?

No, she wouldn't admit defeat so easily. Rezic would have broken the door down had their positions been reversed. She ran to the control panel of the ship and hit the intercom button.

It was pointless, but right now, the only chance she had was a ship hearing her call and coming to their aid. Someone had to be within ten thousand leagues of them. There had to be a patrol along the Black Zone.

"This is the Explorer One, I have a medical emergency and require assistance." Nothing.

"This is the Explorer One, I have a medical emergency. One of our crew is dying and I'm trapped on the bridge. I require assistance. Please respond!" Nothing.

She stared into space and then collapsed to her knees on the floor. Taking hold of Rezic's hand, she squeezed it and smiled.

"Hold on. Someone will come for us. I won't let you die. I won't." She sniffed back her tears and smiled at him. She would never let anything happen to her brother. She wouldn't let him die. "This is the Explorer—"

"Explorer One," a male voice said, deep and crackling. Her heart jumped in her chest, hope making her dizzy. "Leave this space immediately."

Renie frowned, not understanding at first. Leave? A glance at the control panel showed there was no ship within five thousand leagues of her.

"I won't leave. I have a medical emergency. My brother is dying!"

"Explorer One, leave at once." The voice came again, clearer now. "I will not repeat myself."

"I won't leave!" She tried to calm herself so she didn't go through the limited air supply but it was impossible. She wouldn't leave. She didn't even know if she could. "Help my brother, please? I'll give you anything. I have money... riches... I'm willing to pay for help!"

Silence.

Were they gone? Had they abandoned her?

She went to speak again but her voice left her when an enormous silver and yellow ship appeared through the barrier between her and the Black Zone.

Her heart went off the scale and she squeezed Rezic's hand.

What had she called?

The ship dwarfed hers and fear pounded down on her, stealing her breath.

Perhaps this was a bad idea. She hadn't realised that the reply had come from the Black Zone. Perhaps they were better off trying to leave after all. She could set the ship on autopilot, get the door open, and tend to her brother while they travelled to the nearest spaceport.

Releasing Rezic's hand, she grabbed the controls and turned the ship about. Before she could get the engines to full speed, she was going backwards. She pressed the button to switch to the rear view of the ship and her brow furrowed when she saw that the huge vessel was pulling them in. The cargo bay doors were open to reveal an area that her small ship could fit into fifteen times over.

What had she done?

Who were these people?

Were they really going to help her brother?

CHAPTER 2

Renie cradled her brother to her, stroking his brow, and when the ship came to a halt, she gently lay him down on the floor of the dark bridge. The power had gone out during the ship's descent onto the large vessel. Now she was in complete darkness. The strained sound of Rezic's breathing made her feel ill, turning her stomach and filling her head with terrible thoughts. The ship's computer had announced that his life signs were stabilising but she knew better than to believe that meant he was going to live.

The blood on the side of his head was thick and dark, covering half of his forehead and his cheek. He hadn't stirred at all since the meteorites had struck the ship and she feared the worst. An image of the huge vessel that had answered her call for help flashed across her mind. Would they be able to save her brother when she couldn't? She hoped that they could but an ominous feeling had settled in the pit of her stomach on seeing the ship. She couldn't remember ever seeing one like it before, but it had come from the Black Zone and instinct was telling her that wasn't a good sign.

It had commanded her to leave the area. She prayed to Iskara that didn't mean what she thought it did.

Her gaze strayed back to where she knew Rezic lay. Her insides flipped again, stomach churning with fear and anticipation. The air was growing thin again. With no power, the life support system had failed. She stared in the direction of the door and stood. Would they come soon? It was getting hot.

The bridge door opened a fraction. Light streamed in. Renie's heart jumped into her throat and then pounded hard when black claw-like fingers appeared through the gap. She gasped and stepped backwards, hitting the ship's console behind her. The clawed fingers closed around the door and pulled it open with ease. She couldn't possibly have done that. Not even her brother could have. Whatever was coming was stronger than both of them were. She crouched down to be with Rezic and stared at the door, waiting to see the face of their rescuer.

The doors opened fully.

What they revealed was more frightening than her worst nightmare.

Several dark clad soldiers moved into the small space, forcing her to one side. Her eyes didn't leave the man who had opened the bridge door. Standing over six and a half feet, he towered above her, his skin as white as clouds. His long black hair parted over his pointed ears. He barked orders at the men and she frowned when they grabbed her, pulling her around as they searched her body for something.

She glared at the soldiers when they opened the small weapons hold beside the pilot's chair and took the laser guns. Weapons? They were searching her for weapons.

Two soldiers grabbed her and marched her through the ship and out into the cargo bay of the vessel that had her. They roughly turned her on the spot to face her ship and she struggled when she saw her brother on a hover stretcher. Three women and one man were attending to him. She fought harder to escape the men holding her when the others began to walk away with her brother.

"I need to go with him," she said and stamped on one of the men's feet. He snarled and tightened his grip on her, his fingers digging into her flesh.

"You offered payment for your brother's life," a familiar deep voice said and she looked up to see the man who had opened the door to the bridge.

In the bright light of the cargo bay, his eyes met hers, sending a sickening chill through her.

What should have been the white of his eyes was black. His irises were golden, bright and sharp like a hawk's. They studied her and held her at the same time. She couldn't look away no matter how much she wanted to. He stepped out of the ship and she barely held the gasp inside when she saw he had black leathery wings tightly furled against his back. She looked over at the doctors that were taking Rezic away and then at the soldiers in the area. Wings. Black wings.

Her heart beat painfully hard and her gaze slowly came back to the man who had addressed her.

She had never seen one before, but she had been educated well enough to be able to recognise one.

"Vegan!" she growled the word with all the hatred of her species.

The man grinned, an ugly smile that only made his rough countenance more horrifying. He seemed pleased by her reaction.

"Lyran," he said as his hand came to rest against her cheek. He licked his lips. "Wait, even sweeter, a half breed Terran."

Her heart felt as though it had stopped.

His smile widened and she knew what he was going to say.

"Welcome, Princess."

Fighting the men holding her, Renie tried to get free. She needed to get to Rezic and escape the hellish place she had brought them to.

"Rezic!" she shouted after him, desperate.

There was a growl of annoyance and then pain black and sharp split her skull. She faded into the darkness, drifting away.

This was a warm place.

Renie liked how free of hurt she was here, how free of everything. The darkness surrounded her but slowly began to brighten, as though the sun was rising. She watched it, fascinated but numb. Gradually, the dark turned to light and she fluttered her eyes open.

"Rezic?" she muttered, her head splitting, and tried to remember what had happened.

She shot into a sitting position when she remembered that Rezic was hurt and that she was on a Vegan ship and they knew she was Lyran royalty.

She screwed her eyes shut when her head ached even worse, blinding her. Perhaps sudden movements weren't wise after someone had tried to knock your head off. She clutched it and groaned when she slowly opened her eyes to see that she was in a cell. The pale grey wall behind her was solid, a bench running along it that she supposed was a bed. The other three walls of her cell were blue light bars—rows of highly charged vertical energy beams. Lyran vessels had cells that used them but she had never seen them before.

Dreamily and without thinking, she reached out and touched them. They crackled and she snapped her hand back as they burnt her fingertips. Clutching her hand to her chest, she tried to make sense of where she was. The other cells were empty and it was quiet. She didn't know where she was in the ship or where her brother was, or even if he was alive. She didn't know what they wanted with her or what they were going to do to her.

Curling up against the bench, Renie hugged her knees to her chest and checked her hand. She frowned when she saw her communicator band was still there and pressed the button four times, the number she had agreed with Rezic would be their emergency signal.

Nothing but static came back.

"It will not work in here," a male voice said and she jumped, looking around her.

She wasn't alone.

There was someone in the cell beside hers. Renie shuffled over to the bars and tried to get his attention. He was lying on the bench, his back to her and a dark grey blanket covering him completely so she could only see the shape of him.

"Excuse me," she said and held her hand up by the bars, wary of them. "Excuse me... how do you know—"

"Quiet," he said and tugged the blanket further over his head, exposing a pair of heavy dark blue and silver boots at the other end.

Her right eyebrow rose. Such a lazily spoken order wasn't going to put her off. He sounded like her brother after she had awoken him. If Rezic didn't scare her when he was in a mood like that, then this stranger certainly wasn't going to.

Unless he looked like that man had. She had never imagined that a Vegan would look so frightening.

"Excuse me... how do you know it won't work... or even what I was doing for that matter?" She frowned at him. His cell was at a right angle to hers. He had his back to her and she hadn't heard anyone move. How had he known what she was doing?

"The ship is actively blocking communications," he said and his arm appeared from under the blanket. Around his wrist was a device similar to hers. "It was obvious what you would try to do on waking."

Her eyes widened, but not because of the device.

His skin was white but from his knuckles it slowly turned from white to a rich blue colour at his fingertips. He had deep blue claws. The tattered black cuff of whatever clothes he was wearing fell back to reveal tighter clothing in blue and silver beneath.

His hand disappeared back under the blanket.

"Do you know where the medical area is? I need to get to my brother. They're holding him there."

"Quiet." This time his voice carried a note of warning.

Renie shrank back and sighed. Evidently, this man wasn't going to be much help to her. Still, questions crowded her mind and they demanded answers.

"Erm, excuse me?" she said and in one swift move, he pushed the blanket off himself and sat up, facing her.

"I said to be quiet!" he snapped but she was too busy staring to hear what he had said.

She had never seen anything like him. His skin was white but where it neared his hairline it gradually turned dark blue just as his fingers did. His hair was a matching dark blue at the root but slowly changed to black. It hung in loose tendrils, framing his face with tousled strands that made her want to reach out and push them back, out of his face so she could drink her fill of his otherworldly beauty.

A pair of the most fantastic eyes held hers, their pale blue pupil surrounded by black irises fascinating her.

With an irritated sigh, he raked his fingers through his hair, revealing the fact his ears were slightly pointed and the tips of them were also blue.

He was breathtaking. It wasn't the fact that she had never seen a species like him. It was how handsome he was—beautiful enough that her heart beat a little quicker at the sight of him and when her eyes met his, she trembled inside.

Quiet.

She could do quiet when she was looking at him. Words had no place in this moment, no use. They were unnecessary. Sight had command here, and she wanted to do nothing more than stare at him for eternity.

He shivered and his hair fell down across his face. She had never seen someone suffer such a violent shudder before.

He pulled the tattered grey blanket around his shoulders and her gaze fell to his hands and then his clothes. He was wearing black like the soldiers that had taken her captive but his appearance was nothing like theirs.

"Are you a prisoner too?" she said, finding her voice at last and unable to ignore her desire to learn more about him.

He frowned, dark blue eyebrows meeting tightly above those stunning eyes.

"I thought the answer to that was obvious."

She shrugged and dropped her gaze away from his. Loose black trousers covered his legs. They were torn in places. She could see something blue beneath.

Was he wearing something similar to a fight suit beneath the clothes?

He huddled up into the blanket and sighed.

"Do you know where they might have taken my brother?"

"You mentioned the medical deck," he said and his eyes met hers again, sending another warm rush down her spine. She nodded. "Then I suppose he is there."

He wasn't very forthcoming.

"What did they capture you for?" she said and waited for him to tell her to be quiet again.

"Attempting to leave the Black Zone."

"Is that bad?" Since he was answering questions, Renie couldn't stop her mouth from asking them. Perhaps if she broke the ice between them, then he would be more inclined to tell her the location of the medical area, presuming he knew. Her gaze took in his face again, slower this time, in intimate detail. A cut dashed across his right cheek just below his eye. At least she presumed it was a cut. It was a thin blue line. Did he have blue blood?

"Not as bad as being a Lyran in the Black Zone."

His reply startled her and she shuffled backwards a few inches.

"Did they tell you when they brought me in?" she said, wondering what the guards might have said to him and why they would tell a prisoner such information.

"No," he said and pulled the blanket even tighter around him. She got the feeling that he wasn't going to say anything more than that. Perhaps he was a species that could sense things, as Varkans could. She didn't have the courage to ask, so instead she focused on the fact that he was intently wrapping the blanket around him. He banged a fist against the wall. "Turn the heat up!"

She frowned. He was cold? She was boiling in just her thin white shirt, tan waistcoat and brown trousers.

When she moved, a curl of her long black hair fell out of her bun. She poked it back into place and wished she had done something nicer with her hair this morning. She hadn't expected to end up shut in a cell next to a handsome prisoner, especially one who, for the first time in a long time, made her care about her appearance.

"Are you cold?" she said, wanting to break the silence between them again.

He glared at her, as though it was another ridiculous question.

"I thought it was rather warm," she said with a shrug.

With a muttered comment she couldn't make out, he tugged the blanket closer around him.

"It is cold." His voice held a note of command and authority that made her feel as though she should believe it, as though if he said it was cold then it was cold or if he said that deep space was in fact purple, then it was.

"What deck is the medical one?" she said.

"Fourteen," he replied and then paused. His gaze ran over her and then over the room. "I do not recommend attempting to escape. The crew is all male except the medical staff and you have neither the clothing or appearance to pass as a medical assistant. You would be caught in a matter of seconds and your punishment would only be more severe."

"More severe?" she said with another frown. "I'm a princess of Lyra in Vegan space. I don't think my punishment could get more severe than this. They're probably plotting how much to ransom me for right now, or planning my public execution."

He laughed. It was mocking and made her teeth grate.

"Execute you? On whose orders?" He huddled down into his blanket and stared at her, his strange pale blue pupils boring into hers. "Vegans would not initiate another war with Lyra. They have no need to. The galaxy is divided and both are trapped, unable to expand their empires or their technology."

"Lyrans are expanding their technology perfectly well."

"Well enough that you could create your own barrier?"

She resisted a pout. "Perhaps."

It wasn't her place to talk about politics like this, or even something that she was interested in doing, but the way he was talking made her furious. He sounded as though he sympathised with the Vegans and that he was mocking the Lyrans. It was difficult to stop herself from talking about things like her cousin's recent marriage to the emperor of Varka. Lyra had already expanded the reach of their technology because of it. She was sure that soon Lyra could build a barrier like the one Vega had erected, but she wasn't sure there was a need.

"That barrier... I saw a planet out there... or something that used to be a planet. My brother said that it had a high carbon content, as though everyone who had once lived on it had died in a flash." She hugged her knees again as she thought about being back on the small ship with her brother. Where was he? Was he alive? If the Vegans had realised that she was royalty just by touching her, then perhaps they would sense the same about her brother. It was to their advantage to ensure he survived.

"When the barrier was turned on, anything in its path was decimated."

Decimated. Her brother had been right. The barrier had destroyed the planet.

"In time, things that are blocking the barrier or caught in it are eliminated. Vega must keep a clean line between the Black Zone and the rest of the galaxy."

"We were hit by meteorites—"

"Not meteorites," he said, cutting her off. "This ship has a duty. It was sent here to destroy the planet. It was part of that planet that struck your vessel."

No wonder the ship hadn't detected anything before the meteorites were already closing in on them. No wonder there was a ship in the vicinity to hear her distress call.

"I see," she said and stared at her knees. Her hand hurt. She sucked her fingers, trying not to think about how dire her situation was. Her father would pay for her return, but would it be enough? Would the Vegans give her and her brother up so easily?

Would her father give up so easily? She was sure that he would fight for her. If he did, then there was a chance the war with Vega would begin again. She didn't want that. She didn't want to subject the people of Lyra to war again, or to catch another system in the crossfire and have them suffer as the Earth system had.

The thought of billions of people dying as the Terrans had made her sick to her stomach. She clutched it and closed her eyes.

"Are you ill?" the man said.

She shook her head.

"Worried perhaps?"

She nodded this time and rested her chin on her knees.

"If you are a princess, then your brother will be safe."

Those words weren't as reassuring as she had thought they would be. Her thoughts turned to Rezic and she wondered if she would ever see him again. Would they ransom him and then her? What if they refused to hand them over at all? What if her and her brother were about to become pawns in the downfall of Lyra? She hoped her father wouldn't come. She hoped her uncles would be able to talk sense into him.

She had to escape this cell and find Rezic but she knew it was as impossible as her pale friend had said it was. The Vegans would catch her in seconds, and that was if she even managed to escape the cell in the first place. She couldn't see a way past the bars.

"Will you answer one more question?" she said to the man, losing hope more and more by the second.

He nodded.

"What will the Vegans do to me?"

CHAPTER 3

Tres came out of his blanket and looked at her. She was trembling and it wasn't from cold. Warm blooded as she was, she didn't have his problem. She was frightened. He had little experience of frightened females. All of the women this side of the barrier seemed hardhearted and as fierce as the males. Even his mother was vicious. The only female he knew with a modicum of emotion was his sister.

The Lyran female's dark eyes pleaded him for an answer and his heart said she craved reassurance. She was turning to him for help and for hope. He couldn't deny one as beautiful as her, as delicate and scared. Her fear and beauty spoke to him, making her appear as fragile as a Cyoliane butterfly, and tempting him to reach out and cradle her gently in his hands. He wondered at this strange desire.

"I am sure they will release you. Ransoming you would contravene the Treaty of Espacia." He noticed her look didn't change. "They will not harm you."

Silently, he added a promise to those words. He wouldn't let anyone harm her or her brother. He moved to the end of the bench near her, wondering what strange twist of fate had brought her into this side of the galaxy. She seemed too frail to survive in such a dark place but at the same time her black eyes held a trace of determination and there was a hint of strength in the set of her subtly curved jaw. A strange mixture. Beauty and grace joined with strength and resolve.

It was a shame she wasn't strong enough.

His heart said that she could be. He could probably get her to her brother and then to a ship. He knew this class of Vegan fighter well enough to be able to take her through the ducts to the medical deck.

Tres looked up at the ceiling. It shifted from pale grey to a thermal image and then he could see through the panels to the ducts, pipes and wiring beyond. Down the side of the image, thermal readings gave him the temperature of each duct. Below it was an assessment of width, height and other factors.

It was warmer in the duct than it was in this room.

"Is there something interesting up there?" she said.

His gaze shifted to her and, in a matter of seconds, his ocular implants had her vital statistics displayed next to the thermal image of her body. She was hot. Far hotter than he had expected. She was radiating heat at a level that made him consider crossing his cell to the bars, reaching through and taking her hand to warm himself. She was also shorter than he had expected and lighter. If they stood side by side, she would be a good head shorter than he was.

"Only ducts and engineering passageways," he said without thinking and her thermal image frowned at him. His gaze slid down to her chest and he watched her heart pounding. It was beating faster than he had thought it would. As he watched it, it picked up speed. Her body temperature rose. He smiled inside, amused at this reaction to his staring, and then switched off the implants and looked away from her. It was wrong of him to stare, even if she was the most fascinating creature he had ever met.

"Ducts? You can see the ducts?"

He nodded. "On ships this size, they are wide enough for someone to crawl through."

"How can you see the ducts?"

She seemed more interested in how he knew things than how they could help. He tapped the side of his head.

"I have ocular implants, amongst other things."

Her eyes widened and her brows rose in surprise. "Implants? Like cybernetics?"

"Far more advanced than that." He smiled at her. "Does Lyra not have such things?"

Her jaw tensed and he realised that she didn't like it when he spoke about Lyra in a way that made it sound less advanced than Vega or any species on this side of the barrier.

She was even more beautiful when she was angry.

His gaze ran over her again, this time seeing her as she was. Dressed like a male in what appeared to be a white shirt and brown trousers. It didn't suit her. He could imagine her dressed in the raiment of a female, something flowing and soft, in subtle shades. With her hair down, long black locks flowing over her pale creamy skin, she would be stunning, more beautiful than any butterfly.

Tres frowned when her dark gaze fell to her knees, a blush of colour caressing her cheeks. When she raised her eyes again, she gave him a little smile that sent a jolt of heat through him. Not actual temperature, he realised, but something else. Unfamiliar feelings that made him desire to touch her. Touch. He longed to feel her skin against his, to feel a connection to something at last.

A noise in the corridor startled him out of his perusal of her. His eyes shifted to the door of the cellblock and then roamed back to her, unable to leave her for any amount of time. He wanted to look at her forever. He wanted to touch her. Not with gloves on. He needed to feel her soft skin, needed to feel her warmth. He didn't care if it was forbidden. It only made him want it more. He wanted her to touch him. He craved the feel of her fingers on him, hungered for her touch.

The violence and strength of that need surprised him. Never before had he wanted to be touched. Never had he considered that he had been deprived all these years by the law that forbade skin-to-skin contact with him. What would it feel like to have her warm little hands on him?

"The guards are coming. If they find you talking to me, you will be in trouble." He lay back down on his bench, frowning at the hardness of it, and hoped that she would take the hint and be quiet for a while.

She moved to the bench and sat on it, still nursing her hand. She had been foolish to touch the bars. He knew that some Lyran vessels had similar light technology. Perhaps she didn't travel on those kinds of military vessels, or perhaps she hadn't seen any cells in her time. A delicate creature like her would probably want to stay away from such areas.

Or perhaps a protective male had kept her safe from them.

That thought sent a cold spike into his heart.

One as beautiful as her probably had a male.

The door opened, chasing away his thoughts. He sensed her stiffen when the guards passed her cell. They stopped at his.

"It is cold in here," he said, casual and with a smile.

"We have orders to maintain this temperature and inquire whether you will eat now?"

Tres shook his head. "I will not. Perhaps your other guest will."

The two male Vegans looked over their shoulders in the direction of the woman. They grinned and then the smile fell off their faces when they looked back at him. He frowned at them.

"We have orders to starve her, at least until Lyra sends a party to negotiate."

"Negotiate?" he said and then bit his tongue to stop himself from saying anything more. Angering the commander of this ship wasn't wise. He had proven himself to be quite ruthless and a male who followed the rules to the letter. The moment the commander had caught him, he had thrown him in the cells and done everything required to stop him escaping.

"If you try to ransom me it will be a direction violation of the treaty! You will be starting a war with Lyra," the female said.

The two guards laughed and moved to the female's cell. She should have kept her mouth shut. Vegan military officers hated all things Lyran, regardless of how beautiful they appeared to be.

"It's none of your business. Just wait there for someone to come and get you."

"Wait," she said as they started to leave and got to her feet. "My brother."

"What about him?" The first guard glared at her, his yellow eyes intent on her face.

"Is he alive?"

The guard hesitated and looked over at him. Tres held his gaze. The man looked back at her and nodded.

"He is stable. He will be ransomed with you."

She went to speak and then stopped, as though she had got the better of herself at last. They had answered one of her questions. It wasn't wise to ask any more.

The guards left and she moved back to the blue energy bars near his cell.

"Do you believe them?" she said and he nodded. The officers of this ship would ensure her brother's survival. They stood to gain a large amount of currency from ransoming them, but only if her brother were alive.

"Your family must know that you travel together and that you would never enter the Black Zone without reason. Therefore, they would know that you would have been taken together. If they only have you to ransom, Lyra would enquire after your brother. If they discover he is dead, they will not pay the Vegans anything. They will attack."

She flinched at that last word and he could see she didn't want that to happen.

Tres sat up and pulled the blanket around him, muttering to himself about the guards and their orders to keep the cells at such a despicable temperature.

"Are you cold?" she said again and when his eyes met hers, he saw a hint of concern in them.

What kind of warmhearted creature was she that she cared about a male she had only just met? None on this side of the barrier would care about someone they hadn't known for less than two standard Vegan years. He calculated that in his head. By her species, she would've had to have known him for at least fourteen years to reach this level of concern.

He tugged at the collar of the tight suit beneath his looser black clothes, pulling it up his neck until it almost reached his jaw.

"It is cold," Tres repeated but not in the same tone he had used before. This time there was a hint of resignation in his voice that surprised him. Perhaps it was because the guards had flatly refused his attempts to raise the temperature.

"What's that suit you're wearing?" She moved close to the bars and peered at the collar now visible above his clothes. "It looks like a flight suit. Did they capture your ship too? I didn't see another ship in the cargo bay."

Tres reached into the pocket of his loose trousers and pulled out his one remaining glove. He had lost the other to the commander of the ship. Proof of capture he had called it. Sighing, Tres stared at the glove. In his current state, there was no way that he could help the woman find her brother and leave the ship.

His gaze roamed back to her, studying her face as she looked at his hands. His heart beat and then only a few minutes later beat again. He had never felt it race like this, not even when he had been running. Hers was thundering by the time her eyes met his again. His beat again. When compared with hers, it was leisurely at best, but to him it was a giddy fast beat.

"It's a thermal suit." He flexed his fingers while looking at his forearm. His muscles shifted beneath the skintight material and the residual heat they created was absorbed and used to warm his entire arm. "The commander of this ship wanted to ensure I did not get it into my head to escape so he broke it."

Her eyebrows rose. "But you need heat."

"He cares little about such technicalities." Tres slowly stood. It took incredible effort to move his stiff limbs and stretching was painful but rewarded him with a short burst of heat.

She stared at him, silent and pensive.

He wondered what she was thinking behind her beautiful eyes and then remembered what he had been thinking about before the guards had entered.

Her. Males.

Tres frowned at the door to the cellblock and clenched his fists. The thought that she might already belong to another male infuriated him and his heart beat again, quickly followed by another. Two in as many minutes. If a male had her, owned her, then he would fight that male for her.

His eyes grew wide when he realised what he was thinking and he looked down at her. She knelt by the bars, her hands in her lap, her eyes round and dark as she looked up at him. He would fight for her. On this side of the barrier, such a fight would be to the death. If her male was large, Tres could lose, but he would fight regardless. She had him fascinated, a slave to her, enthralled by her beauty and her frailty. He wanted to wrap her in his arms and protect her from the darkness of the universe. He would protect her from anything.

Anything.

"What do your kin call you?" he said and a flicker of shock crossed her face followed by a crimson blush that stained her cheeks. Beautiful. He had never seen a female react to him the way she did. He had never seen a female react like her to anyone. Were all females like this on the other side of the barrier? What was she like compared to them—strong, weak, loving, tender, cruel? He wanted to know. He was so tired of being trapped on this side of the barrier, surrounded by darkness and loneliness.

"Renie," she whispered, as though ashamed to tell him.

Perhaps not ashamed. She cast her eyes downwards into her lap and twisted her fingers around themselves. Embarrassed? Awkward? All new emotions to him. There was none like her on this side of the barrier. Meeting her and experiencing this wondrous array of feeling had only strengthened his resolve to leave the Black Zone.

He moved to the bars and knelt in front of her.

"Tres," he said and slid his hand between the bars, holding it out in what he hoped was a Lyran gesture of greeting. His knowledge of different species' formalities had all collided in his mind and become tangled over the years.

She stared at his hand as though it was going to attack her.

Perhaps he had been wrong.

Her hand slid into his.

Tres's entire body jolted and tensed, a sweep of tingles racing through him, fanning out from the point where her skin touched his. She closed her fingers around his hand, her soft skin brushing his, creating smaller waves of pleasure with each tiny caress. His heart beat hard in his chest, pounding in his ears as he stared into her eyes, absorbing the divine feeling of her body against his. For a moment, he forgot himself, lost in the feel of her hand in his, her gentle touch. He had never been touched before, not skin on skin. Even those who'd had to touch him when he had been a child had worn gloves, and since then he had always been wearing his thermal suit when he had been touched.

Not that he had ever been touched as intimately as this. Anything more intimate than touching his arm or shoulder was forbidden also.

His fingers slowly closed, clasping her hand, and he never wanted to let it go.

"How do you know a Terran form of greeting?"

His eyes had almost closed when she voiced that question. They opened slowly and ambled over her body and then her face to meet hers.

Terran. One of her species then. To think the Vegans and Lyrans had almost destroyed the species that had created her, a stunning dark rose, a flower so delicate he wanted to hold her gently and savour her scent.

"Education," he said as an answer and reluctantly took his hand back, sliding it carefully through the bars.

He could have held hers forever.

His entire body felt warm from just that brief touch but the heat quickly faded.

"Your hands are freezing," she said with a smile that he supposed was meant to make him feel as though that wasn't a bad thing.

She was trying not to offend him.

He smiled at her, showing that he wasn't at all offended. He knew that he was cold compared to her. His species relied on the strong sun of their planet and thermal suits to keep them alive. In deep space, and with his suit broken, he was so cold that it was difficult to move. Painful.

Still, as he looked at her, he found that he didn't feel the cold. He didn't feel the pain. He felt only warmth. A strange warmth that suffused his entire body.

"Tres?" she said and his eyes half-closed on hearing her soft voice speak his name.

He managed a nod in response and clawed the scattered pieces of his mind back together. Something about her made him lose all reason and control. He wished that he was able to get closer to her. He wanted to feel her body against every inch of his and needed to help her get away from this dark place. The Black Zone was no place for her and the Vegan commander of this vessel was intent on hurting her, or at least damaging relations between Vega and Lyra. He had to stop that from happening. He looked around him at the cells. Trapped here, he wouldn't be able to do anything.

"Do you think my brother is going to be all right?" She leaned back against the wall near him and pulled her knees up to her chest.

The vulnerability in her look made him frown and a dark feeling filled him, an urge to escape the cell at any cost to set her free and take vengeance on the commander who had captured her. Her near-black eyes shifted to meet his, sending another bolt of warmth through him. She gave him another little smile, a faint curving of her lips that spoke of hurt. Her brow furrowed.

"He will be all right, won't he?" she whispered, her look almost pleading him to lie to her.

He didn't need to lie.

"Nothing will happen to him," Tres whispered in return and moved closer to her. He leaned his back into the wall and kept his head turned towards her, watching her closely. She was beautifully unguarded with her feelings and the depth of her love for her brother stunned Tres. He was sure that his sister, Tesia, loved him, but it couldn't possibly extend to this. Renie looked as though she would die if anything happened to her brother.

For some reason, that made him a little jealous.

Jealous.

It was a new feeling for him. He had never had a reason to feel it before.

He held a high position within society, so admired and feared that he wanted for nothing. Only his family could refuse him something. Yet he craved more. He stared into Renie's eyes, reading all the love in them. He longed for a life where he was treated differently. An existence where there was more. More. He didn't know exactly what it was that he craved, but he knew that he would find it on the other side of the barrier, away from the Black Zone.

Freedom. Feelings. Life.

All the things he had ever wanted but had never had. The things that he couldn't ask for. The things that were denied him.

He wanted to live. He desired to see how others lived. He longed to experience life in a place less dark than the Black Zone.

Something dawned on him, something that made him feel the depth of his loneliness and the hollowness of his existence, something that made him despair at the thought that he might lose what he had found. He didn't want to go back, didn't want to continue his old life now that he had discovered what was missing from it.

He wanted to live. He desired to see how others lived. He longed to experience life in a place less dark than the Black zone. But he didn't want to do it alone.

He wanted to do it all with a female like Renie.

She was everything that he had ever wanted.

CHAPTER 4

The door opened.

Renie's heart leapt into her throat when the Vegan commander walked in, flanked by two soldiers. He still frightened her. She stood, unwilling to let him see that fear, and walked to the bars of her cell, coming face to face with him.

"We have contacted your family," he said, his eyes showing a smile that his lips hid. He seemed pleased with himself. Renie's heart pounded at the thought that her family were coming. She hated the position she was in, but the knowledge that her father was coming for her lightened her heart and made her feel better. The commander's gaze raked over her and then met hers again. "It will be a while before they reach us. You would be wise to make yourself comfortable."

Renie glanced back at the bench and then at Tres. He was still sitting with his back to the wall, his strange eyes fixed on the commander in a venomous stare.

"You will eat," the commander said.

Renie looked at him, shaking her head. He wasn't going to order her around. She might be his prisoner but she wasn't about to let him take all her strength from her. Tres had refused to eat and she was going to as well. She wasn't going to make things easy on the Vegans. It could be days before her family arrived. When they did, she wanted them to see exactly how poorly the Vegans had treated her.

"What do you intend to do with myself and my brother?" she said, straightening her back and standing tall. She was a princess of Lyra. This commander wasn't going to frighten her.

But her heart thundered in her ears and her palms sweated as she stood before him, staring up into his golden eyes and waiting to hear her fate.

The commander smiled, thin-lipped and evil. "We have discovered something most interesting about your brother. It seems he is in line for the throne."

Renie didn't like the way his smile widened, his eyes narrowing with it. It scared her. She frowned and stepped right up to the bars. She could see in the Vegan's eyes what he was thinking and she wasn't going to let that happen. Rezic didn't care about the throne. He didn't want it. He didn't want to be Lyra V.

All of the malicious thoughts crossing the Vegan commander's face frightened her. They confirmed her fear that he was thinking of hurting her brother. He was going to punish Rezic for being in line to the throne of Lyra.

Her resolve melted away and her brow furrowed. She stared into the commander's eyes, no longer able to hide her fear. He grinned when he saw it and that only frightened her more. The idea that he was feeding off her fear only increased it. Would he hurt her brother just to make her suffer?

"Please," Renie whispered, hating herself for showing such weakness but needing to protect her brother. He couldn't fend for himself. He was already injured. He had been so close to death. If they tortured him for information, he might not survive. "Don't hurt him. Please? I'll do anything you ask of me. Please... just don't harm my brother."

Tears blurred her vision. She couldn't bear the thought of them hurting Rezic. She could almost feel his pain already. If they tortured him, he wouldn't tell them a thing. He would die before he revealed any of Lyra's secrets. She didn't want him to die for a throne that he didn't want. Without him, the galaxy would be an empty soulless place. He was everything to her.

"Please?" she whispered again, reaching up and wishing she could take hold of the bars, could get closer to the commander so he would see that she truly would do anything for her brother. "Take me instead. Don't hurt him. If you want to hurt someone—"

"Enough," Tres snapped in a firm voice, making her jump.

Her head shot around to face him. He was on his feet and approaching the commander.

"The treaty of Espacia forbids this kind of action." Tres stepped right up the bars of his cell, his dark blue eyebrows knit tight into a frown. He was taller than she had expected and when he looked like this, so commanding and confident, she realised how handsome he really was. She moved closer to him, her eyes fixed on his face, wondering what he was going to do.

What could he do?

They were both trapped here. Mentioning the treaty wouldn't change a thing. They couldn't stop the Vegans from hurting her brother. She felt helpless. Useless. Rezic was hurt and there wasn't a thing she could do to help him.

No one could help him.

"You are in no position to speak," the Vegan commander said to Tres.

The determined look on Tres's face didn't change. He held the commander's gaze, unwavering in the face of a man she found so frightening.

"We have contacted your family too," the commander whispered and a flicker of something crossed Tres's face. Anguish? Fear? She couldn't determine the emotion. It was too brief, nothing more than a flash. In less than a heartbeat, it was gone, replaced by a glare so murderous and dark that Renie almost stepped back.

Tres slammed his fists against the light bars, making them crackle and fizz. The commander retreated a step. Tres hit the bars again, his eyes narrowed into dark blue slits. Not a trace of pain touched his features although it must have hurt him to touch the energy bars.

Renie watched in silence, witnessing an unspoken exchange of threats between the two males. She glanced down to see that Tres had his hands clenched into tight fists at his sides. They were steady, not trembling in the slightest. The control he had over his obvious anger was incredible and stunned Renie as much as the hatred in his eyes. He had known what he was doing when he had hit the bars and he hadn't cared about the pain it would cause him. Had he wanted to scare the commander?

Or was it the thought of his family coming for him that had made him react so violently, had made him want to fight?

Tres heaved a sigh and visibly relaxed. Renie's gaze shifted to his face again. He looked calm at last, his head tilted back and his shoulders lowered. His blue pupils remained fixed on the commander though.

The commander grinned, as though Tres's change in temperament was a victory for him.

Tres frowned and then relaxed again.

"If I eat," he said slowly, his voice smooth and calm, "you will leave her brother alone."

Renie frowned now, confused by the exchange. How was Tres finally eating important enough to the Vegans that they wouldn't hurt her brother? If it was true and they would do as he had asked then she didn't care about the reasoning behind it. She looked at Tres and then at the commander. No. Tres hadn't asked the commander. He had told the commander that he would leave Rezic alone.

Was Tres of high standing within society on this side of the barrier? High enough that he could order the Vegan commander? She almost laughed at that. Given their current situation, he couldn't be that important. If he were then the commander wouldn't have been holding him in the cells. If this ship was anything like a Lyran military vessel, then it would have guest quarters. They would have held Tres in one of those if he were that important. Perhaps he was trying his luck. Perhaps he had only risked it sounding like an order to force commander into making a decision.

But still.

How was Tres's offer of eating equivalent to the safety of her brother? It didn't seem like an equivalent exchange to her.

Renie looked at the commander to see what he would do. He looked pensive for a moment and then nodded.

"Bring food for him, and make sure that he eats it." The commander's gaze slid to her and she stepped back, away from him. "If he doesn't, then we go ahead as planned."

Renie swallowed and glanced at Tres. He was looking at her, his expression serene and unwavering. If it was supposed to reassure her, it did, but she still wasn't about to trust these Vegans with her brother.

"You'll leave Rezic alone as promised, yes?" she said as the commander went to pass her.

He paused and looked down at her, across his broad shoulders. There was something in his strange yellow irises that looked like reluctance. He nodded and then stormed out of the room. One of the guards followed him. The other remained in the corner, watching her, his expression empty.

Renie turned to Tres. He had sat down again in the same spot that he had occupied before, leaning with his back against the wall between the light bars of her cell and the bench in his.

She walked over and sat down too. Her hands slipped from her bent knees to the floor and she looked down at Tres's hand. Carefully reaching through the bars, she tentatively stroked the burns on his hand, black marks against white skin.

"I'm sorry," she whispered and looked at him, tears trembling on the brink of falling again. She cursed them, wishing to Iskara that she wasn't so weak. The thought of them hurting her brother made her sick though and she couldn't stop the tears from coming whenever she thought about him. She couldn't lose Rezic. "You're hurt."

Tres's eyes narrowed slightly, a look filling them that made her heart race a little quicker. His blue pupils mesmerised her, surrounded by inky black irises and then the white of his eyes. The soft look in them warmed her, soothed her. She didn't understand any of what had happened between him and the commander and she didn't need to in order to know that Tres had made a sacrifice for her sake. He had protected her and her brother by giving in to the commander.

He had hurt himself defending her.

She tensed when something brushed her left cheek, cold but soft, and then tried to smile when she realised that it was Tres's other hand. He brushed his fingers along her jaw line and his thumb swept across her cheek below her eye, wiping away her tears. He smiled at her when he moved to the other side, catching her tears with his fingers and taking them away.

"I believe you are hurt worse than I," he whispered back at her, his eyes never leaving hers. She briefly closed hers when his fingers paused against her right cheek, his touch light and tender. This was insane. Here she was stuck in a cell on a Vegan military ship with a man she barely knew and she was having what had to be the most romantic moment of her life. She leaned into Tres's touch, wanting to steal every drop of comfort and strength from it as possible.

He took his hand back and she looked at him again.

"My family is coming," she said, more to herself than to him. She needed to make it sink in. Her family were coming for her. Rezic would be safe. Everything was going to be all right. "Your family too, apparently. You seem important to the Vegans."

She studied his face, trying to read his reaction.

"My mother is an important political figure." Tres leaned his head back into the wall behind him. He stared up at the ceiling and Renie wondered if he was seeing it or the ducts. What would it be like to have ocular implants? Could he see through anything? "My family were probably looking for me and that is why the ship picked me up."

Renie's eyebrows rose. "Will they ransom you too?"

"No." He shook his head and looked into her eyes. "As it stands, their treatment of me will probably get them punished... but that all depends on my mother's mood."

"What do you mean by that?" Renie glanced down at her hand where it still covered his. It felt nice. Reassuring. She had never realised that such small contact between two people could have such a profound effect. It wasn't the first time she had held hands, but it was the first time it had deeply affected her, making her feel strangely safe and sure that everything would turn out fine in the end.

Tres frowned. "It means that it may turn out that I am the one who is punished while the commander of this vessel is commended for his actions in capturing and containing me."

"Your mother sounds frightening." Renie managed a smile when he did. He had a nice smile, although they were always closed lipped. She looked at his mouth. The seam of his lips was dark blue. Did he have blue gums? What colour were his teeth? He was so fascinating. She wanted to ask him a million questions but held them all inside, sure that he wouldn't like her probing into his life and treating him as though he was a science experiment.

"She can be at times." He looked up at the ceiling again. Renie studied his profile. His nose was perfectly straight and, for the first time since meeting him, she noticed that he had a slight blue shadowing around his eyes and that his eyelashes were like his hair but in reverse. They went from black at the root to blue at the tip. He suddenly turned his head to face her, his eyes meeting hers. "What is your mother like? Will she be coming with your father on the ship?"

"My mother?" Renie smiled as she thought about her mother and father. "No, she probably won't be with my father. It's not that she wouldn't want to be with him when he came for me. She's probably worried sick about me and Rezic."

She giggled.

"Mother always said that we'd get into trouble one day and father would have to come for us." Her look turned serious as she thought about how scared her mother probably was, and her sister and brothers too. Even her father was probably worried. Perhaps she and Rezic had overstepped the mark by venturing so close to the Black Zone. They only had themselves to blame and she didn't know what she would do if a war started between Vega and Lyra again because of her.

"You look upset," Tres said and she blinked and then looked at him. She shook her head. "Worried?"

"Are they really going to ransom me and Rezic?" she said, needing him to tell her again that everything was going to be fine.

"They would be fools to try. Vega would not condone such actions."

"You seem terribly sure of that," she said with a little laugh and a smile, afraid that he was wrong. "The commander seemed rather intent on getting his dues."

"And he will get them, but it will not be from ransoming you." Tres's hand shifted beneath hers and he held it tight. "Come, you were speaking of your family. I wish to know about them. Is your mother Terran?"

Renie frowned. "You know who I am don't you? You know about my family. Do you know who my father is?"

He nodded. "I know of General Lyra II, but I do not know about you, and... I would like to."

A blush blazed across her cheeks and she dropped her gaze. Her eyes fixed on their joined hands and her face only burned hotter. He wanted to know about her. It was a strange notion. No one had ever really wanted to know about her, but then she had never remained in one spot long enough for someone to ask. Rezic and her had always been flitting from one port to the next, heading deeper and deeper into space that was sparsely populated.

"My mother is Terran," she said after a moment's thought. She wasn't going to deny Tres the chance to hear all about her family, not when it was comforting to speak about them and to remember how much they loved her and that they were coming for her. "She was a princess but no one knew it. When my parents met, she was a slave. My father was given her by a trader. His translator had broken and he didn't realise what was happening until it was too late. My father set her free."

Her eyes met Tres's when his hand tensed against hers. His were wide, staring at her with a curious look that she couldn't quite put her finger on. Was he thinking about their situation? Did he think that he could free her just as her father had freed her mother?

"Your father is a very noble man and has a great reputation that spreads deep into the Black Zone. All of the sons of Lyra are men to be feared. I am learning that their daughters may be just as formidable."

Renie laughed. "Formidable? That's not a very complimentary thing to say to a woman."

Tres's hand left hers. "I apologise." He frowned, staring at the floor near his bench. "I have little experience of speaking to females."

"But you have your mother?"

"My mother is often in other quarters. I rarely see her."

"Oh." A horrible feeling settled in her chest. Perhaps she shouldn't have teased him about his choice of words. He was only being nice to her after all. She should have seen the good in what he had said rather than the bad. His mother sounded quite formidable though. "Don't you have any other family?"

"My sister."

There was a curt edge to his voice that warned her not to probe any further.

"I wish I could speak to my parents. My mother especially. I'm sure that she would want to come with father but he's out in the region of Perseia."

"He is closer to us than he is to Lyra then."

She looked at Tres with a frown. "Are there star charts of my side of the galaxy in the Black Zone? We have no charts of the Black Zone. They end at the line of the Vegan barrier."

"Your space is well documented." His hand came back to hers, his fingers brushing her knuckles. They were still cold but she didn't care, not when it felt so nice and he looked as though he was enjoying the contact between them. He seemed fascinated with her hand. Perhaps it was warmth he was after. She hoped it was something more.

The door to the cellblock opened again and Tres's hand left hers as he stood.

Renie took her hand back and wiped away any remaining trace of her earlier tears before looking up at the corridor of the cellblock. The other guard was back. He had a blue dish filled with something. The guard that had remained with them did something to a control panel near Tres's door and a small opening appeared at the bottom of the bars. The guard with the food pushed the blue bowl through and then the bars closed again.

"Eat." The guard nodded towards the food.

Tres took the bowl and came back to her. He gave her a small smile as he sat down and she peered across into the bowl. It looked disgusting. Inside the blue dish was a thick gooey clear mixture with some kind of pale red strings in it. Tres stuck his fingers into the mixture and stirred it. A blush of purple rose to the surface, rippling through the clear. It smelt foul.

But she couldn't stop herself from watching Tres eat it. He scooped some up in his hand, tipped his head back, and let it fall into his mouth. She caught a flash of blue gums and white teeth and then he was swallowing. How could he eat such a horrible smelling and gross looking food?

Her stomach growled.

She looked at the bowl again and placed her hand over her stomach, trying to make it be quiet. It grumbled again as Tres ate another mouthful of the food. The more she looked at it, the more her stomach rumbled and the more appetising it became. She was starving. It had been a while since she had eaten. Two days or possibly more. She didn't know how long she had been unconscious.

When Tres was halfway through, he stood and went back to the door of his cell.

"Give the rest to her," he said.

The guard looked unimpressed. "Our orders were to make sure you ate."

"I have eaten. Now I am full. I wish for you to give the rest to the princess. If she is ill when her family arrives, your chances of receiving the ransom will be zero."

The bars at the bottom of the cell door lifted. Tres put the bowl down and slid it through the small gap. The guard took it and Renie moved towards the door when a small area of the light bars disappeared. The man pushed the bowl through into her cell. She picked it up and sniffed it. It really did smell foul but her stomach didn't seem to care. It rumbled loudly. She cast a nervous glance at the two guards and then Tres, unsure whether she wanted to eat it in front of them. Not only was she going to have to use her hands, but she wasn't sure if she would be able to keep the food down if it tasted as disgusting as it smelt.

She dipped a finger in and licked it clean.

Her eyes popped wide. It tasted amazing.

Carrying the bowl back to the corner with her, she sat down and scooped a small amount of the stringy goo up. She ate it. It was incredible. The textures and layers of taste were phenomenal, each making some different sense zing and pop. She had never tasted anything like it. It was food fit for a king. Not even the smell put her off.

It was delicious.

The bowl was empty before her stomach was full. She reluctantly turned it on its side and passed it through the bars to the guard. He took it without so much as a glance at her and left along with the other one. She looked longingly after him, wondering if he would come back with more. She could have licked the bowl. She would have if Tres hadn't been watching her.

Sitting back down beside Tres, she sighed.

"Thank you," she said.

"For what?"

She looked across at him, through the shimmering blue light bars.

"For eating in order to help my brother. I admit that I don't understand it, but thank you. I was sure that they were going to hurt him," she said and wondered if Tres would hold her hand again if she placed it down on the floor by her side. "Rezic has no interest in the throne. He wishes we were just archaeologists, like I do. We've never used our positions or our family to get anything."

Tres smiled at her. There was so much warmth in it and his eyes. What was he thinking when he looked at her like that?

He scratched his face, reopening the gash that ran below his eye. A bead of blue blood broke to the surface.

"I think you're bleeding." She pointed towards the cut.

He frowned and raised his hand up, swiping the blood away with the pad of his thumb. Her gaze ran over his tattered black clothes.

"You must have put up quite a fight when they captured you." She shuffled closer to the bars.

Staring at the blue blood on his thumb, he said, "You are not the only one who wishes they were common. I will always fight hard to achieve that which I have set my heart on."

Before she could ask what he meant by that, he had opened his mouth. She stared in fascination as he poked his tongue out. The sight of it stirred a strange desire in her, a hunger to feel it against her. It was blue, as exotic as the rest of him. The glide of his tongue over his thumb was erotic, sensual, igniting fire in her veins as she drank in the sight of it. The fire was fanned into an inferno when he licked his thumb again and she imagined how good it would feel to have that tongue laving her flesh, caressing her. She wanted to feel it, desired his mouth against hers and his hands on her body.

Shaking her head, she snapped herself out of it. She had been up in space too long if the sight of a man's tongue gave her fantasies. Her eyes roamed back to his mouth. But what a tongue. The way he had licked the blood off his thumb had told her without question that he would know exactly what to do with that implement of divine torture if she gave herself to him.

The door opened again and a guard entered. He closed the door and stood in the corner near it. The lights above her dimmed until only the light from the blue bars of the cells illuminated the room.

"Sleep," Tres said, gathering his blanket around him and returning to his bench. He lay down on it on his back, his blanket covering him and his arms below his head.

Renie took the blanket down from the bench in her cell and wrapped it around her as she lay down. The bench was hard and uncomfortable. She looked across at Tres to find him watching her, his skin blue from the lights and his eyes dark. Only their pupils shone strangely, bright as though they fed off the blue light.

"Tres?" she whispered, afraid of raising her voice in case the guard berated her.

"Yes?"

"Do you think Rezic will be safe?"

Silence.

A dark look entered his eyes, one that spoke of strength and belief.

"I swear they will not hurt him. I will make sure of that."

Renie looked at Tres a little longer and then closed her eyes, curling up on her side on the cold bench with her arm as a pillow.

Even though Tres was a prisoner too, she believed him.

He wouldn't let anything happen to her brother.

CHAPTER 5

Tres paced the small cell, his body stiff and aching as he forced himself to move. It was painful, but it did reward him with a little heat. The temperature had dropped again to the point where it was too cold for him to sleep. He tugged the dark grey blanket tighter around him and hunched up. Perhaps he should have asked the guard for an extra blanket before he had left.

The lights gradually came back up. He looked over at Renie and switched on his ocular implants to check her vitals. She was cold, but still warm enough. A desire to somehow get through the bars and curl up with her in his arms settled inside him. He stopped pacing and stared at her.

He wanted to touch her again.

It wasn't just because she was warm. It was so much more than that.

It was so much more than want.

He longed to touch her again, desired it more than anything.

She was so beautiful. Her nose wrinkled in her sleep and she mumbled something as she snuggled into her blanket, drawing her knees up into a foetal position. So enthralling.

He longed to cross the cellblock, kneel beside her, and stroke the rogue strands of her long black hair from her face so he could see it clearly. He desired to watch every nuance of sleep cross her face and wonder what she was dreaming as she fitfully slumbered. He hoped they were good dreams, dreams of freedom, dreams of travelling with her brother, dreams of him. If he had the power, he would see to it that this nightmare ended for her and that something like this would never happened to her again.

Raising his hand, he rubbed his thumb across his fingers. The burns were taking time to heal but they had been worth it. He would do it all again to feel her hand on his, to see the affection she had shown him light up her eyes again as she looked at him. He loved the way her hand had felt in his, and how she had let him hold it. It had been wonderful. The way she had leaned into his touch when he had cleared her tears away had left him desiring her more than ever.

Could she ever want a male like him?

There would be difficulties to overcome. It wouldn't be easy. If she gave him the chance, he would try though. He would do anything for her.

After the commander's visit yesterday, it had taken a lot for Tres to speak to her, to admit that he wanted to know her. It was a step in the right direction he supposed, but it was all moving too slow and he was growing tired of being trapped in this cell, unable to show her that he wanted her.

Unable to save her.

He needed to save her.

There was a shuffling noise as she wriggled under the blanket and then a soft sigh escaped her lips as her eyes fluttered open. Tres remained still, trapped by the wonderful sight of her waking. He wished she had been in his arms as she had awoken, sighing gently as though coming around from a good sleep.

Renie sat up slowly and rubbed the sleep from her eyes. Her delicate hands moved to her hair and she frowned, pouted almost. With a little smile in his direction, she tidied her hair, letting it down so it tumbled around her shoulders in soft dark waves before pinning it back into a loose knot at the back of her head.

She was so beautiful, even when waking.

She stood and stretched. Her white shirt pulled tight across her breasts and Tres felt as though she had punched him in the stomach as he stared blatantly, unabashed. She would be the death of him if she kept doing things like that. He shifted, suddenly uncomfortable in his tight thermal suit. The violent reaction to the sight of her breasts was a new one for him. He had never desired that kind of company before, but as he watched her, he found himself imagining how her breasts would feel beneath his fingers, his lips.

Renie turned to face him.

Tres swallowed and cast his eyes down at his feet. He idly pulled the collar of his thermal suit up again, trying to cover more of his body with it.

"Are you still cold?" she said, her voice soft and mesmerising. He found the courage to look at her again.

She had moved to the bars near his cell and was looking at him with concern in her large dark eyes. She worried about him. He truly had never met someone as warm and caring as her.

He nodded.

"I could probably fix it. Let me take a look." She tipped her head back twice in a gesture that told him to come to her.

He groaned inside. She didn't need to order him to go to her. He would always go to her. He couldn't stop himself.

She knelt down by the bars and he knelt opposite her, looking deep into her eyes for what seemed like hours rather than seconds.

"They did something to the back of the suit." He turned around, moving as close to the bars as possible so she didn't hurt herself on them by having to reach too far.

He removed his blanket, pulled the black jacket off and placed them both on his lap.

Her breathing quickened and he wondered whether it was fear of placing her arms through the bars or trepidation about touching him that made it change. She hadn't seemed frightened yesterday when she had held his hand.

His eyes rolled closed when she gathered his hair in her hands. Her fingertips grazed his ears and he bit his tongue to hold the moan in. Warm shivers danced through him, stirring his body. Her hands brushed his neck and then paused, still holding his hair.

How could touch be so forbidden when it felt this good?

The heat of her wasn't the only reason her touch affected him. It was something deeper, something that enslaved him and stirred his blood.

"You're not wearing a translator." She dropped his hair. Her hands disappeared. He turned, twisting around so he could see her. She touched the small black device in her ear. "Are you speaking Lyran?"

He shook his head.

"Terran?"

Another shake.

"How can you understand me without a translator?"

"I know most languages, just as I know most greetings and many other things. I have been well educated. I even know some dead languages."

Her look turned to fascination. "Dead languages?"

Tres nodded. Dead languages fascinated her? He had thought she would be impressed with his knowledge of the living ones but it was the dead ones that had caught her attention. Females were confusing. What he thought would impress her didn't. What he thought was of no consequence, made her smile.

"Can you write them too, translate them?"

He paused, wondering where she was going with her line of questioning, and then nodded.

"Marshan or ancient Varkan?"

"Ancient Varkan is still spoken by some."

"Marshan then, or old Perseian?"

He smiled at her. "I can read, write and speak those languages."

"How? They've been dead for centuries."

"My education was thorough. There are many I cannot speak though but most have a similar phonetic system or symbolic."

She smiled, a radiant one that drew another hard beat of his heart from him.

"Perhaps if you fix my suit, I will be inclined to tell you more?" Tres said, desperate to get warm again and get her away from the cells. This was no place for her. This dark world in which he lived would taint such a beautiful and delicate butterfly.

She nodded and he turned away again. Her hands touched his back. He swallowed and closed his eyes, heightening the feel of her fingers against him. They were gentle, dancing lightly over his thermal suit as she explored it. What was she thinking? Feeling? He wished he could order her to tell him everything that crossed her mind. He wanted to know if this affected her as much as it did him. He shifted to relieve the tightness of his suit against his crotch.

"Do you have a male?" he said, the words slipping out before he could even consider what he was saying.

"A male?" Her voice was small.

She was going to say yes.

"Not in a long time," she whispered and her hands stilled against his back.

Tres snapped his mouth shut before he could ask whether she wanted one. He knew her enough to tell that she wouldn't be interested in him. She was only making small talk because he was the only one here. He was sure that if there had been a Lyran male in these cells with them, she would have been talking to him instead. No. Something deep inside his heart said that it wasn't like that. She had been so open with him, so unguarded with her feelings, and had touched him. She had sought comfort from his touch. It couldn't be a one sided thing. He was sure that she liked him, but he wasn't sure if she liked him enough.

A frown crossed his face when he ran over what she had said and realised that it implied she had once had a male. The thought of a male touching her made his fingertips twitch, his claws itching to tear the male's throat open.

She went back to work on his suit, humming a quiet melody to herself. The feel of her fingers chased away his dark thoughts and he found himself quietly willing her to touch his skin again, to give him a little relief from his growing hunger. He needed to feel her soft warmth against him. Ached for it.

"Are you certain you know what you are doing?" he said, wishing that he could see what she was looking at and clawing back a little control.

He didn't have a clue about how the suit worked or how to fix it. He hadn't paid much attention during his engineering lessons. Those lessons had taken place in a room near the atrium and he had spent most of his time there staring out of the window whenever his teacher had had his back turned.

"My brother and myself are the only crew of our ship. If things break, we have to know how to fix them. I like to think that I've become quite skilled at repairing things or installing new parts. I'm sure I can fix this." Her hands paused at their work again. A cold breeze against his back chilled him to the bone. She must have opened the suit to get to the same area the commander had accessed.

Sweet mercy she was going to touch him.

Her fingers brushed his bare back and he swallowed hard, unconsciously leaning backwards into her touch so he could feel her better. He wanted her hands all over him, covering every hard inch of his body.

They were warm as they stroked his back, sliding under the suit in a sensual glide that made his heart beat faster.

"You're too far away," she whispered.

He groaned internally and leaned further back. Her warm breath fanned over his back, making him shiver and tremble. Her fingers caressed his skin in mesmerising patterns as she searched for something on the suit. His teeth sunk into his lower lip, biting it hard in an effort to restrain the moan that tried to escape as she swept her thumbs over his back and then breathed against him again.

She was going to be the death of him.

The feel of her hands on him was exquisite, addling his mind and making his head spin as he silently begged her to touch more of him. He craved it. Needed it so violently that he was bordering on turning and trying to break through the bars to get to her. He yearned for her.

Everything about her made him hard and hungry for her. He had never felt such a deep gnawing hunger and desire.

He had never wanted a female like he wanted her.

"Aha," she said and his eyes shot wide when she slid her hand into the back of his suit and then pulled it out again. She hummed, singing a melody that he didn't recognise, and then made another noise of triumph. "There."

Intense heat spread outwards from his back as she closed his suit. It travelled down his spine, its hot fingers creeping around his front and then down his arms. He sighed, content, when his entire body began to warm.

"Thank you." Tres turned to face her. He sat there a moment, basking in the warmth and smiling as it seeped into his body. It was divine.

"They'd only disconnected the wiring."

The way she said that made him feel as though he could have fixed it if he had bothered to try. The idea of exposing himself to the cold for even a few minutes had stopped him though. Even with the suit unable to radiate heat, it was still thermal and had kept him warmer than he would have been without it.

"Tres?" she said and his heart beat again, hard and deep in his chest, turning his blood as warm as the suit was.

"Yes?" He was tempted to say her name. Renie. His courage failed him.

"What do you do for a living?" She carefully pulled her hands back through the bars.

"Living?"

"A job? Myself and my brother are archaeologists... explorers. We travel the galaxy studying dead cultures and abandoned planets."

He vaguely remembered that she had mentioned that yesterday. At the time, he had been too enthralled by her hand on his to listen intently. It explained her interest in his knowledge of dead languages. A skill such as his would be beneficial in her line of work.

"I have none." He smiled again when he realised that he was warm from head to toe. Standing, he stretched and sighed. He removed his trousers, revealing the bottom half of his thermal suit, and tossed the clothes to one side. He looked up at the ceiling and then at the bars that separated him and Renie. "Shall we go?"

She frowned, as though she didn't understand. Did she think that he was going to remain here when he could leave now? He was going to save her, just as he had promised. He wouldn't allow anything to happen to her or her brother.

He walked over to the door bars of his cell and reached through them.

"What are you doing? I'm sure they'll be locked down or alarmed or something."

Tres pulled a wire out from the left wrist of his suit and stretched to reach the control panel. Pushing the wire against the screen, he smiled when Renie gasped as the small bud on the end of the wire opened and extended out to cover the entire screen of the panel in a thin silver film.

Turning his arm so his palm was facing upwards, he tapped the inside of his forearm and the display appeared, hovering an inch above the suit.

"What are you doing?" Renie hissed at him.

"Freezing me to keep me quiet wasn't the only reason they disconnected the power in my suit." Tres tapped a combination of buttons on the long display screen on his forearm. The doors in front of each cell in the block faded. He smiled at Renie. "Stopping me from escaping was the other reason."

Her eyes were bright and wide, full of amazement and awe. She tentatively stepped out of the cell and then went to go to the main doors. He caught her wrist and she stopped and looked back at him. The feel of her skin against his was divine and it was a struggle not to drag her up against his body and kiss her.

"Not that way." He pointed at the ceiling. "This way."

CHAPTER 6

Renie watched in fascination as Tres stood on the bench in his cell and scored a square in the ceiling with his claws. What was he planning to do? She jumped back when he punched the centre of the area he had marked and the entire section buckled under the force of the strike. She hadn't expected such a slim man to be so strong. He was stronger than her brother was and Tres was half Rezic's size.

Before she could ask what he intended to do now, Tres fell forwards so his hands pressed into the floor and then disappeared feet first through the hole in the ceiling. She stared, mouth agape, stunned and trying to figure out what had just happened.

She added acrobatic to the list of things she was discovering about him since fixing his thermal suit. It was little wonder the commander had broken it. Keeping Tres contained seemed impossible. It had taken him only seconds to break free.

His hand reappeared through the hole and then his head followed.

"Come on." He flexed his fingers, as though trying to encourage her.

She didn't need any encouragement to follow him. She was beginning to think that she would follow him wherever he went. Perhaps she could encourage him to join her and her brother. The thought of parting company with Tres was strangely painful.

Renie stood on the bench, reached up and took hold of his hand. A squeak of surprise left her when he effortlessly hauled her into the dim duct.

"We must move fast." He turned and began crawling along the narrow duct.

Renie crawled along behind him, trying not to stare at his backside but finding it impossible as they moved further and further into the ship. He had a nice behind and narrow hips that slowly tapered out into his shoulders. Although he was slim, he was strong. The thermal suit he wore was as tight as a second skin and emphasised his compact muscles in a way that made her imagine him naked.

Her entire body ached at the thought of him nude.

She wondered if he had imagined her naked too. He had asked whether she had ever been with a man after all. There had to be a reason he was asking her and why he wanted to know more about her. His reaction to her touch was another thing. She had seen the way his pale blue pupils had dilated when she had taken his hand and heard the stifled inhale of breath when she had touched his ears. He acted as though her touch was electric. Perhaps it was just because he was cold blooded, but something inside her said that it was more than that. Did he feel the same intense need as she did whenever they touched?

He seemed the adventurous type and she couldn't deny that she was attracted to him. If they made it off the ship, maybe he would join her and her brother in exploring the galaxy. Maybe.

She would do anything to convince him.

She liked the sound of that.

He turned a corner and by the time she had made it there, he was gone.

"Tres?" she whispered, afraid to raise her voice in case a guard heard her. The duct was darker here and she couldn't see very far ahead of her. She slowly moved forwards, her heart beating fast and her arms trembling. What if he had fallen down somewhere? Could his ocular implants make him see in the dark?

There was a blue light shining up from the floor ahead.

"Renie," Tres said and her heart fluttered when his head popped up from the floor. "This way."

He disappeared again.

She moved to the edge of the opening in the floor of the duct. There was light below her. Tres was standing on what looked like a metal grate. Below him was an eerie blue glow. Sitting at the edge of the opening, she took short sharp breaths, trying to psyche herself up into dropping to the floor around ten feet below her. She grasped the edge of the opening and began to lower herself.

A flush of heat washed through her when Tres's hands caught her hips and she let go of the duct when he gently lowered her. Her hands came to rest on his shoulders and her eyes met his as he slowly brought her down to him.

When she could almost touch the floor, he stopped, staring into her eyes in way that made her heart pound.

Impulse battled against sense.

Tres blinked slowly, his blue pupils fixed on her, strangely bright in the dim glow from far below them.

His body pressed against hers, cool and soothing.

His hands held her hips, fingers pressing in and making her ache for his touch.

Impulse won.

"Thank you for helping me," she said and he frowned before smiling.

"I believe we are helping each other," he whispered and her gaze fell to his mouth.

She wet her lips and slowly closed her eyes as she inched towards him. The moment their mouths touched, his grip on her tightened. She kept the kiss gentle, not wanting to startle him or drive him away. It was time she discovered whether it was more than her heat that he wanted. Her lips slowly skimmed over his, tasting their coolness.

The light brush of his against hers made waves of shivers race through her. She wrapped her arms around his neck, leaning in and stroking her tongue over his lips. He groaned and opened his mouth to her. Their tongues touching sent a jolt through her followed by an aftershock of pleasure. His was cool against hers, probing her mouth as he slanted his head and captured her lips.

He turned with her, backing her into the wall. She buried her fingers into his long hair as his tongue caressed her lips and then entered her mouth again. She moaned at how cool his mouth was, his tongue brushing hers and making her tremble with delight. He moved against her and a shot of desire bolted through her.

He definitely wanted her too.

His lips left hers, trailing frantic kisses along her jaw and neck, each one accompanied by a low groan of deep satisfaction. The galaxy disappeared in an instant and there was only Tres, moving her back into a shadowed recess of the walkway they were on and pressing her against the wall there. She moved against him, her body overruling any remaining shred of sense as it begged him to touch her. He pinned her to the wall with his hips, thrusting hard against her. Unable to bear the wait, she kissed his neck and caressed his cheek, matching the fervour of his actions. Desire consumed her until she could only think of acting upon her attraction to him and having him inside her.

He moaned hotly in her ear when she wrapped her legs around him and he covered one of her breasts with his hand. He squeezed and groaned again. She arched into his touch, pleading him to feel her, to strip her and take her. It was insane but she didn't care. The moment she had set eyes on him, she had wanted him. There was no denying her attraction to him now. He had to feel something too. The way he had looked at her, the way he had held her hand, this couldn't be one sided. He had to feel something more than desire. Just as she did.

She went to open his suit but stopped herself.

"What's wrong?" he whispered against her neck, his breath warm now and tickling.

"You'll get cold." It wasn't the only reason she was stopping. What she was planning to do with him in this dark recess really was insane. This wasn't the time to be acting on her desires for him. Yet the danger of being caught only added to the thrill, only made her want it even more. She wanted him. She had to have him. Her fingers toyed with his suit as she memorised the feel of his body against hers and the way his hands gripped her tightly.

Tres tensed against her and then lowered her to the ground. There was a look in his eyes that said that he didn't care if he got cold as he opened his suit. Her eyes widened as he revealed a white muscular torso and then she swallowed as he reached his groin. Her own throbbed when he pulled his erection free of the tight material and she reached out without hesitation to touch it. He flung his head back and hissed through clenched teeth when she ran a hand down the length of him, stroking the soft skin. He was so hard. The feel of him sent a warm rush through her and she wriggled her hips, feeling the slide of arousal in her underwear.

In the name of Iskara, she had never wanted anything more than she wanted him.

Impulse won again. She truly was a daughter of Lyra. She wanted Tres and she was damn well going to have him.

She stifled a giggle when he lunged at her, making fast work of her shirt and trousers. Before she could tell him to slow down, he had pulled her boots and trousers off, along with underwear, and was against her again. He palmed her breasts as his length thrust against her belly. She melted into the wall behind her and closed her eyes, surrendering to him. This was insane, but it felt so right.

His hand skimmed over her flat stomach to the nest of dark curls that covered her mound. Her hands tensed against the wall when he slid one finger between her slick folds. He groaned and she looked at him, watching the fascination flicker across his dimly lit face as he stared down at his hand. Reaching out, she took hold of his length again and his lips parted.

"Renie," he whispered urgently and she felt he wanted to say something. He closed his mouth and moaned instead. The way he reacted to her touch was incredible. The slightest caress had him trembling. She could feel his hands shaking against her. He bit his lip and then took hold of her hand, stopping her. "I... this is all... new."

New?

Her eyes widened. New. As in, he had never done this before. She moved her hand against him again, regardless of his attempt to stop her. Everyone had a first time. At least his would be memorable and hopefully not his only time with her. She didn't want this to be a one-moment thing, she wanted so much more.

No wonder he reacted so strongly to her touch. This was definitely the something else she had sensed earlier.

She felt as though she should say something but couldn't think so she grabbed his shoulders, pulled him up against her, and kissed him. She wasn't going to make him stop or let him make her stop. They both wanted this. She only hoped it was more than a crazy moment for him.

His hands caught her thighs and he lifted her again. She settled her legs around his waist and then buried her fingers into his hair as he lowered his mouth to her breasts. He kissed across them and then licked her nipple into hardness before sucking it into his mouth. She bit back her moan, stifling it so no one heard her. He moved to her other breast, teasing it, torturing her until her thighs trembled.

"Tres," she whispered into his hair and tensed against him, desperate to encourage him.

He looked up at her. Seeing her chance, she reached down between them and took hold of his length.

"I don't think we have time for this to be romantic," she said with a shy smile and he lowered her.

With a combined groan, he slid into her, stretching her body in a way that made the ache inside her worsen. He took hold of her hips and pressed her into the wall, his length pushing up deeper inside her, until she felt as though he was going to break her in two. She buried her face into his neck with his first thrust and found his mouth with the second, swallowing his moans. His tongue tangled with hers, their teeth clashing as their bodies moved against each other, his thrusts so powerful that they slammed her into the wall.

Renie clung to his shoulders, moaning with each plunge of his length into her. He moved faster, deeper, making her quiver. The tightness inside her was growing hotter by the moment and she was on the verge of begging him to make her climax when it crashed over her, sending sweeps of tingles and intense heat through her.

He grasped her hips tighter and thrust harder into her. With a low deep growl that she swallowed in a kiss, he jerked up inside her and came, his length throbbing as he spilled his cool seed.

"Renie," he whispered against her mouth.

She went to kiss him again but squealed instead as he collapsed to his knees, still inside her, taking her down with him.

He trembled against her, shivering. She moved off him and pressed her hand to his bare chest. He was freezing to the touch.

Renie quickly refastened his thermal suit, even pulling the collar up to cover as much of his neck as possible, and then wrapped her arms around him and pulled him to her. His whole body shook in her arms as she rubbed his back, trying to warm him. It made a strange kind of sense that he would be cold now. He had probably used all of the stored energy in his body during intercourse. Now he was back to square one and he needed to get his body temperature back up. It was all her fault. She should have realised that something like this would happen.

Holding him, she didn't care if she was growing cold herself. She focused all of her energies on him, determined to get him warm again. He shivered and held her closer, burying his face into her neck. His breath was freezing against her throat but gradually warmed.

Her cheeks blazed when she thought about what they had done.

She always had been impetuous. It was a trait that everyone in her family shared.

It was one that she wouldn't change for all the world.

Not when it gave her moments like this.

Closing her eyes, she held Tres closer, savouring the feel of him in her arms.

He emerged from her embrace and she looked at him. He had stopped shivering. When he touched her cheek, his hand was warm again. Not as hot as hers, but as hot as he had been the whole time she had known him.

He leaned towards her and her eyes closed again when he kissed her, slow and deep, stirring warmth inside her and bringing a smile to her lips. Perhaps this wasn't going to be a one-moment thing. There was such tenderness in his kiss, so much emotion that she found herself daring to hope that his feelings were the same as hers.

When he pulled back again, she became painfully aware of her lack of clothing and the way his eyes raked over her bare body. As much as she wanted it, this was no time for an encore and she didn't want to hurt Tres again. He stood and held his hand out to her, clearly thinking the same thing. She took his hand and he pulled her to her feet.

Renie dressed quickly, partly because she was cold and partly because she felt embarrassed being the only one half-naked. Tres watched her the whole time. She could feel his eyes on her, following her hands and sometimes on her face. A little smile kept touching her lips, a secret one that he had brought out.

It wasn't just because they had acted on their mutual desires.

It was because he had given her a sign that she wasn't the only one feeling this way.

Now she had to find out the depth of his feelings. Now she had to find a way to ask him to come with her. She didn't want to explore the galaxy without him. Whenever she thought about it now, she could only picture her, Tres and Rezic in their small battered ship.

She was almost finished fastening her shirt when there was a noise. Tres pressed his finger against his lips and edged towards the opening of the small dark recess they were in. She frowned, her heart pounding with adrenaline when she heard voices. Two males.

Tres moved back to her, guiding her into the shadows, and wrapped his arms around her. The warmth she felt whenever he touched her tempered her fear. She rested her cheek against his chest, facing the walkway around the room.

Her breath hitched in her throat when two Vegans passed the opening to the recess and disappeared from view. Tres held her closer, his arms like steel bands around her. When another noise sounded, he released her and went to the end of the recess again. He waved her over.

She poked her head around and looked both ways along the walkway before stepping out to join Tres.

Her eyes widened when she looked over the edge of the walkway and down towards where the blue light was coming from. The height of the drop was stomach turning and there were no railings to stop someone from falling in.

Far below her was a bright blue twisting orb. A large ring encircled it, with a smaller ring inside. Both were spinning fast and in opposing directions. She stared at it, fascinated and trying to get a clear glimpse of the core of the rotating rings.

"What is it?" She leaned forward to get a better look.

"The reactor core of the ship," Tres said without a trace of emotion. He seemed to know a lot about these vessels. "Come away from the edge."

Renie looked up at him and went to take a step towards him. The moment she raised her foot, a shrieking alarm filled the room, so loud that it startled her. She jumped and put her foot down behind her to steady herself.

It slipped off the edge of the walkway.

CHAPTER 7

Renie twisted in the air as she fell. Air rushed against her face and she found herself staring at the reactor core of the ship. The fall seemed to be taking forever and she lost her ability to scream when she clearly saw the centre of the blue orb she was falling into. It was beautiful. It sparkled as though it held a billion stars in its bright depths.

She gasped when something touched her and then her eyes shot wide when she realised it was Tres.

He had jumped after her. He would die too.

"I will not let you die... trust me," he whispered into her hair and held her close, so her cheek was against his. She wrapped her arms around his waist. They turned in the air and then suddenly they were going up instead of down.

Pulling away from him slightly, Renie gasped again when she saw that Tres had wings, white leathery wings that were tinted blue in places. They carried her upwards and then he spread them wide and they began to glide down.

Her brows furrowed.

He couldn't be.

He just couldn't.

She clung to him as they steadily dropped towards the ground far from the reactor core.

"I will protect you, always," Tres whispered close to her ear and she closed her eyes, touched and knowing that he was telling her the truth. It didn't matter what he was or what she was. All that mattered was how they felt.

She couldn't doubt that he felt something for her, not now that he had risked death to save her and that he was promising to keep her safe from harm.

His feet touched the floor first and he slowly lowered her. When her feet hit the deck, he released her and turned away. She watched his wings fold up and then watched in amazement as they shrank and disappeared. The back of thermal suit had slits in it that almost disappeared as they meshed, as though the suit was repairing itself. She hadn't noticed them before and she hadn't known that their wings could disappear. If she had, she might have realised something earlier.

"You're Vegan." She stepped towards him.

Tres stepped away, keeping his back to her.

"I am." His voice carried a weight of sadness.

"Why didn't you tell me?" She tried to step towards him again but he moved away.

She glared at his back and moved quickly so he couldn't evade her. Grabbing his shoulder, she turned him to face her and held his arm.

"You never asked," Tres said with a long sigh and stared over his shoulder at the reactor. There was so much pain in his eyes. What was he thinking in there? "Perhaps I should have told you. Perhaps I did not wish you to hate me."

She frowned. "Why would I hate you?"

"Because of your family," he whispered and then looked at her. "The Earth system was destroyed—"

"Lyrans destroyed it, not Vegans." She cupped his cheek and smiled at him, hoping to reassure him. "Vegans frighten me... I can't deny that. We're told such terrible things about them as children and when I saw the commander, he was everything I'd imagined. But you... I didn't know Vegans could be so beautiful."

He looked down at his feet.

She lowered her hand and took hold of his.

"You're nothing like the Vegans we're told of. I couldn't hate you, Tres, never."

A smile curved his lips, brief but a smile nonetheless. She smiled too, glad that he was listening to her. He was so different to everything she had ever learned about Vegans. He had wings but they were white like his skin, not black as the commanders had been or the stories she had heard. His eyes were different too. Everything about him was different. His ears were pointed but the tips weren't as long as the tips of the other Vegans ears. And he was kind.

He wasn't anything near the cruel picture painted by her education or the soldiers on this ship.

He was helping her.

He cared about what happened to her.

"We cannot remain here." His fingers flexed against her hand. Warmth spread up her arm at the feel of his hand in hers and she hoped he wouldn't let go.

"How much further is it?" High above her the alarms were still sounding.

"Not far, but it will be more dangerous from here on in. We can use the ducts and service passages, but the ship is on high alert. I am afraid they have discovered that we are missing. We must hurry."

She had feared as much. Her hand tightened around his. Before she could utter a word, he was running to the other side of the room. He stared straight ahead, fixed and intent on the wall. What did he see? Did he see the wall as she did or did he see what was beyond it?

What did he see when he looked at her?

Tres held Renie's hand tightly as they crossed the reactor room. Now that it was in his, he was reluctant to let it go, even when he knew that he would have to. They couldn't crawl through the ducts side by side and speed was of the essence. He glanced across at her. She was concentrating on the wall they were running towards, a small frown creasing her brow. She seemed even more beautiful in this otherworldly blue light, her skin washed of colour and her eyes as black as deep space.

When she had fallen, his heart had felt as though it was going to burst. He had seen her drop in slow motion, had tried to reach her before she had slipped off the walkway, but hadn't been fast enough. It had taken less than a second for him to follow her, determined on rescuing her from a painful frightening death. He had meant every word that he had said to her. He would never let anything happened to her. He would protect her with his life, always.

Even though he had known that rescuing her would have won him some sense of gratitude from her, he had still expected her to hate him when she had realised that he was Vegan. Her denial had been beautiful, warming him more than his thermal suit ever could. It hadn't been her words that had touched and reassured him. It had been her eyes. They had held such affection for him and such hurt, as though the thought that he believed she hated him pained her.

They had fallen together in more ways than one.

For the first time in his existence, he desired to live and to take action. Too long he had idled away his hours, not fighting when he believed Vega was in the wrong and not pushing to have his voice heard. No more would he sit back and let things happen. He would make the right things happen. He realised now that his attempt to leave the Black Zone had been nothing more than an attempt to run away from his duties. He had covered it in the lie of wanting to explore the other side of the barrier, to find people like Renie and taste a different kind of life. Now the lie had fallen away and he was left with the stark truth.

He had been running away.

What man of Vega would do such a thing? What a weak fool he had been for believing that leaving the Black Zone would be his best course of action. He should be making himself stronger so he could protect those that needed him, not fleeing and leaving them to fend for themselves.

Reaching the wall, he pulled the wire from the left wrist of his suit and pressed it against the control panel, letting it take over. His fingers danced across the display hovering above his inside left forearm and he smiled when he found the information he was looking for.

"They have your brother on deck fourteen, room nine. He is stable. Conscious. There are two guards posted outside his room."

Renie moved closer, until Tres could feel the heat radiating from her and washing over his skin. Her body pressed into his when she looked across him to his arm.

"I will reassign the guards between here and the room. We will have to take care of the two outside his room. When we have your brother, I will tap into the system again and clear a path to the small fighter ships in the docking bay."

"How far is it to my brother?" she said, her hands tight and trembling against his arm.

"Two decks down. We should be somewhere above him." Tres showed her a schematic of the ship. "We can use the service passageways from here."

A square panel near the floor to his left opened when he pressed a button. He removed the bud from the screen of the control panel and fed the wire back into the sleeve of his thermal suit.

"Come, we must hurry." He took her hand again, leading her over to the access panel.

He looked around them before entering and waited just inside the cramped space for her to get in. When she was in, he closed the panel. The tunnel was larger than the duct but there was still only enough room to crawl. He started off and then paused to look back at Renie.

Her hair was falling down. The messy black wavy strands framed her pale face. A hint of colour touched her cheeks as he looked at her and her gaze dropped to the floor before coming back up to meet his. Was she still awkward about what they had done? Her reaction, her shyness, enthralled him. It made him want to kiss her again.

He turned around, crawled back to her, and did just that. A little gasp was his reward as he cupped her cheek and pressed his lips against hers, capturing them. The kiss was slow and unhurried, a light and sensual exploration of each other laced with an edge of tentativeness. They were both nervous, caught up in this whirlwind of new feelings and a dangerous situation. He closed his eyes and traced her lips with his tongue. Hers was warm as she responded, brushing his and making his arm tremble as it supported his weight.

"Tres," she whispered against his lips, dragging him back to the ship from the place where only they existed.

He slowly opened his eyes and moved back so he could look at her.

"I thought time was of the essence?" She smiled at him and then added, "Not that I don't want to kiss you."

As if to prove that, she leaned towards him and kissed him again, brief but warm and sweet. He smiled at her. She didn't need to prove that she wanted to kiss him. He wasn't worried that she didn't want him or that their moment together meant nothing. He could tell by her reactions to him that she felt the same way as he did.

He turned away and continued along the tunnel, turning to his right at a crossroad. When he reached a hole in the floor and a set of steps leading downwards, he climbed down them and waited for Renie to catch up before crawling along the next passageway. He stopped when he found another set of steps leading downwards.

Tres looked over his shoulder at Renie, pointed down them and then pressed his finger against his lips. She nodded. He went down the steps and crouched in the passageway. Switching his ocular implants on, he looked through the wall to the corridor beyond. There was no one there but when he looked further along, he spotted the two guards. The only exit seemed to be to his left, the opposite direction to the guards. They would have to move quickly to get past them without them raising the alarm.

Tres crawled to the access panel. He pulled it inwards and poked his head out. Far to his right were the two guards. A set of statistics for them appeared down the right of his vision. Their broad builds would slow them down but they were carrying A-Class laser rifles.

He ducked back in and looked at Renie. She looked more frightened than ever. Her heartbeat was off the scale. He could see it pounding fast, spreading heat through her body that made him crave to touch her. He switched his ocular implants off and brushed his fingers across her cheek.

"Wait here," he said and without giving her a chance to respond, bolted out into the hall.

The guards immediately turned to face him, raising their weapons. He ran at them and, as they fired, jumped at the wall and sprang off it, turning in the air and landing on the other side of the corridor as the twin bolts of laser shot down it. Running as fast as he could, he ran up the wall as he reached the guards and kicked off from it. He spun in mid-air, his leg out, and landed a kick on the side of the first guard's head that sent him slamming into the floor. The second guard went to attack him again but he punched him in the stomach. When the guard bent over, Tres grabbed his long black hair and brought his knee up hard to meet the guard's head. The guard slumped to the floor with the other.

"Renie," he said and turned to face the other end of the corridor.

She was already half out of the corridor, her eyes wide. Clearly, he should have told her to remain inside the passageway. He didn't exactly want her to see him fighting. Although it would prove his desire to protect her, it would defeat it too. Protecting her meant never letting her have to see such horrible things.

She ran over to him and was immediately trying to open the door. He tapped the control panel and the moment the door was open enough for her to fit through, she was squeezing through it.

"Rezic!" She bolted straight over to the bed.

Tres moved to stand just inside the doorway. The male on the inspection table stirred and when he opened his eyes, Renie smiled wide and threw herself at him. It wasn't the wisest thing to do to a male in his condition but her brother didn't seem to mind. He was smiling too as he held her close. Tres noticed that they had shackled her brother's feet to the bench that he lay on. The medical officers hadn't been taking any chances with him.

"I was so worried," Renie whispered and Tres tried to hold back his jealousy as he watched them touch each other's faces and smile. He could see all the love in them written clearly in their matching dark eyes. "We have to get out of here."

"How? How are you even here?" her brother said and then looked past her to himself. "Who is your friend?"

"It's a long story. This is Tres. He helped me escape and come here. I called for help after the meteorites struck and you were hurt. Unfortunately, it was a Vegan vessel that answered and they took me prisoner. They're going to ransom us. They know who we are. We have to get off this ship and get out of here."

"Again, how?"

Tres smiled at the sour face Renie pulled. He got the impression that her brother always questioned her actions. He seemed to be a male of sense, one that preferred a plan to the impetuous way that Renie worked.

Desiring to aid Renie, Tres walked over to the opposite side of her brother and took the bud and wire out of his suit. He attached it to the control panel beside the bed and, with a few taps of his fingers, undid the cuffs holding her brother. The two around his ankles retracted first, followed by the one around his waist beneath the blanket.

"That is your how," Tres said as her brother stared up at him. "Come, we must hurry. I will clear a path to the docking bay but I cannot guarantee we will not come across soldiers. We must leave this ship."

Renie helped her brother to sit. Tres was about to leave when her brother caught his wrist.

"Thank you," he said.

Tres removed his hand and looked at Renie. "Thank her. It is for her that I do these things."

A blush coloured her cheeks and she looked away from him. Her frailty and beauty still fascinated him. She could change in the blink of an eye. One moment she was strong and leading the charge, the next she was shy and retreating.

"Come." Tres held his hand out to her. She surprised him by placing hers into it. "We must leave."

"Are you able to walk, Rezic?" Renie said to her brother. "Run?"

"I'll do whatever it takes to get away from these Vegans," Rezic said and Tres felt her hand tense against his.

Not everyone was as understanding about Vegans as she was. He accepted that. Her brother was a prince of Lyra. Hatred of Vega had been bred into him deeper than it had been bred into her.

"Do not believe all Vegans are the way we have been told, brother," Renie said and Tres looked back at her brother to see what his reaction would be.

His dark eyes widened in shock and then slid to him and narrowed. "Vegan?"

Tres nodded.

"A Vegan who will do anything to protect that which he has set out to protect." Rezic's gaze moved back to Renie.

"Argue with me about it later." She held her free hand out to him. "We have to run if we can."

There was a noise like a weapon discharging and then her hand fell from Tres's. Tres turned to see Renie unconscious on the floor and his gaze tracked to the Vegan who had dared to stun her. His claws extended and he launched himself at the soldier. The guard didn't see him coming. In the blink of an eye, he was beside him, his claws dragging across his throat. A moment after that, the man fell to the floor.

Dead.

The second soldier was conscious too and raised his weapon to attack Renie and her brother. Tres picked up the first soldier's weapon, flicked the switch to move it off stun, and shot him through the head. Breathing hard, he stared at the two dead men, his anger crying out for more violence against his kin for what they had done. The death of these two guards wasn't enough to sate his rage.

He slung the strap of the rifle over his head so it fell across his body and turned to face Rezic. The Lyran was holding Renie close to him. Shielding her was pointless now, unless Rezic was intending to protect her from himself. He walked towards the male and crouched beside Renie.

"She will be unconscious for a while. The rifle was set to stun. Thankfully she is too valuable to kill." Tres stroked her forehead and frowned at her, his anger still bubbling like an undercurrent through him, affecting him in a way he was barely conscious of. He only knew that he wanted to kill the commander of this vessel and everyone on it as vengeance for what had happened to Renie. "We must get her away from here."

Rezic went to protest when Tres moved to pick Renie up but he silenced him with a look.

The Lyran wasn't strong enough to be carrying such precious cargo. He would ensure she was safe from harm. He had failed her once. It wouldn't happen again.

Cradling her in his arms, Tres held her tight and close. Rezic moved to the door and picked up the other gun. Tres nodded when Rezic pointed to the switch on the side that would move the rifle off the stun setting. They moved together out into the hall and then ran. The alarms were still sounding and it was only a matter of time before someone came to check on Rezic. They would know that Renie would come here.

Tres led the way through the ship, trying not to jostle Renie too much as he ran. Rezic brought up the rear as they moved through corridor after corridor, heading slowly down towards the docking bay. The journey there was hindered several times by having to hide from soldiers, but it wasn't long before they were standing before the twin doors of the docking bay.

The doors slid open.

"That one." Tres pointed to the one nearest the shielded opening that led to space. Vegan fighter vessels were small but fast. It would carry them out of here quickly and he could easily make it through the barrier before they had a chance to stop him.

They ran towards it and were under fire the moment they came out from between some stacks of cargo. Tres unfurled his wings, wrapping them around Renie in an effort to protect her as he dodged and ducked, avoiding the shots. They would only stun him, but he had to see her to safety. He couldn't let Vega ransom her and her brother. The consequences if it should happen were too terrible to imagine. He couldn't allow another war to start.

The fighter door was open.

Tres looked over his shoulder at Rezic as he returned fire, covering them. In the distance, twenty soldiers stalked towards them and were closing in fast. They wouldn't have time to get out before the soldiers reached the ship.

He looked down at Renie.

He had to protect her.

Pressing a kiss to her lips, he silently promised to see her safely out of the Black Zone. Whatever it took, he would do it. He would kill every soldier on the ship if he had to.

He would protect her.

"Rezic," he said and her brother moved backwards towards him. In the shadow of the wings of the fighter, Rezic turned to face him. Tres held Renie out to him. "Take her and get out of here."

"What about you?" Rezic dropped the rifle and took Renie.

"I am unimportant. Take her. I will hold them off while you escape."

"But—"

"Take her!" Tres snapped and flung his arm towards the fighter's door. "Now. Get out of here."

Rezic stared at him and then walked past him towards the ship.

"Rezic," Tres said and Rezic looked back at him. Tres frowned at Renie, wishing it didn't have to be this way. She had given him the courage to do what was right though and he had to go through with it, even if it meant he never saw her again. He looked at her brother. His brow furrowed. "Take care of her."

Rezic nodded and went into the ship. The door closed and Tres stepped out from the path of the fighter. He stared at the approaching soldiers. The small vessel's engines fired.

Tres took hold of his rifle and aimed it at the soldiers.

The ship shot past him towards the shield.

He looked down the sight of the rifle.

"I will not let you near her."

CHAPTER 8

Someone was stroking her forehead. The motion was soothing, comforting and warming. It lifted the strange black haze from her mind and called her up from the dark depths towards a lighter world. A male voice whispered words to her, encouragement, tenderness, and everything that made her feel safe.

"Tres?" Renie whispered sleepily and opened her eyes. The man slowly came into focus. She frowned. "Rezic?"

She looked around them at the small bunk she was laying on and the empty one opposite. The ship wasn't familiar. It was dark and definitely not the one she and her brother owned.

"Where's Tres?" She had expected it to be him comforting her, sitting with her, not her brother. The cramped quarters and unfamiliar surroundings had to mean they were off the large Vegan ship and on a smaller one. Perhaps Tres was busy flying it. He would want to know she was conscious, although her head was killing her.

"Renie," her brother said in such a solemn tone that her heart clenched and she grabbed his arm.

"Where is he? Is he hurt?"

Was he dead? She couldn't bring herself to ask that question for fear of his answer.

Rezic continued to calmly stroke her forehead.

"The docking bay was crawling with soldiers." He took hold of her hand, peeling it away from his arm. He held it. "He told me to take you and leave. He fought the soldiers to give us a chance to escape."

"No!" Renie pushed him away. She scrambled to her feet, ignoring her spinning head and the way her vision wobbled, and ran blindly forward. "We have to go back for him."

She made it a few paces before Rezic caught her arm. She collapsed backwards into him as her knees gave out.

"You're in no condition to be moving around." He picked her up and she rained her fists down on his shoulders, trying to make him let her go.

"Rezic... please... we have to go back." She gave up when her head ached and white spots danced across her vision. Slumping with her head against his shoulder, she furrowed her brow. Tears gathered and tumbled from her lashes, hot against her cold skin. They reminded her of Tres, of how cool he was to the touch compared to her. "We have to."

"We're no match for them." Rezic held her. She sobbed into his neck and her throat constricted with her tears, making it impossible to speak. He rubbed her back. "Perhaps when we meet up with father's ship—"

"Father's ship!" It lit a spark of hope inside her that chased away her sadness. Pushing herself up, she looked at her brother. "He'll come on the Nexus-Lyra, won't he?"

Rezic nodded.

The Nexus-Lyra was one of the biggest ships in the entire Lyran Imperial Army fleet. Her father, General Lyra II, commanded it. She was sure it was as big, if not bigger than the Vegan ship had been. When they met up with it, she could convince her father to return to the Black Zone with her and rescue Tres.

"How long have I been unconscious?" she said and Rezic sat her back down on the bunk. She stayed there, knowing from his unimpressed look that attempting to leave it again would be unwise. Not only would it anger him, but she would only end up falling flat on her backside. Her head was still spinning after all and she really was in no condition to be running around.

Not even when she wanted to.

She had to get back to Tres and help him out. She wasn't sure what would happen to him. The guards had evidently stunned her. Would they stun him too or would they kill him?

She prayed to Iskara that they would only stun him.

"Over a day," Rezic said and her heart dropped. "We have been in sub-space for much of that. This ship is little and fast."

"How fast?" she said, desperate to hear that her father's ship wasn't far away. She had been asleep for over a day. Anything could have happened to Tres in that time.

"Fast enough that the computer picked up a Lyran vessel within two hundred thousand leagues around an hour ago." Rezic crouched down in front of her and held her hands. "Don't worry Renie. I'm sure that Tres survived. The Vegans didn't seem to want to kill us... but when you were hurt... Tres killed the guards."

Her eyes grew wide. "He killed them?"

Her brother nodded.

Had it been some kind of reaction to seeing her hurt, some desire to get revenge and protect her? Her heart warmed at that thought. He had promised to protect her. He had protected her. He had helped her escape but at what price?

"Rezic?" Renie's eyes filled with tears again. He pulled her into his arms and held her, rubbing her back. "I need father."

The moment Rezic released her, she stood and stumbled along the narrow corridor. Rezic caught her again and she thought he was going to make her sit back down. Instead, he turned her around.

"As usual, you're going the wrong way."

Renie gave him a grateful smile and held on to the wall as she walked. Her legs were feeling better but her head was still a riot of pain and her vision wobbled if she moved too fast.

The door at the end of the corridor opened to reveal a small bridge. Everything was made of dark metal edged with silver. She looked around, wishing she knew how to read Vegan.

"I think this is what you're looking for," Rezic said and she turned to see him pointing at something.

She pressed the small square patch on the display.

The room filled with a hissing sound. It was promising.

"This is Renie Lyra calling for assistance."

She waited. Rezic came and stood beside her, his hand on her shoulder. She looked out of the front window of the small ship at the infinite space. There was no sign of a ship.

"This is Renie Lyra and Lyra V, calling for assistance. Any Lyran vessel in the vicinity, please respond."

A crackling noise made her heart jump.

"This is General Lyra II. I have your coordinates. We will be with you shortly." A pause. "You do not know how good it is to hear your voice."

Tears streaked Renie's cheeks. She knew how good it felt.

Renie raced through the Nexus-Lyra. The moment Rezic had landed the ship, she had bolted out of the door. She dodged past the crew walking along the corridors and burst onto the bridge.

"Father!"

He turned, his smile wide and his arms opening to her. She ran down the steps to where he stood at the helm of the ship and threw herself into his arms.

"Renie," he whispered and held her tight. "Is Rezic safe?"

She nodded, unable to speak. It felt so good to be back on a Lyran vessel and with her father.

"We have to go back," she said and he peeled her off him.

He raised an eyebrow at her.

"Go back?" he said with an air of incredulity, his handsome face a mask of confusion. "I have just got you back. I am not going to go anywhere near Vegan space."

"Please!" She pulled on his arms. "We have to go back."

The door to the bridge opened again and Rezic strolled in.

"Do you know what she's talking about?" Her father frowned, his black eyebrows knitting tight above equally dark eyes. "She's asking me to go back to the Black Zone."

Rezic stopped beside her. "A male, a Vegan, helped us escape. He was going to come with us but stayed to fight the Vegans and give us a chance to get away. Renie desires to go back for him."

"Does she?" her father said and looked down at her. "You want to return to the Black Zone for a Vegan?"

Renie swallowed. It didn't sound good when he said it like that. She knew that having feelings for a Vegan would always be taboo, but her family were judging Tres before they really knew him. Her father especially and he wasn't one to talk. He had fallen for a Terran, the one species that definitely had a grudge against Lyra and the royal family since it had destroyed their system.

"Please?" She pulled on his arms again and gave him her best pout. She hated to resort to such female tactics but she could see he wasn't going to budge on his decision unless she gave it her all.

"No." He removed her hands from his arms.

His eyebrows gathered into a frown and his eyes narrowed.

"I will not take you near that area of space."

Her heart sank.

"Father—" Rezic started but an alarm sounded, cutting him off.

Suddenly, the entire bridge was alive with activity. All fifteen crewmembers bustled around, rushing from one station to the next while her father stood in the middle of it behind the pilot.

"What's happening?" Renie rushed to his side.

"We've detected something, General," a man to her right said.

"A vessel?" her father said.

"Impossible to say. It doesn't seem to be visible in any direction."

"Details!" Her father moved near the front screen of the bridge. "Give me a sweep of space now."

The screen displayed the empty space around them.

"It's large, sir," a female officer near the back called out.

"Coming straight for us," another said.

Renie's heart pounded. What was it?

She moved to Rezic and he placed his arm around her. The feel of it was comforting but didn't alleviate her fear.

"On screen!" her father growled.

The space on the screen changed but there was still nothing there.

Then a bright blue light burst across it and suddenly there was a ship. It was enormous, and silver and yellow. The sight of it made her shudder.

"The Vegans," she whispered and her father looked at her.

"Ready weapons," he shouted and then turned back to face the vessel on the screen.

"Incoming communication," someone near her left said.

"Open a channel."

Renie swallowed, fear making her heart pound as she waited. She kept telling herself that they wouldn't have killed Tres and that they wouldn't be able to take her away from her father again. She was safe on this ship and they would find a way to rescue Tres from them.

"Nexus-Lyra, stand down your weapons," a male voice said.

Her father grinned. She knew he would never follow an order like that.

"Ready weapons and fire on my mark," he said.

"Nexus-Lyra. I have no intention of fighting you. Stand down."

Her heart leapt into her throat.

It couldn't be.

Her father raised his hand and she ran at him, grabbed his arm and held it tight.

"This is Renie Lyra, stand down all weapons. Disengage!"

Her father pulled his arm free and glared at her.

"What in Iskara's name do you think you are doing?" he said, still frowning.

Now she knew where Rezic had got his unimpressed look. When her father frowned like that, they looked incredibly similar—handsome, with black hair and eyes like pools of midnight.

"Put the Vegan commander on screen!" She ignored him and turned to face the screen.

The display flickered and changed to reveal the person on the other ship.

Tres.

He looked different. He had tied his hair back and his clothes had changed. She could see he was still wearing his thermal suit but he wore a tight dark blue thick collarless jacket over it. It was edged and decorated around his neck with silver. Across his chest was a silver sash. She couldn't see anything below his elbows.

Something else was different too.

He seemed to be in command of the ship.

"General Lyra II, I have not come to rekindle a long dead war between our species."

Renie went to step forwards but her father moved in front of her and held his arm out, blocking her path.

"Prince Tres Vega XVI, I have no desire to fight you. Turn your ship around and leave Lyran space. You are in direct violation of the Treaty of Espacia," her father said.

She stared at Tres. A prince? Not just a Vegan but a prince of Vega.

Tres shook his head.

"Fire upon us if you must, but I will not leave here without her." Tres looked at her. "You will have to kill me."

"Tres," she whispered and stepped around her father. She held her hand up to him and Tres smiled at her. "Why didn't you tell me? Why were you in the cells?"

He looked down and frowned. "I was placed there for attempting to leave Vegan space. As heir prince of the Vegan Empire, I am not allowed to leave the Black Zone. No prince of Vegan blood is allowed to enter this space. The treaty forbids it. I wished to experience this side of the barrier but my attempt failed, and then you came to me and made me see that on this side, things are... lighter... and beautiful... and that I had a duty to Vega to lead it into a new era where our side of the barrier would no longer be something to fear."

She could feel her father staring. In fact, she could feel most of the bridge staring at her.

"But you're here now," she said.

"I no longer care about the treaty. I will risk capture and imprisonment for the sake of seeing you again."

"Hang on a minute! Is this who you wanted me to go back for?" her father snapped and she looked at him and nodded. He glared at Tres. "What is the meaning of this?"

"I wish to marry your daughter. To do so, I am willing to surrender the name of Heir Prince Vega XVI and my birthright. I will forsake my lineage."

"No!" Renie moved forwards again. She silently cursed that Tres wasn't here in the room with them. It would be so much easier and they could have made this so much less public. "I'll give up all ties to Lyra and Earth! I'll come to the Black Zone with you."

Tres looked stunned.

Her father grabbed her arm and pulled her backwards. "Now wait a minute! Let's not be hasty. Forsaking this and surrendering that. Who said that anyone had to sacrifice anything?"

Everyone looked at him.

She wondered if Tres felt as shocked as she did.

Her father turned to Tres. "Prince Vega XVI, if you wish to forge new relations with the Lyran Empire then prepare to board this vessel and meet me at the negotiations table. If you are so intent on my daughter's hand, perhaps it is time that Lyra and Vega came to agree a new treaty and era of peace."

She looked at Tres. He nodded, smiled at her, and then the screen went dark.

She turned to her father.

"Go easy on him," she whispered, afraid that her father would see this as an opportunity to bleed Vega dry.

Her father grinned and slapped a hand down on her shoulder.

"A man will do a lot for love and he definitely seemed to love you."

Those words made her so warm and light that it was almost impossible to glare at her father.

Everything in the past few minutes was a blur in her mind, a pleasant haze. In a matter of minutes, she had discovered that Tres was alive, was a prince, wanted to marry her and definitely loved her. If it weren't for the fact that her father was about to wreck her chances with Tres, she would have been on what Terrans called cloud nine.

"You dare use his desire to marry me as an excuse to—" She cut herself off and started walking towards the door.

"Renie, where are you going?" Rezic said as she passed him.

"We're going to meet Tres at the airlock and run away with him. Come on."

Her father stormed up beside her, keeping pace even when she was walking so fast she was almost running.

She stopped and swept her hand through the air in a cutting motion.

"Peace! That's it," she said with a frown. "No bleeding Tres dry because he wants to marry me."

"But the technology. Did you see how that ship arrived, Renie? I'd heard rumours that Vegans could fold space and move from one point to another in hours rather than days. If Lyra could get hold of that... and the barrier—"

"Sir!" someone shouted from the front of the bridge.

Renie and her father turned to look at him and then stared at the display as another blue flash occurred and a second ship appeared. This one was smaller and sleek, but still silver and yellow.

"They can definitely fold space." Her father hurried down to the pilot.

Renie stared at the screen and found herself following him down the steps, curious about the new ship.

"Incoming communication," the man said again.

She stood beside her brother, exchanging a glance that revealed they were both worried about this newcomer. Perhaps they were here to attack, or to make Tres return to the Black Zone.

"Open a channel," her father said. "On screen."

"This is Princess Vega XVI," a beautiful woman said, her appearance similar to Tres's. Her skin was white but turned blue near her hairline. Her long straight hair went from blue to black, parted at the sides by her pointed ears.

Rezic stepped forwards.

Renie raised a brow when she saw he was staring at the screen looking like a Gavaelian carp.

"I believe my brother is en route to your ship. I request permission to attend to him. It is my duty to travel with him wherever he may go." The woman on screen looked around her and sighed. "I had not quite expected it would bring me into Lyran space however."

Rezic stepped forwards again and cleared his throat. The woman's attention moved from their father to him and her eyebrows rose.

"Permission granted," Rezic said with what looked to Renie like a highly charming smile.

He might have pulled off handsome had he been a little cleaner and a little less bloodstained. Rezic seemed to have forgotten that blood caked his hair and covered one side of his white shirt.

"Curious, I had expected the command to come from a superior officer," Princess Vega XVI said, her eyebrows still high.

Rezic adopted a frown that made him look very much like their father and stepped up beside him.

"I am Prince Lyra V. This is my father General Lyra II. Our orders carry the same weight."

Renie stifled her laugh at his lie. Rezic's orders carried barely more weight than her own. Only their father's tolerance was saving them both from being sent from the bridge for commanding his officers.

"Then prepare to meet me at the airlock, Prince Lyra V, and escort me to my brother."

The screen went blank.

Rezic left the room so fast that Renie barely saw him go. She looked over at her father to see him staring towards the bridge doors with a raised eyebrow.

"Deep space has turned my children insane," he muttered and then extended a hand towards her, smiling.

He was still as handsome as ever. When she had been little, she had thought there was no one in the galaxy more handsome than her father was. She glanced back at the screen as she took her father's hand. Now she had found someone more handsome, someone she loved.

And she was getting the impression her brother wouldn't complain about what she was going to suggest. Not if the princess had to go everywhere that Tres went.

Renie walked through the ship with her father, her arm looped through his. When they neared the docking bay, he paused, placed his hand over hers and looked at her so seriously that her heartbeat quickened.

"Tell me honestly, my little angel, do you love this Vegan?"

Her mouth turned dry and she swallowed to clear the sticky lump in her throat so she could answer him clearly.

"I know we've only just met. I heard that the sons of Lyra never took things slow and never took no for an answer. Perhaps the same could be said for its daughters? Sophia married Emperor Varka barely days after she had met him. Miali is going to marry Kosen. I want to marry Tres." She paused and sighed. "I do love him, father, with all my heart."

"What will your brother do now?" he said and began walking again.

She frowned at the doors ahead of her. Rezic was waiting there, pacing back and forth. He had cleaned up and was wearing one of the tight blue and black flight suits of the Lyran Imperial Army. It emphasised his physique, just right for making women stare and realise that he was a true son of Lyra—perfect and handsome.

"I think my brother will be happy for me." She nodded towards Rezic where he waited for them. "I think he might just marry a Vegan too..."

Her father smiled and shook his head. "One Vegan in the family was bad enough."

"Think of the deal you could cut for Rezic's marriage." She grinned and patted his hand. "Technology, father... all that technology."

He rolled his eyes and shook his head again.

"Took your time," Rezic muttered when they reached him.

"I've never seen you move so fast, brother," she teased and smiled wide. "I thought you didn't like Tres?"

"I'm warming to him," Rezic said with a sly smile.

The door opened and she let go of her father's hand when she saw Tres on the other side talking to his sister. He turned to face her and Renie smiled her best smile, fighting the urge to run over to him. She had to behave like royalty, at least until her father had agreed to let them marry.

Tres didn't seem to be thinking along those lines. He strode across the room to her and pulled her into his arms, pressing a kiss to her forehead.

"I am glad you are safe," he whispered against her hair and kissed her again. She smiled at the feel of his cool lips. "I am glad."

Drawing back, she looked up into his eyes, into his black irises that surrounded his pale blue pupils.

"I was so worried about you." She buried her face in his neck. His arms closed tighter around her.

"I had to protect you."

She drew back again and glanced over her shoulder at her father.

"I have to protect you too," she whispered up at Tres. "My father is a tough negotiator. I've told him to ask only for peace but I'm sure he'll ignore me and ask for all kinds of things. Don't let him push you into giving him more than I'm worth... which isn't—"

"Which is the entire universe." Tres cut her off and stroked her cheek. "I would give everything for you to be mine."

"Don't let him hear you say that," she muttered and turned to face her father and brother. "Father, this is Prince Tres Vega XVI."

Tres stepped forward and intimated his sister.

"This is Princess Tesia Vega XVI, my sister and attendant."

Rezic smiled and bowed. "Prince Rezic Lyra V."

Renie looked across to see Tesia smiling and casting a shy glance at her brother. Tres raised an eyebrow.

"Shall we?" her father said and swept his hand towards the door.

She could see the glint of intent in his eyes. There was no way he was going to let Tres off with just a treaty for peace. He was going to add at least a promise of technology sharing to that.

Tres took hold of her hand, the cool touch of his skin against hers chasing away her dark thoughts about shutting her father on the other side of the docking bay doors and running away with Tres. She smiled at him, glad to see him again. Her stomach turned with nerves and excitement.

"I have something to ask you," she whispered.

Tesia and Rezic walked in front of them, deep in conversation.

"What is that?" Tres said and walked with her.

"I'm sure my father will insist on a wedding on Lyra Prime, but after that what will we do?" Her nerves increased as she thought about what she wanted to ask him and whether he would refuse. "Will we live in the Black Zone?"

He frowned. "A delicate Lyran butterfly such as you in the Black Zone? No... not until I have reformed it. I will not risk—"

"What if I wanted to go there... and explore?"

A glimmer of understanding entered his eyes and he stopped walking, turning to face her. "I see. You wish to continue with your brother, exploring the dead cultures on our side of the barrier."

"Yes... and no. I want you to come too. I want to explore with you, and my brother, and probably your sister because I think my brother likes her."

His eyebrow rose again.

"You wanted to come to this side of the barrier to see it, didn't you? You wanted to explore it. Well... how much of your side of the barrier have you seen?"

His look turned pensive.

"Have you seen much outside of the Vega system? My uncle was once an heir prince and he wasn't allowed off Lyra Prime. Was it the same for you?"

"I have been to other planets, but have never been able to freely explore them. I am guarded at all times by at least twenty officers of the Vegan army, and my sister." There was a look in his eyes that made her feel she was winning. "Our appearance makes it clear who we are."

"It does?" Renie looked him over. Tres and his sister did look different to the other Vegans. "Is this a royalty thing then?"

He nodded. "Our genes are slightly different to those of normal Vegan blood."

"So I suppose exploring is off the agenda?" She couldn't imagine his family allowing him to wander the galaxy when it was clear to anyone who knew the Vegan species well that he was royalty. She and her brother were only able to explore because they often went into areas where knowledge of the Lyran royal family was limited to who was ruling at the time.

"Not at all." He took both of her hands in his. Warmth spread through her when he stepped up to her and smiled into her eyes. "I would very much like to explore my side of this galaxy. It would give me a chance to see what needed to be changed, and would bring me the adventure I have craved since my childhood."

"Is that a yes?"

He nodded again. "Yes."

Renie grinned, tiptoed and wrapped her arms around his neck, hugging him. For a moment, she had been convinced that he would say no to her. She never wanted to stop exploring the galaxy but if he had refused, she would have given it up. She wanted to explore, but she wanted to be with him more.

The thought of heading into unknown territory and meeting unknown species was almost as exciting as the thought that Tres wanted to marry her.

Almost.

"We'll need a bigger ship," she said. "Presuming your sister will join us."

A smile tugged at the corners of his lips and he looked towards her father, brother and his sister where they were waiting.

"She will go wherever I go. She shares my passion for exploration and I share your belief that she may grow to like your brother. I wish only for her happiness. As a princess of Vega, she is forbidden to marry until her twin has."

"Twin?" Renie said, hoping he would say what she wanted him to.

"I am her twin. Vegan royalty always has twins. A boy and a girl."

She frowned and began walking with him again. "That takes the fun out of having a family. Now I know what we'll have."

He stopped and she jerked backwards when his hand pulled on hers.

"Family?" Tres said, curiosity in his eyes and voice.

"If you want to... not right now... not yet... maybe someday?"

He laughed at her and she dropped her gaze to the floor, her cheeks blazing over how ridiculous she had sounded. She wanted a family but she wanted to explore the galaxy first. She had said it without thinking, not realising that he would take it so seriously.

"After we have charted the entire galaxy, yes?" he said and she got the feeling that he could already read her.

She nodded and went to walk again but he stopped her, pulling her into his arms.

"Renie?" he said with a serious expression that made her heart pound with nerves.

"Tres?"

He smoothed the tangled strands of her dark hair back, watching his fingers. A look of tender affection entered his eyes and he smiled. She smiled too when he caressed her cheek and his eyes met hers.

"Will you?" he said.

"Will I what?"

He pressed his forehead against hers and cupped both of her cheeks in his palms.

"Be mine?"

Her heart thudded hard against her chest. Reaching up, she held his cheeks and drew back enough that she could see his eyes.

"Always," she whispered.

He tilted his head, dipped his mouth towards hers, and kissed her so slowly that her whole body felt light and warm. It was a tender caress of her lips, a kiss that spoke of love and affection. She melted into it, wishing it would never end and not caring that they had an audience.

His hands caught hers and he lowered and held them.

When he broke the kiss, she stared into his eyes, lost in their fascinating depths and her feelings for him.

"Ready?" she said to Tres with a sideward glance at her father.

"Ready," Tres said and then added, "Are you ready?"

Renie looked back into his eyes. She knew what he meant by that question. He wasn't asking whether she was prepared to face her father, but rather if she was prepared to face a future with a Vegan. She was under no illusion that it was going to be easy. Their union could only promote peace between the species. Even if it upset a few, it would benefit many.

Besides that, she wanted to marry him.

No. She loved him and she was going to marry him.

As long as they loved each other, she could face anything.

She smiled.

Was she ready to walk forwards at his side towards their future?

Taking Tres's hand, Renie held his gaze, seeing her happiness reflected back at her and how wonderful that future would be.

There was only one answer to his question.

"Yes."

The End

HEART OF A COMMANDER

Lieutenant Amerii, one of the beautiful and strong daughters of Lyra, wants nothing more than to prove herself to her captain and the army without her father, Captain Lyra III's, help… except maybe one thing. Van, Count of Aeris and attendant to Emperor Varka has been on her mind since she met him at her cousin Sophia's wedding, and she wants to see him again.

Charged with the duty of meeting the Varkan first fleet at Varka Two, Amerii is pleasantly surprised when the commander turns out to be Van, and he wants her to be the one to join him on his vessel to sign the contract between Varka and Lyra. When she meets him again, he's more handsome than she remembered, and she resolves to risk the violence of his bloodlust to make him hers.

Van is sure bringing Amerii to his vessel is nothing short of dangerous and his fears are quickly realised. Amerii stirs his blood like no other female and he's been battling his bloodlust since first meeting her, desperate to know what love is and to find a way of controlling himself so he can have her, but his feelings for her are too strong to resist, placing his whole crew in danger.

Can Amerii convince Van that he can love and that he's worthy of becoming her mate? Can Van control his bloodlust enough that he won't hurt Amerii when he bites her? And when Van is taken captive by the Wraiths of Varka Two, how far will Amerii go to rescue the man she loves?

CHAPTER 1

Lieutenant Amerii took one final look at her appearance and then left her quarters. She pushed her jaw length chestnut hair from her face, tucking the long fringe behind her right ear, and strode through the ship. It was the largest vessel she had worked on in her career with the Lyran Imperial Army and the one where she had felt least at home. The captain of the Nebuz-Lyra VIII was impossible to deal with. No matter how hard she worked, how much she pushed herself, he seemed to refuse to see her worth. He rewarded the rest of his crew for efforts one hundred times less than her own.

Not that she was bitter.

Amerii refused to let it get to her like that and she refused to raise the matter with her father, Captain Lyra III. In her heart, she knew it would get her nowhere. Her father would see to it that the crew gave her respect, but there would be no feeling behind that respect. It would be a hollow lie. She wanted to win the male crew's respect without having to resort to her father stepping in. She wanted to do this on her own, wanted to make something of herself just as her father and mother had done.

She envied the rapport that a select few officers had with her captain though. She envied it enough that it left her feeling on the outside of that group, looking in at a place where she wanted to be more than anything. She had worked well with her previous captain, but the bond these men shared seemed to go beyond that. She would even say that they were friends.

Her rapport with the captain couldn't be further from what she desired, from what those men had. No matter how hard she worked. It was as though he expected something more from her. She didn't think that she could give any more.

Amerii caught a glimpse of herself in the wall of thick blue glass that surrounded engineering. It was strange to see herself wearing something other than the tight blue and black flight suit that she had become accustomed to. The close-fitting dark blue, almost black, jacket was cropped short so the hem rode level with the waist of her equally deep blue tight trousers. A twin stripe of royal blue chased up the side of her legs from her polished black knee-high boots. The stripes marked the arms of the jacket too, running up from her wrists to her shoulders and from there to her neck. She had never had to wear dress uniform before.

But then she had never been given such an important task.

Walking to the bridge, Amerii went over the greeting procedure in her head, not wanting to mess it up. Her captain had chosen her for this task and she had to get it right. Perhaps then he would begin to respect her and see that she had potential and could be a great officer.

There was another reason why she couldn't mess up this task either. She would be greeting the Varkan commander of the vessel that was coming to escort them to Varka Two. They were to finalise the handover of the planet with the commander. Lyra had to make the right impression.

She had to make the right impression.

The door to the bridge slid open to reveal the curved room that she had seen only once since her transfer to the Nebuz-Lyra VIII. The room fell silent when she entered, the laughter of her captain and the officers dying away. They all turned to face her, their expressions serious. She walked down the curved steps and past the communications post to reach the group.

Each of the five men's gazes raked over her and then rose back to her face.

Sometimes she couldn't decide whether it was because she was a woman or royalty that they treated her so differently.

"Lieutenant Amerii," her captain said, his expression still stern.

Amerii looked at him, wondering if she would be a captain by the time she reached his age. Silver touched his temples, streaking his black hair. His dark eyes held hers. There was cruelty in them that rivalled her father's when he was angered. She almost sighed when she thought about him. Perhaps she should have remained on his ship where they had treated her like an equal, not an inferior. She had wanted to make something of herself though, and she couldn't do that under his command.

"You are late."

Amerii had been expecting that. She was late by fifteen minutes. His gaze lingered on her face and she knew what he was looking at.

She just didn't know why he looked so unimpressed.

"Are you here to do your duty, or to attempt to win yourself a Varkan husband like the king's daughter?"

A frown threatened to crease her brow but she stopped herself. The malice in his voice annoyed her but not as much as the laughter of his officers did. Her hands clenched into fists at her sides.

Swallowing her feelings, she bowed her head. "My apologies, Captain. I only wished to make the right impression on the Varkan emissary."

When she straightened, her captain was smirking. She didn't need to be able to read minds to know what he was going to say. It was going to be another snide remark about her attempting to snag a Varkan male.

He opened his mouth to speak.

"Incoming communication," the young man behind her said.

She silently thanked him for sparing her the embarrassment of having her captain make fun of her and then added thanks to the Varkans for interrupting too.

Her captain left her, barking orders at the officers on the bridge.

"Is it them?" He glanced at his first officer. The younger man was leaning over one of the displays at the side of the bridge. He pushed his long black hair from his face and nodded.

"It's the ship of the fleet."

"On screen," her captain said.

Amerii looked up when the view of space shifted to reveal the Varkan vessel. It was still at a distance but it was already huge, black and ominous. Two bulky halves were joined down the centre by a domed section and in front of that was an array of spiked blocks that slowly created a point, each a weapons port. It looked as dark and deadly as the species that had built it. It also looked as though it would dwarf her ship and the rest that followed.

Her thoughts shifted as she stared at the ship and she found herself recounting what her captain had said. Her cousin Sophia was her best friend and she despised her captain for showing such disrespect towards her and their family—the royal family. She touched her cheeks. And she wasn't wearing make up to catch a man. It was barely a hint of eyeliner and lash darkener and a little colour to her lips. It was purely because she wanted to make a good impression.

Sophia's wedding came back to her and Amerii found herself thinking about the Varkan that she had met there. It had been a year since the celebration but she still thought about him sometimes. She doubted that she would ever see him again though. He had said that he was the emperor's attendant. A secret smile touched her lips. Perhaps, since she was already all the way out here in the Varka system, she would visit Sophia and the children on Varka Prime. Maybe she would run into him there.

"Lieutenant Amerii, pay attention!"

Jolted back into the room, she rushed to her captain's side, cringing inside over angering him again.

The screen changed to reveal the Varkans. There were three of them, all wearing the black high stand-up collared jackets that she remembered seeing the Varkans in at Sophia's wedding. Two of the men were standing behind the third, seated, man. All of them were wearing black visors that covered the top half of their heads, the two curved sides of the visor sweeping to a point in front of their noses. She looked at the one at the front. He had to be the commander.

Stepping forwards, she recited the greeting she had practiced, speaking the old language of Varka in a show of respect for them and their history.

The commander smiled.

There was something familiar about his mouth.

Van sat up and paid more attention when he realised who the female addressing him was. His dark red gaze ran over her, his perusal safely hidden by his tinted visor. She had said the words of greeting perfectly, although with a slight tremble to her soft voice that declared her nerves. The snug deep midnight blue dress uniform she wore emphasised the curves he had noticed that night over a year ago. Curves that had captivated him until she had turned in his direction and he had seen her face. Her beauty was unparalleled. Not in all his long years had he seen one with such angelic grace and features.

The nerves reached her eyes and her fingers flexed. It dawned on him that she was waiting for his reply. She had captivated him again and he had been so lost in refreshing his memory of her that he had forgotten to say his part of the greeting. She threw a glance at the male who wore the insignia of a captain. The male glared at her. Her cheeks coloured and she turned back to face him. She wasn't nervous because he hadn't replied. It went beyond that. She drew a small device out of her pocket and began to frantically look at it.

Van stood the moment that he realised that she thought she had said something wrong. She had spoken it perfectly, right down to the accent on some of the more difficult words. When he removed his visor, her sky blue eyes came back to the screen.

A smile curved her lips, the same shy one she had shown him at Regis's wedding. She had looked beautiful then. She seemed even more beautiful now.

His breathing quickened when her cheeks coloured again. This time it wasn't shame that tinted them but something else, something entirely more alluring. He cursed the distance between them, wishing she were here in front of him, not on another ship, and struggled with the sudden surge in bloodlust. It had never come on so strong before, not even in the midst of battle. He had never wanted anything as much as he did her. She had haunted him since the first and only time he had seen her.

In all their time apart, he hadn't forgotten how she had made him feel that night, how he had found himself desiring her. It burned in his blood. It pervaded his dreams. It stripped control from him until he verged on becoming a slave to his bloodlust. He had spent long nights fighting his bloodlust, battling for control over it even as he surrendered himself to his feelings. He had tried to learn to let go, to accept the terrifying feeling of not being in control of his emotions, but it was far harder than he had ever expected. He didn't think he would ever be able to do as Regis had done. He didn't know if he could love.

When he saw her, it was all he wanted in life.

He wanted to be able to love.

"What is the matter, Lieutenant Amerii?" Her captain's tone was more than displeased. Van looked at the male, a piteous example of Lyran breeding, and contemplated ripping his head from his body as payment for speaking to her with such disrespect. "You must have said something wrong."

"My apologies," Van said and all eyes were back with him. He bowed his head. "Welcome to Varkan space. The greeting was spoken with perfection and a true sense of belief."

Amerii bowed her head. Her cheeks darkened further. This reaction to him was interesting. Fascinating. It threatened to steal control from him.

He blanked her captain and stared at her, fixated, watching every subtle change in her body language and studying every emotion that flickered across her face.

"The younglings are doing well. They have inherited many traits from their father and are strong." Van warmed inside when her gaze came back to him just as he had desired. He knew that talk of Sophia and Regis would always have her rapt with curiosity and would hold her attention. "Sophia is well and plans to visit Varka Two when work has been completed and your troops are settled."

"Thank you." She bowed her head again. Her small smile when she looked back at him told him how grateful she truly was for this information about her friend and relation. He had realised back at the wedding that she and Sophia were very close.

"Take your place again, Lieutenant Amerii," her captain said and Van frowned at him, unimpressed by the interruption.

The captain squirmed under his glare, fidgeting in a way unbecoming of one of his standing. A Varkan commander would never behave in such a way, showing their fear. Still, it was probably this male's first time seeing a Varkan. He didn't look as though he had seen any action within Varkan space.

If he had, he would know better than to break into a conversation between a Varkan and another. He would know how dangerous it was, especially between a male Varkan and a female he desired.

"Varka requires a representative of the Lyran Imperial Army to sign a declaration of peace. The representative should be the highest ranking Lyran on your ship." Van furtively glanced at Amerii.

The captain stepped forwards.

"I will be honoured to begin this new era of peace between our species." His broad smile was wholly irritating.

Van's expression remained emotionless. "You are not required. Only the highest-ranking Lyran will be transported here to complete the contract for Varka Two. You are not that person."

The captain's eyes darkened with his frown. Van ignored him and looked at Amerii again.

"A transport will come to collect you."

"Now..." The captain moved forwards, his anger visible in the tight lines of his face. "Lieutenant Amerii ranks below a captain."

"Royalty always outranks an officer of the army, Captain." Van signalled the two men behind him to go to the transport ship. "Even if Princess Amerii is a lieutenant of the Lyran Imperial Army, in Varkan space she will be treated as her true title dictates. Royal blood is honoured above all others."

The captain spluttered something but Van blanked him again and looked at Amerii.

"The transport will be with you shortly. I hope you will find it comfortable enough, your highness." He bowed to her, holding it for long seconds before rising again.

He turned away and ended the transmission without another word. It had been foolish of him to insist on her being the one to sign the contract. Even though she did outrank the captain, he had asked her purely because he desired to see her in the flesh again. That need would only lead to trouble. Seeing her in the flesh would only stir his bloodlust and bring it out. It would be almost impossible to control his desire when she was near. It would be dangerous for his crew and for her.

Van clenched his fists and strode through the ship.

He had to remember his place. He couldn't treat her as though she was only a female, a normal citizen that he could speak to openly and perhaps even act upon his desires with.

She was a princess of the Lyran royal family. He had no place speaking to her outside of formal situations.

He had no right to want her.

He closed his eyes as his bloodlust rose inside him.

He cursed under his breath and let his control slip.

Right or no right, he would have her.

CHAPTER 2

Amerii sat patiently between the two escorts as the small shuttle docked with the Varkan vessel. Nerves fluttered in her stomach at the thought of seeing him face to face again. Van. Count of Aeris. Apparently a commander too. She smiled inside at this twist of fate and thanked Iskara for his helping hand.

The shuttle jerked her. A clunk and a hiss announced that they had docked. One of the escorts left them and she looked at the other one. He was wearing his visor so she couldn't see his expression but she could tell from the compressed line of his lips that he wasn't the talkative type. The other one she had met at Sophia's wedding had been like him.

Amerii had decided back then that there were two types of Varkan. The talkative and the non-talkative. Sirus had been silent, composed, distant almost. She hadn't seen him speak to anyone except the Varkans. Regis had been amiable, smiling and the centre of attention, which she had expected since it had been his wedding. Van had been, well, she didn't quite know where to place him. He had talked and laughed well enough with Regis and Sophia, and even Sophia's family and some of the other guests.

With her, he had been different. He had hovered somewhere in between the talkative and non-talkative personalities she had assigned all Varkans. There had been moments when he had smiled at her, laughed at something she had said, or said something amusing himself. But there had also been times when he had fallen quiet and simply looked at her. Those were the times that she remembered most. She remembered the dark red of his eyes as they had held her captivated, unable to look away. They had shown her something that stayed with her.

A hunger that made a shiver bolt down her spine and her whole body come alive.

After the wedding, she had spoken to Sophia about it. Sophia had given her the information pads on Varka that she had received from Regis and had told her that Varkans had something called bloodlust and because of that bloodlust they kept a tight rein on their feelings.

It was then that Amerii had decided her two types of Varkan were wrong. It wasn't that one was talkative and the other not. It was that one was willing to relinquish a little control, enough to be amiable while still controlling their bloodlust, and one wasn't willing.

Regis had accepted lack of control and had found another way of controlling his hunger. Van had only been able to do it for short periods. Since he had spoken to her the longest, she had seen the result of that, the change between his amiable side and his hunger. The other one, Sirus, hadn't relinquished one iota of control.

For some reason that frightened her.

Just as the man opposite did.

Was he unwilling to relinquish control because he didn't want to feel, or because he feared his bloodlust would be too strong to contain should he feel?

She was thankful when the other man returned and announced that it was safe to exit the shuttle. Standing, she fixed her appearance, took a deep breath and then nodded to the two men. Both stared at her, their hands held in tight fists at their sides. For a moment, she thought that she was going to have a problem and then they turned and led the way through the shuttle.

Amerii's heart pounded. It probably wasn't a good idea to let it go unchecked. Her nerves could be affecting the Varkans. They would be able to hear her heartbeat. It might bring out their bloodlust. She cursed Van for choosing her to come to the ship and sign the declaration but at the same time thanked him for showing her the respect so few did, and for giving her a chance to see him again.

Stepping out of the vessel, she nodded when her two escorts bowed and left. The docking level was enormous. She had been too full of nerves to look out of the window during the flight. From the size of this deck, the ship had to dwarf her own vessel.

"Your highness," a familiar male voice said, its timber deep and warm, laced with a slight echo.

A blush touched her cheeks as she bowed her head and closed her eyes in greeting. It had been a long time since someone had referred to her as royalty. She never had been able to get used to it. She was happiest just being Lieutenant Amerii.

Although Captain Amerii sounded far better.

"Count of Aeris." She rose, her eyes coming up to meet his. He still wasn't wearing his visor.

Her heart thudded against her chest. He was as handsome as ever, his beauty otherworldly when combined with his incredible dark red irises. His hair had grown long, tied back at the nape of his neck, and she swore he was taller than she remembered. He stood almost a head taller than she did.

"Call me Van." He swept his arm out to one side, a smile curving his deliciously kissable lips.

Iskara must have made him to tempt her. She had never witnessed such perfection. Not even on Lyra Prime or Lyra Six. Her mouth turned dry when she thought about Lyra Six, one of the universe's foremost pleasure planets, and looked at Van. Females of mating age would flock to the planet if he were working there.

She would be there every day, all day.

"Protocol dictates that as an envoy of Lyra, I—"

"I insist." His voice was firm enough that she felt that insistence. He wasn't going to take no for an answer.

"Then I insist that you call me Amerii," she replied and he looked uncomfortable. She added, "Or at least Lieutenant Amerii. I am not royalty when I am serving Lyra after all."

"You are not?" He frowned, as though he couldn't bring himself to believe it. It was part truth and a lot lie. While she was on her ship, she wasn't royalty. She was the rank assigned to her. While off the ship or onboard any other vessel of non-Lyran ownership, she was royalty. He didn't need to know that though. She couldn't have him calling her 'highness' all the time. She liked the way her name sounded on his lips. The slight echo and hunger that he said it with made her flushed with heat.

She nodded.

He stared at her, deep red eyes mesmerising her, and the universe fell suddenly silent and seemed incredibly warm. Her heart pounded steadily, a beat that she breathed to, her lips parted. Her mouth felt dry again. A small gasp escaped her when his eyes lightened for a brief flash and then darkened again.

Sophia had warned her about that.

Bloodlust.

Her pulse quickened.

"We are ready for you," Van said and Amerii swallowed hard, unable to tear her eyes away from his. He helped her by turning his back to her and striding towards a door in the far corner of the deck.

Clearing her throat, she hurried after him, struggling to swallow her heart back down again. Her hands trembled as she tugged at the hem of her jacket, nerves getting the better of her. Her father would scold her for being so weak. He had raised her to be strong like him. She normally was. For some reason, Van made her edgy, and it wasn't because she was frightened.

In fact, it was something other than fear or concern. She trembled for another reason.

When he looked at her like that, as though he wanted to devour her, as though she made him lose control, she found herself wanting him to.

She found herself wanting him.

All that hunger and desire directed at her made her blood burn.

Van paused at the door and turned to face her. When he smiled, she saw his teeth, saw his pointed canines gleam in the dim light. The sight of them sent a shiver of anticipation through her followed by a flash of a fantasy. She had dreamt about those teeth.

She had dreamt about being with him, their naked bodies entwined, and his fangs in her throat.

Heat suffused her body and she tingled with the prickly warmth of desire. It swept over her skin, making her clothes feel too tight and restrictive. She swallowed to clear her dry throat and tugged at her clothes to relieve herself of their irritation.

"Is something the matter?" Van stepped up to her, looking down into her eyes, close enough that she longed to reach out and place her hand against his broad chest.

She ached to step into his arms, wrap hers around his neck, and bring his mouth down for a kiss that would be the undoing of them both.

She coughed and shook her head.

"Maybe I'm coming down with something," Amerii muttered, thinking it was a reasonable excuse for her fluctuating heartbeat, blazing cheeks and trembling.

Van moved closer, his eyebrows knit tight, dark lines against his moon-white skin.

"Then I will have quarters arranged so you may rest once the declaration is signed."

Amerii shook her head, her eyes wide. Staying on the ship was a bad idea. Being close to Van was a bad idea.

"I don't want to be an inconvenience, really. I can sign it and then hop back to my ship and rest there."

"I insist," he whispered.

Amerii found herself dazed and nodding in agreement as she stared at the beautiful bow of his lips.

He insisted after all. He seemed to insist a lot. Could she become insistent too? Did it work both ways? If she insisted that he kissed her, would he?

She was royalty after all and he seemed to place great importance on that.

Did that mean he would do as she had asked or refuse because she was royalty?

By the time she had come out of her thoughts, he had moved away and was waiting by the open door. She went to him, her gaze skimming over the knee length black jacket he wore. It was almost as snug as hers was. It fitted tightly across his chest and dipped in at his waist before flaring out into loose tails. He had been wearing something similar last time she had seen him. His polished black knee high boots matched her own.

When she reached him, he moved on, leading the way through the ship. She tried to think of something to talk about but failed. He had already told her that Sophia and the children were doing well.

Younglings he had called them. They had inherited their father's traits, which she knew was a delicate way of saying that they too had bloodlust, fangs and red eyes. She wished she could see them and Sophia. She longed to hold them before they grew. She had never held a baby before but whenever her mother spoke about the day that she had been born, it sounded magical. Perhaps it had to be your own child to experience such a wonderful feeling. She glanced at Van again.

His gaze slid to meet hers but he said nothing. Their eyes remained locked as they walked and she wondered if he felt the same as she did. Did a jolt run through him whenever their eyes met? Did he think about her? Did he dream of her?

Amerii couldn't stop dreaming of him—fantasies so wild that she woke in a sweat with her heart thundering. Several times the brainwave monitors on the panel beside her bed had reported unusual neural activity and had suggested she report to the medical officer. She had ignored it every time. She really didn't want to sit with the doc and explain to him that she was having highly charged erotic dreams about a man she had only met once.

"Is Regis well?" she said to break the silence.

Van turned his head fully to face her. "He is well and enjoying some time with his family. The whole of Varka Prime has been celebrating their birth for many months now."

"Is that usual?" She hadn't read anything about royal births. The Varkans placed such importance on royalty that perhaps it was normal. On Lyra Prime, they only celebrated a royal child's birth for one day.

He nodded. "It will most likely continue until they have had their first feed."

She frowned and then her eyes widened when she realised that he was talking about blood.

"How will they know?" She was pleased that she had him talking but, at the same time, she wished that she didn't have to ask so many questions. She was beginning to sound ignorant about Varka and she didn't want him to think that was the case. She thought about impressing him with her knowledge of Varka and his species but decided against it. Looking like a swot probably wouldn't get her anywhere either.

"The first feed is public."

"Oh." Her eyebrows rose. They were going to feed the younglings in public. "I think I remember reading something about this."

It was Van's turn to frown and he stopped walking, moving to face her. "You do?"

Amerii smiled nervously, hoping that she remembered it right so he would continue to be so impressed. "Yes... younglings of the royal family are fed from their father first, aren't they? It's something about strengthening their blood so they... live forever."

"You paused." Van stepped up to her. "You paused before speaking of eternity."

"It's just... it's a strange concept to me." An embarrassed smile tugged at her lips. "Lyrans live a long time, but to live forever..."

Van raised his hand as though to touch her and then lowered it again. "I can understand it would be difficult to comprehend. Sophia shares Regis's immortality now. He has gifted it to her."

"Are you... I mean, is every Varkan immortal?"

"It is not true immortality." His look softened. "We live many times longer than any other species that we have met and can give a member of another species the ability to also."

The way his dark pupils narrowed on hers made her heart thunder.

"Regis made Sophia live forever... will she need to—" Amerii cut herself off, afraid to ask about blood in case she offended Van. She knew that Varkans believed the universe saw them as monsters for their feeding habits. It was probably unwise to mention it. She didn't want to shatter this sense of ease between them.

"She will not need blood. The eternal kiss only grants her a longer life. She is unchanged. You need not fear for your friend." His voice held darkness that said the sense of ease between them had already been shattered.

"I don't!" she said quickly, cursing him for thinking that she was frightened of his kind or anything they could do. His right eyebrow quirked. "I just... I find it... fascinating."

His other eyebrow joined it and he stared at her so intently that her cheeks coloured under the scrutiny.

"Fascinating," he whispered, as though tasting the word, savouring it. "You find my species interesting?"

Amerii nodded and cast her gaze downwards, looking at her boots. His appeared in view, the toe of them incredibly close to hers. His hand rose and he placed the backs of his fingers under her chin. The soft brush of them made warm tingles dance down her neck. She followed his silent command when he brought his hand up and raised her chin. Her eyes met his and she nibbled her lower lip when she found him smiling at her. Her body mourned the loss of contact when he released her chin and she barely stopped herself from showing it.

"You do not fear us, as your captain does?"

Her eyes widened. He had noticed her captain's fear just as she had during their journey here. Half of the crew feared Varkans and didn't want to be working with them.

She shook her head. "I have no reason to fear you."

His smile widened and a glimmer of bright red flashed across his eyes. "There are reasons you should fear me."

Her chest heaved with her breathing and her throat felt tight. She held his gaze, desperate to show him that what he spoke of didn't frighten her either. Sophia had told her about what had happened when Regis had been in the grip of his bloodlust. He hadn't hurt her. It was only others that needed to fear him.

Just as it would be only others who would need to fear Van.

He wouldn't hurt her.

At least that was what she told herself.

"Not you... others perhaps, but not you. I have no reason to fear you."

He tilted his head to one side, his dark gaze penetrating hers. She continued to hold it to show him that she was telling the truth—she had no reason to fear him. He really didn't frighten her.

"I am pleased to hear that." He looked to his left and she realised that the two escorts had rejoined them.

Van held his hand out, intimating the door. Stood just inside the room were two young females. They were beautiful, their pale faces framed by long soft black waves of hair. Their deep red eyes were rimmed with black, their long lashes making Amerii envious of their looks. They nodded to her and then looked to Van. Van said something she didn't understand and the two women smiled and nodded again.

Amerii's feelings moved beyond envy to jealousy, especially when Van continued to look at them for long seconds.

"We are ready for you," the women said in unison and bowed.

Amerii swallowed her anger and all feelings with it. She had been foolish to let herself get caught up in Van. He wasn't the reason that she was here and she shouldn't have let herself behave so openly with him. His easy conversation and manner with her had probably been the result of him taking his cue from her and not because he liked her in anyway.

He was Varkan.

She was Lyran.

It was best she remembered that and why she was here.

She had a duty to do, a task befitting of royalty, and she was going to do it well and get back to her ship.

Amerii walked into the room, sat in the chair that the two beautiful females drew out for her, and stared at the contract. She read every word that was written in her own tongue, ignoring the Varkan translation. It seemed fair enough to her.

They could create a base station on Varka Two but ownership of the planet remained with Varka.

With a trembling hand, she picked up the electronic quill, and again swallowed her feelings. Her duty here was to Lyra, not to her heart, no matter how much it protested and tried to make her change her mind.

She signed the space below the Lyran translation.

Princess Amerii Lyra.

That was who she was. It was foolish to let herself get caught up in a fantasy. Her dreams of Van were just that—dreams. They weren't reality. She didn't know him and he certainly didn't know her. She frowned at the contract, wondering what was wrong with her. Was this all jealousy speaking or were there other emotions at play too?

Disappointment.

That one rung truest of all.

She had been starting to think that Van might like her, that his words about her being frightened of him had been because he felt a hunger for her and desired her blood. The two females now flanking her were a reality check that she had badly needed. She realised now that she had been wrong.

Amerii pushed the contract across the table to Van. The second he had finished signing it, she stood, bowed and walked out of the door.

The corridors passed in a blur as she hurried through them, breathing hard and struggling to get a grip on her feelings. They burned inside her, a heady combination of disappointment, jealousy, anger, and self-reproach.

The metal floor of the corridor rang with each heavy step she took, her pace swift with the intent of reaching her destination—the shuttle.

Another set of boots rang out on the walkway.

Amerii pulled on her top, breathing faster in an effort to stop her head from spinning. Her clothes were too tight. She tugged at them, pulling a face when she found no relief. Her chest heaved against the jacket. Her temperature rose. She frowned and pulled at her jacket again, desperate to breathe.

She couldn't breathe.

Idiot.

"Princess Amerii!"

Van.

She doubled her pace and her head felt heavy as she burst through a door onto the docking level.

"Princess Amerii," he called again, his footsteps closing in.

She silently called him an idiot too and then her anger rose again, breaking through the restraints that had been holding it inside.

He grabbed her arm. She spun to face him, yanking his hand off her and pushing it away with all of the violence burning inside her.

"Get your hands off me!" Amerii shoved him backwards, a small part of her aware that she was damaging relations between Lyra and Varka but the larger part controlled by the maelstrom of her emotions. She blinked and tried to focus.

Van wavered in front of her.

She pulled at the collar of her jacket and went to move backwards but stumbled as her legs felt weak.

She couldn't breathe.

Her damn clothes were too tight.

Panic shortened her breaths. Van wobbled in her vision and then suddenly he was close to her, his voice distant to her ears as he shouted. Her eyelids dropped and comforting darkness loomed up from below her.

She fell backwards into it.

CHAPTER 3

Van paced near the foot of the bed in his living quarters, wearing a trench in the plush black material that lined the floor. He pressed his knuckles to his lips, his eyebrows drawn in a permanent frown. The doctors had left a long time ago but Amerii showed no sign of stirring. She lay on top of the covers of his bed, her colour only a little better than it had been in the docking bay where she had passed out. He was tempted to call the doctors back again, convinced that their assessment had been wrong.

She couldn't have fainted because of a panic attack. There had to be something more to it.

She had mentioned that she was feeling unwell. Perhaps she was truly sick but didn't know it.

The doctors had removed her jacket and boots in an effort to give her the air she needed. She had been pulling on her clothes when he had followed her along the corridor. Perhaps their assessment was right. The jacket had been incredibly tight after all. Maybe it had been lack of air that had made her unwell.

This was all hideously new to him and it made him realise how fragile a Lyran was when compared with his species. There were no known illnesses on Varka and sickness was rare. His need for air was low so tight clothing like her jacket would not affect him. If it did feel too tight, he would have simply removed it.

Van closed his eyes when he realised that he had made a grave mistake.

Pressing the button on the collar of his jacket, he said, "Increase air density by point eight."

"Yes, Commander," came the reply.

Van took a deep breath of the cooler thicker air. He had noticed on Lyra Prime that the air density was higher than that of Varkan planets. The same thinness of air had been applied to Varkan vessels too, allowing them to travel further without need to clean the filters on the environmental control.

Effectively, it was his fault that she had fainted. He hadn't recognised that bringing her, or any Lyran, onto a Varkan vessel without a period of adjustment would be dangerous. Sophia had travelled to Varka Prime on Regis's vessel, where she had probably grown gradually accustomed to a change in the air.

Amerii had only had a short journey from her ship to his in which to adjust. To her body, it would have been as though she had gone from walking on the ground of Lyra Prime to walking the highest mountain on the planet in the blink of an eye.

Anger at himself coiled tight in the pit of his stomach. His claws extended. How could he have been so foolish? His rush to have her onboard his vessel had placed her at risk. He should have thought things through, taking into account every factor about a Lyran, and then sent the shuttle for her. What if she hadn't only fainted? What if he had hurt her?

She murmured in her sleep and Van went to her side, closely watching her face for a sign that she would wake this time. Her hair was shorter than he remembered, spread out across his pillow in straight chestnut waves highlighted with lines of gold. He hesitated a moment and then touched her cheek. She had cooled down and her colour had returned enough that she was no longer as pale as him.

Her lips parted in a sigh and he swallowed hard before drawing his fingers down her cheek, stroking it lightly. He trembled inside at the contact and the way it pushed at his control, urging him to let go and to make her his. She didn't belong to him. She would never want to belong to someone as lowly as a count. He had no place wanting her, a princess, when he was below that level of rank himself. Her family wouldn't condone such a poor match and he knew that they would expect her to marry well, as a princess deserved.

Her eyelids fluttered. Was she dreaming? He studied her face, taking in the subtle curve of her jaw and her soft cheeks, the fine arch of her dark eyebrows and her long eyelashes. The sensual curve of her full lips was tempting—angelic but devilish at the same time. Something as beautiful as her could never want a monster like him. He wasn't Regis. He couldn't love and he didn't have a kingdom to offer to a beautiful maiden. He had nothing.

Amerii shifted and sighed again, her soft breath fanning his hand. He swallowed shakily and ran a trembling thumb across her lower lip. His eyes half-closed and he growled, on the brink of losing control. She was so warm and soft, so delicate. His teeth began to extend. Taking a deep breath, he clawed back control and shut down the emotions he had allowed to slip through the steel bands he normally held them with.

Had her lack of oxygen been the reason for her strange behaviour too? One moment, they had been on easy terms with each other and the next, she had become cold and distant. He frowned as he remembered her reaction to his touch. She had turned on him. Why? He couldn't believe that it was purely her need for air.

When her eyes fluttered again, he took his hand back and waited.

Her eyes opened to reveal her rich aquamarine irises. The dark flecks in their depths had fascinated him when he had first met her. None of his kind had such patterns in their eyes. They were a flat colour, only darker around the edges. Hers were full of changes and warmth. He could stare into them, studying the subtle differences between each, for eternity.

"Are you feeling better?" he said, voice low so he didn't startle her.

She blinked and drowsily looked around her at his room.

"I fainted?" she said with a small frown as though she couldn't quite remember.

Van nodded. "Our air was too thin for you. I apologise."

"Apologise?" She swallowed with effort and looked up at him. "Why?"

"I should have thought to change it for you. It has been adjusted now. I have informed your captain that you will rest here until you have fully recovered."

Her frown stayed. "Not your fault."

Her voice was quiet, almost beyond his hearing. He bent towards her so she didn't strain herself by speaking to him. It would be another black mark against him if she did. As the commander of this vessel, he was responsible for her during her time here. He had failed to recognise the effect the air would have on her. It was his fault.

"I will make a formal apology to Lyra—"

Amerii touched his hand, silencing him and making him stare down at her delicate fingers where they rested against his. Hunger rose inside him at the light touch. The scent of her filled his lungs and his mind, intoxicating him. He breathed deep and struggled for control over his rising bloodlust. This wasn't the time. He had already hurt her, put her at risk, and he wouldn't allow that to happen again.

"No apology. I knew the air was thin. I... it was my fault. Stupid feelings. Sometimes they're a burden."

He didn't understand but she didn't look as though she would appreciate him asking her to explain.

She slowly sat up and cast another glance around his room, her gaze eventually coming back to him.

"It must be nice sometimes."

He didn't understand that either. She looked down at her white vest and then her feet, and then around the room again. Her gaze stopped on her jacket where it rested on a low square cushion beside the bank of windows.

"It must nice to be able to control what you feel." Her eyes came back to meet his. "I wish I could do that."

Van frowned at her and then stared pensively at the bed for a moment before bringing his eyes back to hers.

"I think it must be nice to not have to control your feelings." He looked out of the window at the Lyran vessel, unable to say these things while looking at her. "You do not have to control what you feel, but you can if you put your mind to it. If I did not control how I feel, then the bloodlust would take control of me. It is a constant battle, but one I am learning to... I am trying to change."

His eyes roamed back to her.

Amerii's expression softened and then her mouth opened to form an 'o' as her eyebrows rose.

"Like Regis?"

He nodded.

She frowned at the bed and was silent for a few seconds. Those seconds felt like an eternity as his heart beat against his chest, filling the dreadful stillness of the room.

"You want to feel it too?"

"I have been practicing." He paced across the room, coming around to stand in front of the window. "Regis has been teaching me but I am afraid that I am no good at it. Sometimes my bloodlust is too strong."

"Perhaps it isn't your bloodlust that is the problem," Amerii whispered into her knees as she drew them up to her, wrapping her arms around them and hugging them to her chest. She looked at her feet, wriggling her toes. "Perhaps it's fear stopping you."

"Fear?" It was an alien word to his tongue. He had never uttered it in any context relating to himself before. Varkans didn't fear. They were fighters.

Violence and bloodshed came as easy to them as breathing. They were born soldiers.

"Fear is just another emotion. What if when you're practicing, you fear letting go in case the bloodlust takes you?"

He had never noticed any such fear during his experiments with surrendering control of his emotions. He had only noticed an overwhelming thirst for violence and blood. He couldn't discount it though. Sometimes he was less willing to lose control. Sometimes the consequences crossed his mind and they were horrifying.

Other times, his head was full of her. The bloodlust easily controlled him those times. His hunger was too strong to resist.

Just standing here right now was becoming increasingly difficult.

He looked out of the corner of his eye at her, watching her push her chestnut hair behind her ear. The action exposed her neck and his gaze travelled over her pale creamy skin. Perfect. Untouched. It could be his. She could wear his marks as Sophia wore Regis's.

The room brightened and Van turned his back on her, aware that his eyes were changing and not wanting her to see them. He took long deep breaths, holding each one for a moment before exhaling so he could claw back control. His hunger abated and he closed his eyes, thanking the gods for their mercy. If he lost control near Amerii, his only option would be to knock himself out, if he was even conscious enough to do that. He wouldn't allow himself to hurt her.

He looked at his arm, remembering her reaction to his touch. She had pushed him away. She had been angry for some reason. It hadn't been her lack of air.

"Van?" she said and he heard her move off the bed. Before he could turn to face her, she had padded softly across the room to him, her footsteps a bare whisper. She stepped around him, hesitated a moment, and went to the window. "My ship looks tiny from here."

Small talk. Regis had warned him that females made small talk when they feared asking something. She had come to him with a question and had shied away from asking it.

"She is not a large vessel." Van moved to stand beside Amerii at the window. She fidgeted, picking at the hem of her top. "Once the doctors have confirmed you are well enough, I will have you escorted back to your ship."

She looked at him and then back at the ship. There wasn't any sign that she liked or disliked that idea.

"Van?" she said again and he faced her, hoping it would help her voice her question. Small talk was all very interesting but he had no patience with it, not when he wanted to know what she needed to ask.

"Your highness?"

Her frown said that she didn't appreciate his falling back onto treating her as royalty.

"Amerii." He stared into her eyes. Hers widened and her cheeks coloured. The sight of such a sweet reaction to him stirred his blood and he again found himself fighting his bloodlust. An image of her in his arms flashed across his mind—her body bare and neck exposed to him as soft mewls escaped her lips. He swallowed, clenched his fists and shut his feelings down.

She avoided his gaze and nibbled on her lip. Seeing that she was going to make small talk again, he stepped towards her, closing the gap so much that she looked at him.

"There is something bothering you," he whispered and relinquished a slither of control over his feelings so she would see his concern was genuine. "You left the room in such a hurry. I was worried you were not feeling well."

"Worried?" Amerii's eyes searched his, their rich blue depths questioning him. He nodded. "You truly have been practicing."

"Are you unwell still?"

"I'm fine." She toyed with the hem of her white top again. "I just... I couldn't... I didn't... I mean... I realised that perhaps I was acting out of place."

She spoke her last sentence in such a cold distant tone that it drew a frown from him. Again, she had changed on him in the blink of an eye.

"Amerii, what is wrong?" Van fought the temptation to reach out to her. His heart said to touch her. One touch and she would understand him, she would know what it was that he felt and would hopefully respond as she did in his dreams. He couldn't do it though.

One touch and he might lose control.

It was hard enough just being close to her right now. He didn't know how much more he could take.

"I..." She closed her eyes and turned her face away from him, lowering her head. "I'm an idiot."

Van stood silent, knowing that she wasn't finished. She was building up the courage to say something, to ask something that he could sense was important to her. Her heart was beating rapidly and her emotions were so intense that he could almost feel them.

"The women," she whispered and her cheeks darkened with the shame that he could sense in her. "They're beautiful, Van."

Women? The alteration in her attitude towards him had been because of women? He wished Regis were here. All of his crew had little experience of the opposite sex and none had ever had contact with a member of the opposite sex who was also of another species. He didn't understand.

Amerii turned away from him fully, her arms wrapped tight around herself.

Women.

Beautiful.

The answer hit him hard, sending his eyes wide.

She thought that he would want such inferior females as those under his command?

Van stepped up behind her, took hold of her shoulders with trembling hands, and turned her swiftly to face him. She stumbled but regained her footing. He frowned down into her eyes, trying to discern whether he was right. They swam with tears.

Foolish Lyran.

He raised his hands to her face, cupping her cheeks, and wiped away her tears with his thumbs. His hands shook, the feel of her soft warm skin triggering a war within him, a battle to control his bloodlust.

"Amerii," he husked, his voice tight with his fight against his hunger. He stepped into her, so their bodies were pressed against each other, desperate to slake a little of his desire with the sense of contact. He ran his hands down from her jaw to her neck, caressing the delicate curve of it. The room brightened and an intense wave of bloodlust crashed through him. "You do not know how much I want you."

CHAPTER 4

Amerii stared into Van's eyes. Their bright crimson depths and the strain in his voice told her exactly how much he wanted her. Her heart beat hard against her chest, her body quivering under the intensity of his touch and the heat of his gaze. She swallowed and pressed her hands into his chest, against rock hard muscles that trembled with restraint. He was fighting it.

He dipped his head towards her and her eyes closed as their cheeks brushed, sending a shiver of anticipation through her. His lips caressed her jaw and then trailed downwards towards her throat, his breath hot against her skin.

She swallowed again, waiting, aching to experience what Sophia had called exquisite when she had spoken of being bitten.

Van's mouth closed over her neck and Amerii shuddered when his tongue brushed her skin.

A second later his lips, hands and body had broken contact with her. She opened her eyes to see that he had moved away from her and was standing by the window, his breathing heavy and his eyes still vivid red.

"Leave," he said in a gruff voice.

Amerii didn't understand. One moment all of her fantasies had been coming true and she had felt as though Van really did want her, and the next he was distant and cold.

"Leave!" He turned his back on her.

His shoulders shook violently.

Why had he suddenly changed? Was his hunger too strong for him to control? Perhaps she had been wrong. Perhaps he might hurt her if the bloodlust took hold of him and he couldn't control it. She had thought it would be others in danger, not her. Nerves fluttered in her stomach but she slowly walked towards him, intent on soothing him if she could. She had brought out this hunger in him. Maybe she could ease it and help him.

"No," she whispered and he looked over his shoulder at her, his expression solemn. "I don't want to leave."

"You don't know what you do to me," he said, his voice so low that she barely heard the words. She edged closer, her movements slow so she didn't startle him into reacting. He laughed—a self-mocking one that made her wonder what he was thinking. "I cannot do this... I don't... I am not worthy and you are royalty... you... Amerii, you don't know how dangerous I am."

Amerii swallowed her fear and stepped up to him. With a steady hand, she reached up and touched his back. His eyes closed and he inhaled slowly.

"I think I know," she whispered in a soft tone, full of the warmth she felt inside. "I believe that you won't hurt me. You don't."

Van frowned, his eyes still closed, black lashes brushing his cheeks. Her hand trailed upwards, brushing the ponytail of his long black hair aside. When her fingers reached his neck, he tensed. She stroked the pale skin above his collar and then his ear. He turned, leaning into her touch.

"You won't hurt me." She didn't know whether she was saying that to him or to herself. "I know you won't."

"Amerii," he muttered and opened his eyes. They slid to meet hers, filled with incredulity. "You do not fear me? You do not think I am a monster?"

She shook her head and stepped around him, trailing her fingertips along the line of his strong jaw. He was beautiful even when he looked so frightened. The sight of his fear made her want to comfort him, to show him her own feelings in the hope that he would find some reassurance in them. She wanted him to know that she truly didn't fear him and she didn't think he was a monster because of his bloodlust. His eyes narrowed, dark red and penetrating hers, searching deeply as though he needed to see the truth in them. She cupped his cheek and held it.

"I have never feared you, not once since I met you that night, and I have never thought you a monster," she whispered up at him, holding his gaze.

His gaze shifted to her throat and then back to her eyes.

"Would it help if I said I wanted to feel it... that you have no idea how much I want you too?"

His eyes narrowed and brightened.

Evidently, it would help.

"I've thought about you ever since that night, Van. I've dreamed of you."

"Dreamed?" he husked, his voice echoing eerily, and moved closer to her, his eyes zeroing in on her neck again. "Tell me... tell me this isn't wrong... tell me I am not overstepping the mark... tell me what you dreamed."

He certainly was embracing worry at least. Fear and worry. Both negative emotions. Amerii wanted him to feel others, ones that were positive. Happiness, desire, love.

Love.

Regis had been teaching Van to lose control so he too could achieve that feeling.

So far, Regis was the only Varkan capable of love. If she could, then she would help Van know it too.

"Tell me," he pleaded as his hands caught hold of her upper arms and he neared her.

"This isn't wrong." She closed her eyes when he kissed her jaw. Tingles swept through her, hardening her nipples against her white vest. "This isn't wrong and you aren't overstepping the mark. It doesn't matter that I'm royalty. I'm free to fall in love with whomever I choose."

"Love?" he whispered against her throat, his voice tight again. "Tell me what love is. I fear I still do not understand it."

Amerii smiled and sighed as his lips caressed her neck, soft and slow, tender and warm. He was so gentle with her. He worried so much about her. He didn't want to hurt her and had tried to protect her from himself. Perhaps he already knew love but couldn't recognise it.

"Do you feel as though you're flying and falling at the same time?"

Silence.

"Yes."

Her heart beat harder. "Then this is love. Love is flying and falling at the same time."

Her eyes shot wide when he licked her neck and then his teeth scraped it a moment later. He wrapped his lips around the graze, encircled her waist with his arms, and pulled her close to him. She tilted her head to one side, her hands pressing into his chest. Each brush of his tongue over the small cut made her shiver. His body trembled against hers.

"Van?" The hunger in her voice surprised her. "Do you want to bite me?"

His breath shuddered against her neck. "More than anything."

She frowned. "Then why don't you?"

She could tell that he was holding back. He wanted more than the tiny drop of blood he must have taken from the scratch. She wanted more than that too.

He kissed along her shoulder, caressing it with his fingertips and pulling the strap of her white vest down.

"It is not that simple." He kissed her collarbone. "I cannot bite you there."

"Somewhere else?" She was aware of how desperate that made her sound but she didn't care. She wanted to feel him bite her. She wanted to feel his need for her and know that this wasn't a dream. Dreams. He had asked her to tell him about them. "I've dreamt of you biting me."

Van groaned and his arm around her waist tightened, pressing her so hard against him that she could barely breathe.

"You always bite me... it always feels... I can't explain it."

"Try," he whispered and licked the cut on her throat again. "Try for me."

"Divine," Amerii said and he moaned and bucked his hips against her. Her eyes widened at the feel of his hard length against her stomach. The thought that she was affecting him so much with nothing more than simple words gave her the confidence to say a little more. "Divine... exquisite... like nothing I've ever experienced before."

"Where," he muttered, his voice trembling. He kissed up to her jaw and she tilted her head to one side. "Tell me where I bite you."

She had never had to say things like this before. It was embarrassing and only made worse by the fact that she was talking about her fantasies with the object of them.

She cleared her throat and stroked his chest, slowly moving towards the buttons of his jacket. She needed to feel him skin on skin with her. She wanted to see the svelte body that she knew his uniform concealed.

He kissed her shoulder.

"Here?" he whispered and she nodded. He took hold of her wrist, stopping her attempts to get him naked, and kissed the inside of it. "Here?"

She nodded again.

His hands grazed her stomach. "Here?"

She bit her lip and nodded.

He stepped up to her and pressed a solitary kiss to her throat. "Here?"

She moaned her reply.

"More than once?"

"Almost every time." She trembled when he closed his lips around her throat and sucked. She ached for him to bite her, her body tightening and yearning for his touch.

"Do you know what a bite here means?" His voice was a sultry whisper in her ear, sending warm shivers dancing down her spine.

Amerii shook her head, her hands going back to work on the buttons of his jacket. When she had it open, she dipped her hands inside, pushing the two sides of his jacket apart. He was naked beneath it. She groaned at the feel of hard muscles and tight sinew. Filled with a need to see what she was touching, she pushed him gently backwards, and furrowed her brow when she saw his body.

In all her times on Lyra Six, she had never seen such a perfect example of masculinity. Every muscle was taut and pronounced, but not overly developed. His body was lithe and powerful, calling to her on a base level where she had no control. She wanted to taste every inch of his flesh, to spend long hours exploring his body. She wanted to feel that body against hers, filling her, knowing that it would be every bit as wonderful as she had imagined.

Van pulled her back to him.

"If I bite you here." He spoke the words between kisses against her throat. Each kiss made her temperature rise a little more until she was burning with need. "It means that you are mine."

"Yours?" In her desire-hazed mind, she liked the sound of it. She kept her mouth closed tight though, not wanting to voice her thoughts. He had said that he wouldn't bite her there but she knew that it didn't mean that he didn't want to. It meant that he didn't feel worthy of staking a claim on her. His mention of her royal status hadn't gone unnoticed. She didn't care that she was royalty. As far as she was concerned, she chose who she wanted to be with.

Given time, she was sure that she could change his mind and convince him to bite her on what was clearly a sacred place. Sophia had said that Regis hadn't bitten her neck the first time. Van had been close to it. He only needed a little encouragement.

If her neck was the most intimate and meaningful place that he could bite then she wanted him to bite there.

She slid her hands inside his jacket, capturing his waist. His lips coursed along her throat and she groaned when she felt his teeth again, scratching her flesh in the most tantalising and intoxicating way. She leaned her body into his, hungry to feel him against her.

His hands mirrored hers, grabbing her waist and holding her tight, as though he didn't want her to escape his grasp. She wasn't going anywhere.

"Bridge to Commander Aeris," a crackling voice said, so loud that it shocked her and she jumped.

Van continued to kiss her throat, his grip on her increasing to the point where it bordered on painful.

Amerii swallowed when his mouth closed around the scratch and he suckled her skin. He couldn't be getting much blood from so tiny a wound. She gasped when he sucked harder, rocking his body against hers. He was going to leave a bruise. She'd had what her father had affectionately called 'hickies' before and she was heading for a new one now, and judging by the desperate way Van was sucking on her neck it was going to be black, ugly and highly noticeable.

She couldn't go back to her ship with a mark like that on her neck. A bite she could probably hide, but she didn't think her collar would reach high enough to cover all of this.

"Bridge to Commander Aeris," the voice said again.

Van released her neck and gave a deafening roar. She flinched away and he instantly pulled her to him, smoothing her hair in a clear effort to soothe her. His heart was thundering. She rested her head against his bare chest and listened to it and his heavy breathing. He was trying to regain control.

After long moments of silence, he said, "Commander Aeris to the bridge. Go ahead."

"Nebuz-Lyra VIII is requesting permission to continue to Varka Two."

"Time?"

"Sixteen point five nine point three. Designated time for departure to Varka Two approaching."

Van released her and held her upper arms, his gaze lingering on her neck. Amerii touched it, caressing the point where he had been suckling. His gaze shifted between her eyes and her throat and he looked torn between doing his duty and continuing with her neck. He growled at the ceiling and she noticed that his teeth were longer than before. Her heart pounded. How close had he been to biting her?

She wanted to block his way when he walked away but couldn't move. She kept still, watching him collect her jacket and boots and bringing them back to her. Her smile was weak and small when she took them.

"Will you be alright?" His low tone of voice betrayed his disappointment.

Seeing everything that she was feeling reflected in his eyes, she dropped her things. He frowned and she stepped up to him, wrapped her arms around his neck and kissed him. His hands instantly claimed her waist and a moment later, his body was against hers, his kiss stealing her breath. Their tongues touched, sending a jolt through her and drawing a moan from him. She tiptoed, slanting her head so she could deepen the kiss. Their tongues tangled again, a smooth warm caress that set her body alight with desire.

The intercom beeped.

She slowed the kiss and then stepped back, fighting to catch her breath. Her eyes met his dark red ones. They burned with hunger but showed no sign of bloodlust.

A smile curved her lips as they tingled from the kiss.

"Now I'll be alright," she said.

Picking up her things, she dressed, her eyes only ever leaving Van for a few seconds at a time. He sat on the bed, watching her with that same intense look of need. A man had never looked at her with such intensity before. It made a blush touch her cheeks and she couldn't help smiling.

He hadn't given her the bite that she had wanted, but she knew now that he did feel something for her. He wanted to bite her. She could wait a little longer to live out her dreams.

When she had finished buttoning her jacket, she looked at him. He rose from the bed and crossed the room to the door. She looked around the room and then at him.

"Amerii." The warm tone of his voice carried a hint of affection. He walked back to her and took her hands. "I will do it if you believe me worthy and wish me to."

"Do what?"

His look turned serious. His gaze shifted to her neck and then back to her eyes.

"Bite you..." His eyes brightened, a flash of scarlet that faded a moment later. "There."

"Do you want to?"

He frowned, his eyes narrowing with it. "I have no place courting royalty... but I wish to. I cannot stop thinking about you Amerii... I have tried hard to change for you."

Her eyes widened. For her? He had changed himself for her. He wanted to feel something and experience love.

He wanted to love her.

"Van," Amerii whispered and he leaned forwards, every ounce of desperation showing in his eyes. "I don't think you're unworthy... any man who has fought so hard to change himself deserves to be loved for his effort... but then... I would have loved you even if you could not love me in return."

"You love me?"

She thought for a moment and then nodded. "I do... I do love you."

He swallowed and looked uncomfortable. "I think I love you too... I have this need inside me, a desire to protect you, to hold you close and keep you safe from the universe. Is that normal? Is that love too?"

She smiled and nodded. "That's love. A burning collision of need, fear, hope, trepidation and a desire to protect."

"Flying and falling, as you put it," he said with a broad smile.

She sighed and touched his cheek.

"Flying and falling."

CHAPTER 5

Van led the way onto the bridge. The walk to it had been long and quiet as he had struggled to regain total control over his feelings. Amerii's admission of her desire to have him bite her neck had sent him over the edge and he had feared that he would lose control and hurt her. Her choice to remain with him, to kiss him after he had left such a terrible black welt on her neck, had given him a strange sense of comfort. A smile touched his lips. Everything that Regis had told him of, he was feeling for Amerii. It was a mindless series of urges, of needs so strong that he couldn't deny them. He had no control over them. They had total control over him. It was a wonderful sensation but frightening at the same time.

Flying and falling.

That was what Amerii had so aptly named it. He couldn't have thought up a better metaphor himself.

All of the crew on the domed bridge rose from their various positions and saluted him as he walked down towards the screen. Amerii walked in behind him. Thankfully, the collar of her jacket hid most of the bruise on her throat. Only a tiny fraction showed above it. It wouldn't be enough for her captain to notice, or any of his crew. It would look like a shadow from her hair.

Van took a deep breath and looked up at the image of the Nebuz-Lyra VIII on the screen. Two other ships had joined it. Departure time for Varka Two was imminent.

"Your highness," he said without looking at Amerii.

A sense of calm filled him when she came to stand beside him and his gaze fixed on the mark on her throat for a moment before he looked back at the screen. He needed her close. The crew didn't seem to suspect anything but he had tasted her blood. There was a chance that his crew might be able to smell her blood and he couldn't risk them reacting to the scent. He didn't want to fight his own men but if they dared go near her, he wouldn't be able to stop himself from protecting her. He would turn as dangerous as Regis had. The bloodlust would make him violent.

He was behaving exactly as Regis had back on Lyra Prime. On their return to Varka Prime, Regis had lent him the fables of love that he had collected and he had read them all. What he was experiencing certainly matched the feelings contained in the stories and his behaviour matched Regis's. It seemed like love. Amerii had said it was.

It was a strange collision of feelings, not particularly enjoyable at times like now when he was considering the outcome of any attempt to hurt Amerii. The bridge would be a bloodbath. He didn't think Regis would forgive him if he slaughtered thirty of Varka's finest soldiers for the sake of one female.

"Incoming," someone said and Van snapped back to the galaxy.

"Go ahead." He stood tall, his focus fixed on the display as it changed to show the captain of the Nebuz-Lyra VIII.

Weak male.

Perhaps he would slaughter him too for daring to offend Amerii and treat her as inferior.

His eyes brightened and his teeth extended a fraction. He drew a deep breath and reined his feelings in.

"Commander Aeris," the man said in a cold tone. "I would like to proceed with the mission as planned if all went well with the signing of the declaration."

Van frowned when he noticed that the captain didn't even acknowledge Amerii, let alone ask about her state of health.

A Varkan would have asked that first. They would have placed the mission second to royalty. He glanced at Amerii. The fact that her captain had overlooked her didn't seem to surprise her.

If it didn't bother her then he had no right to feel bothered by it. He tilted his head back and glared at the captain of the Lyran vessel. It was hard to ignore his desire to kill the man, to control the urge to make him suffer for his treatment of Amerii. If she showed a hint of hurt, he would butcher this male. He would be unable to stop himself.

"All hands prepare for departure. Escort the Nebuz-Lyra VIII and its comrades to her destination." Van held the Lyran's gaze, trying to see if he was satisfied now that they would be continuing to Varka Two.

The male's attention moved to Amerii at last.

"Lieutenant Amerii, return to the Nebuz-Lyra VIII."

She opened her mouth to respond but Van stepped forward and stole the captain's attention.

"Her highness is in no condition to return to your vessel and we have been stationary too long. We have received reports of recent Wraith activity in the area. They would attack any small vessel. We will rendezvous on the surface of Varka Two at the assigned coordinates."

He held his hand up and the screen returned to showing the view outside the ship.

"Depart as planned. Maintain alert status. If anything moves out there that isn't part of this convoy, I want to know about it." Van waited for his crew to salute and then turned on his heel to face Amerii. Her eyes were wide and full of shock. Was it because of his actions? He would have been a fool to allow her to cross back to her ship when he didn't know if Wraiths were waiting in the darkness.

He would have been a fool to let her go so easily.

Holding his hand out, he intimated the door of the bridge. She nodded and walked ahead of him. He scanned his crew for any sign of trouble and then followed her out into the corridor. They walked in silence. It grated on his nerves. He wanted her to speak to him again, to talk as openly as she had in his room. He could sense her nerves. Was it their destination that frightened her or was it a reaction to his desire to keep her on his vessel?

"Amerii," Van said and she looked up at him. A smile graced her lips, the sight of it relieving some of the tension in him. "Are you hungry?"

Her expression turned thoughtful.

"We may have some protein packs," he said and she paled and gulped.

"It's fine. I'd rather go hungry than eat those."

He stopped dead and she walked a few steps before stopping herself and looking back at him. The thought that she would rather starve than eat a protein pack was a disturbing one. He had no experience of them but surely consuming one was preferable to becoming weak. He couldn't allow her to starve herself. A frown married his eyebrows at the thought but then he reminded himself that her wish was his command. If she did not want to eat, it wasn't his place to force her. He only wished that he could find an alternative source of sustenance for her.

"I am sorry." Van bowed his head, feeling foolish for not allowing Amerii to return to her ship where she could have eaten. Now she was going to starve with him and grow weak. He should have been more responsible and thought things through. In his haste to have her near to him, he had again placed her in danger.

She smiled, wide and warm, her blue eyes shining with it. He could drown in those. They reminded him of the pure Lyran skies. He had never seen skies like them before, not in all his life, and he had never thought it possible to capture something so beautiful, so powerful, in something as small as irises.

"There isn't anything to apologise for." Amerii walked back to him.

"We have no other food besides... blood." He waited for her smile to fade but it remained constant. He wondered what amused her when it widened a little. Her fingers against his startled him and he frowned down at their hands where they touched and then looked into her eyes. They swam with gratitude.

It dawned on him that it was because he was worried about her.

Her hand shifted against his, sending his eyes falling to her mouth and his heart beating faster. He wanted to kiss her again. The feel of her warm fingers against his, soft and tender in their caress, made him surrender a little of the vice-like grip he held his emotions in. He wanted to kiss her and he wanted her to know his feelings from it.

His fingers closed over hers and he pulled her to him, into his arms where she belonged. He wrapped them around her and she leaned her head back, her lips parting in silent tempting invitation. He lowered his mouth to hers and brushed his lips slowly and lightly against hers. Warmth chased through him, his lips tingling where they caressed hers, his body burning where her hands pressed against his chest. She leaned into him and he tilted his head, his tongue parting her lips to tangle with hers.

It was divine but frightening to realise how much these new emotions ruled him. More than hatred and violence ever could. With these feelings, he felt as though he was falling uncontrollably but it was so exhilarating that he could be flying, just as Amerii had said. It was incredible. It was intoxicating.

It was everything Regis had said.

And at the same time, it was so much more.

Amerii moaned quietly into his mouth as their tongues tangled, hers gliding sensually along the length of his, drawing more of his feelings from him. The smooth brush of her lips over his stole more of his control and a creeping sensation spread over his neck and down his spine. A strange surge in awareness followed it. After that came the familiar itch of his canines and claws, and a growing hunger for violence.

Bloodlust.

He tried to contain it but it was too strong, pushing at the restraints and whispering tempting words to him. Amerii's tongue stroked his canines and all sense of control shattered.

Two people were approaching.

Terrible timing on their part.

Stepping back from Amerii, he glared at them, his chest heaving as he fought for breath and control. He needed control.

No.

He needed violence. Violence and blood. Then he would have his sweet relief. He would have his most heartfelt desire.

He would have Amerii to himself.

If he killed these two officers that were approaching him—this odious male and female that were exchanging a glance—then he would have Amerii to himself again. He growled when they both looked at Amerii, a look in their eyes that spoke clearly of amusement and disgust. How dare they look at her like that? How dare they think to judge her for his actions?

His eyes narrowed.

His teeth extended.

The officers stopped dead and looked at him, their own eyes wide.

The male officer's eyes moved back to Amerii.

With a roar, Van launched himself at them. He knocked the female to the side, slamming her into the wall of the corridor, and rushed headlong into the male. The female landed hard on the deck in a crumpled heap. The male barely had time to raise his hands before Van barrelled into him, tackling to the ground. Van growled as he locked his hands around the male's throat. How dare he look at Amerii?

Amerii was his and his alone. He wouldn't let such an inferior male look at her like that, wouldn't surrender her to any male. She was his.

His hands closed around the male's throat, choking him. The male's eyes slowly brightened, turning crimson. Van grinned and throttled him. Yes. A fight for Amerii. He would show this male that he was stronger and the male would leave her alone. He would prove his strength to Amerii and she would become his mate. A female desired a strong mate. One who could protect her.

He would protect her.

A strange light sound punctured the rushing noise in his head—the sound of his heart pounding and his blood thundering through his veins. He ignored it, intent on making the male pay.

The male's eyes were vivid red now, fixed on him, starting to narrow.

A fight they would have.

Van growled when the male pressed his feet into his stomach and kicked him off, sending him into the wall. He picked himself up and retaliated, launching himself back at the male. The male swiped at him, catching him across the face with his claws. Van threw a punch at him at the same time, his fist slamming hard into the male's jaw and knocking him off balance.

The female was getting up.

The light sound came again, stronger this time. A word perhaps? Someone speaking to him? In the haze of the bloodlust, he knew no voices, not even his own. Someone he knew? It was familiar but gone in an instant, swept away by the scent of fear and blood. His lust for violence increased—an incredible thirst that he was dying to slake.

He went to knock the female back down, flinging his arm out to backhand her, but someone else was suddenly there.

His eyes widened.

His hand stopped a hair's breadth from her face.

Amerii.

Her eyes were large and round, her mouth open in shock, and her skin was the colour of stars.

With a growl, Van caught her around the wrist and pulled her into his arms, wrapping them tight around her. Her hands pressed against his chest. She was shaking.

He had frightened her.

The knowledge of that allowed him to drag back a modicum of control, enough for the haze of bloodlust to lift and for his senses to come back.

"Please stop," Amerii whispered against his chest, a light sound in a dark world.

It had been her voice. She had been trying to speak to him, to make him stop.

Breathing hard, Van willed his heart to slow, and methodically shut down his feelings one by one until he was finally in control again.

The female was helping the male officer up. Van looked at them both as they turned to face him. The male wiped his hand across his face, clearing blood away from his lips. Van's jaw tensed and he couldn't bring himself to look into the male's eyes. It wasn't guilt making him look away. It was a desire to retain control. If he looked at the male, he would lose it again. The bloodlust would demand his head for the way he had looked at Amerii as though she was a potential mate for him.

The two officers saluted him.

Van cleared his throat and slowly released Amerii, allowing her to come out of his embrace but not letting her go completely. His arm remained around her, keeping her close.

"My apologies." Van bowed his head. "I was not in control of myself. Please report to the infirmary and have them attend to your injuries. I will report my actions to Emperor Varka and ask his forgiveness."

The two officers bowed and went to pass him.

He hesitated a moment and then frowned.

"Halt." He cursed himself for what he had done. He couldn't risk the ship discovering what had happened here, not because it would disgrace him, but because it would disgrace Amerii. "If you speak of this matter to anyone, there will be consequences. As a member of royalty, Princess Amerii deserves your kindness. Refrain from discussing what you witnessed here."

They nodded, saluted, and then walked away in dead silence.

He knew they wouldn't dare speak of what had happened to anyone. Every member of his crew were loyal Varkans, placing royalty above all else, and obeying all orders given to them. They would probably never even mention who had attacked them in the first place. Matters of bloodlust were rarely spoken of. Varkans protected the identity of those who had suffered and hurt another Varkan because of it, for the simple reason that they wanted the same courtesy extended to them should they come under the influence of it.

Amerii touched his hand, the light caress dragging him out of his dark thoughts. He turned to face her and was surprised to find her smiling.

"I am sorry. I have not only compromised you but I have frightened you," he said and placed his hand over hers.

"I knew that you wouldn't hurt me." She sighed. There was no trace of fear in her eyes as she looked at him. "I only wanted you to stop before you killed that man. I understand why you did it—because you wanted to protect me... because I am yours... it shocked me, that's all. I promise. I wasn't scared."

She smiled wider and shook her head as she reached up and swiped her thumb across his cheek. The action made him aware of the cut that dashed across it. It stung as she caressed it and when she brought her hand away, he couldn't help looking at the blood on it. What had he done? Not only had he compromised her, but he had attacked his crew. He closed his eyes and his jaw tensed. How could Amerii want a monster like him? He had been so close to hitting her. Lost in the haze of the bloodlust, he had barely been able to stop himself. If he had hit her, he didn't know what he would have done. Such a low, violent creature wasn't worthy of her. She deserved better. She deserved a prince, a male who would keep her safe from such a violent world as his, from such a dark heart.

His fists clenched.

He would kill any such male.

Amerii was his. Without her, he couldn't function, couldn't think or even breathe. The thought of her leaving made his throat tight, stealing his air. The idea that she might think him a monster now that he had proven himself one made his heart clench. It ached in a dull strange way. He rubbed the spot above it on his chest, trying to alleviate the pain.

"You have seen me for what I am now," Van whispered at his hand, rubbing the same patch of his sternum. The pain wasn't going away. It was only getting worse. "I am a monster, Amerii, a creature of bloodshed and destruction. I am a beast unworthy of you. You would do better to risk the Wraiths and return to your ship than to remain here with me."

Her hand appeared in view, steady as a rock as she placed it over his where it continued to rub his chest. He stopped, looking at the way she had curled her fingers over his and checking her with his senses. She was surprisingly calm, only a hint of anger lacing her scent.

"You are not a monster," Amerii whispered back at him. She stepped closer, narrowing the gap between them. He could feel her heat, could hear her heart beating steadily, and feel her soft breath on their hands. "Look at me, Van, please?"

The imploring edge to her tone made him do just that. Lifting his gaze, he looked into her eyes and saw tears shining in their blue depths. Not tears of fear, but of sadness. He checked her again and realised that what he had thought was anger was actually sorrow.

"You were defending me." Amerii's hand left his, coming up to capture his cheek. The touch was light, tender, and the pain in his chest dulled a little. "I don't think you're a monster... or unworthy of me. I wanted to see you again. I even thought about going to see Sophia and Regis because I thought perhaps you would be there."

His heartbeat doubled at that confession.

"You did?" Van needed to hear her say it again, needing her to tell him that she still had feelings for him and that he hadn't frightened her away. The daughters of Lyra were strong, but was she strong enough to love him? Regis had discovered love and had found a way to temper the bloodlust around Sophia, but Regis was far older than he was. Royalty aged slower than normal Varkans. Van didn't know if he was strong enough yet to do as Regis had done, or whether he would ever be strong enough.

And Amerii deserved to be loved.

"I did... I wanted to see you Van. I was so happy when you appeared on that screen. I was so happy when you asked me to come here. I'm still happy now. Nothing has changed. I know about Varkans, enough to prepare me for anything that you might do. Sophia has told me all about the bloodlust and how Regis reacted. I wasn't surprised by your reaction to the male, and I know if it had only been the female you wouldn't have reacted so strongly. You were trying to protect me from the male... because you see me as yours. I want to be yours."

He went to speak again but she tiptoed and kissed him. It was sweet, tender, and he couldn't help responding to it. His arms slid around her waist and he tugged her against him, so the full length of her body pressed into his. He leaned into her, kissing her with more force than before, hungry to taste her and to feel her body on his. Her hands caught his shoulders and she moaned into his mouth.

He pushed her off him, getting the better of himself. Looking down at the floor, he cursed himself for kissing her again in the hall.

"It is my duty to protect you while you are on this vessel," he whispered to their feet, afraid of looking at her in case he couldn't stop himself from kissing her again. His hands shook as he fought to restrain the feelings that she brought out in him. The subtle taste of her blood filled his mouth, its memory as potent as the reality had been. His eyes brightened as his teeth extended slightly. She wanted him. She wanted to be his. He could make her his. He compressed his lips, grinding his teeth together in an effort to stop them from changing further. The hunger subsided with the memory of her blood. "That includes not exposing you to comments about your personal life."

Her fingers grazed his cheek, sending a warm shiver across his skin. "Is it your duty, or your desire to protect me? It looks like desire from where I'm standing."

Her voice was so sultry a whisper that he had to look at her. Her eyes were wide, their enchanting sky blue depths darkened by her enlarged pupils. He wasn't the only one the kiss had aroused. He could sense her hunger, could feel it in her touch and see it all in her eyes.

Taking her hand, he held it tight, feeling it shake in his. She knew as well as he did that they stood together on a precipice, facing a point of no return, and neither knew where it would take them. He didn't know if he could control himself in the heat of the moment. Something about Amerii, about his feelings for her, made his bloodlust difficult to control. He only hoped that his feelings towards her would protect her from the bloodlust when it overwhelmed him.

His eyes held hers, his heart thundering as his mind raced to imagine the feel of her body against his, and the bloodlust began to push at the boundaries of his restraint. To feel everything that he wanted to, to show her what he wanted to, he would have to relinquish control. He wasn't afraid. He believed now, just as Amerii believed.

He wouldn't hurt her.

He wouldn't allow himself to.

His eyes brightened and he held her hand tighter.

"If you wish to see desire... I can show you just how much I feel for you."

CHAPTER 6

Amerii stumbled along behind Van as he marched down the corridor. She knew where he was taking her and she wasn't afraid, not even if her heart was threatening to burst out of her chest. She ignored it and held his hand. His vice-like grip on her was painful but she endured it, knowing that he had little control over himself. She had seen his eyes change. She had never seen them so bright or so full of conflict. There was violence in their depths, but fear and love tempered it. This was a leap forward for both of them, and she wouldn't fool herself into thinking that it wasn't a dangerous one. She had faith in Van though. He had been practicing relinquishing control since they had first met a year ago. In that time, he must have made substantial progress. He had made enough that he could kiss her without hurting her but when he had tasted her blood earlier he'd had trouble maintaining control. He had bordered on violent when his crew had interrupted them and had almost killed the officers back in the corridor.

Sophia had told her that Regis had fought the palace guards when he had been lost in his bloodlust. He had wanted to kill them because they had interrupted him. Perhaps it was vital to make sure that didn't happen when she was with Van. Maybe if she locked them away and removed all possible methods of communication from the room then he would be all right and wouldn't perceive any threat to her. Once her blood was in his system, and she suspected what he had in mind would involve biting, he would become unpredictable. The bloodlust would take him completely. There was no doubt about that. When it did, she had to remain calm and she had to pray they weren't disturbed. The thought of Van hurting his crew because of her was sickening. She hadn't wanted to be responsible for that and she didn't want it to happen again.

They reached his door and it opened as though it had recognised him. Amerii tripped on her feet when Van pulled her inside and clung to his arms to stop herself from falling. He held her elbows and helped her stand again.

The door closed.

"Amerii," Van whispered in a tight voice full of emotion. She looked up into his vivid red eyes. "Do not fear me."

Amerii shook her head and brought her hand up to touch his cheek. She could feel him shaking. He closed his eyes and leaned into her touch.

"Know that I am yours to command. Even in the haze of the bloodlust, I may still respond to you even before I have claimed you as rightfully mine. I heard your voice back in the corridor. If you are frightened, do not hesitate to stop me."

Amerii liked those words. Yours. Claimed. Mine. They had a beautiful ring of certainty about them. They sounded strong and fixed, unwavering. She was his. He was hers. Once he had placed a claim on her, then she would never have to fear the bloodlust again.

Sophia had told her that too.

When they were bonded, Van would no longer perceive everyone as a threat to her when he was in the bloodlust. He would be able to assess the danger and act accordingly.

He would no longer see every male as a potential mate for her.

It was that desire to protect what was his that would make him dangerous until they were bonded.

She went to the door and frowned at the control panel beside it. It was totally different to any she had ever seen.

"Do you wish to leave?"

Those whispered words carried pain that cut deep into her heart. She spun on the spot to face Van and shook her head again.

"No, Van... never." Amerii went back to him when she saw all the hurt in his red eyes. She touched his cheek again and he brought his hand up to claim hers, holding it tight as he pressed a kiss to her palm.

It was strange to see so strong a man act so weak. A desire to protect him in return rose inside her and she wrapped her arms around him, hoping that her embrace would give him the reassurance he needed. He buried his face into her neck, his hands claiming her waist and pulling her body flush against his.

"I wanted to lock the door." She ran her fingers through his fine long black hair. "Maybe cut communications so we'll be truly alone."

"Amerii," Van whispered into her neck. "As the commander of this vessel, I must maintain contact with my crew."

She frowned and then smiled. "Would you cut communications if a member of royalty ordered you to?"

He came out of her embrace and looked deep into her eyes. "An order?"

Amerii nodded. She had to make sure that no one could disturb them, or at least ensure that she had stopped every possible method of interruption. She couldn't do anything if someone was foolish enough to knock on the door.

Van left her arms and walked past her to the door. He pressed a series of buttons on the control panel and then turned to face her. She bit her lip, nerves churning her stomach as she watched him remove his communication device from his collar.

She swallowed when he followed that by removing his jacket, revealing his bare torso. This was really happening. Everything she had fantasised about was on the brink of coming true. With trembling fingers, she undid the fastenings of her jacket and walked towards him. It felt as though this was her first time again. She hadn't been this nervous about sex in years.

Then again, she hadn't had sex in years. Every male in the fleet avoided her and she wasn't naive enough not to realise why. Her father had ordered all Lyran males of mating age within the army to keep their hands off her. It was a good job that she and her friends had visited Lyra Six all those times or she really would have been facing her first time. As enjoyable as being royalty was, it certainly had its downsides too. Usually when a man realised she was a princess, they were quick to run in the opposite direction. She didn't think her father was that frightening, and it wasn't as though she had to marry every man she was intimate with.

But then, she would marry Van in a heartbeat.

He stepped up to her and pushed her open jacket off her shoulders. The feel of his hands grazing her arms sent a warm shiver of pleasure through her and her eyes half closed, her lips parting.

"Are we alone now?" she whispered, lost in the feel of his touch. Her jacket fell to the floor.

His hands skimmed up her sides, fingers brushing the undersides of her breasts. She sighed and furrowed her brow, her mouth turning dry.

"Yes," Van husked in a voice so low it sent her trembling. His breath was hot against her cheek as he moved closer to her and lowered his hands to her sides again. This time when he brought them up, he raised the hem of her white vest with them. His hands brushed her bare stomach, sending a powerful jolt through her that made her hands tremble with the need to touch him.

She had to feel him and feel this was real.

Her touch was a tentative caress at first, tracing the line between his pectorals. Her eyes opened, her gaze tracking her hands as she flattened them against his chest, her fingertips pressing in. He tensed his muscles. They were rock hard, sending an ache to her stomach that made her hunger rise. She wanted to feel every inch of him, wanted to lose herself in the moment and the pleasure she knew that he could give her. There wasn't a man like him in the universe. None of the men of Lyra Six compared to Van.

Her fingers trailed lower, charting the pronounced muscles of his stomach with a light caress. Van trembled beneath her wandering hands, his breathing shaky. A glance into his eyes revealed they were vivid crimson, intently fixed on her face. He pushed his hands up and under her vest, claiming her bare breasts. She bit her lip to stifle the moan that tried to escape her when his thumbs brushed her pebbled nipples. Sparks shot out from their hardened points each time this thumbs tortured them. She pushed her breasts into his hands, eager to feel more than his hands on her. Her mind raced to imagine how it would feel to have his mouth on her, his teeth teasing her nipples and tongue torturing her.

"Touch me," she begged, arching into his palms, aching inside.

Van growled and pulled her vest off. The chill air sent a wave of goose bumps washing over her skin. Her heart pounded as he pulled her into his arms and picked her up. She clung to him, peppering kisses across his cheek, his forehead, his neck, anywhere she could reach. She bit lightly on his collarbone and he stilled. The air in the room seemed to shift, turning heavy and hard to breathe. He threw her down on the bed, towering over her, his eyes red and intense. His fingers stroked the point on his neck where she had bitten.

Amerii's breathing quickened as she stared into his eyes, seeing his feelings battling inside him. Biting him might not have been her greatest ever idea.

With a low rumbling growl, he covered her body with his, his hands claiming her wrists and pinning them to the bed.

A little more dominant than she had expected.

She wriggled to get free and his grip tightened. His lips parted to reveal sharp teeth. The shine left his eyes, making her feel as though he was no longer conscious of what he was doing. He lowered his head towards her and she gasped when he kissed her. Rough. Passionate. Everything she had imagined it would be and so much more. His mouth slanted over hers, his tongue thrusting into her mouth. She tried to respond but he was too fierce. Their teeth clashed. Too hungry. She submitted to him, hoping he would calm down. A flash of pain burst in her lip and her eyes widened when she tasted blood.

Blood.

Van's kisses grew hungrier, deeper, stealing her breath and turning her giddy. She pushed her arms up but he growled and shoved her wrists harder against the bed. Wrestling her mouth free of his, she turned her head to the side, breathing hard in an effort to clear her head. It spun but she wasn't frightened. She knew in her heart that Van wouldn't hurt her. He was just caught up in the moment and the bloodlust.

"Van," she whispered to her arm, staring at his right hand where it tightly gripped her wrist. Her hands were pale. He was holding her too tight.

His body pressed against hers and she moaned internally at the feel of his hard arousal grinding against her groin.

"Van?" she whispered again, hoping he would hear her wherever he had gone off to. She didn't feel as though he was here with her. He had said that she might be able to get through to him when he was lost in the bloodlust. She hoped that he was right.

He dipped his head and kissed her neck, constantly returning to lick the arch of it above her collarbone. It tingled and then she felt nothing. Whenever his tongue brushed it now, it felt as though he hadn't touched her. It felt missing, numb.

Her eyes widened as it hit her.

She couldn't let him do that when he was like this. She wanted it but she wanted him aware of what he was doing when it happened.

Amerii pushed her arms up, hoping to get his attention. He growled and pressed his body harder against hers.

"Van!" she snapped and he paused at last.

He slowly drew back and blinked at her, the shine back in his red eyes along with a look of confusion.

"Are you with me?" She furrowed her brow, hoping his answer would be yes.

He looked at his hands where they gripped her wrists and snatched them away, moving to kneel on the bed between her legs.

"I..." He swallowed visibly and stared at her.

Sitting up, she took hold of his hands, wanting him to see that he hadn't overstepped the mark and she wasn't angry with him. She smiled, kissed his fingers, and brought his trembling hands back to her breasts. His pupils narrowed and then widened when he palmed her breasts, his breathing heavy.

"My neck is numb," she said with another smile.

His gaze flickered to it, his eyes brightening.

"I..." he started again.

Seeing that he was on the verge of another apology, Amerii caught him around the back of his neck and pulled him to her. Her lips claimed his, her kiss slow and gentle, an effort to keep him calm. His thumbs grazed her nipples, arousing them again, sending tingling waves over her skin. She slowly leaned back, taking him with her, until she was lying on her back with him on top of her.

His hands moved down over her stomach, skimming her sides in a way that tickled her, and then ran along the line of the waist of her trousers. She bit her lower lip and looked down at his hands, silently urging him on. When he looked as though he was going to spend the whole journey to Varka Two just skimming his fingers back and forth along her belt, she stepped in and undid it and then her trousers. He pushed himself up when she brought her legs up and shoved her trousers down them. They hit her boots. An awkward smile settled on her lips when Van sat back and helped her by removing her boots. She probably should have taken those off first.

Naked, she felt a little exposed when his dark red eyes trailed over her body, making her burn wherever they touched. She went to cover her breasts but his growl stopped her. Instead, she found herself toying with her nipples just to see the hunger in his eyes.

His hands went to his belt and he was naked before she could make out what was happening. When he went to cover her body with his again, she pressed her hand to his chest, stopping him. She wanted to see him in all his glory. He was magnificent, his body as breathtaking as she had imagined it. Pure lithe muscle and strength knelt before her, his hard length thrusting eagerly from its home of dark curls, enticing her.

She sat up and leaned forwards, pushing him back. He frowned at her but she didn't give him a chance to protest. Whatever words he had been on the verge of saying came out as a garbled mutter as she wrapped her lips around the sensitive head of his cock and sucked it. He thrust forwards into her mouth and she took him in deeper, suckling his length and imagining how good it would feel when he was inside her.

His hands claimed her shoulders. She moved closer, wrapping her hand around the base of his length and moving it in time with her mouth as she sucked him. His fingers tightened against her, bordering on painful and then crossing that border into true pain when his claws penetrated her flesh. She released his length and gritted her teeth.

His grip loosened. His eyes were wide when she looked up at him. They were bright red too, shining, speaking to her of his hunger. He wanted blood. She glanced at her shoulder. He had drawn it. Where each of his claws had broken the skin, a drop of crimson trembled. She smiled up at Van and touched one of the cuts. When blood coated her fingertip, she brought it to her mouth and sucked it clean, her eyes locked with his the whole time.

She was playing with fire but she wanted him to bite her. She knew him well enough now though to understand that he would need a little convincing while he wasn't lost in his bloodlust.

She crooked a finger.

He licked his lips.

He had drawn blood. It was his duty to clean it up and kiss it better.

She smiled, wide and seductive. Her eyes narrowed on his.

His gaze flicked between her eyes and the cuts, his breathing turning heavier with each passing second. She needed to get him to bite her before he lost control completely.

Her eyes shot wide when he tackled her to the bed and began hungrily licking at the cuts, sucking occasionally. His movements were frantic, desperate, and made her realise how hungry he truly was for her.

His tongue traced the marks and then he kissed down her body, his hands roughly gliding over her breasts and then her stomach.

"You still with me?" she whispered, afraid to ask but needing to.

He nodded and she could see in his eyes that he was fighting the bloodlust. He moved down her and, for a moment, she thought he was going to kiss the apex of her thighs, but then he did something far more erotic.

He bit her just above the hip.

The only warning she had was a sweep of his tongue, a momentary sense of numbness, and then his teeth were in her. She arched off the bed and cried out as a wave of pleasure crashed over her, so intense that her head spun and every bone in her body became liquid. She trembled against him, her body humming and throbbing as though she had just climaxed. He locked his arms around her, feeding greedily, each pull on her blood sending another wave through her. She writhed against him, her groin slick with need and her abdomen aching for release. He growled against her skin and bit deeper, tearing another cry from her throat as she shuddered with her climax.

He hadn't even touched her there.

He had made her climax with just a bite.

Amerii melted into the bed, too warm and fuzzy inside to care what happened to her. A lazy smile wound its way across her lips and she sighed, her focus scattered to the four edges of the galaxy. Van continued to drink for a while, slower and deeper now, a pace that matched how she felt, and then released her. He licked the mark on her hip and she smiled at the ceiling, stretching her arms out and toying with the short strands of her hair.

Van appeared above her.

She smiled at him too.

His lips were red. Stained by her blood. She pulled him down and kissed him, tasting herself on them, wanting to know what it was about blood that made him wild. His hard length pressed into her groin and she raised her hips to it, rubbing herself against him. He moaned into her mouth and then broke the kiss.

"I need you," he whispered against her neck as he kissed and licked it.

She needed him too.

"Hmm... come and get me then," she said on a sigh, still a little delirious from her orgasm.

"Are you... I mean, do we need to..."

Her smile widened and she managed to open her eyes properly.

"My father insisted that I had sterilisation injections." She had wanted to reassure him but the mention of her father seemed to make him even paler. She touched his cheek. "I choose who I love, remember?"

193

Van nodded, frowned and then reached between them. She shuffled up the bed and watched as he guided his length into her. Their sighs combined as he eased in, deep and slow, and she hoped he would be able to keep control. The tight lines of his face spoke of restraint as he withdrew and thrust in again. He had tasted her blood without losing his mind but that didn't mean that he would remain calm. Anything could send him over the edge.

His body covered hers and he buried his face into her neck.

Anything.

He licked her throat and she felt it turn numb.

Or perhaps he didn't need a push. Perhaps he had already made his decision and was only holding back the bloodlust for her sake. He hadn't hurt her so far, not really. She had expected more than just a few minor scratches.

She moaned and her mind went blank when he thrust deeper into her, his pace increasing, and he breathed hard into her ear. His hands closed over her shoulders and she wrapped her arms around him, skimming her fingers over the shifting muscles of his back. She arched into him, tightening her muscles around his length as it drove into her, so deep that her insides coiled tight, ready to explode again. A few more thrusts and a warm rush burst through her, her body convulsing around his.

Van growled and she squeaked when he pulled out of her, turned her over onto her front and pulled her hips up. He thrust into her from behind, harder now, so deep that she lost her mind a little more with each plunge of his length. She pushed herself up onto her hands and bit her lip, moaning each time their hips met. He growled again and she sensed his restraint snap. His fingers tightened against her hips, clinging to them as he pounded into her, seeking his own release. She clenched his length in her depths, hoping to help him find it, loving the feel of him thrusting into her. She felt every ounce of his power in each thrust, every ounce of his strength.

It felt divine.

Her breasts wobbled back and forth with each deep thrust, her moans combining with his and filling the room along with their hard breathing. She closed her eyes when her insides began to tighten again and begged him not to stop. He moved faster, deeper, taking her out of her mind. Close. She was so close.

With a roar, he came, filling her with his warm seed. He grabbed her around the ribs and pulled her up so her back was flush against his front, his length still inside her. She ached and writhed against him, desperate for release again. It had promised to be mind blowing.

Van made sure it was.

He snarled and then sunk his fangs into her neck. Intense pleasure tore through her and she convulsed against the restraint of his arms as she came, her whole body quivering with her release. The universe turned bright white. Her ears rang.

Pain was the first thing Amerii felt on coming back to the galaxy. Her neck hurt with each hard pull Van made on her blood but it felt good at the same time. She leaned back into him, unable to resist as he drank deeply from her. She sighed when he began to slow and then shivered when he withdrew his fangs and licked her neck.

Her neck.

He had bitten her there.

Van released her and she collapsed into the bed, dreamily touching the pronounced bumps on her throat.

With a sleepy smile, she looked at Van. He looked troubled. She crooked her finger at him, wanting him to come to her. He hesitated a moment and then lay beside her. She didn't press him into speaking.

There were no words that could convey what this moment had meant to her, and she knew that he would find it impossible to find the right words too.

She lay close to him and smiled again when he carefully lifted her, moved the covers away, and then settled her down on the bed. He pressed a kiss to her forehead and lay beside her before covering them both with the blanket. She snuggled into his back when he rolled onto his side, her forehead pressing against his shoulder.

Her hand skimmed down his arm and she smiled. It was all a little overwhelming, but she knew that it was so much more so for Van. She could feel the tension radiating through him. What thoughts were troubling him? She ran her fingers back up his arm, her touch light. She hoped it comforted and reassured him as she intended it to. Moving closer to him, she pressed the length of her body into his and kissed his back and shoulders, memorising the feel of his skin beneath them and the warmth of him.

"Van?" she whispered against his back, afraid of disturbing him but wanting to reassure him as best she could.

He was silent for a long time and then said, "Amerii?"

"I love you." She pressed another kiss to his back and wrapped her arm around him, her hand splaying out against his chest. "Nothing will change that."

Silence.

"Van?" she said, her voice trembling now. He was still so tense. She wished that he would turn towards her. She wanted to see his face and look into his eyes when she said these things. Pulling on his arm, she tried to force him to roll over and look at her. "Turn around."

He did and she moved backwards to give him room. His eyes were dark as he looked into hers, full of conflict. She stroked her fingers over his brow and then down his cheek, smiling at him the whole time.

"I love you," she said again and the tension in his expression lifted a little. "I'm glad that I'm yours now... your mate... there's no one else that I want as mine."

He swallowed, frowned and pulled her close to him as he rolled onto his back, growling possessively. She pressed a kiss to his chest and then looked up and studied his beautiful face as he fell asleep, wishing with all her heart that he didn't feel so unworthy of her.

She hoped that things would be different now.

Now that she was his.

CHAPTER 7

Amerii shifted on the seat of the small shuttle as it descended into the atmosphere of Varka Two. She looked herself over for the millionth time, wondering what her captain was going to make of her outfit. Van had insisted that she change into a black armoured suit. It was tight to her skin, the thick material lined with some kind of liquid metal that responded to impacts. She had discovered that when she had been prodding it whilst walking and had bumped into Van, forcing her finger into the chest area of the suit. It had instantly hardened and then became soft again. Varkan technology certainly was incredible.

Her gaze roamed to Van where he sat close beside her, a huge black heavy artillery laser rifle cradled in his lap. He wore a suit similar to hers. It mimicked his muscles perfectly, giving her every reason to remember how good he had looked naked. She wet her lips.

"We will arrive shortly. It will be day in the area where the old base station is situated," Van said and she noticed that he seemed uneasy about that.

Varkans didn't like the daylight. The other Varkan soldiers in the transport shuttle with her and Van were already wearing their black visors in preparation.

Van's sat on the seat beside him.

"The area is shielded as per Varkan regulations but the facility is old. We must be on our guard."

Amerii nodded, knowing exactly how to read between the lines of what he had said to the meaning beneath. It wasn't just information or a warning. It wasn't just that she would see firsthand Varka's method of filtering the light to protect their sensitive eyes, or the fact that Wraiths used to inhabit the planet and could return at any moment to attack them there.

It was that he was worried about her and that he would do all he could to protect her.

He placed his hand over hers where it rested on her knee and closed his fingers around it, holding it. None of the other Varkans seemed to notice or they were doing an admirable job of pretending they hadn't seen this sign of affection from their commander towards a Lyran. Van squeezed her hand and she looked back at him.

She was surprised when he leaned towards her and whispered something in her ear that she didn't understand. It wasn't Varkan. It was another language. Perhaps the old Varkan language but no words that she was familiar with.

He kissed the spot on the neck of her armoured suit that was directly over the marks on her neck. She smiled and blushed, that blush turning to a blazing fire when she realised that all of the soldiers opposite her were now facing her direction. Van kissed her neck again, whispered something else, and moved back into his seat.

She glanced at Van, glad that he was all right with what had happened between them and that he seemed more comfortable around her now. She placed her other hand over his where it covered hers and held it.

The pilot announced they had entered the facility docking area and, a moment later, they touched down, the thrusters of the small vessel deafening her as they fired to stop its descent.

Van's hand left hers and went to his gun. He stood, slung the strap of his gun across his body, and motioned to his soldiers. She didn't understand what any of the elaborate gestures meant.

When the soldiers had filed out, Van offered her his hand. She placed hers into it and stood, looking into his eyes as he smiled and brushed her hair from her face.

"Remain close to me, Amerii." His dark eyes gave her the impression that he was thinking about violent things. Was he really that worried that the Wraiths would attack? Lyran reports indicated that they had been quiet in this area for some time now. "I will not let anything happen to you."

She leaned into his touch, seeking its comfort, and then closed her eyes as she pressed a kiss to his palm.

"What did you say to me that you wanted those men to hear?" she said with a sly smile, seeing straight through him.

When her eyes met Van's, there was an awkward look in his.

"That you are mine, and only mine, and I would not share you with any male."

"Mmm." Amerii pushed his gun aside before wrapping her arms around his neck. "I don't want to be anyone else's. I only want to be yours."

He smiled, exposing his sharp teeth. "Truly?"

She nodded. "There's no other man in the universe for me. I love you."

His eyes widened and then closed as he leaned in to kiss her. She sighed against his lips as they touched hers in a sensual caress that heated her blood and made her heartbeat quicken. She frowned over the loss as they left hers and looked at him.

"What about your father?"

Amerii's frown stuck. "I'm really not interested in my father in that way."

"I am being serious."

He looked it too. She stroked his cheek, enjoying the sight of him so deadly serious and intense. His red irises were brighter than they had been a moment before. Had he been thinking about her blood while they had been kissing?

"My father will be fine." She released him, walked a little way towards the exit of the shuttle and then paused, looking back at Van with a wide smile. "Of course, he won't make it easy on you at first."

Van paled.

"I'm joking," she said and he glared at her. She made a mental note that Van didn't like jokes. When he walked towards her, she went to leave the shuttle but his hand on her arm stopped her.

"Take this," he said and she turned back to see him holding out a small laser rifle.

He really wasn't taking any risks.

She slung the strap of the rifle over her shoulder and weighed it up. It was a good weapon. She had shouldered a few rifles in her time and this had to be the finest and most balanced one she'd had the opportunity of using.

A glance at Van made her blood boil with desire. He stood tall, back straight, holding the massive rifle. The armoured suit he wore really did make him look as though someone had stripped him and painted him black. It was a divine sight. She blushed when she remembered that he was all hers now, and she was his. She touched her neck again, her fingers hovering over the point where he had bitten. His gaze shifted there, boring into it and heating it until it matched the fierce temperature of her blood.

She wasn't sure how she was going to break it to her parents. Her mother would understand but her father was protective of her, and then there were her uncles. Sebastian, the king of Lyra, would understand. After all, it was his daughter Sophia who was married to Emperor Varka. Balt might not be too upset since his eldest daughter Renie was marrying a Vegan, but her youngest uncle, Remi would. He had suffered both physically and emotionally because of the Varkans and the war. She doubted that he would be able to bring himself to see past Van's role in that war, just as he couldn't bring himself to speak to Regis.

"Come." Van dragged her out of her thoughts.

Amerii pushed them to the back of her mind. When the time came, she would deal with them. Until then, she had a mission to focus on and a job to do. She followed Van out of the shuttle and watched two small Lyran vessels land, sending plumes of gritty black sand into the air. The ribbons twirled like smoke, drawing her eyes upwards to the dome. The sky was dull, nothing like the one she was used to seeing back on the planets of Lyra. She wondered if she could stand to be always under a dome, locked away from the sun and the sky. If Van were with her, she probably could get used to it.

The dome on Varka Two had its purpose though, and it wasn't only to protect the Varkans' eyes. It regulated the temperature of the station and protected its occupants from the harsh rays of the Varkan sun. Apparently, it was almost twice as strong as the sun of Lyra and because of Varka Two's proximity to it, the dome was essential. Without it, the temperature would be near impossible to bear.

Nothing could survive here.

She remembered the Wraiths.

Something could live here, but it wasn't something she wanted to meet.

The dome protected against that too. At least, she hoped it did. It looked weak in places as her eyes scanned the perimeter. They would have to fix it.

She walked forwards with Van and, as he joined his men, she noticed that he had put his visor on. The two sides of it swept around to form a point a short distance from the tip of his nose, a line running directly over the top of his head where the sides joined.

When her captain stepped out of the first Lyran vessel, his first officer at his side, Amerii saluted and stood straight. Her captain raised an eyebrow at her apparel and her heart beat harder as she prayed to Iskara that he wouldn't make a scene. She didn't know how Van would react if he did, or if he treated her any less than Van thought royalty should be treated. She had seen his disapproval both when she had been on her ship and Van had first met her captain, and when she had been on the Varkan vessel and her captain had ignored her.

She hoped that he would ignore her now.

"Commander Aeris, we are ready to begin our inspection."

"We will split into two groups. I will escort you, your first officer and Princess Amerii. I am sure you wish to tour the facility. My officers and those left of yours will inspect the facility and decide upon any repairs or changes that will need to be made to accommodate Lyrans. All officers are to maintain a state of alert. We do not know if the Wraiths have returned. I would order your men to remain close to mine." Van's deep voice carried a note of authority that practically challenged her captain to disapprove of his plan.

Amerii waited to see how her captain would respond. A momentary flicker of something crossed his face, something remarkably similar to irritation or anger, but quickly disappeared when Van stepped forwards. Any sign that her captain was going to speak out against the plan or attempt to take leadership of the mission faded along with his courage and his colour. His skin paled, turning almost as white as Van's.

Van grinned, revealing sharp teeth.

"Shall we?" Van held his hand out to one side.

He walked ahead of them, his massive rifle constantly at the ready. Wherever he turned his head, he turned it. Did he really think the Wraiths might attack here? The barrier was thin in places. It was possible that they could get through and Van had mentioned that there had been sightings of them in this area of space.

Was this the reason Varka had insisted on escorting them to the planet and remaining with them a time rather than letting them arrive on their own? Lyra had never fought Wraiths before. The Wraiths had never attacked them during the insurgences or the war before that. She had only read sketchy data on them before Sophia had married Regis and Varka had made their military data available to Lyran soldiers. She had read all about them then, wanting to know what sort of species it was that shared the Varkans' planets.

They sounded terrifying.

Creatures that were like ghosts, able to appear and disappear in the blink of an eye, impossible to hit without the correct weapon.

She hoped she didn't meet one.

Her captain moved and she followed him, walking beside his first officer. Van dropped back to walk alongside her captain but near to her too. He turned his head slightly towards her, clearly glancing in her direction. She knew what he wanted but she couldn't do it. It wasn't her place to walk beside her captain. Van had to understand that to her captain, she was a lieutenant, not a princess.

Van dropped back again as they entered the building and even though she couldn't see where he was looking because of his visor, she could feel that his eyes were on her.

He explained, seemingly to her alone, his attention always with her, about the rooms they were passing through. This complex had been the stronghold of Varka on this planet many years ago. They hadn't used it since Lyra had withdrawn and it had returned to Varkan hands. There was a corridor and steps leading downwards that Van went straight past without explaining. She knew why. There was only one place that he wouldn't want to take her or her comrades. The cells. She could read his silence as clearly as her captain and first officer would be able to. They had held many Lyrans in this complex once and even though Varka Two had returned to Varka over fifty years ago, there were still those that would have had kin held in those cells.

If they had ever caught her uncle, they would have held him here and tortured him for information. While that thought disturbed her, it didn't change her feelings towards the Varkans. That time was long over and peace had long reigned between their species. Lyrans had captured Varkans too and tortured them. She took a deep breath and told herself that was the face of war.

It was a face that she hoped to never see.

They came out into a long wide room. The lights above were dim but it was bright enough for her to see that Heavy Armour suits lined the walls. She had never seen one in real life but had read all about them. She walked over to the nearest suit and ran her hands over the bulky black frame, shaped reminiscent of muscles, and down the arms. The sleek black helmet stared lifelessly down at her. It was incredible. If a soldier were to wear this, they would be well protected but completely unhindered by the suit. In fact, judging by the complex array of pistons and fluid tubes, the soldier would be able to move faster and with more strength than they normally had. The metal was cool under her fingers. Varkan steel. There was nothing stronger in the galaxy. Van would look incredible in it.

Her exploration halted when she remembered that a Heavy Armour had taken her uncle Remi's arm and years later a Heavy Armour had almost killed him and his friend, Jericho, during the insurgence.

"Is something the matter?" Van said close to her elbow and Amerii shook her head. He touched her cheek, the caress soothing but unsettling at the same time. She tried to push the thoughts out of her mind but couldn't. "Terrible things happen in wars, Amerii. Varka and Lyra have moved into an era of peace. No longer will these weapons hurt those of our kin."

Her brow furrowed and she leaned into his touch, trying to find the comfort in it and his words.

"It's just... were you here?"

She wished she could see his eyes as she looked up at him. She wanted to be able to read his feelings in them. She needed to see if he was being honest with her.

"For the eighty-seventh and the one-hundred-and-twelfth combats... the ones in which your uncle was involved?"

She didn't know if that was what the Varkans had called them but nodded.

"No. I was on Varka Prime with Regis. I have been here once in my lifetime and that was to eradicate the Wraiths."

The knowledge that he hadn't been here slaughtering Lyrans didn't comfort her as much as she had thought it would. Her eyes darted about his visor, trying to see through it to his eyes.

"Van?" she said in a small trembling voice.

"Amerii... I have never fought a Lyran. Neither has Regis. It does not mean that we were not involved though. Just as you have never fought a Varkan, you have been involved by blood in those fights."

Amerii frowned. He was right. How could she feel such negativity towards Van and the Varkans because of what had happened to Lyrans when it had been Lyrans who had instigated the war and had attempted to take Varka Two from its rightful owners? She had absolutely no right to feel this way.

"I'm sorry." Amerii closed her eyes when he stroked her cheek, his touch light and warm. "It's a little overwhelming."

"I would rather you had remained on the ship," he said on a sigh and she looked up at him again. "I do not like you being down here. I do not trust your captain's ability to protect you."

She smiled at Van. Out of the corner of her eye, she could see her captain and the first officer staring at them. She stepped back, remembering her place and not wanting to be reprimanded. Her behaviour was far from how it should be. She was here as a lieutenant of the Lyran Imperial Army, not a love-struck woman with her man.

"You seemed very interested in the Heavy Armour," Van said, his voice a bare whisper.

A blush crept onto her cheeks and she turned her back on her captain so he didn't see. Van moved closer to her, coming to stand slightly behind her, half of his body against hers. Her blush deepened. He leaned down and whispered into her ear.

"Would you like to see me in one?"

His rifle pressed against her back as he leaned in and stroked her neck with his free hand. Her eyes half-closed, fixed on the Heavy Armour as her mind raced to imagine him in it. He really would look incredible.

Her captain cleared his throat.

"Will all of the Heavy Armour suits be removed?"

Van stepped away from her and she gathered herself while he walked along the row of suits.

"We will leave them here. The weaponry they carry has been modified since the war. It was altered to be effective against Wraiths."

Amerii looked at the armour that she was still standing in front of. It held a large assault rifle. She had thought it was just a regular laser rifle. It looked no different to the one Van held, only a lot larger.

She realised that the one she held was just a smaller version of his rifle. They were all anti-Wraith weapons.

"We will continue our tour this way." Van walked ahead of them. She looked at the armour for a few seconds more, curious as to how it would feel to wear one, and then followed the group.

At the other end of the room, bright light filtered in through open doors. Van paused and looked back at her.

"The garden here is beautiful and I am certain that it could be altered to grow food for the soldiers."

She came to a halt just behind her captain and peered through the bright open space, trying to make out the garden beyond.

Something moved.

Her fingers tensed against her gun, but when she didn't see anything move again, she decided that it was probably just the light and her focusing too hard on trying to see what was out there.

"When we have briefly toured the garden, we will—" Van went rigid and then turned, his gun coming up fast.

Before Amerii could even shout his name, three incredibly tall white figures had appeared and disappeared.

Van was gone.

CHAPTER 8

Amerii ran to the end of the room and out into the garden. She couldn't see Van or the white figures anywhere. She turned on the spot, her breathing fast as her heart thundered against her chest. They had taken him.

Wraiths.

A Varkan commander would be valuable to them but there was no knowing what they would do to him.

She had to get him back.

She ran back into the room, passing her captain and the first officer, and looked around her.

"Lieutenant Amerii, what are you doing?" her captain said.

Her eyes fixed on the Heavy Armour suits.

"We must go after them," Amerii said, out of breath as her body trembled with the adrenaline.

"How?"

She didn't know. Her hands shook against her gun and she cursed the tears that threatened to fill her eyes. She was a princess of Lyra. This wasn't time to be weak. It was time to be strong and prove to herself and her captain that she was capable of great things.

Two Varkan officers came rushing in, their speed incredible as they ran towards her. They halted barely three feet from her and lifted their visors. It was the two who had accompanied her on the shuttle from her vessel to the Varkan ship.

They glared at the far end of the room.

"Wraiths have Commander Aeris. We must get him back," she said and they nodded. She looked at the Heavy Armour and ran over to one of the suits. "These work, yes?"

They nodded again.

"Good." She began opening it, prising the two sides of the heavily armoured chest apart.

"Lieutenant Amerii, what do you think you are doing?" her captain said, his voice stern. "This is a Varkan matter."

She turned on him. "It happened in our base station. It is as much a Lyran matter. Unless you want to be the one to tell Emperor Varka that his attendant has gone missing and we did nothing to rescue him?"

He paled. "Attendant?"

She nodded and frowned. "Not only an attendant but a close friend of Regis's... and my..." She pulled the collar of her armoured suit down to reveal the marks on her throat. The two Varkans bowed their heads. Her captain's eyes shot wide. "My mate. As a subject of Lyra, you will follow my orders and step aside."

Before he could respond, she clambered into the Heavy Armour. It closed around her, sealing her in. The helmet covered her head. She slid her arms into the suit's and flexed her hands, seeing the robotic suit's hands move in perfect synch with hers.

"Can you even work that thing?" the first officer said.

"If you'd paid the remotest bit of attention to me you would know that I'm as skilled with technology as my mother and as headstrong in battles as my father." She scowled at him and then moved her foot forward. The Heavy Armour's foot landed with a loud thud on the floor, the whining sound of the parts moving like music to her ears.

The two Varkans suited up and she nodded in thanks to them for their assistance. They would know this planet better than she did and could probably give her a few pointers about the suit. She was good with technology but reading Varkan was beyond her. Not that she was about to admit that within earshot of her captain.

Amerii stomped past her captain and first officer, building to a steady run that sounded like thunder. The suit responded beautifully to every move. She didn't even have to exert much effort to make it run faster than she ever could.

The two Varkan officers passed her and she spotted a hole in the barrier ahead. She squeezed through it after them and followed their lead as they flanked her.

"Where would they have taken him?" she said over the intercom.

"North Sector has always had high Wraith activity. The shield from here to there and over that sector is low since the area hasn't been used in almost a century," came the reply and the one to her right nodded.

She took a deep breath, shouldered her rifle and ran as fast as she could towards the area now flashing on the map in the bottom right corner of the red screen in front of her. The landscape took up the rest of the screen. Overlaid onto it were diagnostics of the terrain and atmospheric readings.

Dust rose around her as she ran, her focus fixed on the distance, on the buildings that shimmered in the heat haze.

She had to get to Van.

She had to save the man she loved.

The ground slammed into Van's face, smashing his black visor. Or did he slam into the ground? Everything that had happened over the past few minutes had been a blur, a whirlwind of colours and sounds that had disorientated him.

"Commander Aeris," a thin voice echoed in his head.

Van blinked his eyes open and tried to focus. Bright light burnt his eyes. The sun. He could feel it on his face, strong and searing. He squinted up at it. It filtered in through a hole in a ceiling and wall. Where was he? His eyes watered as he tried to assess his surroundings. The building was old, dilapidated. The North Sector?

"It has been a long time since our paths have crossed," the voice continued in his head.

Cruskin.

"A Lyran curse... they truly have tamed the mighty Varkans with their female."

His thoughts shifted to Amerii. Would she be safe back at the complex? Did the Wraiths have her too?

"Another Lyran female? This one the victor over your own heart?"

Van cursed in Varkan this time, in the old language that Wraiths had never been able to understand. He despised them and their way of being able to invade minds. No thought was safe, not unless he constantly thought in the old language and that wasn't possible. Instinct made him think in the Varkan language that he had been raised with.

"Perhaps we should have taken her." The echoing voice held a note of amusement.

The Wraith meant to provoke him but instead had given him a clear indication that Amerii was safe, or at least she wasn't here.

Van tried to get onto his knees. Before he could manage it, something was around his throat. Hauled off the ground and suspended by his neck, he stared up at the Wraith who had captured him.

The ethereal white figure stood at least a male taller than himself, his humanoid-shaped body shifting with the breeze but his grip as solid as stone.

The face shimmered in and out of focus, long and thin, trailing away in a wave of white that danced like hair in wind. Empty dark eyes shifted into sharp relief, a wide hollow smile following. As it moved into the light, the rest of the Wraith's face came into focus and Van's eyes settled on the deep groove in his neck.

J'nir kis'kl reatlnnfir.

Only this Wraith was worthy of the strongest Varkan curse.

It was little wonder the Wraith had mentioned that their paths had crossed many moons ago.

Van had been the commander of the fleet that had wiped the remaining Wraiths off the face of Varka Two almost a century ago. Those Wraiths had included this male's family. A Wraith commander.

He had thought that he had killed him too.

The Wraith's grip on Van's throat tightened. He choked and tried to grasp at the burning hot ribbons of smoke that held him. His fingers passed straight through. Van cursed again. This was why he hated Wraiths. While they could touch you, it was almost impossible to touch them. That was the reason Varkans had made weapons that would disintegrate their particles.

"What do you want with me?" Van said in a strained voice.

The face above him shifted to reveal a wide grin. He could see straight through his mouth to the blinding sky beyond. His eyes stung and he longed for his visor. He could show no weakness though. Wraiths fed off weakness.

Regardless of the pain it caused him, he let his bloodlust take control, his eyes brightening and the world brightening with them. He growled at the Wraith.

The Wraith's smile widened.

"I want to kill you. I desire to avenge my kind by destroying you and every disgusting creature in that facility."

Van snapped, violence surging through him at the thought of the Wraiths touching Amerii. He growled again, his teeth sharpening as he lost all control. He wouldn't let them touch her. He lashed out with his claws, cutting through the Wraith's arm in a desperate attempt to escape. The pale smoke shifted and then regrouped. Van struggled, flailing his legs and scratching at the Wraith.

"It seems we have determined our first target. A love for a love, Commander Aeris," the Wraith said coolly.

The Wraith turned away to look back at others who shimmered behind him. "Seize the girl."

No.

Van roared, his feet slammed into the ground and he launched himself at the Wraith.

He wouldn't let them touch his Amerii.

The Wraith's hand slipped from around his throat and Van struck at him, growling with frustration when his hand went harmlessly through the Wraith's body. Van tried again, a growing lust for violence burning inside him. The Wraith would pay for what he had done and for threatening to hurt Amerii. He wouldn't let anyone near her. He would protect her with his life if that was what it took.

A surge of bloodlust stronger than he had ever felt crashed through him and his teeth elongated. The world brightened until it was painful, the sunlight turning everything white. He didn't care. Violence. Death. Bloodshed. It would all be his. The Wraith would die this time. He would make sure of it.

The Wraith backhanded him and he slammed into the wall, hitting the floor a moment later. His head spun but he immediately pushed himself back up onto his feet and launched himself at one of the other Wraiths. A quick glance around revealed that the other Wraith had gone. Only the commander and one subordinate remained. He would give anything for an anti-Wraith weapon around now.

A hot prickling feeling crept down his spine and out along his arms. It burned deep in his chest. Rage. The bloodlust was taking complete control. He couldn't stop it. Even as he battled it, it grew stronger, pushing at the boundaries of his mind and overcoming it.

Darkness filled him.

The world drained of colours and sound.

And then it turned as red as blood.

He had never experienced this before, the other side of bloodlust. He had never crossed the threshold to the place where it ruled him and his actions, trapping him in his own body.

He hit the wall again and before he could get up and attack, the Wraith commander had grabbed him around the throat. Van sneered at him, swiping with his claws, growing increasingly frustrated each time they passed through the Wraith without inflicting damage.

Damage.

Blood.

Destruction.

Death.

He wanted it all. He wanted to feel his enemy's blood on his skin. He wanted to smell it in the air. He wanted to see the light of life fade from his eyes.

Van stretched out, shoving his hand deep into the Wraith's chest. The Wraith commander recoiled, dropping him, and screamed in fury. Van grinned.

It seemed that Wraith's weren't so impenetrable after all.

He threw a punch towards the Wraith's chest again, aiming for the same point that he had attacked a moment ago. He had felt something in there. A heart perhaps. Some vital organ that the Wraith couldn't easily shift into smoke. The Wraith blocked his attack and the other one left him. Van growled at him, angered by the fact he was escaping and the fact that he knew where he was going.

He wouldn't let them take Amerii. His weakness had placed her at risk again. A sense of shame mingled with the rage inside him, pushing his blood to boiling point as he grew angry both at himself and at the Wraiths. What if they had taken Amerii, his mate?

"Mate?" the Wraith commander said, an amused ring to his words. "You have mated with a Lyran female."

Van growled and leapt up, trying to hit the point over the Wraith's chest again. The Wraith swatted him away, catching him in the stomach and sending him crashing into the wall again. He hit the floor hard, every bone in his body aching from the impact. Pushing himself up, he told himself to keep fighting, to prove that he wasn't weak and to restore his honour by protecting his mate.

"Soon she will be here... I will have her brought to us so you can watch her die as I watched my family..."

Van sprung off the floor and punched straight through the Wraith's chest. His fingers closed around something and a victorious smile twisted his lips when the Wraith screamed again. Before he could get a better grip, the Wraith's hand was around his throat, pulling him away. Van kicked out at him, growling and struggling to get free. The Wraith's eyes narrowed into a black look, his grin widening.

Van slammed into the floor again, his back pressed hard against it, the Wraith's hand still locked tight around his throat. He grasped at it with both hands, trying to take hold of it as he choked. The world dimmed a little.

"Perhaps I shall make you pay a little first. Your precious Lyran female could be dessert," the Wraith said with a lascivious smile.

Before Van could retaliate, the Wraith had struck him hard in the stomach. Van doubled up, choking as he tried to breathe and winded from the punch. The Wraith hit him again and he shut his feelings down, taking the beating without making a sound. The Wraith could hit him all he wanted, could rip him apart, but he wouldn't give him what he wanted. He would show no weakness. No matter what happened to him. He would not give the Wraith the satisfaction of seeing him weak.

His senses receded, the bloodlust fading as he started to lose consciousness.

Tired and throbbing with pain, Van slumped against the dusty floor, saving the remaining shreds of his strength. If they captured Amerii, he would need the last of his strength to save her. He would find a way to protect her.

The Wraith released his neck and kicked him in the side so he rolled onto his front. He grimaced as the Wraith took hold of his wrists and pulled his arms behind his back, locking something cold and solid around his wrists. Varkan steel. Van smiled at the irony of that. The Wraith commander must have found the cuffs in the facility. What Van had once used on his enemies was now being used on him. It was what he deserved for his weakness. The Wraith pulled him up so he was kneeling.

Van hung his head forwards.

He should have been on his guard. He shouldn't have let Amerii distract him. By allowing her to do so, by pandering to his desire for her attention, he had placed her at great risk. He was weak. Shameful.

Out of the corner of his eye, he saw one of the other Wraiths return.

His head felt heavy.

His body felt broken.

But his heart held on, unwavering, strong, even as he feared he would never see Amerii again.

"Commander," the new Wraith said. "Three Heavy Armours are coming this way."

The last thing Van saw was the Wraith commander's grin. The last thing he felt was his forehead slamming into the ground. The last thing he heard was gunfire.

Darkness swallowed him.

Amerii screamed as she blasted her way through the small dusty settlement, her Heavy Armour pounding the dirt. This hadn't looked like a particularly dangerous area when they had been approaching but her two Varkan friends had immediately begun firing their laser rifles. The moment the shots had hit the buildings, white shimmering beings had appeared and attacked them. She remained sandwiched between the two Varkans, shooting at any Wraith that dared get into her line of fire.

When she hit one, it shrieked and seemed to destabilise, falling apart before her eyes. She shot another and moved forwards, intent on reaching Van. More Wraiths crowded the passages ahead of her. He had to be that way. They were protecting it.

"This way." She motioned to the Varkans. One caught the arm of her Heavy Armour and held her back.

"Cover yourself, your highness," he said and she frowned at him.

She turned in time to see the other Varkan step forward and shoulder his rifle. It built up a charge, whining high as the end of it glowed red. The moment he released the shot, she fell backwards into the Varkan behind her, the blast knocking her off her feet. She stared in amazement as it tore through the Wraiths, killing most of them in an instant and leaving the rest missing limbs.

She hadn't realised that she could do that with her weapon.

Her comrade behind her pushed her back onto her feet and she followed the first Varkan into the building.

He collapsed in front of her eyes and she barely had time to leap to the side and avoid the green blast that had ripped through him. The other Varkan landed heavily with her, covering her. He fired at the Wraith, disintegrating it and then stood, pulling her up off the floor. She ran to the other Varkan and pulled the Heavy Armour over.

Blood covered the inside of the visor.

Amerii swallowed hard.

"He is gone, your highness. We must move fast," the other one said.

She had never seen anyone die. Before she could take it in, the remaining Varkan was forcing her to run. She gathered herself and shouldered her gun again, intent on reaching Van even though she was petrified. Suddenly she was frighteningly aware of how fragile she was compared to her enemy and how much danger Van was in. She had to get to him before it was too late. A part of her said to ask her comrade what the Wraiths would do to Van but she couldn't find her voice. Fear stole it. What if he said that they would kill him? She didn't think that she would have the strength to continue if those words left his lips. And she had to keep going. Even though her legs were tiring, becoming tense from the adrenaline turning to fear, and her heart was missing beats as it pounded hard against her ribs, she had to keep going.

She had to save Van.

She wouldn't let them take her mate from her.

A galaxy without him was one she wanted no part of.

Setting her jaw, she straightened up, raised her gun and locked it tight against her shoulder, and stormed forwards. Van was in that building. She knew it. There she would find him and she would save him.

The Wraiths would pay for what they had done.

As they entered the building, she blasted any Wraith that appeared in her field of view, her eyes darting about the screen as she struggled to understand the readings. In the bottom right corner was an image of what was happening behind her. The Varkan officer was bringing up the rear, his aim impeccable compared to hers. Her gun shook in the Heavy Armour's hands, a reflection of her own trembling. She fought against it, but her fear was overwhelming. Now was a time to be strong. Her blood was strong, her lineage that of kings and generals. She was strong. It was time that she proved that to the world, even if no one saw it. It was time she proved it to herself.

She broke through into a new area and fired off several rounds, holding the trigger to build a stronger charge than normal. The bolts tore through the Wraiths, clearing her path, and she pounded on.

An alarm flashed in the corner of her screen. Two fighter ships were outside. A sonar image of them came back. She breathed a sigh of relief when she recognised them as Lyran. She would have to thank her captain when she returned. He must have called for the fighters the moment she had left. It would have taken them some time to enter the atmosphere from the Nebuz-Lyra VIII.

She frowned when she saw that the path behind her was empty. Turning, her eyes widened when she realised that she was alone. She couldn't see the Varkan officer. She turned on the spot, scanning for him. They must have been split up. There was no time to go back to find him. She had to keep going.

She had to find Van.

She moved through room after room, sometimes having to shoulder her way through the doors. The Heavy Armour was too wide for some of the corridors so she had to find another way around. The building was a maze, half of it collapsed into nothing but rubble. Most of the ceiling was missing. The bright sun blazed down, blinding her sometimes in the seconds that it took the visor of the Heavy Armour to react and darken.

A heat signature appeared on her screen and she moved towards the red blip, her gun at the ready.

Turning a corner and entering a room, her heart leapt into her throat when she saw the owner of the heat signature.

Van.

He knelt on the floor, his arms restrained behind his back and his head hung forwards. Bright light shone down on him. On the floor beside him were pieces of his visor. The screen of the Heavy Armour assessed his vitals and she was relieved to see that while his injuries were severe they weren't life threatening. She moved towards him, intent on rousing him and getting him away before more Wraiths appeared.

Just as she was about to bend down to break his restraints, something slammed into her and she flew across the room. The Heavy Armour hit the wall, knocking it down. She landed in a heap on top of the splintered blocks, her heart thundering and her breathing fast. Lifting her head, she scoured the room.

Only Van.

That couldn't be right. Something had hit her. She was sure of it.

The red screen of the Heavy Armour said different. There was nothing there except Van, and he was still unconscious.

Besides, she didn't think he was strong enough to throw a Heavy Armour across the room. There was something else here. Something phenomenally strong.

Getting to her feet, Amerii slowly scanned the room again. The diagnostic showed nothing out of the ordinary. Walls, ceilings, doorways, and Van. Everything she could see was apparently everything there was.

Not even the sonar was showing anything different. The corridors around them were empty.

She stepped down from the broken wall and began towards Van again.

"You certainly are persistent," a voice said, deep and menacing, straight into her head.

She turned as quickly as she could in all directions. Nothing.

"I dare you to try again."

Ignoring the threat in the voice's tone, she walked towards Van. She lifted the gun, locking it tight into her shoulder and moving with it the way she had seen Van move with his rifle. Wherever her head turned, she turned the gun.

Still nothing on her screen.

Her breathing was loud inside the helmet, hot too. Her heartbeat pounded in her skull. Her left arm ached from where she had hit the wall.

Although the Heavy Armour had taken the brunt of the impact, it had still hurt her.

The moment she was within arm's reach of Van, she was struck again and sent skidding across the floor.

"Foolish," the voice said, taunting her. "Did you think I would allow you to free him? I am not finished with him."

Amerii got to her feet again. Still nothing on the screen. She was beginning to get annoyed now. Whoever owned the voice should have the guts to show his face. She ran over his words in her head. Not finished with Van? He damn well was. There wasn't a chance in Madjar that she was about to let anyone hurt him now that she was here.

Her eyes widened when a bright shape shimmered across the screen of her helmet and disappeared.

A Wraith?

"Very perceptive," the voice said in her head. It had an amused ring to it. "For a Lyran."

She gasped. How did it know that?

"You think in Lyran... a female? Let me see... the princess dear Commander Aeris was so worried about... his mate."

Amerii tried hard not to think anything but it was impossible. Her thoughts flashed back to that moment in Van's bedroom when he had claimed her as his mate and bonded with her.

"Disgusting." The Wraith shimmered into being right next to her.

Before she could look up at its full height, it had backhanded her, sending her crashing to the ground again. Her legs twisted in the suit and she cried out when the muscle in her calf burned with pain. Gritting her teeth, she pushed herself back up quicker this time. She raised her gun and aimed at the Wraith. With a roar, she fired round after round at it, tracking it around the room as it appeared and disappeared, dodging her.

This Wraith wasn't like the others. Instinct told her that it was in command, that it had been the one to take Van from the compound. She lifted her laser rifle higher, looking down the sight at the room. The moment the Wraith appeared, she aimed for its right hand side and just as she pulled the trigger moved her aim across it to its left. The Wraith moved straight into the path of the round and let out an unholy scream as it tore through its arm. Amerii grinned.

Her victory was short lived as the Wraith appeared in front of her, grabbed the arm of the Heavy Armour and hurled her towards the far wall. She hit it face first, cracking her head against the inside of the helmet. A warm liquid trickled down from a throbbing hot patch on her right temple. She screwed her eyes shut as her mind spun, waiting for it to come to a halt. The blood reached her cheek. It tickled but she couldn't wipe it away with her hands inside the suit.

When her mind had stopped spinning, Amerii picked herself up and then picked up her laser rifle. The heavy gun had taken a beating, but it still seemed to be functioning. The sensors on the Heavy Armour showed that the Wraith had disappeared. Was it waiting for her to try to reach Van again?

It seemed to enjoy hurting her.

She turned to face Van where he still knelt on the floor. He looked terrible. She could barely recognise him through the blood that coated his face and neck. It seemed the Wraith had enjoyed hurting him too. Her mate.

She shouldered her rifle again.

The Wraith would pay for that.

Just as she took a step towards Van, the Wraith appeared in front of him. It seemed more real this time, more than just a drifting cloud of white. It had form, shaped like a humanoid but at least twice as tall as any species she knew. It had eyes, hollow holes that held no emotion, and a smile that set her teeth on edge.

It bent towards Van and grabbed his hair, hauling his head up.

"No!" Amerii shouted and ran at the Wraith, the Heavy Armour's steps like thunder on the dusty ground. She took aim. Her finger closed around the trigger. Her heart missed a beat.

Before she could release the round, the Wraith was in front of her, past the muzzle of the rifle. She could only watch in horror as it reached towards her, everything moving in slow motion, and its hand moved straight through her visor and into the helmet. Hot burning fingers closed around her throat.

Amerii stared up into its hollow eyes.

As it squeezed her throat, she brought the gun back and fired.

A dark smile crossed the Wraith's face and then faded. Amerii's breathing quickened as she blinked and stared up at it. The hand disappeared from her throat. Its face turned elusive and began to disintegrate, drifting away in the breeze. She stared into its eyes as they narrowed and then blinked out of existence.

She still stared long after it had gone.

Her heart beat hard.

Her breathing was shallow.

Her body felt numb.

A noise snapped her out of her shock, bringing back the sound of gunfire outside the old building and the bright sunshine that beamed down at her from the hole in the ceiling.

She turned and lowered her head to look at Van. He was conscious, looking up at her as he knelt on the floor.

Her heart clenched at the sight of his face so beaten and bloodied. A cut split his lip and it had swollen. His left eye was almost closed from the swelling around it and a nasty gash ran across his eyebrow, over the tender skin of his eyelid. Long strands of his hair had stuck to the blood on his face. She wanted to clear them away and look after him. She wanted to tell him that things would be fine now that they were together again.

There were cuts on his throat and in the fabric of his suit on his arms and chest. She thanked Iskara that the suit seemed to have sustained the bulk of the damage and protected him. Tears filled her eyes but she fought to hold them back. This wasn't over yet. They still had to get him back to the compound and she had lost the other Varkan soldier.

Walking towards him, Amerii smiled when he moved so he could continue to look up at her, even though he probably couldn't see her through the darkened visor.

She knelt down on one knee. It hit the dirt hard, sending a jolt through her. It wasn't easy to perform delicate moves like kneeling in the Heavy Armour.

Reaching around him, she broke the metal restraints on his arms, the Heavy Armour making them look as brittle as glass.

"Thank you, soldier." Van gripped the arm of the Heavy Armour, pulling himself up onto his feet.

She held him steady when he wobbled and frowned.

"I owe you much," he said, voice quiet and hoarse. "Give me your rank and I will see to it that Varka hears of your bravery."

There were bruises on his throat, as though someone had been throttling him. She swallowed, feeling the ache in her own throat. That Wraith had paid for what it had done, but she didn't feel any better. She wanted more. She wanted to bring it back so she could fight it again and make it truly pay for inflicting such terrible injuries on her mate.

"Soldier?" Van said.

Amerii smiled to herself when she realised that he thought she was a Varkan. She pressed the two sides of her helmet and it extended outwards and then opened up to reveal her face. Van stared at her, his eyes wide and his lips parted in shock.

"Amerii?"

She nodded, amused that he needed her to confirm that.

"What are you doing out here?" He frowned. "You are hurt."

He stepped towards her and she closed her eyes briefly as he wiped the blood from her cheek and temple. The sweep of his fingers was gentle, tender. It filled her with warmth and drew her tears out of her. She sniffed them back and told herself to be strong. The sight of Van so hurt scared her though. She wished she could hold him, could feel his arms around her, but she couldn't in the suit.

Looking at him, she found he was staring at his fingers and the blood coating them. His eyes brightened to vivid crimson. She could see the battle within him.

"I'm fine," she said, wanting to alleviate his anger and soothe him. He looked at her, right into her eyes, and his frown melted away, his irises darkening back to normal. "I'm just glad that you're okay."

Her brow furrowed as she looked at him, seeing all his injuries and wishing there was something that she could do about them.

The Varkan officer she had lost came thundering around the corner.

He walked into the room and kneeled before Van. Amerii noticed that his suit barely made a sound as his knees hit the dirt. He clearly had better control over the Heavy Armour than she did.

"We came to rescue you," she said with an affectionate and soft smile, holding her hand out to Van. "If you're ready to go, I really think we should. I could carry you if you wanted."

Van frowned at her and the Varkan soldier looked up in her direction. She didn't need to see his face to know that he would be scowling too. Insinuating that Van was weak was becoming quite amusing. She liked how he reacted to it. She liked the way he looked when he frowned. It added to his handsomeness.

He touched the hand of the Heavy Armour, frowned again, and then touched her face instead. His hand was warm against her face, soothing as he held her cheek and looked into her eyes. He nodded.

"I am sure I can last the journey back to the station." He glanced up at the sun, his eyes narrowing to slits, and then looked at her and the soldier. "We will need to hurry. The sun is a long time from setting."

She closed her helmet and then turned to lead the way. She knew what that meant and even though her heart said to, she couldn't refuse him. If he wanted to run, then they would run. She wouldn't risk the sun damaging his eyes by making him walk.

"Keep between us. Lyran fighters are waiting outside to cover us."

Amerii walked back out into the corridor, her eyes on Van for a moment where he walked between her and the Varkan officer. She would see him back safe. She wouldn't let anything happen to him.

Never.

Amerii walked into the infirmary, smiled politely at the nurses, and went into the small room where they were holding Van. Holding was the right word. They'd had to restrain him to stop him from trying to leave the bed. He was nowhere near ready for duty again, even if he insisted that he was.

She snuck into the room, as quiet as she could so she didn't wake him. He looked better today. Many of the cuts were now healed, the swelling had disappeared, and his skin had a little more colour, or at least as much as she had come to expect of it. It had been four days since the Wraiths had captured him.

The Lyran fighters had escorted them back to the complex and had then returned to blanket bomb the North Sector. She had gone with Van to his vessel, but not before her captain had taken her aside.

It seemed she had finally impressed him and that he was recommending her for a long overdue promotion. His apology had been so sincere that she hadn't been able to speak for several minutes and had only been able to salute him.

He had also given her leave to remain by Van's side until he recovered. She was grateful for it but even if he had refused, she would have gone anyway.

She sat beside Van on the black covers of his bed and stroked the hair from his face. The monitors above him showed him as stable now. A red gauge read ninety-seven. Apparently, it meant he was close to being completely healed.

She gave a shy glance at her wrist and the marks on it. In the shuttle en route to the ship, she had fed Van. The Varkan officer who had rescued him with her had told her that even a small amount of her blood would help increase Van's healing speed.

She had given him all she could without passing out.

"What are you thinking?" a drowsy voice said, the sound of it warming her right down to the marrow of her bones.

"About you." She looked into Van's eyes.

Their dark red irises still spoke of fatigue. She smiled and caressed his cheek. His hand came up and claimed hers, bringing it down to his chest.

"I wish you would not worry so."

He could say that a million times and it wouldn't change a thing. She would always worry about him.

"I'm not the only one who worries." She moved closer so she was sitting near his ribs. He rested one arm across her lap, holding her hand with his other. "Regis is en route."

Van rolled his eyes and sighed.

"He claimed it was so Sophia could see me as planned, but I think it's for your sake that he's coming. Sophia said he was packing the moment he heard you were injured."

Even though Van looked unimpressed, she could see that Regis's concern had touched him.

"I didn't tell him," she whispered, afraid to raise her voice now. His gaze shifted to her throat, to the marks hidden beneath the collar of her tight blue and black flight suit. "I thought it was best you told him and it was done face to face."

"Have you told anyone?"

She nodded.

"My captain knows. Your crew knows. And when you were... while you were sleeping... I contacted my parents."

His hand tensed against hers. "And?"

She smiled at the tremble in his voice. Her fearless Varkan was afraid of the one thing in the universe that she would always be able to protect him from—her parents.

"My father wishes to know if all Varkans claim their women first and ask for their hand after."

"Is that a bad response?" he said.

"He wished to meet you. I told him that he already had. My mother reminded him about a certain young Varkan who had spent half the night talking to his daughter. He remembered you rather vividly then. It seems he has heard all kinds of positive things about you. Regis has been talking to my uncle, Sebastian, and in turn, he has been telling my father. It sounds rather like a plot to me."

Van frowned. "Regis."

"You didn't happen to mention why you wanted to learn love, did you?"

He shook his head. "He also noticed that I had spent a long time talking to you though."

"You'll have to thank him for the groundwork on my father. It seems he approves of you and will be looking forward to discussing tactics with you at our wedding."

"When we return to Lyra?"

She shook her head this time and patted his hand. "He's on his way here. We're already heading to Varka Prime where the ceremony will take place. Regis will meet us halfway and we will transfer to his ship. You'll have around six days to prepare to meet my father. Will it be enough? I had always read that Varkans were fearless..."

His eyes narrowed into a glare.

"I do not fear your family," he said with a grim expression.

"That's the spirit." She smiled even though he frowned at her.

"How did your captain find out?"

Pulling the collar of her blue and black flight suit down, she touched the marks on her throat. "I showed him these."

Van's eyes brightened, sending a flush of heat through her.

"Hungry?" Amerii whispered, her own and different form of hunger rising. He looked at the door and she glanced there. Before she could stop to consider how naughty the thoughts crossing her mind were, she was at the door and locking it. She crossed the room back to Van and moved to kneel on bed. He groaned when she straddled him.

His eyes followed her hand and she lowered the fastening of her flight suit to just past her breasts. She pulled the collar of it to one side to expose her neck.

He pulled her down to him, his grip on her waist firm and his tongue caressing her throat. Closing her eyes, she leaned into him, sighing out her breath.

"Are you well enough for this?" she whispered, afraid that she might hurt him.

"Stop worrying so much," he muttered and she did when he kissed her, his mouth warm against hers, his kiss persuasive and electrifying.

Returning the kiss, her lips caressing his and her hands pressing into his shoulders, she thought about her future now.

She was sure that when she reached Varka Prime, she wouldn't want to leave it again. She would want to remain there with Sophia and her family, and with Van.

Her father's wedding gift had been leave from duty and she intended to spend it on Varka Prime. He had given it to her when she had admitted how frightened she had been on the battlefield against the Wraiths, and how horrifying the sight of death was.

She had almost asked her father to discharge her.

Before she could voice that request, he had told her of his first experience in close combat, and how scared he had been on seeing death for the first time and being injured.

It had made her realise that he had grown from his experience, and he had found a way to deal with the things that happened in war. It had changed him, but for the better. He had become stronger, and she knew that she could become stronger too.

Instead of asking him to discharge her, she had requested a transfer to one of the ships that would remain in Varkan space assisting the rebuilding of the base station on Varka Two. Van would be heavily involved in the project and it would mean that they could spend time together and she wouldn't have to give up her dream of becoming a captain. Perhaps she would even make it to the rank of general one day.

Her father had granted her request and had told her that she was strong, even when she doubted it. She was like her mother.

That had made her smile. She had always thought she was like her father, always seeing him as the stronger one out of her parents. Now she could see that she was like them both.

Her strength and resolve had come from both of them. She was a good soldier and she knew that she could make something of herself, could help her fellow soldiers and could make a difference just as her parents had. With Van at her side, she believed that she was strong enough to make the rank of captain.

But first there was the matter of getting married.

It had been her request to have the wedding on Varka Prime. She hoped that once they were there, Regis would grant Van time away from his duties and they could spend their leave together on the planet.

She pulled back and stared into Van's eyes.

"Van?"

"Amerii?"

"When we're married... what will my gift be?"

He smiled as though he knew the answer that she wanted. She wanted what Sophia and Regis had. She wanted the gift that Regis had given Sophia.

"The only gift I can give that is worthy of you," Van whispered and pulled her back down to him. He kissed her throat and then her ear. He whispered into it, "Eternity."

Her eyes closed on hearing that word and she smiled.

Soon the kiss he placed on her throat would be one that would last forever and give her a gift beyond her imagination.

A gift that she wanted above all others.

Van.

For all eternity.

"Amerii," Van husked against her throat, kissing up it towards her jaw. She smiled lazily and held his mouth against her.

"Yes, my love?" she whispered and dipped her head to kiss his neck.

He took a deep breath.

"I love you." There was a tremble to his voice that made the usual echo that laced it even stronger.

Amerii stopped and pulled back, a blush on her cheeks. "You do?"

Van nodded, a nervous look in his eyes that was quickly chased away by hunger when her hands came to rest against his chest.

"I love you too." She leaned forwards, kissing him again and feeling light and hot inside. He loved her. She had seen it all in his eyes. He had realised his dream of feeling love. He had changed himself for her. Her stomach flipped and jigged, her heart thumping against her ribs. "How does it feel?"

He swallowed hard, pushed her off him and smiled into her eyes.

She smiled back at him. He was so handsome and he was all hers.

His smile widened.

"Like I am flying and falling at the same time."

Her smile widened too on hearing her description of love on his lips. She knew that feeling well.

With a sigh, she leaned down again and kissed him, whispering against his lips, "Like flying and falling."

But more than that.

It was flying and falling.

And knowing that Van would always catch her.

Always.

The End

HEART OF AN ASSASSIN

Princess Natalia, one of the beautiful and strong daughters of Lyra, has spent her whole life on Lyra Five behaving just as a princess should, except for one thing. After her daily duties she sneaks out at night to sing in the bars of Lyra Five, pretending to be someone else. Natalia loves to sing, more than anything else in the galaxy, until the night that Ixion, the handsome commander of the royal assassins, comes to the bar to bring her home.

Ixion is the only man Natalia has dreamed of since she first saw him seven years ago, but she's sure he doesn't notice her and she's determined to change that. But Natalia couldn't be more wrong.

Ixion has loved his elusive princess, Natalia, since the night he revealed himself to her, and now he faces a daily struggle between his duty and his heart, between hoping a princess could love him, an assassin and man of no rank in society, and fearing that she loves another man more worthy of her heart.

When Natalia insists on going to the spring festival, Ixion is ordered to ensure her safety, just as she hoped, but things don't go as smoothly as she had planned. An explosion in the port triggers a battle between the purist factions and the imperial army and Natalia is caught in the middle of it.

Will Ixion be able to protect Natalia? Will Natalia be able to convince Ixion that she loves him and that the passionate night they share won't be their only time? When her family discovers she's in love with an assassin, will Natalia be able to save him or will Ixion face a death sentence?

CHAPTER 1

Natalia lifted her head and almost stopped singing when she spotted him sitting alone at a table at the back of the dark and crowded club.

What was he doing here?

Without missing a beat, Natalia continued to sing to the gathered Terrans but his presence played on her mind, making her movements restrained. She pushed rogue spikes of her black hair off her neck, trying to cool down while still looking as though she was dancing. Nerves fluttered in her stomach, keeping time with the fast bouncy music. She twirled and the moment she faced front, her gaze snapped back to him.

He stared at her.

The room was too hot. Her eyes darted to the exits either side of the stage. She struggled to keep singing under his watchful gaze.

What was a royal assassin doing here?

Was he here for her, and if he was, why had they sent him?

The song faded. Natalia gave a quick bow and then fled the small stage. No time for the usual talk at the end of her set tonight. The applaud ceased when a door slid shut behind her. No time for an encore.

She had to get away.

Natalia turned down the corridor to her changing room, hurrying along it as quickly as she could manage in the platform-heeled metallic pink boots. The door to the changing room slid open and she hit the pad to shut it behind her. No time for a shower. She stripped off the small shiny pink and white top, the long gloves, and the tiny shorts and stuffed them into the black bag that she always brought with her. She tugged on her long deep blue dress and fumbled with the fastenings across the front, struggling to tighten and tie the ribbons with her trembling fingers. When she was done with her dress, she grabbed her hair, twirled it around into a knot at the back of her head and pinned it roughly into place.

What was he doing here?

Did her father know about her singing?

Her breaths shortened and came faster when she thought about how angry her father would be if he discovered that she had been singing in the slums of Lyra Five. Her mother would kill her.

Maybe the assassin was just in the club to relax like all the other patrons. Maybe she was mistaken.

Natalia stormed along the corridor towards the exit that led to the narrow street at the back of the club. The palace was far away but she was going to run all the way there, even up the steep hill on which it stood overlooking the city. She would be in her rooms within the hour. No one would know that she had been gone.

She sent a prayer to Iskara that she was mistaken and it wasn't him. The bright lights on the stage could easily have turned someone else's face into his. It might not be him.

No. It was definitely him. The lights hadn't been that strong and she had taken a good look at him. She had only seen his face once before but it was enough. You didn't forget a royal assassin.

She had to get home. Perhaps he hadn't recognised her. No one else did. Renie was the more famous of them and Natalia always looked different when attending public events and around the palace. He might not recognise her.

The beaten grey metal back door slid open as she approached.

Natalia froze in her tracks, her heart hammering.

"Princess Natalia," he said, voice deeper than she had expected.

It sent an odd tremor through her.

Ixion stepped forward. Head to toe in black, and with his dark hair, he was a sight to be seen. His clear purple eyes fixed on her as he moved into the corridor, blocking her only exit. The muscles of his lithe body shifted beneath his tight black uniform with each step.

Natalia's palms sweated and her skin turned tacky. She clutched the bag over her shoulder and tried to see if she could pass him. It was too hot in the building. She longed to drink in the cool night air and to return home to her apartments in the palace. She wanted to pretend that she hadn't been caught.

"I don't know who you mean." The quiver in her voice ruined her denial.

"Princess Natalia."

Her heart fluttered at the way her name sounded on his lips—soft and sensual. She had never heard him speak before, didn't know anything about him or any of the royal assassins.

She tried to move past him but he shifted to block her path, towering over her. She didn't even know where he was from. He wasn't Lyran or Terran. None of the assassins were. They were a different species entirely.

Natalia tried the other side but he blocked her again.

She stared at his knee-high black leather boots and hunched up, clutching her bag with both hands over her right shoulder. It was no use. While she had never seen him close up or more than once, he had clearly seen her a lot of times, enough to recognise her when others hadn't. She supposed that was part of his job. He and his men were often used as stealth bodyguards for her family.

"Did father send you?" She gave up her attempt to lie. It probably didn't do to lie to a royal assassin. Although they worked for her father, they were still deadly and mysterious, giving off an air of men who would gladly kill anyone if they were offered the right price.

Natalia corrected herself. Ixion wouldn't. He had been with her family since she could remember. She had heard his name repeatedly from when she had only been a child. He was loyal to her family.

Her eyes scanned up the length of him, over taut muscles that were only emphasised by his uniform, until they reached his face.

Ixion shook his head, causing finger-length strands of his black hair to fall down across his pale forehead.

In a way, he looked Minervan, but she knew that he wasn't. No Minervan had eyes so vivid and purple.

"Mother?" she whispered, hoping he would say no. She didn't want to upset her mother, not after what she had been through with Renie and Rezic's kidnapping by the Vegans.

"None at the palace know." His voice was as smooth as the ocean of Lyra Five, and almost as deep.

Natalia exhaled long and slow, and then frowned at him. "You knew."

"No one of importance knows," he said as though correcting himself and her.

No one of importance? He was part of the palace and an important part of it in her eyes.

He placed his right hand to his chest and bowed his head, closing his eyes. His hair fell forwards, a mass of long spikes that hung in front of his face.

"It is not safe, my lady. We must return to the palace."

Natalia tightened her grip on her black bag and nodded. At least she wouldn't be frightened on her way home tonight. Sometimes some of the men had too much cheap Lyran Aquan and came around back to serenade her with lewd suggestions and offers. She didn't think that they would dare approach her when Ixion was by her side.

His eyes opened and he looked up at her through the strands of his hair, his purple eyes cool and impassive. When she blinked, he straightened and turned, moving out into the alley.

Natalia followed.

They walked along the main street of the city. It ran straight to the palace and she could see it standing tall in the distance on top of the hills, lit up in the dark. Its pale stone towers shone brightly, like something out of the fairytales her mother had told her as a child. The waterfalls thundered down from arches at its base to the river one hundred feet below.

Her cousin Sophia had told her that the emperor's palace on Varka Prime was similar to hers, but a lot spikier and darker looking. She had looked up a picture of it and had decided that her palace was far superior. There was nothing in the galaxy that could compare to the beauty of her home. She loved it with all her heart, even when it felt like a prison at times.

Turning her attention away from the palace, she looked in the windows of the small redbrick buildings that lined the main street. The stores sold all kinds of goods, from junk to antiques and food to clothes. They were a treasure trove when they were open during the day hours and a place that she loved to wander around with her attendants in the rare times they had managed to escape the palace alone. There was always something new and fascinating to find.

In one of the windows was a pretty painted card advertising the upcoming spring festival. Natalia wanted to go to it but had never been allowed. Her attendants went every year and always came back with stories of wild animals and even wilder men, and of beautiful clothes and bolts of stunning coloured silks and materials. She loved to make her own clothes. Her outfit that she sung in at the club was one that she had made and certainly one that she had kept hidden from her parents. Her mother would have Snrikiks if she ever found out about her singing.

Natalia snuck a glance at Ixion. The street was only lowly lit by the tall glowing white lights that hung from the roofs of the shops but it was enough to see his face. He was younger than she had expected considering how long ago she had first heard his name and far more handsome. She didn't remember him looking this good the only time she had seen him but then he had been far away, not close enough for her to see any real detail. She had noticed his eyes though, couldn't forget the rich clear purple of them and the way they had fixed on her, intent and unnerving her back then. When they had settled on her tonight, she had felt no fear. She had only felt a strange stirring deep inside her and incredible warmth that had suffused every inch of her body.

They turned down a side street and came out by the river. The lights were brighter here, making the rapidly running water sparkle like diamonds. Two large passenger freighters passed overhead, one going towards the city port and one away, the tinny whine of their engines loud in the night. She wondered where the one leaving was going as it moved into the distance and struggled upwards. Out of the planet for certain and probably only to another one in the Lyra system, but she imagined that it was going somewhere far away, to a place that she had never been.

To one where Ixion might have come from.

She looked at him again, as furtively as possible so he didn't realise that she couldn't keep her eyes off him. He was incredible. His straight nose, the delicious curve of his dusky lips, and the strong square line of his jaw made his profile so noble that she could imagine that he was a prince from some distant planet. The light shone off his purple eyes, making them bright. It wasn't just his profile that made him regal. It was the way that he held himself. He walked with his shoulders back and chin tilted up, a confident stride that spoke of assurance. No man was a threat to him. More than a prince. He looked like a king.

Her gaze flickered to the palace. He was certainly more of a prince than two of her older brothers, Aiden and Ciel, and possibly more than her oldest brother Rezic.

Natalia glanced at Ixion again and then up at the crescent moon and the stars beyond. Where did Ixion come from? How old had he been when he had joined the royal assassins?

She had first heard his name when she was five. That was twenty Lyran years ago now. Ixion didn't look beyond fifteen years older than her. She wanted to ask him about his species but didn't dare converse so freely with him. A princess wasn't supposed to talk to those outside her circle, even if she wanted to know about them more than anything in the world.

If she knew what species he was, she could look it up on her computer pad at home and learn more about him. She could find out whether his species aged differently to Lyrans, like the Varkans and Vegans did. He was no species that she recognised. She had never met another man like him. Everyone seemed so ordinary in comparison.

He was quiet as he walked beside her but she could sense that he wasn't deep in thought. He was aware of everything, his hands remaining constantly near the two long daggers strapped to his thighs. Did he think that she was in danger? The streets were empty. They hadn't seen a soul since leaving the entertainment quarter.

The light shone on him again, making the delicate royal Lyran blue embroidery around the cuffs of his black stand-up collared jacket glimmer.

Natalia realised that he hadn't been out tonight without reason. If he had been off duty, he wouldn't have worn his uniform. It was obvious to any who knew about the Lyran royal family that he was an assassin. He had been on a mission, or he had wanted to be seen.

That was a strange notion for Natalia. Ixion was their best assassin. She had only seen him once in her lifetime and they had been in the same palace since she was a child. She had seen other assassins several times, which had led her to believe that the one time she had seen Ixion, he had wanted to be seen.

He had wanted her to see him.

Just as he had wanted her to tonight.

Her parents hadn't sent him. He wasn't on a mission from the palace. He had sent himself. A chill raced through her but she wasn't frightened. In fact, she felt strangely honoured that Ixion had chosen to retrieve her and bring her home safely.

It wasn't his duty to do such things, but he had done it nonetheless.

Which meant he was telling the truth when he said that no one at the palace knew.

"What were you doing in the city?" She hoped that he would just think that she was making small talk and wasn't probing for answers.

"Following you." His eyes remained forwards, his deep voice emotionless.

Her heart thumped against her chest. Following her? He must have seen her leave the palace and wondered where she was going so late in the day. She always left after dinner and it was getting dark then at this time of year.

"Why?" That question came out blunter than she had wanted.

Ixion looked at her. He blinked slowly but not a trace of emotion showed in his eyes.

"I have noticed you leaving the palace at night for several months." He faced forwards again and a frown married his eyebrows. "It is dangerous at night in the city right now."

Was it? It didn't seem any different to usual but he would know better than her. The only city matters that she was involved in were balls, openings and festivals, and any other ceremonies. Her father kept her and her siblings away from news that he thought might upset them. Was something going to happen? If it did, the palace was well protected. The bridges over the wide moat would rise and the shield would activate to cover the entire area in a dome. If something happened, she would be safe, but it still frightened her when she thought about it.

Her city had always been peaceful. The only violence she had ever witnessed was drunken fights outside the club.

"So you came for me?" she said in a quiet voice, distracted by her thoughts and the idea that Ixion had feared for her safety. He nodded. "Thank you."

His purple gaze slid to her. "It is my duty to protect you and your family."

She stopped and turned to face him. "It is also your duty to tell my family what I have done, is it not?"

Ixion came to a halt and slowly moved to face her.

"Are you going to tell my father?" Natalia's heart clenched at the thought. Her father would be so angry with her for going out into the city after dark and singing somewhere so public without any guards. She bit her lip and stared into Ixion's eyes, waiting to hear her sentence.

She would do anything to keep him silent.

A frown creased her brow when a voice at the back of her mind asked exactly how far she would go to silence Ixion.

The pale light of the streetlamp shone down on his face. His gaze held hers, steady and intent, his stunning purple irises stirring something deep inside her. She pressed a hand to her stomach as it warmed. Her heart fluttered against her ribs like a butterfly, trembling in its attempt to break free and fly to him.

He was so mysterious and handsome, and she had never experienced anything like the pull she felt to him. It was deep, making her chest and stomach hot, and tingles dance along her nerve endings whenever his eyes met hers.

"We must keep moving," he said at last.

Natalia shook her head. "No. Not until you promise not to tell my parents."

His eyes darkened as he frowned. He looked as though he was going to refuse and then slowly nodded.

"But you must promise me something in return." Those words held a sense of foreboding and she knew what he was going to say. She didn't move, didn't want to agree to his terms, even though it would mean trouble if she didn't. "You must stop leaving the palace to sing."

It hurt to agree to that, to sacrifice the one thing that made her truly happy and feel free, but she nodded nonetheless. She had no other choice. She was asking a lot of him by making him promise to keep her habit secret and go against his duty to inform her parents of any danger to the family. The least she could do was promise that she wouldn't put herself at risk anymore.

With a heavy heart, Natalia followed him over the bridge that led to the palace grounds and through a side gate. No one was on the other side and it wasn't a gate that she was familiar with. Was it one that the assassins used? She hadn't been paying attention to whether Ixion had a key for it.

Looking up at the palace towering above her, she tightened her grip on her sack of clothes and sighed. So much for freedom. She was reduced to singing in her room again and living the life of a princess.

They walked up through the gardens and she followed Ixion when he branched away from her normal path and took a barely visible one through the low flowering shrubs. It twisted and snaked its way through the garden and she was surprised when it came out right by the door to her apartments.

She looked back, trying to see the path, but the night stole her vision and made the path invisible—just as it made Ixion invisible. She could barely see him in the low light from her apartments. He lingered in the shadows away from her door, on the main path that led to the back of the palace.

Natalia looked into his eyes, wondering if he would keep his promise and whether she would ever see him again. Twice in her life, he had allowed her to see him, and this time it had affected her deeply. She wanted to know more about him and how he came to be at the palace. She wanted to know why he had come to escort her back rather than sending a guard, and why he would keep her secret when it went against his duty to do so.

Most of all, she wanted to know him.

He placed his right hand against his chest and bowed. "Goodnight, my lady."

With that he disappeared into the night before she could even realise he was gone. She blinked and stared at the spot where he had been.

She pressed her hand against the panel beside her door. The light flashed blue and the twin arched glass and white wood doors to her apartments opened. She looked back into the garden, trying to catch a glimpse of Ixion.

She knew that he was still nearby. She could feel him watching her, just as she had felt his eyes on her at the club.

"Goodnight," she whispered and then walked into her apartments, knowing that she wouldn't be able to sleep tonight.

Not when her heart and mind were full of Ixion.

He made her feel things that she had never experienced before.

For the first time in her life, she wanted to know a male's touch.

Ixion's touch.

CHAPTER 2

Ixion tilted his head back and looked up the impressive height of the central courtyard of the palace to the blazing blue sky above. It was hard to tell what time it was. It seemed to be moving slowly today, dragging its heels as though the sun didn't want to set. He wished it would. Today had been nothing short of torture.

And he couldn't keep his mind off Natalia.

Every shy glance and smile she had given him had been replayed in his mind at least a thousand times since he had left her last night. His concentration was shot, enough that he had agreed to something without thinking it through. Something he was regretting.

Aiden collided with Ciel and burst into a fit of laughter when his older brother fell, his backside hitting the white flagstones of the courtyard hard.

Ixion's jaw ticked.

How could the beautiful and elegant Natalia be related to such buffoons? Her older brothers were both fools, good for nothings that didn't know the meaning of work or study. Ixion pressed his fingers to the bridge of his nose.

"Again… without the tomfoolery," he ground the words out from between clenched teeth.

A curse rolled off Ixion's tongue when the two men ignored what he had said and began to play fight with the wooden swords that he had provided for use in their lesson today. When their tutor returned from his urgent business, Ixion was going to have words with him. Aiden and Ciel were impossible. They lacked even basic manners and their fighting skill was atrocious.

If they continued to vex him much longer, he was going to have to intervene and show them how quickly they would lose in a fight for their lives. He couldn't hurt them but he could bring them down several pegs. It would take him no more than ten seconds to disarm and pretend to kill them.

Ciel brushed his black hair from his eyes, smoothing the strands back into his long ponytail, and thrust the wooden sword at Aiden. Aiden was two years younger than Ciel but they were both broad of build and tall, a strange mixture of their mother and father, just like the family's firstborn, the twins Renie and Rezic.

Rezic showed as much responsibility towards his species as the two younger brothers did. Ixion didn't think much of Renie's exploits either. As the first princess of the family, she should have remained on Lyra Five and attended to her duties.

Being an elite member of the royal guard gave him access privileges to the family's schedule. All of the appointments that were assigned to her brothers and sister, Natalia attended. She went to all of the ceremonies and receptions, and read through most of the invitations and letters that came to the palace. Her brothers and sister could learn a lot from Natalia.

Her schedule was punishing but she endured it because she felt a responsibility towards her people. A true princess—kind, warm hearted, open and beautiful.

Aiden bumped into him. Ixion gritted his teeth and pushed him away, barely stopping himself from hitting him as he desired to. He sighed and looked up at the patch of sky again, willing the time to pass so he could escape to somewhere quiet where he could be alone with his thoughts.

"Again. From the top. The moves that I showed you, if you please, my lords." His words gained a sharp edge at the last, his frustration getting the better of him.

He had never had direct contact with Aiden and Ciel before, but had heard about their disrespect towards the palace staff. Having witnessed it firsthand, he found himself struck by a longing to beat some manners into them.

Just at that moment, a breath of fresh air swept through the room.

Natalia.

She looked at him with wide startled eyes and then lowered her gaze and hurried forwards. Beautiful Natalia. His impossible dream. He had allowed her to see him once when she was eighteen and could still remember how she had looked at him—frightened but fascinated. He had guarded her ever since, although she hadn't been aware of it. When she had started sneaking down into the city last year, he had considered stopping her straight away but then he had seen how happy it made her to sing and he hadn't been able to through with it. Things were different now though. Back then, it hadn't been dangerous for her to be out alone at night. Now she was attracting attention from the wrong crowd—the kind who would kill her if they realised who she was.

"Where are we scurrying of to?" Aiden stepped in front of Natalia. She frowned up at him and tried to pass but he blocked whichever direction she went.

She turned around and swept the two long strands of hair that framed her beautiful face out of her eyes. Ciel stood behind her, his sword resting on his shoulder and a wide grin on his face.

"I'm busy," Natalia said on a sigh. "Just get out of the way."

There was a tired edge to her voice that spoke of stress. Ixion had seen her schedule for today and it was as gruelling as ever. By now, she would have been working straight for six hours and would have travelled down into the city for a council meeting about the festival. Her brothers were being nothing but cruel by delaying her.

"Don't go." Ciel grabbed her around the waist from behind. He lifted her off the floor and she slid downward in her pale pink accented white empire-line dress. It rode upwards, exposing her legs to the thigh. "Play a while."

Ixion swallowed hard. Iskara. It was wrong of him but he was thankful to Ciel.

Natalia struggled, flailing her legs, and Ixion couldn't take his eyes off them. The white stockings she wore made his heart thunder. His elusive princess.

He looked away, berating himself for taking such liberties. Natalia was a princess. It was wrong of him, a lowly assassin, to look at her like that.

A dull ache settled in his chest. It was wrong of him to love her. It was torture.

"Get off me," Natalia said and then Ciel cried out in pain.

Ixion's head snapped around. Ciel was clutching his shin, hopping around the courtyard as Aiden laughed. Natalia stood with her hands on her hips, glaring at both of her brothers. She huffed and straightened out the loose knot of black hair at the back of her hair and the frowned.

Ixion was about to go to her when she stooped, picked up the wooden sword that Ciel had dropped and stalked towards her brother. She snatched Aiden's sword from him and shoved it into Ciel's hand. Her brothers stood at least eight inches taller than her and were three times as broad, but she wasn't intimidated in the least.

"Play?" She held the wooden sword out in both hands. "Is that what you think this is?"

Ciel and Aiden exchanged a confused look.

"All you two ever do is play, and I'm going to prove it. I bet you can't beat me. Nothing that Ix—your tutor says goes into that thick head of yours."

Ixion smiled inside at the fact that she had almost said his name. He wasn't surprised that she knew it. Since he was head of the royal assassins, he was often spoken about by her father and the members of the elite guard.

He was also silently thankful that she intended to beat some manners into her brothers for him.

Ciel looked wary and then straightened to his full height, his cocksure smile back on his face. Aiden patted him on the shoulder and gave him a look that said it should be an easy win.

The moment Aiden had stepped aside, Natalia launched herself at Ciel. Ixion had never trained any of the royal family to fight but knew that the daughters had been trained to the same level as the sons. Clearly, Natalia had given her tutor and lessons the attention they deserved because Ciel was immediately on the back foot, desperately blocking her thrusts and strikes.

The look of sheer determination on Natalia's face only made her more beautiful. Her emerald green eyes sparkled with satisfaction when she landed a blow and a smile curved her delicate rose lips. Ixion pressed a hand to his chest, willing his heart to be still when it raced at the glorious sight of her. She fought with grace and speed, and with immeasurable elegance fit for a princess. She was stunning. If she hadn't captured his heart before that moment, she would have claimed it then.

Ciel tried to dodge her wooden blade and swing at her but she ducked and kicked his legs out. He crashed to the floor. Before Ciel could recover, her white booted foot was on his chest and her sword was against his throat.

The sound of clapping echoed around the room.

"Stunning," a deep warm voice said, reflecting Ixion's thoughts. He turned at the same time as Natalia and her brothers to face the newcomer. General Lyra II. Ixion immediately pressed his right hand against his chest and bowed his head. "My sons would do well to listen to their tutor's instruction since their little sister has beaten them."

General Lyra II halted in front of them as Aiden helped Ciel up off the floor. Natalia hid the sword behind her back, a deep blush staining her cheeks.

"You will never make officers if you do not apply yourself to your studies," General Lyra II said with a saddened expression.

Ixion didn't think that Aiden or Ciel wanted to be in the imperial army. Neither of them showed any inclination to do anything besides playing the fool.

"Natalia." General Lyra II turned to face his daughter. She looked up at him with wide eyes that held a trace of fear. Her father was an imposing figure but Ixion didn't think that she had a reason to fear him. He hadn't said a word about her singing in the city clubs. He would take that secret to his grave for her. "I would like you to come with me. I need to discuss something with you before I leave to meet Renie and Rezic at the edge of the system and escort them home."

Natalia nodded and handed the fake sword to Aiden.

Ixion kept his head bowed but watched her as she passed. She was frightened. Why? Was she expecting some sort of retribution for her behaviour today or was it something else?

The town clock chimed the hour, the sound of the bells carried on the still warm air. Ixion saluted Aiden and Ciel and left. Rather than heading back to his quarters and reporting for duty, he followed Natalia and her father. It went against his duty to spy on General Lyra II but he had to know what he was going to say to Natalia, because whatever it was, it scared her.

They disappeared into her father's chambers and Ixion hung back. He couldn't stand by the door and listen. It was too obvious. There were rooms adjoining her father's office. He looked around the wide arched stone corridor and then went into one. It was a grand drawing room. He had been in it once before when he had first arrived and the general and Natalia's mother had greeted him and the others. There was a door that joined it to the office where Natalia and her father were. Ixion walked over to it and leaned his head against the dark wooden door, listening.

"Several potential suitors have contacted me."

Ixion wished that he hadn't heard those words right. He closed his eyes and leaned harder into the door, until his skull ached.

"Suitors?" There was a high note of panic in Natalia's voice but something told Ixion that her father's suggestion wasn't so wholly unexpected.

She was mating age after all and her sister was to be married. It made sense that her father would start to think about finding her a husband too.

A husband?

Ixion felt sick. He had watched Natalia for seven years. Had fallen in love with her. Now he was going to have to stand by and watch as she was married off to some whelp of a male for the sake of the prosperity of Lyra and good relations with whatever species the male was from. It turned his stomach.

He pressed his hand to the door, wishing that he could see Natalia's face so he knew what she was feeling. Did the thought of suitors frighten her?

"Send them away," Natalia said and something slammed into something else. Her fist? It sounded as though she had hit something. "I want no suitor!"

"Natalia... my sweetest angel of Iskara... you are twenty five. When you turned mating age it was only a matter of time before you attracted the attention of suitors. You are beautiful, the very image of your mother, and it will be a sad day for me when you marry."

Ixion's fingers curled into a tight fist. How could her father talk like that when he was clearly going against her will just by entertaining the thought of allowing males to court her?

"You will be waiting a long time because I refuse. I will not have males peddling their wares for my heart!"

There was such force behind those words that Ixion was sure her father would be shocked by the outburst. Couldn't he see that she hated the very idea of having suitors come to the palace to court her?

The silence in the room next door stretched on. Ixion's breathing was slow and steady even when his heart beat fast with anticipation of what would happen next. He needed to see her face so he could read her feelings. Years of watching her had given him the ability to see the emotions she felt even when only a tiny trace of them showed on her face. He could see beyond it to her heart.

Looking down, he frowned at the old-fashioned brass handle and lock. He crouched and peered through the keyhole. He could see part of Natalia. She was facing towards him, staring intently at her father, her hands pressed against the wide wooden desk.

"Natalia." Her father's tone was cautious. "Is there someone already?"

Ixion's eyes widened. He watched Natalia closely. Her blush gave her away.

"Tell me, Natalia."

She shook her head and lowered it. Her fist came up and pressed against her lips. Ixion silently begged her to say the name of the male in her heart. He wanted to know who he had to kill. If it was anyone other than him, foolish dream as that was, he would see to it they disappeared.

The door opened behind her and a tall man stepped in, dressed in a tight blue and black flight suit. He saluted.

"I must leave," her father said and Ixion heard a chair move. Her father appeared in view and then stopped beside her, facing his officer. He placed a hand on her shoulder and turned his head towards her. "We will speak of this in a few days when I return."

With that, he walked away. Natalia remained in the same spot, hunched up and with her eyes closed. The pink stain on her cheeks darkened, as though she was thinking of the male who had stolen her attention. Ixion's heart darkened at the same rate as her cheeks, jealousy coiling deep within it. He had never wanted to kill a male more. He had never wanted to kill anyone at all for his own sake.

He stood and reminded himself that it wasn't his place to do things outside of his orders and his duty. Following Natalia into the city had broken the rules of a royal assassin, along with his failure to report her actions. He couldn't break any more rules without drawing attention to himself and bringing dishonour to his family.

As difficult as it was for him, he had to maintain his distance from Natalia and stop fooling himself into believing that something might ever happen between them. A princess would never fall in love with an assassin, and she would certainly never marry a man like him.

When she married, it would be to a king, a leader of men and a public figure that people looked up to. A male of the standing that she deserved.

It wouldn't be to someone who didn't even exist in the eyes of universe.

It wouldn't be him.

CHAPTER 3

Natalia sighed for the hundredth time and stared out over the beautiful city as the sun set. Golden light cast an unearthly glow over the tiled roofs of the town and the tall tower of the city hall, turning them warm and peaceful. She had seen pictures of the towns that had once stood on Earth and one in particular reminded her most of her city. A place they had called Prague. She was sure that the city architects must have studied the towns of Earth when they had designed hers.

The waterfall cascaded below her, dropping the hundred feet to the pool at its base. The sun turned the water golden as it flowed out into the city, following the intricate network of canals.

In the town square, she could see them setting up the festival but it was too far away to get any real image of what it would look like. She longed to go there once in her lifetime, to wander around the stalls and see the entertainment with her own eyes. Hearing about it from her attendants wasn't enough. Every year it sounded more exciting, and every year she wanted to go more.

A small sleek blue and silver fighter vessel lifted off from the royal port and circled around the palace before heading upwards.

Her father.

She glared at the ship, glad that he was gone. Suitors? What was he thinking? She didn't want him to try to pair her off in the same way her cousin Sophia's father had.

Natalia rested her elbows on the white stone balustrade of the balcony and propped her head up on her hands. Suitors?

She wanted to be free to choose her own husband just as her older sister Renie had. Renie would return soon with her twin Rezic. Natalia couldn't wait to see them again, and meet the Vegan prince that Renie was going to marry, but the excitement was dampened by her father's proposition to find her a suitor.

A suitor!

Natalia turned her glare on the city. She didn't want males offering her planets and systems and monies or power. She wanted to be left alone. She wanted to be free.

She wanted to sing.

The sun touched the horizon and she looked down at the entertainment quarter. With the setting of the sun, the city would be changing. The stores would be closing and the bars opening. It was a different world down there after dark.

A deep longing to go down into the city to the club grew in her heart but she told herself that she couldn't. Singing made her forget her worries and made her happy. It was the one thing that made her feel free.

It was the one thing that she had promised she would give up.

She couldn't go down into the city. She had sworn to Ixion that she wouldn't go there anymore, even though she desperately wanted to. It would break her promise with Ixion and he might tell her parents this time. She couldn't outsmart a royal assassin of his standing. No matter which way she chose to go, he was bound to see her and stop her.

It was useless.

She couldn't risk it. If Ixion told her father, he might keep her locked in the palace until he found a male to marry her off to.

Soft steps on the white flagstones made her tense. She imagined it was a handsome male dressed in black, a dangerous male who made her giddy just from looking at him. The person came to stand beside her.

Not a male at all.

Her mother.

Natalia looked at her, managing a smile. Her father was right. She was the very image of her mother. Their black hair and bright green eyes matched perfectly. Her brothers and sister all looked more like their father. Perhaps that was why her father doted on her so much, because she looked like her mother. But then that didn't answer the question burning in her heart. Why had her father decided to start accepting proposals for her?

"Missing your father?" Her mother smiled but Natalia could see the strain in it. Her mother was missing her father at least.

Natalia took the small black translator bud from her ear. Sometimes it was nice to speak to her mother without it.

"No," Natalia said in Terran. Her mother removed her translator too.

"Have you two been arguing again?" Her mother's look was gentle, concerned, and it lifted some of the weight from Natalia's heart but made her feel weak at the same time. If she cried like she wanted to her mother would understand, but what kind of princess cried over something like this? She had always been the strong one, the responsible one, and that wasn't going to change now.

Natalia looked out at the city again.

"Are there really suitors contacting you?" Her voice trembled but she held it together. She wouldn't cry over something like this.

"He told you then?" Her mother sighed and placed her arm around Natalia's shoulders. She squeezed them and Natalia closed her eyes, feeling as though her future had already been determined and her sentence pronounced. Her father really did intend to take proposals from suitors. "Don't worry. He won't go through with it."

"How do you know?" Natalia leaned her head against her mother's shoulder, needing the comfort.

"Because he has mentioned it before and nothing came of it. He won't give you up so easily... at the moment he is just overwhelmed. He didn't expect you to grow up so quickly and be noticed so soon after you turned mating age."

There was a little comfort in those words but not enough. Her father could be unduly stubborn when it came to his duty and he would see finding her a good husband as one of his duties, even when she was willing to beg him not to. In that respect she was much like her father. She would do her duty and what was expected from her, even when it broke her heart.

"I don't want a suitor," she mumbled, her heart heavy again.

"And you won't have one." Her mother held her closer. "Renie and Rezic will return soon and we will all be together again. The preparations for Renie's wedding will keep him distracted. We can make sure that we reach the letters before him and get rid of any ones from suitors. If they contact him directly through the imperial army, we will simply have to bide our time. Renie's wedding will satisfy him and it is only a few months away."

A few months. In that time, her father might have given his consent to any number of the suitors who were bound to contact him via channels that she couldn't access. Neither her nor her mother had the clearance required to enter the imperial army's computer system.

She considered asking Rezic for help but thought the better of it. While her eldest brother could access the system, he was bound to be on her father's side. Mentioning it to him would only bring it to her father's attention again.

It was better to sit and wait just as her mother had suggested.

"Don't stay out too long. It will be cold tonight." Her mother squeezed her shoulders one last time and then left.

Natalia looked up at the darkening sky. Today had been such a good day too. For the first time in a long time, she had enjoyed doing her duty and had been happy without resorting to singing. Why had her father had to spoil it by talking to her of suitors?

She should have told him who she had thought of when he had asked her if she had a male. Her father would have had Snrikiks if she had announced that the male she wanted wasn't of royal blood or high status.

It was an assassin.

Ixion.

He had been on her mind all day. Every meeting that she had attended had been made a little easier because she had been thinking of him. She had relived their walk back to the palace from the city hall, telling her guards that she wanted a little air. She had retraced their steps and remembered the way that he had looked at her. It still made her heart race.

But there was no hope for a princess and a royal assassin.

Her father would have laughed at her once the initial shock had passed. He would have thought that she was joking.

Renie was going to marry a prince and her father would expect no less from her.

With another long sigh, Natalia started singing softly, hoping to lift the pain from her heart.

Only tonight, singing didn't make her happy.

For some reason it made her feel sad.

CHAPTER 4

Natalia's heart missed a beat and her pulse quickened when Ixion and two other men in similar black uniform stepped out of her father's day chambers. One of her mother's attendants had told her that they would find her there. Whenever her father was away, her mother took care of household business. Did she have business with the royal assassins? Ixion was their commander. Natalia didn't know the other two but they looked the same age as Ixion, if not a little younger.

She quickly smoothed her sky blue empire-line dress down and slowed to a more measured and demure pace. It had taken her three hours to dress this morning, two and a half hours longer than usual, and the reason she had taken such care was now talking to his men right in front of her. If he had noticed her, it didn't show on his face as he stood with his profile to her, discussing something that she couldn't hear.

Her steps didn't falter as she walked towards him, her hands clasped in front of her. Her two attendants walked a step behind her, silent support that she badly needed. They were the closest she had to friends, two women that she had known since turning ten. They shared everything with each other and they were always there to support her when she needed them most. Today was one of those days. It wasn't just because she had resolved to find Ixion and see him again, but because she had decided that she was going to go out. She was going to go to the festival and her mother wasn't going to stop her this time.

Ixion was only steps away from her now. Natalia willed him to look at her, to see her. She knew that he wouldn't but she wanted him to. She had made so much effort with her appearance today and it was all for him.

Just as she passed, she heard the shift of his boots on the stone flags and felt his gaze on her. Her mouth turned dry and she resisted the temptation to look at him. Playing hard to get was something that her attendants had always told her about whenever they had talked of males but it was more difficult than she had imagined. Her strength failed as the guards standing either side of the double door reached over and opened it. Her gaze slid to the side and a thrill bolted through her when she found Ixion's clear purple eyes fixed on her face.

"Natalia." Her mother's voice jolted her out of her reverie and she stepped into the room with her two attendants.

The doors closed.

"Whatever brings you here?" Her mother sat back down on the royal blue and silver couch, spreading her long cream satin gown across it.

Natalia could see past the smile plastered on her mother's face. She was always sad when her father went away. The worry lines between her mother's fine black eyebrows made Natalia sigh. She went over to her mother and wrapped her arms around her shoulders as she sat down beside her.

Her mother's smile faltered.

"He'll be back soon," Natalia said with a real smile, hoping to brighten up her mother. "It's only an escort mission within the Lyra system this time and if he encounters any trouble, he'll survive. He's too stubborn to die on the battlefield."

Her mother laughed. "You are right but it still doesn't stop me from worrying about him. Balt's stubbornness is the reason I worry so much."

Natalia understood that. Her father wasn't likely to turn tail and run if he encountered any resistance. He would fight to the end for Lyra.

She took hold of her mother's hand and squeezed it as she tried to think of a way to broach the subject that she had come here to raise. It was difficult now that she knew her mother was worried about her father. She didn't want to increase that worry by suggesting that she was going to go to the festival.

Natalia looked at her two attendants where they waited by the door. They nodded.

Perhaps they were right. Her plan might actually go better now that her mother was worried and she was sure that nothing would happen to them down in the city. They would only be there a few short hours and if things went to plan, they wouldn't be alone. They would have the best protection in the galaxy.

"Mother... I am going to go into the city today." Her heart fluttered and she could barely meet her mother's gaze.

Her mother's emerald eyes were wide, fear shining in them. "But the festival is in full swing and there are reports of potential unrest amongst some of the purist factions."

For a moment, Natalia's heart faltered and she almost said that she would stay in the palace. Ixion had spoken of danger in the city but Natalia hadn't realised that it was so bad. The purist factions hated Lyra and wanted revenge for what it had done to the Terran species. Years ago, the Earth system had been caught in the war between Lyra and Vega. It had been decimated and the Terran people scattered across the galaxy, orphans in space. Her father had met her mother, the last Terran princess, by accident when she was a slave and they had fallen in love. Her mother had united her people again and it had been so peaceful on Lyra Five, their new home world, that Natalia had thought the Terran people's hatred of Lyra had been healed and its sin forgiven.

Clearly it hadn't.

Natalia looked at the door. Was she willing to take the risk in order to see the festival and Ixion? As a Lyran princess, she would be a prime target for the purist factions. Her death would trigger the war that they wanted. That war would be a massacre. Her father wouldn't hesitate.

She swallowed the dry sticky lump in her throat and clenched her fists. She would be safe in the city. Nothing would happen to her.

"Is the military on alert?" Natalia's voice trembled the tiniest amount.

Her mother nodded. "They are posted in town and the palace is also on alert."

Was that why her mother had been speaking to Ixion? The royal assassins would be used if there was an attack on the palace.

"Would you stop me if I tried to go?" She needed to know. Her mother hadn't disapproved of her desire to go to the festival. If she was against it, she would have said as much rather than just pointing out the potential danger.

Her mother shook her head, the beautiful black ringlets that tumbled from the back of her head swaying in time with her movements. Natalia's own black hair was down today, falling loose around her shoulders in black waves. She never wore it down in public. It was always tied back, centre parted with each half plaited from the parting directly above her nose to the nape of her neck where it met and joined into one long plait or held in a bun. Today, she had been careful to wear it in a way that would help disguise her identity. She wore it in the way that she did sometimes when she sung at the club.

"No one will recognise me as royalty." She stood. "I want to see the festival just once in my lifetime."

"You are of mating age and able to be responsible for your own actions. I will not stand in your way if you want to do this. I have often wanted to see the festival myself." Her mother stood and placed her hand on Natalia's shoulder. Her expression turned pleading. "Just be careful and be alert."

Natalia nodded.

"Ixion!" The loudness of her mother's voice startled Natalia and she turned the moment the doors opened, her eyes immediately fixing on Ixion where he stood between them. It was exactly as she had hoped. Her mother would ask Ixion to guard her, trusting his skills above those of the guard. Guards would draw too much attention. No one would see an assassin.

Ixion placed his right hand against his chest and lowered his head. "Your highness?"

Natalia had expected him to call her mother 'my lady' as he had called her. His deliberate use of 'your highness' for her mother made her feel as though his use of 'my lady' for herself was more intimate, as though she commanded him more than her mother.

"Princess Natalia has expressed a desire to see the festival," her mother said and Ixion's gaze shot to Natalia, as though he couldn't believe that she would do such a thing. It made her nervous. Did he really think the threat of conflict was that real? Did he fear for her safety? "Take two of your men and shadow her and her attendants. At the slightest sign of trouble, you will get them out of there and bring them back to the palace."

"Yes, your highness." He bowed lower before backing out of the room.

The doors closed.

Natalia's heart thumped.

Was she really going to risk her life in order to have Ixion notice her?

Perhaps her father was right.

A male had already captured her heart.

Ixion leapt over the narrow divide between the buildings on the main street of the city. His gaze never left Natalia where she walked below him on the street even though his attention was spread wide, monitoring everything for a sign of danger. He signalled his two men where they ran over the rooftops on the opposite side of the street to him. They nodded and disappeared, reappearing in the crowd below.

The people were still spread out at this end of the street, but the market square ahead of them was packed. It would be difficult to keep an eye on the princess and her attendants from the rooftops.

She reached the start of the festival, passing under the large colourful banner that marked the boundary and the first of the stalls.

Ixion watched her closely as she moved through the gathered people. She was beautiful. Her gown pushed her breasts up and the tight short pale blue jacket she wore only emphasised them all the more. The glossy waves of her long black hair spilled over her shoulders, free for once rather than drawn back. At the palace, she had looked at him long enough for him to notice the black kohl that lined her rich green eyes, emphasising the shape of them and her long lashes. She was beautiful enough to take his breath away, but it was difficult to see her like this, knowing what her father had planned and that she may already love another.

It was torture and he longed for her to end his misery and silence his heart forever.

She had a very sensual way of moving, her hips swaying enough that it would be noticed, more so than usual today. It was as though she knew she was being watched, or she wanted to be watched.

The males in the crowd were certainly out to satisfy her desire to be seen. The way they looked at her made Ixion's blood burn. His fingers twitched against the two blades strapped to his legs.

Two young males at a stall called her over, showing the fine pottery they were selling. Another male at a stall opposite called to her too, holding up a bolt of pure blue silk and smiling.

Ixion stroked the blades, picturing their quick deaths at his hands. He hated the lustful and unabashed way they raked their eyes over Natalia, lingering on her cleavage and daring to look into her eyes.

Natalia shook her head and moved on, her hips swaying enticingly with each step, drawing his attention to only her, so much so that he started to forget to focus on the crowd and look for danger.

He was no better than those males. Her sensual air and beauty had him lusting after her too.

No. It was more than lust.

But whatever it was, it was pointless, just as the males attentions to her were. They could compete for her attention all they wanted but in the end, she would belong to none of them.

Ixion watched her stop at a stall with her two attendants. All three of them wore empire-line dresses but the two attendants' ones were noticeably different. The material was poorer quality and made the fineness of Natalia's evident to everyone. The colour was also dull, the dark haired maid in cream and the redhead in a pale green. Natalia wore sky blue.

It turned his stomach.

Sky blue would be the colour she wore at her wedding.

Her father's conversation with her came back and Ixion stared at Natalia, wondering who the man she had blushed about was. Did she already have someone in mind? Had other males been contacting her, males worthy of her love and attention? That turned his stomach too. The whole affair made him want to turn his back right now and walk away. Pride and duty kept him still, forcing him to continue along a path that would inevitably break his heart. It was a path that he had to tread. An assassin had no right to desire or love a princess and it was time that he realised that. His duty was everything. To turn his back on it was to disgrace his family.

She had moved on and he was thankful that his men had followed, blending into the crowd.

Two older males at stalls next to each other competed for her attention, offering her sweet candy and sugary drinks. She took some from both of them. When her dark haired attendant tried to pay, the men waved them away, smiling and laughing.

Did they think that giving her free things would win her heart?

Ixion's jaw ticked.

If that were the case, he would kill every suitor her father sent her way for her. It was the only thing he knew how to do. He couldn't offer her fine goods and fancy delicacies. He could only kill.

That was all that he was good for.

Natalia stopped at another stall, this time managed by an older woman and selling jewellery. The stones didn't seem particularly expensive, nothing more than cheap trinkets, but they excited Natalia and her two attendants. The dark blue hangings on the stall were stitched with silver stars, providing a beautiful backdrop for Natalia as she turned and showed one necklace to her companions. A myriad of emotions crossed her face as the bright sun made the deep purple heart-shaped stone in the pendant sparkle. They fascinated him. He had rarely seen her express her emotions and let them show. She looked at the tag on the pendant and frowned when her attendant checked her purse. Disappointment flitted across her face. Clearly she hadn't expected the festival to be so expensive.

They moved on, heading deep into the crowd where there was barely any room to walk and away from the rooftop on which he stood. He couldn't track her from above anymore and he was growing tired of seeing the males vying for her attention. He needed to be closer to her, wanted her to be his so much, even when he knew that he couldn't have her.

Ixion disappeared and reappeared next to the stall that sold the jewellery. Looking down, he spotted the necklace that had made Natalia's eyes shine and frowned at the price. It was expensive. The price tag was far more Lynans than it was worth. But she had seemed to like it.

Reaching into his jacket pocket, he took out all the Lynans that he had. He never bought anything with his wages. It accumulated in the Central Bank of Lyra. What he had in his pocket was this week's pay and wasn't enough to buy the pendant. He looked at the old woman and then in the direction that Natalia had gone. She had stopped two stalls away.

His hand went straight for his blade when someone touched his money where it sat on his upturned palm. He stopped himself from drawing it when he saw it was the old woman. She smiled at him, as though she knew why he wanted the pendant, and took some of his money, not nearly enough to cover the cost of the necklace.

"Tk'llsoi nkayk utteaiosolance."

Ixion stepped back, glaring at her, shocked by the language that she had spoken.

She offered the pendant with a broad warm smile.

"Akkati nem utteaiosolance."

His hands shook when he went to take it. The clear purple heart was warm against his fingers and slowly turned black when he touched it. Variance stone? He stared at the old woman. How had she managed to lay hands on something from his home world? No traders went there. She nodded and smiled. Her words rang in his head.

A heart for an assassin.

How did she know him?

An assassin deserves love too.

She didn't know him at all. If she did, she wouldn't say such things to him in his own language.

Her eyes shifted, the edges of her irises turning purple. Perseian. Their own language then. He had never expected to meet another Perseian outside of the royal assassins, not here on Lyran soil so far from home and definitely not a female.

He bowed, pocketed the pendant and followed after Natalia, trying to shake off the unsettled feeling inside of him. It had been twenty Lyran years since he had left Perseia. In that time, he had forgotten things about his home world, things that came back to him now.

He shook them away and focused on Natalia.

The crowd was closely packed but he moved through it with ease, never breaking his cover or being seen and always aware of his surroundings but focused on Natalia.

She pointed to something a short distance away and tugged her attendants there. Ixion slipped through the crowd and stopped when he saw her. She was laughing. It had been so long since he had seen her laugh. Years. It was a relief to see her smiling again after her confrontation with her father.

Ixion moved closer, wanting to see what had amused her. Her eyes lit up, glittering like the precious stone from which they had stolen their colour, and she laughed again.

He looked at her hands as a portly middle aged Lyran female placed a small bundle of pale blue fluff into them. A head immediately popped out of the mass of feathers, wide blue eyes taking in the Natalia as she stared back at it. It pecked at her with its dark blue beak and then wriggled as though settling down for a sleep in a nest.

A baby Friskin.

They didn't have such things on his planet. It was bleak and lifeless, barely able to sustain his species let alone any wildlife, and situated beyond the point where the markets roamed.

There was so much life on Lyra Five.

He narrowed his eyes on Natalia, almost smiling along with her as she laughed and stroked the Friskin now settled and sleeping in her delicate hand.

There was so much life in her.

It only made him love her more.

Natalia turned and stopped when her eyes fell on him. Her hand continued to stroke the Friskin even though her concentration was clearly on him. The laughter fled her lips, replaced by a shy smile that barely tilted the corners of her rosy lips but filled her green eyes with startling warmth.

It tugged at his heart.

Such a smile for him?

He was tempted to look around and check that she was really looking at him and not one of the more worthy males present, but didn't want to shatter a moment that he knew would live in his memory forever.

No matter what happened, he would always have this moment. This smile would always be his.

He took a step towards her.

The universe exploded.

CHAPTER 5

A hot shockwave slammed into Natalia's back, throwing her to the ground. She held the baby Friskin to her chest, protecting it, and angled herself so she landed on her shoulder rather than her front. Blood rushed through her ears, her heart thundering as she tried to make sense of what had happened.

Her two attendants were immediately covering her, their bodies protecting her from any further damage. Her head spun and a ringing sound replaced the rushing blood in her ears. She could barely hear the shrieks and screams of the crowd over the noise. Every bone in her body ached when she tried to move.

Suddenly she was on her feet, the baby bird still clutched safely in her hands, and was moving. She stumbled along, her legs shaking and weak, and looked down at the black-gloved hand on her arm. Her gaze tracked up a black-clad arm to its owner.

Ixion.

He said something to the other two assassins and they were gone, leading her two attendants off in different directions.

The crowd pushed at her, increasing her panic to the point of hysteria. Weapon's fire rang out around the square and she ducked her head, clinging to the small animal in her hands. Its frightened heartbeat almost matched the speed of her own but she wouldn't let anything happen to it.

Ixion pulled her down a side street where only a few other people were running from the scene. Natalia looked back to see black smoke curling up into the air and the military rushing in. So many people must have died. The heat and force of the blast had been incredible and she could see that it had come from the spaceport. She had been over two hundred metres from the port. The bomb must have decimated anyone near it.

Adrenaline made her shake and she only managed to keep going because of Ixion's unrelenting grip on her arm. If he hadn't been with her, she was sure that she would still be back in the square, shell-shocked by the blast.

Heavy weapons fire made her flinch. Deep thudding echoes alerted her to the approach of armoured suits—metal robotic armour that soldiers piloted. One appeared at the end of the alley, blocking it completely, the suit making her think of a huge man. It moved towards them, massive assault rifle raised.

Ixion ducked down another alley, heading away from it and towards the palace.

The palace.

She wished that she had stayed there.

Smoke loomed ahead of them and the sound of fighting was getting stronger rather than weaker. She gasped when they came out in the midst of a skirmish and only had time to see one man gunned down before Ixion was running with her again, this time towards the ocean. The palace was getting further away.

Tears filled her eyes, a mixture of fear and reaction to the smoke. It burned her lungs but she kept running, holding the Friskin close to her chest. They were all in this together now and she wasn't going to let anything happen to any of them—not her, not the Friskin and certainly not Ixion.

Natalia looked across at him where he ran a step ahead of her, his gaze scanning everything. He turned again and she wondered how well he knew the city. She had never seen these side streets before. They were barely wide enough for them to run down.

The palace stood in the distance. She held the Friskin in one hand and lifted her dress with the other, determined now to keep running and get back to her home. Ixion's grip on her loosened, as though he had sensed her resolve to live, and he ran faster.

"My attendants," she huffed and promised herself that, if they made it back alive, she would start running around the palace grounds to keep fit.

"Safe with my men. We must get you back to the palace." Ixion didn't sound at all out of breath.

A wide road lay ahead of them. Natalia stopped in the middle of it when she saw the soldiers running along it towards them. They would help. Ixion grabbed her arm.

"Not a wise place to stop." He pulled her forwards.

Shouts filled her ears and she turned and saw a group of civilians running at her from the other end of the road. No, not at her. At the soldiers. They raised their weapons and Natalia ducked as she ran. She had barely made it into the alley when laser fire shot down the road. One hit the wall of the building to her right, sending brick exploding outwards.

"Keep moving," Ixion said in a grim voice.

She looked up at the palace. They were close now. She could see the bridge ahead of them.

Her eyes widened when it began to lift. She ran harder, desperate to reach it in time, even when she knew it was impossible. Ixion had to grab her to stop her from attempting to leap for it when they reached the moat. He pulled her back, tightly holding her arm.

Along the length of the moat, all of the bridges were rising.

They were too late.

The last bridge clunked into place and the pale blue shield flickered into life.

Natalia's breathing quickened. She had to get back in. She needed to get back into the palace where it was safe. The whole city had gone insane. Everyone was fighting or running for their lives. She didn't want to be out here anymore. She wanted to be back in her room. She wanted to be with her family.

"Ixion reporting in."

Natalia turned to look at him. He had the black band around his wrist close to his mouth, his eyes fixed on her.

"We hear you, Commander." Came the reply.

"Inform her highness that Princess Natalia is safe and contact us when the gates are open again."

What was he doing?

Natalia grabbed his hand and pulled the device to her mouth. "Lower the bridge!"

Ixion snatched his arm back. "Belay that order. I will report in at nightfall."

The communicator crackled and Ixion pressed the button.

"What are you doing?" Natalia tried to grab his arm again but he held it behind his back. "Tell them to lower the bridge!"

"I cannot do that. Lowering the bridge would leave the palace open to infiltration." His tone was soft and Natalia stopped trying to reach his hand. He was right. She couldn't risk her family for the sake of getting back in. There was fighting everywhere. In the time it took them to lower and then raise the bridge again, any number of people could make it over into the grounds. The shield would be down too, leaving the palace vulnerable to aerial attacks. Ixion took hold of her arm. "I promise you, my lady, that I will keep you safe."

She warmed from head to toe at those words and the fiery look in his eyes. She had no doubt that he would protect her and keep her safe. In fact, she trusted him with her life.

And with her heart.

"We must move." He took her by the elbow and led her away from the palace.

Natalia glanced back at it, afraid that her family were in danger and needed her, and that her mother would be worried.

She must have slowed because Ixion stopped and looked at her. "Do not fear."

It was easy for him to say. It wasn't his family in there and he was trained to kill. What good would she be if they were attacked? She would only prove a distraction for Ixion. He would want to keep an eye on her to ensure that she was safe. It could be the opening that would see him killed.

She looked up at the sky.

"Do you think my father knows?" she whispered.

"Standard protocol dictates that he would be contacted in the event of an uprising or emergency. The moment it had happened, they would have sent word." His tone started out empty but grew warmer, until it became so soft that it comforted her. "He will be on his way back, my lady. The skirmish will not last. You will be in the palace again before dawn."

Natalia nodded and then let him lead her away. He took her through the back streets, avoiding the areas where they had run into conflict before. When she began to recognise some of the streets, she realised where he was taking her.

The entertainment district.

She looked towards it where it lay downhill from her and then over at the spaceport far to her right. The single black column of smoke that the bomb had caused had been joined by others. The smell of burning wood filled the air. Some of the buildings were on fire. Her city was burning.

Ixion's hand tightened against her elbow and she looked ahead of her again. Some men were coming. They had no weapons that she could see but they didn't look friendly.

Natalia's eyes widened when Ixion turned with her and pinned her against the wall, his hands firm against her shoulders. She was about to ask him what he was doing when one hand shifted to her cheek, moving her hair across her face, and his lips pressed against hers.

Her eyes went even wider and then slowly slipped to half mast as Ixion kissed her, his mouth slanting over hers, turning her blood to fire and making her heart race quicker than fear ever could.

She was too stunned to kiss him back, could only manage small jerking movements with her lips, was drowning in the feel of his against her and her first kiss.

His mouth left hers and she remained leaning against the wall, her head tilted back in silent invitation, her mind spinning from how good it had felt to have a man kiss her.

To have Ixion kiss her.

His hands slipped from her face and shoulder.

The world slowly came back. The first thing she noticed was the small baby Friskin wriggling in her hands. She released her grip on it a little, apologising to it without words. The second thing she noticed was Ixion had moved away from her and was looking along the alley. She turned there and saw the men had passed them. Ixion had kissed her to protect her identity and give the men reason to ignore them. Her heart thumped hard against her ribs, refusing to slow while the memory of the kiss lingered.

"Are you alright?" He turned to her. The moment his eyes met her wide ones, he dropped his gaze, lowering his head a fraction too. "Apologies, my lady, for assaulting you in such a manner. When we return to the palace, I will confess to my handling of you and—"

"Stop." Natalia didn't want to even think about what punishment he would suffer if he confessed to kissing her. He had done it to protect her, and it wasn't as though it had been bad. She had enjoyed it. "Don't apologise."

His eyes widened now and shot up to meet hers. She could read the unspoken question in them. She wanted him to kiss her?

A blush scorched her cheeks and she moved away to avoid his scrutiny.

"We should keep moving," she muttered weakly and, a moment later, he moved past her.

As they walked, Natalia stroked the small blue Friskin where it lay nestled between her hand and her breasts, hoping to soothe it. She was thankful that Ixion didn't look back. She couldn't stop blushing while she considered the answer to his silent question. Did she want him to kiss her?

She wanted it more than anything.

Ixion walked out of the back room with a small empty shipping crate that he had found, trying to get his thoughts off the idea that Natalia might want to kiss him. She had responded to his kiss in only a small way, enough that he could believe that she hadn't like it. He had believed it until she had told him not to apologise. Her blush had made his heart race. The idea that she wanted him to kiss her again was firmly lodged in his mind. He groaned inside. Iskara, he would dearly love to kiss her again.

He placed the box down next to Natalia where she sat on the stage of the empty club, nursing the baby bird. When he removed the lid, Natalia frowned at the bare plastic interior of the crate and then looked up at him. She held the Friskin out to him and he took it, wondering what she was going to do.

It didn't surprise him when she removed her small blue jacket and placed it into the crate, moulding it into a warm nest for the bird.

It was just like Natalia to be so thoughtful and kind. She had been protecting the baby bird since the bomb blast, keeping it close to her heart. He had heard her whispering soothing words to the animal, as though it understood her. He smiled and looked down at the bundle of fluffy feathers in his hand. It was calm, curiously watching Natalia work to make it a comfortable bed.

When she was done, Ixion handed the Friskin back to her and she carefully set it down in the makeshift nest. It investigated the new environment for a few seconds, pecking at the jacket and the tall solid sides, and then settled down.

"Thank you." Natalia stroked the bird.

"There is no need to thank me. I was only carrying out orders." He sat down on the other side of the crate.

Natalia pulled her feet up onto the stage and hugged her knees. Her gown had short sleeves and the club was closed so there was no heating. It had taken them several long minutes to find out how to turn some of the spotlights on. The owner had given them the pass code for the back door and told them to lock up after them. Ixion could understand why he had wanted to get away. The battles outside showed no sign of dying out. The weapons fire and shouting were only growing louder and more violent.

Ixion slipped down from the stage and came to stand in front of Natalia. He removed his jacket and placed it around her shoulders.

The tight black vest he wore beneath his jacket wasn't enough to keep him warm, but the princess needed heat more than he did. If he allowed her to become cold and catch an illness, it would be a black mark against him and would be a violation of his duty.

And his feelings.

Natalia touched the lapels of his jacket where they met in front of her chest and then looked at him. Her gaze dropped to his body and she frowned at something.

"What are those?" She reached out to touch the two black leather and metal cuffs that covered his forearms and he stepped back so she couldn't.

He didn't want her anywhere near such things.

He looked at them, turning his arms so the underside of his forearms were upwards, and the mechanics of the devices were visible. The short retractable blade in each gleamed brightly under the spotlight, as though they had never been used. They had caused so many deaths.

Natalia looked curious, her eyes fixed on the devices.

"Do they come out?" A little line appeared between her eyebrows as she peered at them, craning her neck so she could see better. "Show me."

He thought about not showing her and then acceded. Her words could be considered an order. He had to obey.

Without looking at her, he tilted his hands back to trigger the devices. The two blades shot out, extending past his fists, locking in place. Natalia's eyes were as large as twin full moons.

She didn't look horrified though. She looked fascinated, just as she had done the first time she had seen him. He pushed the tips of the blades up with his fingers and they shot back into the cuffs.

"Where do you come from?" Natalia glanced at his wrists and then at the blades strapped to his thighs. "I have never seen such weapons or the methods you were teaching Aiden and Ciel with swords."

Ixion's heart gave a hard beat. She had been watching him teach her brothers? He hadn't taught them anything when she had been present. She must have been watching them from the gallery around the courtyard on the first floor of the palace and she had done so stealthily enough that he hadn't noticed her.

"I am Perseian." Speaking the name of his species made him remember the pendant that he had bought Natalia, one which he would never have the audacity or courage to give to her but which now resided close to her hands in his jacket pocket. His gaze flicked to it and then to her hands. She was toying with the sleeves of his jacket, her slender fingers tracing the blue embroidery around the cuffs. "These are the weapons I was raised with. The only ones that I have needed since I took the trials as a child."

"You went through trials when you were a boy?" She drew her knees up again, wrapping her arms around them and looking up at him. He was thankful that her hands were away from the pockets of his jacket.

He nodded.

"Tell me about them."

Ixion tensed. He didn't want to tell her about them. She didn't need to know about the things that he had done.

"Is something wrong?" She frowned.

He bowed his head. "My lady, I request you give me leave to refuse your request."

She giggled. "Why should I grant your request to request that I give you leave to refuse my request?"

He frowned. She was playing with him. The things that he had done were no laughing matter. If he told her, she would never look at him again. She would fear him. He sighed, pressed his right hand against his chest, and closed his eyes.

"My lady does not need to know the things that I have done, only that I will protect her."

She was silent for a long time. He didn't dare look at her. It had taken him a strangely large amount of courage to say those words. He had told her earlier that he would protect her but now it felt different to say such a thing. It felt as though he was confessing that there was something deeper than his duty behind his reason for protecting her.

"I would like to know." Her voice was small.

He looked at her, right into her green eyes, trying to see if she was telling the truth.

"Why?"

She toyed with the fastenings on his jacket. "So I will know you better."

He bowed his head again. "I am unworthy of such a thing."

"Indulge my whim then and tell me because I am asking you to."

"An order?"

"If you prefer it that way." There was an edge to those words that said she might order him to do other things if he was lucky. He could only pray to Iskara for such an elusive dream to come true.

"Then I will do as my lady asks." He drew up a chair and set it down in front of her.

Just as he was going to sit down, a loud blast shook the building. Natalia gasped. One of the white spotlights went out and then blinked back into life. The baby Friskin made a purring noise.

Ixion reached into the crate and stroked it. It settled immediately. He glanced at Natalia. Her eyes were wide and fearful again. He wished he could soothe her fear so easily.

Perhaps talking to her would keep her mind off the fighting outside.

He sat down on the chair and thought about what to tell her. Only the truth would do, although he would omit some parts.

"Tell me about the trials," she said in a tight voice.

If she feared the fighting outside, then telling her about the trials would only scare her more, but she had ordered him.

"They are a rite of passage on Perseia. I was the only survivor out of nineteen others who shared my birth date."

"That's terrible. What happened to them?"

He leaned back in the chair. "I killed them."

Her eyes shot wide and she gasped again. Her mouth opened but he beat her to speaking.

"It is the way of Perseia." He hoped it would make her see that he'd had little choice in the matter. "All males of eleven years—"

"Eleven!" she shrieked, cutting him off. She looked horrified. "They made you kill at eleven?"

Clearly his people were not well documented and she didn't have access to any of the palace personnel files or information about the royal assassins. He had thought that she would know where they all came from and how they arrived at the position.

"I joined the Lyran royal assassins at age fifteen and was the commander here by twenty-five." He didn't hold back now. He wanted to see how she would react to the knowledge that Perseia had always supplied Lyra with its elite assassins and how they were raised so they were good enough for her family. He wanted to see if she would finally be frightened of him rather than fascinated. If she did change towards him, it would put an end to his feelings once and for all. "I was bred to kill."

"You were so young." She leaned towards him, her expression full of concern.

"All Lyran royal assassins join at the same age when our training is complete."

"Are they all Perseian?"

He nodded.

"Does Lyra dictate the age at which they are put into service?"

He nodded again and she paled. She looked down at her hands where they rested in her lap and then up into his eyes.

"And you joined at fifteen. Why?"

"Lyra takes all of the sons from specific bloodlines and has done for generations. My father served Lyra and my grandfather before him, going back hundreds of years." He paused for breath, thinking about his family and how he had rarely seen his father. Assassins could only return to Perseia once every two years. Most mated in that time in the hope of gaining a son to carry on the bloodline and the honour of being a royal assassin. His father had been a commander on Lyra Prime. Ixion had only seen him four times in his entire lifetime. "I was expected to continue the tradition. My bloodline will expect me to... mate... and bear a son that will carry on the name and become an assassin."

Natalia fell quiet, her fingers twisting the fine blue material of her dress. Did she finally see him for what he truly was? A killer, unfit for a princess such as her, and someone that she should fear rather than seek to know more about.

"Did they make you take the trials?"

He wondered if it would make a difference if he said that they had even though they hadn't.

"No," he said and she looked at him. "All males take part in the trials. There is no option to not take the trials because all would do it regardless. The trials are to gain our honour. It is the first step on our path to upholding our families' names."

"But so many die."

"They did not die, my lady. I killed them."

"Why?" There were tears in her eyes.

He cursed the sight of them and the way they made his heart ache to comfort her. "Because it is the way of my people and because I had to maintain the name of my bloodline. Failure was not acceptable. None of my bloodline has ever died in the trials."

"Do you regret what you did?"

"Not now. It was them or me and I have done far worse things since."

"In the name of Lyra," she muttered and sighed. A tear slipped down her cheek. He longed to brush it away. "Have you killed many for us?"

He nodded. Hundreds. If asked, he wouldn't confess though. He didn't want her to know how many lives he had taken, not when she struggled to come to terms with the nineteen lives he had taken as a child. If he told her how many he had killed in the name of Lyra, she would only cry.

The sound of distant weapons fire filled the oppressive silence.

"I'm frightened," she whispered.

"Of me?" That thought hurt. He had wanted her to be frightened but the idea that she actually might be made a dull ache settle in his chest.

Natalia reached into the crate and stroked the baby bird. "No."

That word was like a sweet elixir to his heart.

"What frightens my lady?"

She looked at him and then at the doors far behind him at the back of the dimly lit club.

"This fighting."

"I will not let anything happen to you. The battles are growing quieter. It will not be long until the military has them under control. It is safe here."

Heart of an Assassin

"With you," she whispered with half a smile. "You wouldn't let anything happen to me."

His heart warmed at her belief in him and her trust. She was right. He would never allow anything to happen to her.

He was surprised when she tilted her head back and started singing softly. The melody was one that he recognised but hadn't heard in a long time. She had been singing it the night that he had first heard her. He had been en route back from his first mission as a commander and she had been walking the garden, the only light that of the crescent moon and the bright stars. She had been barely fifteen then but her voice had been beautiful. Only not as beautiful as it was today.

He had listened to her many times throughout her childhood and even more often when she had reached eighteen. He had allowed her to see him then, to know the presence of the assassins and to see how she reacted to him. She had been so fascinated that she had stopped singing. Her beauty had stopped his world from spinning. The moon had been shining down on her, highlighting her pale gown and the silver threads that ran through her hair, holding it back. He had fallen for her then. She had looked like an angel.

With a voice that matched. No.

"Iskara's angels have no voice to compare to yours," he whispered, unsure whether he wanted her to hear.

She faltered and looked at him. Her voice died away and he cursed himself for speaking. She was looking at him with such questioning eyes. They demanded answers and he would give them to her.

"I have always listened to you sing." He somehow managed to hold her gaze and keep his voice steady. "You have a beautiful voice... although I preferred it when you were younger."

She frowned. "Why?"

"Because your songs were only for my ears then."

Her lips parted, her mouth falling open as she blinked at him. Iskara, he wanted to kiss her. He wanted to confess everything—he loved her more than anything. No male could ever love her as he did.

Crimson touched her cheeks and she averted her gaze.

He cursed again. He hadn't wanted her to turn quiet or be ashamed. He should have kept silent and let her sing. She had obviously been trying to calm her nerves and he had ruined it with his foolish words. As though a princess could ever love someone like him.

She pulled his jacket closer around her, her fingers slipping into the pockets to hold it closed. He froze when she frowned and looked down at one of the pockets. She reached a little further in and his heart stopped.

Natalia slowly pulled the pendant from his jacket pocket and held it up in the light.

Her eyes shot to his.

Ixion swallowed hard.

This was going to go horribly wrong.

251

CHAPTER 6

Natalia stared at the heart pendant dangling in front of her, still shocked from finding it. Why would Ixion have the pendant that she had set her heart on at the festival but hadn't been able to afford?

Her heart whispered that he had bought it for her but that didn't make any sense at all. Ixion couldn't afford to buy such an expensive item and, even if he could, why would he buy it for her?

She slipped down from the stage and came to stand in front of him. Staring down at him, she waited to see if he was going to explain. She knew that he wasn't a thief but she needed to hear him say it. She needed to know why he had the pendant that she had wanted.

"Princess Natalia." The sound of her name spoken in his deep voice sent a shiver tripping down her spine and her stomach warmed. "I can explain."

She touched the stone at the same time as he did. It turned black. He snatched his hand back and the heart turned purple again.

She hadn't realised that it could do such a thing. No wonder it was expensive. Whatever it was made from, it wasn't a cheap stone that could be found anywhere. She had thought that it was just purple glass.

"Why do you have this?" Her voice shook almost as much as her hands. The pendant jiggled, the heart swinging in a small circle.

"I…" He lowered his head. The long finger-length black strands of his hair fell forwards to hide his face. She wished he would look up at her again so she could read the reason in his eyes because she was beginning to fear that he was going to leave her with no explanation. "Forgive me."

She frowned. Forgive him? His tone had held such a solemn note, one that spoke to her heart and told her to do as he had asked, even though she didn't know why he wanted to be forgiven.

"I should not have bought it," he said to his knees. "But the Perseian took a little money and handed it to me. She spoke to me in my own language and made me foolishly believe in something which is impossible… I never intended to give it to you. Doing so would break—"

"I forgive you." Natalia didn't want him to continue. If he was going to mention his duty and his position then she had to stop him.

She knew that he had been watching her the whole time since she had left the palace but hadn't realised how closely. He must have seen her at the stall and seen the disappointment she had felt on realising that she couldn't afford the pendant. Taking a look at the scant silver Lynans in his jacket pocket, she realised that he probably hadn't been able to afford it either. Had the woman given it to him for only a few of his Lynans because he was Perseian or because she had realised why he had wanted it?

The woman had made him believe something that was impossible. What was that something? Did it have anything to do with her?

Natalia looked at the pendant. It was beautiful, but what made her smile was the fact that Ixion had bought it for her because he had seen her disappointment.

"Thank you," she said and he looked up at her, his clear purple eyes as bright as the stone that she held. "No one other than my family has bought me a present before."

He frowned. "No one has bought you this. Only your family are worthy of buying you gifts."

Natalia's shoulders slumped. She hated the way he talked about himself as though he didn't exist. He had done so the night he had come to take her home from the club and he was doing it again now. She wanted to tell him that she thought he was someone of consequence and that he wasn't a nobody. He existed to her, in her heart.

"Can I keep it anyway?" She closed her fingers around the heart and held it to her chest. "Can I say that it means a lot to me and order you to believe it?"

An order was probably her only way of making him believe it.

She swallowed her nerves and stepped closer to him, so they were toe to toe. She looked down into his eyes and then leaned over, swept his black hair from his forehead, cupped his cheek and kissed him.

It was barely a meeting of lips but her stomach flipped and her heart raced. She brushed her mouth over his and was surprised when he responded with force. His hand caught her wrist, bringing her closer and holding her there. His lips grazed hers and then he slanted his head and his tongue stroked the seam of her mouth.

Natalia felt giddy when she parted her lips, allowing his tongue into her mouth, and clumsily tackled it with her own. It was thrilling to kiss him like this, to have such deep intimacy between them. His tongue slid sensually against hers, stroking it and her teeth. Her breathing turned rough and her blood heated. The kiss became choppy, a clashing of lips and bursts of tongues. Her nipples tightened against her dress and fire pooled at the apex of her thighs. Iskara. She wanted him.

Suddenly, the kiss was over and he had drawn back into the chair. His eyes were dark as he stared at her, full of passion and something else.

Anger?

Natalia struggled to level her breathing, absorbing the calamity of sensations and feelings inside her. Renie had told her that males could make the female body do funny things but she had never imagined that it would feel like this, that she would feel as though her body was taking control and leading her actions.

"Why did you stop?" she breathed, still trying to get hold of herself.

His black eyebrows knitted into a heavy frown and he stood, pacing a short distance away from her.

"I am an assassin… under your father's command no less—"

"Stop!" She didn't want to hear it, didn't want him to find a reason not to kiss her when she knew that he wanted it as much as she did. He looked over his shoulder at her with hurt in his purple eyes. She had never wanted him to look at her like that. It hurt her heart. It made her realise what he had wanted to say. "Don't mention my father… or the palace… or that I am a princess… because I wish that I wasn't and I have done from the moment I met you."

He turned now, a stunned look replacing the pain in his eyes.

Natalia turned away, unable to see him when she said this because she feared it wouldn't make a difference. She was frightened that she would lose her nerve. Ixion was the only male that she had ever wanted. She couldn't bear it if he rejected her because of her title.

"I wish I wasn't a princess." She lowered her head, uncurled her fingers and looked at the purple heart resting in her hands. Ixion's heart. She wanted to take hold of it and not let it go, wanted to make him see that it didn't matter what titles they bore, because she loved him and she knew that he had feelings for her. "I just want to be Natalia... I want to be free to sing wherever I want to and do whatever I want."

"What is it that you want so badly that you cannot have or do now?" he said close to her ear and she closed her eyes, relishing the way it felt to have him near. It was comforting and warmed her heart. He made her feel safe. He made her happy. "To sing?"

She shook her head, turned to face him, and looked deep into his eyes. "You."

His eyes narrowed, the passion in them reigniting, and then she was in his arms. They were tight against her back, crushing her to his chest. His mouth descended, claiming her lips in a fiery kiss that scorched her heart. She closed her eyes, tilted her head back, and surrendered to him. His tongue plundered her mouth and she fought back, stroking it with her own. The sound of his deep moan made her shiver with delight and empowered her. She slid her hands up his chest, the pendant tangled around the fingers of her left hand, and looped her arms around his neck.

The sound of weapons fire drifted into the distance, the hard beat of her heart drowning out all noise. Ixion's hands settled against her sides, fingers pressing in hard as though he wanted to hold her forever and never let her go. She wished that he wouldn't. She wanted to be his forever. She wanted to give him every part of her—her heart, her body and her soul.

His lips trailed fire down her neck and she leaned back, sighing at the ceiling as his silken tongue traced sensual patterns on her flesh. He travelled lower, his hands coming up to press into her back as he placed soft kisses on the curve of her breasts. Her nipples tightened against her dress and she found the courage to unleash her first moan. It felt so good that she did it again. Ixion responded by tugging at the short bodice of her dress. Her breasts spilled out when he undid the dark blue ribbons that held it closed across them.

She gasped when his lips latched onto her right nipple, tugging it into his mouth. Her wide eyes fell shut again when he suckled and laved the pert nub, sending warm sparks skittering across her skin. She buried her fingers into his hair, clutching him to her breast, wishing he would never stop.

Instinct made her lift her leg and wrap it around his backside. The move put her off balance and she crashed to the floor with him on top of her.

"Natalia?" Ixion's urgent tone made her opened her eyes. There was an overwhelming amount of concern in his. "Are you hurt?"

Natalia shook her head and blushed when she realised that he was on top of her, between her thighs, her leg still hooked over his backside.

Before she could even think of something to say, his mouth had claimed hers again, his kiss fierce and demanding. She responded as violently, desperate to taste him and feel him against her.

His hand skimmed up her thigh, pulling the skirt of her dress with it, and then moved down again. The next time he touched her, it was with only her stockings between them. His hand was warm as it stroked her thigh, making her tremble with need. She responded by sliding her tongue along his, brushing it over his teeth and then nipping at his lower lip. He moaned again, his breath hot against her face.

"Natalia," he husked and a shiver danced through her.

She liked the way he normally said her name but she loved the way he said it in the heat of the moment, breathed soft against her skin and telling her of the depth of his passion and hunger.

Natalia raised her knee and his hand slid lower, grazing her backside. He propped himself up on his other elbow and lowered his head to her breasts again. The feel of his tongue swirling around her nipple was torture but one she willingly submitted to. She tilted her head back and arched her body into his, forcing her breast against his mouth. He wrapped his lips around the pert nub and sucked.

A moan escaped her, loud in the empty club.

"Natalia," he whispered against her flesh again and she ran her fingers into his hair.

He disappeared. She frowned and then her eyes widened when he pressed a kiss to her inner thigh.

Iskara.

He was going to kiss her there? Renie hadn't mentioned anything about that kind of thing.

Natalia's breathing quickened, anticipation making her tremble, and she stared at the ceiling. Waiting. Ixion placed a trail of kisses along her thigh, marking his path to the centre of her flesh. She gasped when he pressed a kiss to the thin silk of her underwear, directly over her mound, and then groaned when he laved her clit through it.

A wave of pin pricks chased over her skin and she couldn't stop herself from reacting, from lifting her knees and letting her legs fall open. He licked again, rougher this time, and she flung her head back.

"Ixion." Her fingers scrambled for purchase on the floor.

He groaned against her, as though the sound of her uttering his name so passionately had thrilled him.

A cold draft caressed her backside when he pulled her underwear off and her heart fluttered. He was really going to kiss her there.

She tried to prepare herself but nothing she could have done would have made her ready for how it felt when his tongue found her slick flesh again. He ran his tongue up the length of her and swirled it around her clit, sending jolts through her and making her whole body tighten. The warm feeling inside her abdomen turned to fire and an ache filled her, a desperate need to find release.

He licked down to her opening and then back up again. It was maddening. She clawed at the dirty floor, writhing against him, unable to stop herself from thrusting herself against his mouth as he suckled and licked. The feeling within her reached bursting point.

Ixion flicked her pert nub with his tongue.

Stars exploded in front of her eyes.

Her already rough breathing turned choppy.

Her heart hammered.

Ixion appeared above her, licking his lips. She grabbed him around the back of his neck, dragged him down to her, and kissed the breath out of him, tasting herself on his lips. He moaned into her mouth and she answered with one of her own. Her whole body felt lax but as she kissed him, his hands moved over her body—skimming her thighs one moment and caressing her breasts the next—reigniting the hunger she felt for him.

She wanted him.

She wanted to give all of herself to him.

Her hands slid down his sides and settled on his backside. It was taut beneath her fingers, the muscular globes delighting her. She could easily imagine how beautiful he would be when naked, but the room was cold even with her clothes on. She definitely couldn't imagine him wanting to strip for her.

Gaining some courage from the eager way that he was kissing her, she brought her left hand down and around his hip. She tensed the moment her fingers found the hard evidence of his arousal and then relaxed a little when Ixion moaned. She kept her hand firm against him when he thrust, rubbing his erect length against her palm. Bigger than expected. Renie hadn't said much about that either, only that males varied. Her tutor had said even less than that. It was a miracle Natalia even knew that some species' males had parts like this.

Ixion moaned and shuddered against her, his lips leaving hers. His face was beautiful—his eyebrows knit into a tight frown of concentration, his eyes closed, and his lips parted as he breathed roughly. Whatever he felt when she stroked his cock, it felt good enough to make him want to just stop everything and take it all in, to savour the sensations.

Her fingers found the clasps of his trousers and she struggled to undo them. He tensed and she thought that he would stop her, but instead he leaned to one side and helped her. She craned her neck, looking down the length of their bodies, eager to see him in all his glory and to see what she did to him. She had aroused him. She had made him want her. Now all she had to do was make him go through with it. Renie had warned her about that bit. It was going to hurt and he was going to know.

He startled her out of her thoughts by taking hold of her hand and guiding it to him. She wrapped her fingers around the rigid shaft and watched as he moved her hand up and down its length, stroking him. It felt good. Clearly it felt good to Ixion too because he moaned with each stroke of her hand.

Her gaze settled on his hard cock.

She wanted that inside her now. She wanted them to be one at last.

Bringing her hand down, she forced him to follow, and raised her knees again. Ixion's eyes shot to hers and she stared into them, wanting him to see how much she needed this and wanted him. She wouldn't regret it. Her heart was his and her body would be too.

He lowered his hips, removed her hand from his length, and guided himself to her slick opening. She tried to relax but it all happened so fast that she didn't have a chance. Before she could even draw a deep breath, Ixion had buried his length inside her. She bit her lip to stifle her cry as pain shot through her and closed her eyes, squeezing tears from them.

"Natalia." He sounded more than a little shocked.

Did he think that she had visited the pleasure planet like Renie had? Most of her family either lost their virginity there or had some lovers from the planet come to them. She hadn't wanted that. She had wanted her first time to be with someone she loved.

"Sorry," she said through clenched teeth.

Ixion peppered her face with kisses, erasing her tears with his lips and thumbs, and kept still inside her.

"You should have told me, sweet Natalia," he whispered against her skin.

He would have stopped her if she had. He would have started spouting stuff about her being a princess and him not being worthy. She hadn't wanted that. He was worthy. He was the only man she would ever love.

The pain began to subside and she opened her eyes, finding herself staring into the beautiful purple depths of his.

Lifting her hand, she stroked his cheek and then smiled. "You would have stopped."

The look in his eyes said that she was right.

"Don't stop... I want you to have this... me... like this." She was close to pleading him to move, to take her mind off the pain and dark thoughts that were creeping in at the corners of her mind. This wouldn't be their only time. She wouldn't marry another. She would only marry the man that she loved, if he would have her. There was no one as worthy of her love as Ixion. "Kiss me."

He did. He dipped his head and brushed his lips over hers, his kiss sweet and slow. Her heart warmed and her body relaxed under the gentle ministrations. When Ixion withdrew and slowly eased back in, she felt no pain, only raw pleasure. She moaned her encouragement.

His pace quickened and she deepened their kiss, sliding her tongue into his mouth, her body on fire as Ixion moved against her.

His moans joined hers, each thrust punctuated by one. Natalia closed her eyes and wrapped her arms around him, clinging to him as he thrust into her, each one making her body tighten a little more until she was close to begging him to make her climax. She wanted to feel him climax inside her, wanted this beautiful moment to be complete.

Ixion touched her ear and she didn't realise that he had removed her translator bud until he whispered words against her lips that she didn't understand. They were passionate sounding, hungry things that made her blood burn even though she didn't know what they were. It was a beautiful language. It made her heart sing.

His hands caught her shoulders and he moved deeper, thrusting all the way in, taking her out of her mind. Her body tensed but release seemed so far away. She raked her nails down Ixion's arms and then threaded her fingers into his hair. She kissed him hard, her teeth knocking against his with each thrust of his body into hers. He uttered something deep and rough, and then jerked hard up inside her. His cock throbbed, his warm seed spilling into her. She tensed her body around his length and the hard pulsing of it pushed her over the edge. Her hips convulsed against his, her thighs trembling with her climax and a warm haze suffusing every molecule in her body.

Ixion continued to kiss her, slower now and softer, spreading the warmth inside her and making her smile. She could feel his emotions in it and they soothed her heart.

She wasn't the only one in love.

CHAPTER 7

Ixion pulled the blanket closed over Natalia's front and tucked it around her shoulders as best he could with one hand. His other arm was under her head, his beautiful princess's pillow. She slumbered on, unaffected by his coddling, her face the picture of serenity.

The night had fallen silent shortly after he had found some blankets and she had fallen asleep in his arms on the stage. The fighting had stopped.

The only sound now was Natalia's soft steady breathing and the small noises of the Friskin as it moved around in the shipping crate beside them.

Ixion sighed and carefully lifted each rogue wave of black hair from Natalia's face so he could see it clearly. She was beautiful. His elusive princess.

The heart pendant he had bought for her lay resting against her bosom, almost slipping into her dress. She had asked him to put it on her after they had made love. Everything had been so perfect that he had almost fooled himself into believing that things would be different now.

They couldn't be.

If her parents discovered what she had done, they would be angry with her.

If her parents discovered what he had done, they would execute him.

The black band around his wrist crackled and then a voice came over it. The palace was secure. The riots in the city had been quelled. They were safe to return.

Natalia's nose wrinkled and she curled up against him, as though she had heard those words and didn't want to go back to the palace. It was a nice fantasy. When he told her that they could return, she would be happy, not sad. He stroked his fingers across her forehead, not wanting to wake her yet. He wanted to have this moment last a little longer, wanted to imprint it all on his memory so he would never forget a second of it.

Her eyelids fluttered and then lifted to reveal her bright clear green eyes. A shy smile touched her lips and a hint of colour reached her pale cheeks. He smiled back at her, continuing to caress her, not wanting her to leave him yet.

Or ever.

"There was a noise," she muttered, her voice filled with sleep.

Ixion wanted to tell her not to worry about it and to return to sleep but her eyes were growing brighter and more awake by the second. She rubbed her face and then frowned.

"I must look terrible."

His smile widened. If terrible was looking like an angel, then she looked terrible.

She pulled the black waves of her hair from her face and slowly sat up. Her arms crossed over her chest, hands grasping the dull grey blanket near her shoulders to keep it around them.

"Is it morning?" She looked around.

"Almost." Could he tell her to stay with him? Was that a foolish thing to do? There was no chance for an assassin and a princess. He was a dead man when they returned to the palace. No matter how hard they tried, if they continued to see each other they wouldn't be able to keep it secret. His position meant that he would often see her father and family. He didn't think he could hide it from them, this sin that he had committed.

Would she even want to keep it a secret? A female of her standing deserved a man that stood on a similar level, far above the one that he could reach. The commander of the royal assassins was the highest echelon he could attain, and it would never be enough. Her father wouldn't condone an assassin courting his daughter.

"We should leave." He stood, stooped and picked up the crate with the baby Friskin in it. It was Natalia's now, he supposed. She would look after it and it would probably remind her of him, just as the heart pendant would.

He hoped that she would never forget him.

That was all he could ask for.

Without another word, he opened the door to the club and stepped out into the still-dark street. Dawn was only minutes away but the sky showed no sign of lightening. Clouds of smoke drifted overhead in the ink-blue sky, the last signs of the riots. When they returned to the palace, he would have to file a report to General Lyra II about what had happened and would find out how much damage had been done to the city. Whoever had planned the riots was going to become his next target.

Natalia walked in silence beside him as they headed back towards the palace. The baby Friskin shifted around in the box, looking up at him occasionally with wide blue eyes full of curiosity. It was probably wondering where Natalia had gone. He had heard that Friskins grew attached to people and Natalia had protected it from the fighting and shown tender care towards it.

The palace loomed ahead of them, bright golden in the light of the sun now peeking over the horizon.

Natalia wrapped her arms around herself and stared at the floor. What was she thinking? Did this hurt her as much as it did him?

When they crossed the bridge into the palace grounds, passing the guards, he felt her glance at him. He wanted to look at her too, but doing that would draw attention from the guards that were going about their business. He had a duty to protect Natalia from any rumours that might spread if he looked at her, showed any sign of affection towards her.

He had neglected his duty once already. He wouldn't do it again.

They walked up through the garden to her apartments and she opened the door. He handed her the box with the Friskin in and she looked sad as she took it. Tears rimmed her eyes with sparkling diamonds and he longed to wipe them away, to tell her not to cry for him because he wasn't worthy of such a thing.

Ixion took a step back.

His fists clenched and trembled with restraint. Everything he wanted stood before him, beautiful in the pale light of dawn, and he couldn't have it. In order to protect her, he had to do this, even though it would hurt them both.

He had to leave her.

He had to disappear from her life and never let her see him again.

Natalia placed the crate down just inside the door and closed it. She stood on the threshold, facing Ixion, hating the fact that they were back at the palace. Tears trembled on the brink of falling but she wiped them away, not wanting to look weak in front of him. There was so much pain and sadness in his eyes as he looked into hers that she felt it too. When he took hold of her hands, it was with a solemn look, one that made her heart ache.

"Goodbye." That softly whispered word pierced her heart like a shard of ice, turning her cold. It felt as though he was saying it forever and they would never see each other again.

Not wanting it to be over, she stepped between his arms, tiptoed and kissed him.

She didn't say goodbye. He walked away without so much as a backward glance and a tear slid down her cheek, hot in the cold morning air. She would never see him again.

Her hands trembled when she curled them into fists. Her heart hurt.

Suddenly the palace garden looked like a dark and dead place. The building towering at her back felt like a prison. Her title was a collar around her throat.

She hated everything.

Everything but Ixion.

Why couldn't she have been born a normal woman who was free to choose who she loved?

She stared at Ixion's retreating back. He disappeared into the staff quarters of the palace.

Why couldn't she be free to love him?

Something moved at the corner of her vision and she turned sharply to see a woman standing in the garden below her. Her long blue hair and milk-white skin shone in the light of dawn, a face Natalia had never seen before. Intruders?

Natalia stepped back towards her apartments. Her heart pounded.

Had the female seen her and Ixion?

Natalia's eyes widened when a male that she recognised walked down the path to the female. His dark hair, handsome face, and clothing of white shirt and tan trousers were unmistakable. Rezic. Her eldest brother had returned which meant that her father and sister had too. The female was one of the party. A Vegan.

The female spoke to him. Natalia could only see her lips moving. The distance between them was too great for her to hear what was being said. Rezic turned a frown on Natalia. She panicked.

He strode up through the garden, his frown remaining fixed on his face, making him the picture of their father. The female followed him. Her unusual appearance went unnoticed by Natalia. She could only focus on her brother and the look in his eyes.

"I heard the strangest thing." There wasn't a trace of amusement in his voice. "Princess Tesia informed me that you were kissing someone."

"Leave me alone." Natalia backed into the door and fumbled for the pad that would open it. "And keep your spy away from me!"

The door behind her opened and she darted in, closing it straight in Rezic's face. He banged on it, making the glass shudder in the frame.

"Come on, Natalia, confess! I'll find the man." The note of amusement finally laced his voice.

Natalia cursed him for finding this something to laugh about. It wasn't a joke. She loved Ixion with all of her heart. Why did all her family have to treat her as though she was nothing more than a plaything, someone to do their duty for them while they had all the fun? Why couldn't she have fun for once? Why couldn't she be free?

Her eyes widened in horror when the female with Rezic gave a very detailed report of what she had seen.

Rezic was quiet for a few seconds. The pounding of Natalia's heart filled the silence.

How could the female have seen that much at that distance?

"An assassin!" The force and anger in Rezic's voice shocked Natalia enough that she stepped back from the door. "Natalia! Open this door now!"

"No!" Her voice shook but she held her ground. She wouldn't do as he asked because she was afraid that she would confess if she did.

"Fine." His tone was calm and measured. It only meant one thing. He was up to something. "If you will not confess… I will find your assassin myself."

Natalia gasped. He wouldn't.

She looked out of the door to see that he was gone and so was the female.

He would.

Panicked, Natalia grabbed her long coat to protect her from the morning chill of the palace and put it on. She lifted the crate with the Friskin in off the floor and placed it on her bed so it would be safe while she was gone, and then ran to the door.

By the time she had reached the central courtyard, most of the assassins were lined up and Rezic was pacing the length of them.

Her heart stopped when her father chose that moment to walk through.

"Inspecting the troops?" he said in an amused tone. "That isn't like you, son."

"No." Rezic's voice was dark. "I am looking for someone who took something dear to the family."

"A thief?"

Natalia's fingers closed around the heart pendant. If they discovered what Ixion had done, he would be punished, or worse. She prayed to Iskara that Ixion wouldn't come but knew that he would. He was commander of the royal assassins. It was his duty to be here.

She would have to stop this madness before he arrived.

Dashing between her brother and father, and the gathered assassins, she flung her arms out either side of her to block their way. They both frowned at her. Her father looked confused.

"Please don't do this, brother." She wasn't above begging him if it would protect Ixion. "Leave it alone… you're worse than Aiden and Ciel."

"Confess then, little sister." There was a strange look in Rezic's eyes. It was hard to tell whether he was joking or not.

At that moment, Ixion walked in.

Natalia looked at him, her heart aching. Tears welled up.

"I only wanted to be normal... free of the tight bonds that hold me prisoner, tied to a destiny that I don't want. Is it too much to ask?" She looked at her brother and the tears in her eyes slipped down her cheeks. His look softened and then changed completely to one of remorse.

"I didn't realise... I thought it wasn't serious or I would never have—"

"Serious?!" She cut him off and glared at him. Her blood boiled and she couldn't contain herself. She stepped towards her brother. Her voice was a snarl. "What would you know of serious? You spend your whole life gallivanting around the galaxy, fleeing your duty as Lyra V. You have never had to dance at the balls or meet the new commanders or bestow gifts upon the populations of Lyra. You shirk your duty at every turn! And while I hate mine... I do it... and I'll do it even when it breaks my heart." Her eyebrows furrowed when she looked at her father, her anger overwhelmed by the sadness and pain in her heart. She clutched the heart pendant tightly. "I'll marry someone I don't love because I'm a princess and a good marriage is expected of me."

Stepping back, she lowered her gaze away from her father and brother's stunned ones and turned away.

"I guess we can't all be as fortunate as Renie."

With that, she ran away, unable to hold back her tears any longer.

Ixion stared in the direction that Natalia had run, touched by her words but angry, upset that her family had hurt her so much. Both her brother and father looked shocked. Her words had hit their mark but Ixion didn't expect them to have much effect. Natalia was so different to her family. She bore so much pain and stress for their sake when none of them would do the same for her.

"She always did speak her mind and tell the truth." Rezic was the first to speak. The sound of his voice made Ixion's fingers curl into tight fists of barely restrained anger. He wanted to teach Rezic some manners too. Clearly Rezic had thought Natalia's feelings were nothing other than something to be laughed at. He was worse than Aiden and Ciel. "I never saw it the way she did."

Remorse. It wasn't enough for Ixion. Rezic deserved to suffer for hurting Natalia.

"I never knew," General Lyra II whispered to the floor and Ixion looked at him, able to forgive him in part because of how pained he sounded. The expression of sorrow on his face was a silent confession of the feelings in his heart. He truly hadn't been aware of Natalia's feelings and what the family were doing to her. "I never knew that she was so unhappy here."

Ixion had heard enough.

Her own family hadn't noticed something which he had seen that night seven years ago. This palace was a prison to her and she only wanted to be free—like her brothers and sister were.

He stormed past Rezic and General Lyra II, intent on going to see Natalia, intent on doing what they should have been—comforting her.

"Where are you going?" Rezic's voice was loud in the courtyard.

Ixion stopped, turned on his heel, and stared him down.

He considered the repercussions of what he was about to say and then threw them all away, no longer caring what happened to him.

"My lady needs me. My duty—no—my heart has long been pledged to her. I will not stand by as you do and let her suffer!"

Rezic's eyes narrowed into a glare. "Insolence!"

Ixion took a deep breath to control his anger and walked back to Rezic. The prince backed off a step, moving closer to his father.

"I am staring at insolence... a man who does not do his duty, even when a woman does hers when she hates it. The males of this family are weak and unworthy of the general. His daughters have inherited all of his strength!" Ixion didn't back down even when Rezic's hand moved to the laser pistol hanging at his side. "I have watched Aiden and Ciel become spoiled and watched an heir prince turn his back on his people. Weak fools who don't consider the outcome of their actions... how it all falls to Natalia to lift the name of their family."

Rezic's hand closed over the pistol's grip. General Lyra II's hand against his chest stopped him.

"I have long felt the same. I have neglected my role within this family," he said and Ixion looked at him, surprised that he had found the strength to confess such a weakness. "I have not given my sons the upbringing that they needed."

Ixion stepped back. "That is your problem, your highness. I cannot linger."

He turned and walked away. Rezic shouted after him, ordering him to stop, but he kept going. With a heavy heart, he removed the commander's insignia from the arm of his black dress uniform and dropped it to the floor.

He couldn't work for a family who would hurt Natalia.

His feet knew the way to her apartments, leaving him free to lose himself in thought. The repercussions of what he had done would be tremendous, but it had lifted a heavy weight from his heart. Natalia must have felt the same when she had confronted her eldest brother and father.

Reaching her door, he knocked and waited. After a few seconds had passed, it opened inwards and Natalia poked her head around it. Her eyes were sore and red, her cheeks stained with tear tracks. She stepped back and allowed him to enter, closing the door behind him. His gaze followed her as she went to the end of her bed and stood there looking lost.

His heart ached.

Nothing he could do now could make his punishment worse.

He walked to her, wrapped his arms around her shoulders, and held her close to his chest. She sobbed against him, her hands pressing into his chest, and her body trembling in his arms. He pressed kisses to her hair and whispered soothing things, not wanting her to cry over her family or him.

"It is over for me, Natalia," Ixion murmured into her hair and she looked up at him through wet eyelashes. With a slight smile, he wiped away her tears with the pad of his thumbs and cupped her cheeks. "I will likely be executed for the things that I said to your brother and father."

Her eyes grew wide and then a spark of warmth filled them. "Thank you."

"They deserved it—"

"No," she interjected and dropped her gaze to his chest before shyly raising it up to meet his again. "For last night... for giving me a moment of normality and letting me experience love."

Her voice hitched on that final word and he ached for her, to see the hurt in her eyes and know that she was thinking this was the end for them.

"Do not speak like that." He rested his forehead against hers. Her breath was soft and warm on his lips, so close to his. "I will not leave you here."

She drew back, shock flittering across her face.

"I will take you away to a place where you can be free." He held his hand out to her. It shook and he cursed it. Now wasn't the time to look weak in front of her. He wanted her to see how strong he could be for her, how he would protect her from a life that made her miserable, and would do anything to bring her happiness. "We can go somewhere no one will look for you."

"No." It was the answer that he had expected deep in his heart. She wasn't one to run away. "I can't leave... I have a duty to my people. They need me now more than ever."

He touched her face, immense sadness filling his heart. "Then I will watch over you... somehow... we will be parted but I will always watch over you."

Tears streamed down her face and she hiccupped on her sobs. "I don't want you to leave."

But she couldn't leave with him. To remain here would be a death sentence for him. The pain in her eyes spoke of confusion and fear.

"I don't want to have to choose between you and my family... am I so bound by my title that I can't even escape when offered the chance?" She turned away from him and wiped the backs of her hands across her face. "I have a responsibility... but I love you."

Someone knocked at the door.

Natalia said nothing.

Ixion stepped up behind her and hesitated a moment before placing his hands on her shoulders.

"I love you," he whispered, knowing that she needed to hear him say it, and that it would comfort her through whatever darkness lay ahead of them. "I have loved you for seven years. I have watched you all that time, watched over you, and nothing will change that."

He pressed a kiss to her hair and then walked to the door. His hand shook as he opened it, expecting to find her brother and father on the other side.

It was neither of them.

Renie's face was a picture of deviousness and excitement. She pushed past him, bursting into the room and going straight to Natalia. Ixion raised an eyebrow when a young man followed her in at a more refined pace. White skin and blue hair. His eyes were wrong somehow, with bright blue pupils and black irises. Was this the prince of Vega that Renie was going to marry?

Ixion had never seen such a strange looking male. He appeared nothing like the pictures Ixion had seen of Vegans.

"I have a shuttle in the royal port," Renie said in a rush of words. "Yellow and silver. It can fold space. We can take you both to Vega and Tres will protect you!"

Tres? Ixion looked at the male. He didn't look particularly strong but there was a confidence about him that said looks were deceiving.

"I heard about what happened," Renie continued in a blur. "Rezic is furious."

"And father?" Natalia's tone was solemn and calm.

Renie shook her head.

"We cannot flee," Ixion said and Renie looked at him, her dark eyes large and round, reflecting her confusion. "Natalia refuses to."

"You're insane. Rezic will kill Ixion."

"It would be interesting to see such a fight." The Vegan drew his gaze down the length of Ixion. "This male seems competent at killing."

"It would go against my creed to raise a hand against one of this family." Ixion frowned at the thought. No matter what they had done, he couldn't dishonour his bloodline by hurting Natalia's family.

"I'll go," Natalia said and everyone looked at her.

"To Vega?" Renie sounded as surprised as he felt.

Natalia shook her head.

"No. I'll go and speak to father." Determination flashed in her green eyes and Ixion knew that she would give her father another piece of her mind. "If he refuses to let me live my own life... then I will leave... but I can't leave without fighting for what I want."

Ixion's heart thudded against his chest. She was going to fight for him? His beautiful princess loved him that much?

"Then I am going with you." He looked her straight in the eye. "As your personal protector."

He wouldn't let anything happen to her.

Natalia's palms were sweating as she walked through the wide corridors of the palace, Ixion at her side. She kept trying to find something to say to him, but her thoughts weighed her down. What if she couldn't convince her father to grant her some freedom? What if by going to see him now, she was condemning Ixion to death? Her father could easily have his personal guards with him. The four of them could overpower Ixion. It was a thought that made her ache inside and want to tell Ixion to leave on the shuttle that waited for them in the royal port. She couldn't bear the idea of losing him.

Ixion stopped in front of the door to her father's chambers. She didn't bother to knock. She barged straight in and relief swept through her when she saw that her father was alone, sitting at his desk, looking straight at her as though he had been waiting for her to arrive.

Her nerve almost failed but the feel of Ixion close by strengthened her resolve to face her father. She had been silent too long. She wouldn't hide her feelings anymore. It was time that her father knew how hard this life was for her and how much it would hurt her if he made her marry someone that she didn't love.

She came to stand before him, her gaze unwavering. Ixion closed the door and remained near it, as though guarding her from anyone who might intrude.

"Ixion gave me a lot to think about," her father said and she was tempted to look at her assassin but kept her eyes fixed on her father's. "As did your mother when she heard about what had happened."

Natalia's heart missed a beat. She smiled inside, pleased that her mother had chosen her side just as she had hoped that she would. She was sure that her mother had mentioned more than just what had happened today. She would have mentioned his whole idea of finding Natalia suitors too.

"I have long let my children run wayward, but I need a firm hand to guide them… one that will be willing to stand up to them." Her father stood and his gaze shifted to the door. "One like Ixion."

She heard him move and couldn't stop herself from looking at him this time. He seemed shocked by her father's words, as surprised as she felt. Was her father granting Ixion a reprieve?

"I saw Aiden and Ciel in a light I did not like the other day, and saw my daughter's strength, and I knew that she was fighting with a reason. You." Her father picked something up off the desk and held it out in Ixion's direction. Ixion moved across the room to her and stared at her father's hand. It was his insignia. She hadn't noticed that he had lost it. Had he cast it aside after seeing the way her family had treated her? "You are free to return to us without repercussion… if you will train my sons in combat and help me turn them into men worthy of their titles."

Ixion didn't move. He stared at her father, his purple eyes impassive and emotionless.

"What of Natalia?" he said in a calm tone.

Her father looked at her. "My daughter has long done the duty of her brothers as well as her own. From this point forward, she will guide them also, ensuring they take responsibility and behave as expected of their status. Ixion will be assigned to her—"

"Assigned?" Natalia broke in and snatched Ixion's hand, holding it tight. She was ready to flee with him right now if her father was daring to suggest that they go back to normal, that she give Ixion up. "I don't want Ixion to be assigned to me, just like I don't want my husband chosen for me. I love Ixion and I will be with him, even if that means we leave the palace."

Her father held his hands up. "I have already had one daughter threatening to give up her title in order to marry the man she loved… and one is enough. I had intended to say that Ixion will be assigned to you as whatever you choose him to be—your personal assassin or future husband."

Natalia blinked, stunned into silence. She was sure that she had heard him wrong. Her father was stubborn, just like his brothers, and it wasn't like him to back down so easily and give in to someone else. It could only mean one thing. He really did dote on her as much as her mother said. He loved her and wanted her to be happy.

Ixion's hand tightened against hers. She looked at him, into his warm eyes that smiled at her. He reached out and brushed her cheek with the backs of his fingers.

Her eyes slipped shut and she leaned into his touch, savouring the softness and the love behind it.

The galaxy faded away until there was only them, standing so close to each other, joined in a tender caress.

The door slamming snapped her out of the moment. Her gaze darted to it. Renie stood in the doorway, her laser pistol drawn, with Tres beside her.

"Are we leaving?" Renie said in a hurried tone.

Natalia wondered if her older sister was actually prepared to hold their own father at gun point.

"We're staying." Natalia smiled at Ixion. He placed his arm around her shoulder and drew her close.

"I believe you must congratulate your little sister," her father said and Renie's eyes went wide.

"He agreed?"

"It was his idea." Natalia still wasn't quite able to believe it. Her father wanted her to marry Ixion. She looked at her father, wondering if he was going to burst out laughing any moment now and tell her it was all a joke.

Her father smiled. "I wouldn't have parted with you for a lesser male. I have no fear of your happiness or safety when Ixion is with you."

Natalia blushed and then grinned at her sister when it finally sunk in. "I'm getting married!"

Her father laughed. Tres said something which she didn't understand but hoped was congratulations.

"Double wedding!" Renie grinned right back at her.

Natalia hesitated and looked at Ixion. He towered over her, the tendrils of his black hair obscuring his eyes. His gaze slid down to meet hers and she waited with bated breath to hear what he would say.

"You haven't asked me yet." She felt a little awkward about how carried away she had been. Ixion might not want to marry her.

His arm left her shoulders, making her feel cold, and then he took hold of both of her hands, standing before her. His eyes held hers, steady and confident, but something lurked in their clear purple depths.

"Natalia... my princess... I am not worthy—" He pressed his finger to her lips to silence her when she went to speak. "Will you ever learn not to interrupt?"

Her father laughed again. The suspense was killing her. She didn't want him to outline just how unworthy he felt of her love and what she wanted to share with him. She wanted him to marry her.

"I am not worthy of a royal wedding. My status is not that of a prince or even a noble. I am merely an assassin, a servant of your family." He hesitated and then sighed. "I want to marry you more than anything and make you happy, but I cannot stand before the population and bring dishonour to your family by marrying you at a royal wedding."

Natalia's heart sunk. The thought of having such a grand wedding and sharing it with her sister had been like a dream, but it wasn't everything. She would be happy to marry Ixion here in this room in front of the few gathered. She was about to say so when her father spoke.

"I have a solution. Come here."

Ixion released her hands and did as her father had ordered, walking around the large desk to stand before him. Her father took down one of the swords that hung above the grand marble fireplace behind him and turned to Ixion.

"Kneel."

Natalia raced forwards, afraid that her father was going to hurt Ixion. She stopped in her tracks when he said a few words in Lyran and placed the tip of the sword on one of Ixion's shoulders and then the other.

"Rise, Lord Ixion. Knight of Lyra Five. Commander of the royal assassins."

Ixion stood, looking confused. "What does it mean?"

"It is something from my mother's species' past." Natalia went to Ixion and smiled up at him when he looked at her. "A lord was a noble title of the Terran species. A knight is a protector of the realm."

"A noble?" A smile slowly curved his lips.

"Will you consent to the wedding my daughter deserves now?"

Ixion nodded. "If she will have me, I will marry her in front of the whole galaxy."

Natalia grinned, threw her arms around Ixion's neck, and kissed him breathless.

If she would have him?

She would be a fool not to accept his offer and have him.

"Yes," she whispered against his lips, giddy with excitement and love. Ixion held her close, his lips barely grazing hers.

He was everything that she wanted.

Her Lover.

Her Lord.

Her Knight.

But above all else…

Her Assassin.

The End

ABOUT THE AUTHOR

Felicity Heaton is a romance author writing as both Felicity Heaton and F E Heaton. She is passionate about penning paranormal tales full of vampires, witches, werewolves, angels and shape-shifters, and has been interested in all things preternatural and fantastical since she was just a child. Her other passion is science-fiction and she likes nothing more than to immerse herself in a whole new universe and the amazing species therein. She used to while away days at school and college dreaming of vampires, werewolves and witches, or being lost in space, and used to while away evenings watching movies about them or reading gothic horror stories, science-fiction and romances.

Having tried her hand at various romance genres, it was only natural for her to turn her focus back to the paranormal, fantasy and science-fiction worlds she enjoys so much. She loves to write seductive, sexy and strong vampires, werewolves, witches, angels and alien species. The worlds she often dreams up for them are vicious, dark and dangerous, reflecting aspects of the heroines and heroes, but her characters also love deeply, laugh, cry and feel every emotion as keenly as anyone does. She makes no excuses for the darkness surrounding them, especially the paranormal creatures, and says that this is their world. She's just honoured to write down their adventures.

To see her other novels, visit: http://www.felicityheaton.co.uk

If you have enjoyed this story, please take a moment to contact the author at author@felicityheaton.co.uk or to post a review of the book online

Follow the author on:
Her blog – http://www.indieparanormalromancebooks.com
Twitter – http://twitter.com/felicityheaton
Facebook – http://www.facebook.com/feheaton

Made in the USA
San Bernardino, CA
09 October 2016